THE DAMSEL'S INTENT

The QUILTING CIRCLE Series

The Widow's Plight
Book One

The Daughter's Predicament
Book Two

The Damsel's Intent
Book Three

THE DAMSEL'S INTENT

The Quilting Circle Series

By Mary Davis

The Damsel's Intent
Published by Mountain Brook Ink
White Salmon, WA U.S.A.

All rights reserved. Except for brief excerpts for review purposes, no part of this book may be reproduced or used in any form without written permission from the publisher.

The website addresses shown in this book are not intended in any way to be or imply an endorsement on the part of Mountain Brook Ink, nor do we vouch for their content.

This story is a work of fiction. All characters and events are the product of the author's imagination other than those stated in the author notes as based on historical characters. Any other resemblance to any person, living or dead, is coincidental.

The author is represented by and this book is published in association with the literary agency of WordServe Literary Group, Ltd., www.wordserveliterary.com

Scripture quotations are taken from the King James Version of the Bible. Public domain.

© 2020 Mary Davis
ISBN 9781-943959-81-5

The Team: Miralee Ferrell, Alyssa Roat, Nikki Wright, Cindy Jackson
Cover Design: Indie Cover Design, Lynnette Bonner Designer

Mountain Brook Ink is an inspirational publisher offering fiction you can believe in.

Printed in the United States of America

Dedication

And the Lord God said, It is not good that the man should be alone; I will make him an help meet for him.
Genesis 2:18

Dedicated to my son, Ben. I'm so proud of you!

Acknowledgments

A special thanks to Miralee Ferrell for believing in my story and being a great editor, to Nikki Wright and Alyssa Roat for marketing help, to Lynnette Bonner for my beautiful cover, and to Sarah Joy Freese and WordServe Literary Agency. I'm so thankful to work with each of you!

One

Washington State, Late Fall 1893

"Nick, there's something you should know. You ain't no boy like your cousins."

In buckskin pants and shirt, Nick sat across the wobbly, pot-marked table from Sarah Combs, the only neighbor for miles around. "I know. Grandpa said I'd be the *man* of the house when he passed over into heaven, which he did a few weeks ago. You being our only neighbor, I came to you for advice. We buried him, but I'm not sure what to do now. I'm not skilled enough to look after Rolfy and Bucky through the winter. Grandpa always got us what we needed. He'd leave for a day or two and come back with flour and coffee and the like. I don't know how to do that."

The grizzled old lady, tough enough to survive alone in the mountains, sucked in air through the gap between her two front teeth and shook her head. "You miss my meaning. Your grandpa meant well—was trying to protect you—but he's done you a disservice by keeping you hid away up in the mountains. You ain't no man. You're a woman like me."

"A woman? Why didn't he tell me that all along?" Nick leaned forward on the table. "Grandpa grabbed my arm and his last words were, 'Go to Kamola and find a husband. I should have told you sooner, but Nick, you're not a fell...'Then, he breathed his last. I don't know what he was trying to tell me. Why would he claim I was a man, then tell me to get a husband? That isn't right. I figured that maybe *man* was a general term for humans or person, and *woman* was another sort of man. I don't think I know the real meaning of the words man and woman. I'm all kinds of confused."

Sarah rubbed her lips, like she was trying to form the right words. "He was probably going to say you ain't no feller. Your full name is Nicole. It's a right pretty girl's name. I told Ike he shouldn't be dressin' you like them boys and telling you, you was just like them."

"I've known for a long time I'm different from my cousins." Maybe that was why she'd felt a connection with Sarah, because they were both women. "But Grandpa would never talk about it. He'd get real upset if I asked, so I didn't. I let him call me what he wanted to."

The older woman patted Nick's hand. "He's afraid someone might hurt you iffen they knew you were a girl. There be some pretty mean folks out there, and he did what he thought best for you. Now, I'm not one to do much trusting of outside folks, but it's time for you and your cousins to move into town."

"Move there? Leave the mountain?" A fear coiled up inside her, ready to strike. "I've never lived anywhere else."

Sarah nodded. "It's time."

Nick's insides wiggled as though she'd swallowed a snake. Grandpa never spoke well of town. "Grandpa wouldn't approve of us moving there, but I'll visit—just to see what it has—get provisions and come right back. Can you take me?"

"Sorry. I can't go to town. Follow the crick all the way down. You'll see the place. Aunt Henny can help you better than me. Take your cousins with you."

"I cain't take the young'uns. I'll leave them in the cabin. Will you check on them while I'm gone?"

"Rolfy's what—twelve now? Bucky's seven?"

Nick nodded.

"And you're seventeen or eighteen?"

"Turned twenty on my last birthday."

"I didn't realize it had been so long." Sarah shook her head. "But still too young. It's best if you and the boys move into town. You're not gonna find a man to come up here with you. There's a loose floorboard under your grandpa's bed where he stashed some money. You take that and find Aunt Henny. She's good people. You tell her I sent ya. She'll help ya."

The next day Nick trudged down the mountain. Sure wished the mule hadn't died. At the tree line, she stopped short and ducked behind a lodge pole pine. A whole passel of cabins dotted the landscape. Big ones. She'd never seen the likes. There must be seven or eight of them. All bunched together. Horses pulled carts with four wheels. What did a person need with four wheels? Was this that Kamola town Sarah told her about? She said there would be a lot of people. Nick had never been around other folks besides her grandpa and cousins, Sarah Combs, and the occasional trapper or hunter passing by.

She ventured out of the forest, scurried up a knoll and onto the heap of rocks to get a better view of this Kamola and the cabins. She kept her rifle in her hand. Grandpa said to never set down your gun lest a grizzly surprise you and your gun's too far away.

She gasped at the sight. Far more than eight cabins. A whole mess of them. Too many to count. What were so many doing together? The horses and carts moved along on the spaces between the cabins. Some of the bigger ones had two and four horses pulling them. Lots of people roamed all over the place. How was she supposed to find one person in that mess? Like a colony of ants crawling all over an apple core.

Sarah had said for her to ask someone.

Nick best get to it. Time was wasting. She marched along the slope of the knoll and strode toward the town of cabins and people and horses and carts. Was this a hopeless task?

The first couple of cabins she came to had white board fences all the way around them. When she came to a whole string of buildings attached together, she stepped up onto the long wooden walk along their fronts. These ones had large windows. She'd never seen glass so big. Grandpa's cabin had two, small, four-paned windows, and when the bitter winter wind blew, they let in all the cold. How did people stay warm with windows the size of walls?

She peered through the glass.

One man lay in the strangest chair or was it a bed?

He had shaving soap on his face. Another man held the razor blade, scraping off the white foam and whiskers.

She walked on to the next one.

A man handed a brown-paper wrapped box to a lady. The next building had all manner of things stacked around in rows and rows—cans, lamps, blankets, fabric with pretty flowers, stripes, or plaids on them. Sacks with the words—flour, coffee, and sugar spelled out on each. This must be where Grandpa got everything he brought to the cabin. She would need to buy a mule and come with the cart to get everything they would need for the winter.

These were the strangest homes she had ever seen. How did people sleep and eat with all those trappings?

She stepped off the porch as a man on horseback galloped along the dirt pathway.

"Hey, mister?"

He rode right on past without even stopping or saying good day. Grandpa always taught her to say a greeting to people.

Two women dressed in clothes like Sarah's, but cleaner and without patches, headed toward her. Maybe one of them was Aunt Henny.

Nick tipped her hat. "Howdy. Do you—"

The women gasped and darted across the open stretch between the long cabins.

That wasn't very neighborly. Nick never would have done that to Sarah or the occasional trappers and hunters.

"Begging your pardon?" She said to the next man who sidestepped around her. Now she knew why Grandpa said towns were evil places. When a person wouldn't greet another, it wasn't worth the effort it took to speak. She should skedaddle back up to the mountains.

At a noise, she spun around and faced a horse square in the chest. It startled and reared. She ducked and rolled out of harm's way and landed on her feet with her rifle at the ready.

The horse settled, and the rider rode off down the long dirt patch.

A deep voice behind her said, "Nice move, kid."

Nick swung around.

The man laughed, deep and warm, and put his fingers on the end of her barrel, pushing it away from pointing at him. He was fine-looking and had a friendly smile that did something funny to her insides.

She lowered her gun. "Sorry about that."

"No problem. You moved pretty quickly out of the way of that rearing horse. A lot of people would have frozen and gotten themselves injured under those hooves."

"Grandpa always said, 'move fast or die.'"

"Words to live by." An amused twinkle flashed in his blue eyes. "If you're interested in work, I can always use someone like you who is fast on their feet and quick-thinking."

"I'm not after work." Finally, someone who would speak to her. "I'm looking for Aunt Henny. Do you know where I can find her?"

"Sure. Everyone knows Aunt Henny, but I've learned she's not really anyone's aunt."

"Then why's she called aunt?"

"I've been wondering the same thing." He unwound his horse reins from the hitching rail. "Come on. I'll take you to her. You planning to stay at her boarding house?"

"No, sir." Nick fell into step beside him. "She's gonna help me find a husband."

"A what?" The man stopped and snatched Nick's hat.

"Hey, give that back, thief."

"I declare, you're a girl under all that dirt and buckskins."

"Am not. Grandpa said I was to be the man of the house after he passed, but Sarah said I'm a woman."

He doubled over laughing. "Girly, you are no man."

"Stop calling me that." She swiped her hat from his hand and smashed it onto her head. "Are you going to take me to Aunt Henny or not? Point me in the right direction. I'm a good tracker. I'll find her."

"Oh, I'll take you there, all right." He tried to stifle his laugh, but his snicker still came out. "I can't wait to see her face."

Regardless of his beguiling smile, she determined not to like this man laughing at her the way he had. But he had been the only one kind enough to offer her help, so he couldn't be too bad.

Henny turned the pie crust dough out onto her floured worktable in her kitchen and picked the sticky bits off her fingers.

Boots clomped on her porch.

She let out a frustrated groan. Why did a new boarder have to show up while her hands were gloppy?

The anticipated knock sounded.

"Just a minute. I'm coming." She grabbed a towel and wiped what dough she could off her hands. She covered the knob with the towel and turned it, opening the door.

That new rancher Shane Keegan and a buckskin-clad boy stood on her porch. "Good morning, fellows. What can I do for you?"

"This here...fella? is looking for you." Mr. Keegan swiped off the boy's hat. "But he's a she."

The boy-er girl grabbed her hat. "You need to stop doing that." Her nearly black hair had been cropped short like a boy's. Hacked, really, to above her shoulders. Between her hair and her clothes, no wonder Mr. Keegan thought she was a boy.

Henny pushed the screen open with her elbow. "Won't you both come in?"

Mr. Keegan tipped his hat. "I'd love to, just to find out what this is all about, but I have a lady to see. Good day, Aunt Henny. Good day, kid." He tromped off the porch laughing.

The girl did look a bit unusual but nothing to laugh at. Henny would like to say she'd seen worse, but she couldn't recall that she had.

The girl entered.

Henny closed the door and pointed to the entry to the parlor. "Stand right there. I'll return in a moment." She washed the dough off her hands as quick as she could. Who knew what that girl would get into? She drew two glasses of water and cut two slices of spice cake, set the lot on a tray and grabbed two tea towels.

When Henny re-entered the parlor, the girl stood in the exact spot she left her in. Surprising. "You didn't move."

"No, ma'am. Grandpa said when he told me to do something, I was to do it without question. That's the reason I'm here. He said come into town, so I did."

Henny's calico cat sauntered across the room to investigate the new arrival. "That's Miss Tibbins."

The girl crouched and held out her hand. "Hello, kitty."

The cat approached cautiously, then her tail puffed out three times its normal size. She hissed and strolled away.

"She doesn't normally act like that." Henny set the tray on the serving table in front of the settee.

"I probably have all kinds of strange smells on my buckskins she's not used to."

Still, Henny didn't think it was any reason to hiss. She draped one tea towel on the seat of a padded chair and the other on the backrest. "I hope you don't take offense, but your...clothes are a bit dusty." That was being kind. "Have a seat?"

"I don't mind. I can sit on the floor if you'd like."

"No. That won't be necessary." Henny didn't know what to make of this girl.

She sat. "You have a real nice cabin. I never saw one so big. This town's full of cabins like this. You must have a passel of kin in your family."

"No. No family. This is a boarding house. I rent rooms to travelers and people who don't have or need a home." Henny sat on the settee and handed her guest a glass and a plate. Did she know how to use a fork? "Water and cake. I thought you might be thirsty and hungry."

The girl's eyes widened. "I sure am. I haven't had cake in ever so long. Must be three years or more." She took the plate and glass. "Thank you, ma'am." She guzzled half the water, then took a large chunk of cake on the fork and shoveled it into her mouth without dropping a crumb.

She knew what a fork was used for, said "thank you" and "ma'am." Someone had taught her a few things.

"What's your name?"

"Nick. No, wait. Sarah told me to tell you my full name. Nicole Waterby."

"Sarah Combs?"

"Yes, ma'am. She's our neighbor."

"Our?"

"Me and my cousins."

Henny resisted the urge to correct her grammar. "I didn't realize Sarah had any neighbors. I thought she was up there all by herself."

"Have to go a bit farther up the mountain to get to our place."

"How old are you?"

"I turned twenty last month."

"How old are your cousins?"

"Rolfy's twelve. I left him in charge while I'm gone. Bucky's seven."

"Two boys, then?"

"Yes, ma'am."

"Mr. Keegan said you were looking for me?"

"Keegan? Is that his name? He was the only one who would even look at me, let alone talk to me. Everyone else gasped as though they had seen a rabid coon and hightailed it away from me. But Mr. Keegan was right nice. He brought me all the way here. Nice, except for him taking my hat and laughing."

"Did Sarah send you? Is she all right? I worry about her."

"Sarah's right as rain. She sent me here on account of my grandpa passed away."

"I'm sorry to hear that."

"He was pretty old. He told me to take care of my cousins—on account they are younger than me—and to go to Kamola to fetch me a husband."

Henny nearly choked on her cake. She coughed and patted her chest. "A husband? Did he tell you how to do that?"

"He was pretty bad off by then. He just made me promise to do it so I could take care of the young'uns." Nicole leaned forward. "Is there a special place I go to get a husband? Cuz I'm anxious to get back up the mountain."

Mercy. This girl needed help.

❦

Shane rode down the main street of Kamola, fresh from the cattle drive. He'd sent his men on ahead to his ranch to check on things. He didn't want to waste any more time finding out Miss Isabelle Atwood's answer.

Before he'd left two months ago, he'd asked to court her, when he returned, with the intention to marry. He knew it had been quick, but he liked her a lot, and he didn't want another man to steal her away while he was gone. He wanted to make her his wife and take her to his ranch outside of town. Though he hadn't thought about taking on a wife before Isabelle fell into his life, he decided he'd rather like to have a wife.

He'd gone to the bathhouse to wash off the trail dust and grime and bought new clothes so she wouldn't think him uncivilized. He shook his head and chuckled, thinking about that buckskin girl. She certainly was an unusual creature. But girl or not, he could use a fast-thinking hand like her. Maybe he would talk to Aunt Henny and find out more about her.

He rode up to Isabelle's house, one of the larger ones in town, but by no means the wealthiest family. He knocked.

A maid answered the door. "May I help you?"

"Um. I'm here to see Miss Isabelle Atwood." Was that the correct way to make that kind of request for someone of her station?

She opened the door wider. "Come in."

He stepped inside the foyer.

"Wait right here." The maid slid open a pair of pocket doors, disappeared inside, and closed them behind her.

An expensive-looking rug covered the marble floor. He skirted around it. A dark-wood, curved staircase ascended to the upper level. This was one swanky place. Could Isabelle ever be happy stuck way out on his ranch? Muffled voices leaked through the doors, but he couldn't tell what anyone said.

The doors slid open, and Isabelle appeared. "Mr. Keegan, it's so good to see you." She crossed the entry and slid open doors on that side. "We can talk in here."

Mr. Keegan? That couldn't bode well for him. He followed her into a room that appeared to be a study with heavy furniture, dark paneling, and cases of books.

"I'm glad you caught me here." She sat on a little couch and pointed to a chair. "Please have a seat."

As he did, his stomach knotted. This meeting would give direction to his future. One way or another.

The maid entered with a tray and set it on the coffee table. "Anything else, ma'am?"

"No, thank you."

The maid curtsied and left.

Isabelle poured tea from a china teapot into two china cups and handed him one. "How did your cattle drive go?"

"Real well. I got a higher price per head than I anticipated." He took a swallow of the warm brew. "I think you know why I've come." No sense dawdling.

She gave him a sweet smile. "I do."

"I'm not gonna like your answer, am I?"

"Shane, I care about you a great deal."

"But you aren't going to marry me."

"I'm not in love with you. I don't know if I could be happy way out of town on your ranch. You deserve someone who wants all the same things as you. Someone who finds living on your ranch as exciting as you do."

"Did you marry the man your folks wanted you to?" He hoped not. She hadn't been enthusiastic about him.

"No."

"That hotel clerk? You're in love with him, aren't you?"

She nodded. "I am. How did you know?"

"You were always talking to him, always around him, and he gazed at you the way you deserve to have a man look at you. I don't think I ever looked at you quite that way. Maybe that's why I proposed. So he couldn't steal you away."

"But he did."

Shane shook his head. "He can't steal what wasn't mine to begin with. He obviously makes you happy. I can see it on your face. Is he going to marry you?"

She held up her left hand. "He already has. I'm so sorry. I wanted to tell you, but I didn't know how to reach you on the cattle drive."

"No reaching a man on a drive." He stood. "I'll be going."

She walked him to the door. "I hope you find the perfect woman. You deserve someone special."

The image of the buckskin girl popped into his head. She was special all right, but not necessarily in a good way.

He opened the door. "Isabelle, thank you for telling me yourself. You could have easily had your maid relay the information to me...or your father."

"I couldn't do that to you. You mean more to me than to treat you inconsiderately."

"Good day, Miss Isabelle." He walked down the steps and out to his horse.

Though in his heart, he'd known he was never good enough for someone like Isabelle, her refusal—even as kind and sweet as it was—still stung.

What should he do now? On the drive he had a purpose—return to Kamola and court Isabelle. Now, he would simply head out to his ranch. That seemed lonely somehow. It never had before. Isabelle had changed his way of thinking. He would need to change it back to his solitary way of life. He could do that. Make ranching everything again. He'd been foolish to think otherwise.

Two

NICK WAITED IMPATIENTLY IN THE FANCY chair in the fancy room. She'd finished the delicious spice cake. How long was this elderly lady going to sit there jawing? Nick needed to return to the hills and care for her cousins. They'd be fine for a day or two but had a penchant for getting into trouble. Neither of them had a lick of sense when it came to making decisions.

They'd once poked a stick into a hornets' nest before they realized it wasn't such a good idea and got several stings each. The bigger problem was that Nick had gotten stung for their troubles. Grandpa said he oughta tan their hides in spite of their stings. One strike of the switch for each sting Nick had received on their account. Ordered them to each pick out a switch, and Nick was to carry out the punishment. She hadn't had the heart to strike them. But she knew Grandpa had decided the punishment to get the gravity of their poor decision to sink in. They needed to learn what they did affected others.

As the pair stood before her and handed over their choices of switches, she weighed her options. They were due three strikes a piece. She gave them a choice. Complete a whole list of chores or feel the switch on their backsides. If they started complaining about the work or didn't do what they were supposed to, she held the threat of the switches over their heads. Grandpa put the sticks on display over the fireplace as a reminder. She'd gotten a full month's worth of extra chores out of the pair.

Nick took a sip of water and let her gaze jump from one dainty, pretty thing to the next around the room in Aunt Henny's house. Sun glinted off a red glass lamp, and silver candlesticks flanked a white mantle clock with painted roses. A crocheted doily on the table at her elbow beckoned her. Sarah had tried to teach her how to make one, but Nick could never remember what to do from one visit to the next. The times were too short and too far apart. Nick wasn't fit to be in such a place. She belonged in the barn, not in here. But she longed to fit in, even just a little.

"Do you like that doily?"

Nick jerked her hand back and snapped her head up to look at the older woman. "I'm sorry. I shouldn't have tried to touch it."

"No harm was done."

"I appreciate your kindness. If you could tell me where to find a husband, I'll not bother you any longer."

Aunt Henny took a deep breath and let it escape. "I'm afraid it's not that simple. Finding a husband isn't like buying a horse. It takes time."

"How much time? Winter is going to set in soon."

"Weeks. Months even."

Nick couldn't wait that long. "But I must return to my cousins. I can't be leaving them alone that long."

"You need to bring them to town. You all can stay here with me."

"I don't know. I don't think Grandpa would have approved." But Sarah had told her to move to town too. "I suppose we could for the winter then move back up on the mountain come spring."

"I think once you've lived in town for a bit, you'll like it and want to stay."

"I'm not sure about that. It seems so closed in having all these cabins so cramped together, but I wouldn't mind seeing what it's like for a while."

Aunt Henny gave a nod. "Then it's settled. Tomorrow we'll take my wagon and retrieve your cousins."

Grandpa wouldn't like this one bit, but he wasn't here, and it was him who had told her to get a husband. "If we stay here through the winter, you'll help me find a man to marry?"

"I would be happy to help you." The older woman waited a long moment, gazing at Nick before speaking again. "About that. I mean no offense, but the way you're dressed isn't going to help you find a husband, if that is what you truly want. Any man who would take you up on your offer to be your husband, as you are dressed now, likely isn't a man you want to be married to. Do you have other clothes at your cabin? A dress perhaps?"

Nick shook her head. "Nope, just this and my summer clothes, a pair of britches and cotton shirt."

"How about we pour you a bath and get you something clean to wear? I could find a dress for you, if you'd like?"

Nick had never worn a dress. She'd once held one up to herself at Sarah's, but Grandpa had told her to get such foolish thoughts out of her head. "But it's not spring. Don't you know a person could die by taking a bath this time of year?"

Aunt Henny gave a soft laugh. "People take baths year-round."

Nick stared at her. "All year?" She did like the feel of warm water. "Do you take a bath any time of year?"

"I do. I took one a few days ago."

And this woman is still alive.

"The important thing is to stay warm until your hair dries, so you don't get chilled."

Nick never dreamed of taking a bath more than once a year. Maybe she would like town after all. "Tell me where the bucket is and point me toward the creek, and I'll fetch the water."

"No need. I have a storage tank behind my stove." She motioned toward the kitchen. "When the stove is lit the water is heated and during the night the hot water helps keep the house warm. We only need to pull out the tub and fill it."

Nick pushed to her feet. "Can I see it? The stove with the water? I can't imagine. How does the fire stay lit with the water in there?"

"The water isn't in the part of the stove that has the fire. Come look." Aunt Henny rose slowly and limped.

"You don't have to. I can see walking troubles you."

"I broke my leg a few months ago. It gets stiff when I sit for a spell. I need to keep it moving so it doesn't quit on me all together. It's getting better and better all the time."

Nick trailed behind the woman. The kitchen was in a whole other room, not just a corner of one big room. The floor had white and red tiles in a checkered pattern. Grandpa had brought a few of these kinds of tiles up to the cabin that he used to put pans and kettles on to keep them from burning the table. "Do you put hot things on the floor?"

"No. Why would you ask that?"

"The tiles. We used some of these to put pans on after cooking."

Aunt Henny smiled. "They are good for that. I have a few I use that way as well." She tapped her foot on the floor. "These are set into the floor and make it easier to clean."

"I sure wish I had these on the floor of the cabin. It'd be so much easier to scrub when the boys track in mud. But then it's hardest on them, because they are the ones who have to get on their hands and knees to wash it. Though I've spilled my share of things I had to mop up with a towel. Not easy."

"I do like it, but this is what you came in to see." Aunt Henny pointed to the back of the kitchen stove. "I'm heating up the stove anyway to cook. The fire doesn't have to do any more work to make the water in the tank hot."

Nick leaned in closer to gander at the one-foot by three-foot tank attached to the length of the stove. She put her hands on her hips. "Well, isn't that something. I've left a pot of water and a kettle on our stove to always have hot water ready, but I never thought to have something so large."

"What do you say about us pulling out my tub so you can take a bath?"

"Right now?"

"Right now. My boarders won't be home for some time."

Nick relaxed into the idea of the hot water on her body, but the pleasure was short lived. "It won't do any good if I put my dusty clothes on again."

"Like I said, I'll find a dress for you. Would you like

that?"

"I would." What would it be like? She was ready to find out.

"Let's get you in the tub, then I'll go see what I can find for you to wear."

In not much more than a jackrabbit minute, the tub, sitting next to the stove, was filled with warm water and sweet-smelling bubbles.

Nick gingerly touched the white foam. "I'm supposed to get in all that?"

"Yes. It's called a bubble bath. You'll like it. I promise."

She drew in a deep breath. "It smells pretty."

"It does, at that. You can lay your clothes on a chair and climb in while I find you a dress." Aunt Henny left.

Nick shucked her clothes and slipped into the hot water. The scent of the bubbles wrapped around her like a hug. This would be the best bath she ever had.

Aunt Henny returned with two dresses, one peach and the other yellow. "Which one would you like?"

They were both so beautiful. "If it's all right, the yellow one. It reminds me of the buttercups in the meadow near our cabin."

The older woman smiled. "The yellow one it is. I thought the black trim on this one would go especially nice with your dark hair." She set the dress on another chair from Nick's buckskins. "Would you like me to help you wash your hair?"

"Yes." The warm water soon streamed over her head and felt heavenly. In a jiffy, her hair was washed. "That man who brought me here?"

"Mr. Keegan."

"Do you think he would be my husband? Since I've already met him and all."

Aunt Henny coughed and patted her chest. "Courting takes time, and you need to let the man ask you."

"Why?"

"Because that's how it's done."

"Can't I get a husband by asking and bartering?"

Aunt Henny's mouth moved about before she answered. "I suppose you might be able to find one that way, but you might not like who you end up with, and then you will be stuck with him. It's better if you take your time and get to know a man first."

Get to know a man first. That made sense.

In no time, Nick was all clean, but didn't want to get out of the still warm bath.

Aunt Henny draped a towel over the back of a chair she'd scooted close to the tub. "What I like to do, after I'm all washed, is to linger in the warm water and let it relax my body."

"Can I do that? Don't you need to use the water for the next person?"

Aunt Henny shook her head. "This one's all yours. I'll return in a little bit and help you out."

Nick hunkered down until the bubbles tickled her chin. Between the cozy bath and the hot stove right near her, she was toasty warm. She'd never had a bath like this before.

An hour later, Nick stood in a bedroom upstairs that Aunt Henny said she could sleep in. The woman had directed her in dressing and helped her get into all the layers of clothing but wouldn't let her peek in the mirror. Layers and layers—pantaloons, slip, petticoats, chemise, and corset—until finally the dress slipped over it all. As Aunt Henny tied a bow behind Nick at her waist, Nick glanced over her shoulder at the standing mirror.

Aunt Henny shifted into her view. "No peeking. You'll see soon enough. It needs to be taken in a bit, but it will work for now." A moment later the older woman stepped in front of Nick. "All done. You can look now."

Nick turned toward the mirror. A strange but familiar young lady stared back at her. "Is that girl me?"

"She is."

She twisted one way, then the other, and squinted at her reflection. She hardly recognized herself cleaned up and in a dress.

"Don't you like the dress? I can get the other one if you prefer."

Nick blinked away her blurry vision. "No. I like this dress. I never imagined..."

"It is quite a difference, but you look beautiful."

Would Mr. Keegan think so? "Thank you so much. Are you sure this whole room is for just me?" It was nearly the size of Grandpa's cabin.

"This will be yours while you stay here. When your cousins arrive, they can use the one next door."

"Oh, you don't have to do that. We can hang a blanket or something to divide this room."

Aunt Henny touched her arm. "You are a young lady. You shouldn't be sharing a room with boys."

Nick liked the idea of her own room. "I have a lot to learn, don't I?"

Aunt Henny smiled. "You'll get there."

⁂

Shane moseyed out of town on Huckleberry, his sorrel stallion, toward his ranch. His thoughts kept drifting to the buckskin girl. She was quick and had fire in her eyes when he took her floppy hat. Spunky. His mouth pulled up on the corners.

How old could she be? When he'd thought her a boy, he would have guessed fourteen or fifteen at the most. But as a female, she was a young lady, maybe as old as nineteen or twenty.

When his ranch came into view, the land and livestock weighed as a heavy burden instead of the blessing he'd viewed it to be when he'd first received it. After this winter, he would sell the place. He had liked owning his own place, but now it felt as though it was tying him down. He had an itching to be on the move. Interest in Isabelle Atwood had waylaid that feeling, gave him a sense of longing for something he'd never had before. Family. But now that dream was gone. He would enjoy his warm house over the cold winter before he headed out to the open country. There was something out there for him. Something calling him. Something—but what?

He'd been disappointed to not see the buckskin girl again. He'd stopped by after visiting Isabelle, but Aunt Henny said the girl—Nicole Waterby—was indisposed. Whatever that meant. Probably for the best. She'd been the most interesting female he'd met in...well, ever. And he knew nothing about her. Only an interesting life would explain her attire, her handling of a rifle, her agility, her spunk, and the fire in her eyes when he swiped her hat. He chuckled. Next time he was in town, he'd have to do that again to ignite her spark.

As he approached the edge of his place, his collies, Roxy and Pepper, one tricolored, the other black and white, sprang from their resting place on the porch and raced out to greet him.

His foreman, Handley, met him in the yard between the house and the barn. He'd inherited the man along with the ranch and a few hands. "I take it your delay in town with Miss Atwood went well."

Shane swung down. "Actually, it didn't. She's married. Why would you think it went well?"

"That dopey grin on your face. If Miss Atwood isn't the cause, then who is?"

A certain buckskin-clad filly flashed in his mind. "No one. Just glad to be home." At least for now.

"Sure."

To keep Handley from scrutinizing him further, Shane crouched and petted his dogs. Nicole was more of a boy than a girl. Intriguing, yes, but totally unsuited to even consider courting...unfortunately.

Three

THE FOLLOWING MORNING, IN THE DIM dawn light, Henny's breath came out in white puffs. The barn offered little in the way of protection from the cold. She and Nicole planned to head into the mountains early. She'd left a simple breakfast of hard-boiled eggs, biscuits, and jam for her two boarders.

First stop would be Sarah Combs's, then on to the cabin the young lady had grown up in. The girl had made quite a transformation from buckskins and dirt to a young lady all cleaned up in the yellow calico dress, straw bonnet, and with her hair brushed. Too bad Henny hadn't been able to talk her into wearing the dress today. Nicole had said it wasn't fitting for a trip into the mountains. Perhaps not, since she wasn't used to wearing a dress. Henny hoped she could talk the girl into remaining in town permanently. For now, her stay would only be for over the winter. If nothing went wrong today. *And* if her cousins would come without a fuss. Were they actually boys? Or were they girls too?

Nicole helped Henny hitch the horse to the wagon. Hopefully, Henny's small buckboard would be big enough to transport all of Nicole's and her cousins' belongings. Leaving even one thing any of them deemed important could mean the difference between them staying safely in town or suffering through the cold winter in the mountains. If they returned, Henny might never get them into town again. Mountain people could be very set in their ways, so unwilling to try something new.

Nicole walked the hitched horse out of the barn. "I certainly appreciate you helping me retrieve my cousins and letting us stay with you."

"It's no trouble, dear." It was Henny's duty to help

those she could. She glanced across the street. A well-dressed man stood there, studying Henny's house.

Maybe she would have another boarder soon. The extra money would be nice. She would tell him to return later, but her movements must have caught the stranger's attention. He shifted his gaze to her, ducked his head, and hurried off. That was odd. Maybe he would return later, but no time to dwell on that now. She climbed aboard the wagon, and Nicole clambered up next to her in her buckskins. Thank goodness the girl had washed them. Henny had hoped to keep the girl in a dress, but best not to push her too much until her cousins were safely in town as well. Though Nicole seemed to like wearing the dress yesterday and was eager to learn, she might get fed up with all the changes and decide town life was too hard to get used to.

Henny snapped the reins and set the wagon into motion.

A few hours later, the wagon crested a rise, and Sarah's one-room cabin came into view. Everything was dusted white from an overnight snow. The frosty ground crunched beneath the wheels.

"Hello!" The frigid air made her voice loud enough to be carried to the cabin. "It's Henny!"

"And Nick!"

It wasn't wise to surprise mountain people, as they would most likely shoot as a way of greeting.

The old woman stepped out onto her porch, shotgun in hand, and waved Henny forward. When the wagon was close enough, Sarah approached and took hold of the harness. "Good thing you called out. I've had trouble with some scalawags."

It surprised Henny how spry the woman was, being twenty years older than herself.

Sarah scowled at Nicole and shook her head. "You was supposed to be gone. But since you're here, you might as well come inside."

After setting the brake, Henny climbed down. The leg she'd broken this past summer ached in the cold. She rounded to the rear of the wagon. "I brought you supplies."

Sarah flashed her gap-toothed grin. "You's always thinking of me."

Henny, Nicole, and Sarah loaded their arms and tromped inside the toasty cabin.

The warmth wrapped around Henny, inviting her to sit a spell. She couldn't stay long. Not if she expected to complete her mission of retrieving those boys and returning to town by dark. She would allow herself a few minutes to get the chill out of her sore leg. "Thank you for sending Nicole to me. Why didn't you ever tell me you had neighbors up here?" Henny might not have worried so much about the woman.

"Ike wanted it that way." She inclined her head toward Nicole. "Her grandfather. Nick, would you fill my bucket at the crick and water the horse?"

Nicole grabbed the pail and skedaddled.

Once the girl slipped out of earshot, Sarah turned on Henny. "Why'd you brung her up here fer? It was all I could do to talk her into goin' into town. Now she's back and won't likely never leave."

Henny understood Sarah's concern. "She's agreed to stay with me through the winter. I'm hoping she'll decide to remain there for good. We came to retrieve her cousins."

Sarah brightened and slapped the table. "Well, that is somethin'. I's wonderin' what I was gonna do about them boys."

"So then, they are actual boys?"

"Yep. Little scamps half the time."

"Did her grandfather never take her into town?"

Sarah shook her head.

"Why keep her tucked away up here?"

Sarah's expression turned sorrowful. "That goes back to Nick's mother, Maeve, Ike's only child. When he first come here with her—she must have been about fifteen—he'd just bought the land. He was going to set up a logging business. A lot of good timber up here. Maeve disappeared for a week. When she was found, she'd been beat up real bad. Terrible things done to her. I helped Ike take care of her, and she healed—at least on the outside. She was never right again. It broke him inside. It was obvious before long that she was in a family way. Nick couldn't have been more than a year and a half when her ma finally left their cabin and went out in the woods with a shotgun."

"That's terrible. The poor girl. Both Nicole and her mother."

"Nick don't know. All she knows is her ma died when she was young."

"Why didn't Ike take his daughter and live in town instead of up here where those awful things happened to her?"

"She wouldn't leave the cabin...until *that* day. She was the one who insisted upon dressing Nick like a boy. Ike was never right after he lost Maeve."

"How heartbreaking. What about the boys? If his daughter was his only child, how can Nicole have cousins? Second cousins?"

Sarah shook her head. "They are a completely different story. Honestly, I don't think they're any relation to Ike. He just showed up with them one day. They were all battered and bruised, clinging to each other, a seven-year-old and a two-year-old. They've done real well these past five years. They're good boys mostly."

So, Nicole's grandfather snatched them? Did their family know? "You don't know who they belonged to?"

"Nope. And I didn't ask."

"What if they have family who have been looking for them?" A person couldn't just take someone else's children. Henny had never heard of anyone missing a pair of boys five years ago.

"What if it were that family who had been mistreating them? They didn't deserve them."

But what if they weren't the ones? No use belaboring the issue now. Henny would ask around in town. For now, the important thing was to get them there. She would figure the rest out later. "How long will it take to get to their cabin?"

"About a half an hour on foot."

"What about with the wagon?"

"You can't get a wagon through. You can drive it a bit of the way. My mule and cart can make it. It's narrower."

"Can we take it? I want to get as much of their things as possible so none of them wants to return for something important."

Sarah raised her head higher. "Smart of you. We'll get the wagon as far as we can and take the cart the rest of the way. Hopefully, everything will fit in with no more than one or two trips between Ike's cabin and your wagon."

Henny hoped so too. The faster they could get everything and head down the mountain, the better it would be.

Sarah swung on a heavy leather duster that looked as though it had been her late husband's. "Don't be thinking the girl will be a burden on you. She can pay her own way as well as the boys'. Ike owned this mountain. It's hers now."

Even though her leg still ached, Henny stood, prepared to leave the warmth behind. "The whole mountain?"

"At least this face of it. She'll need to check with the land office." The older woman hefted her shotgun and held the door open for Henny.

Nicole quickly hitched up Sarah's cart to her mule, and the three headed out, Sarah and her cart in the lead. About ten minutes in, Sarah stopped.

Nicole jumped down. "This is where you'll leave the rig. Wagon's too big to go between the trees. It's another half a mile or so."

No closer? But if the wagon wouldn't fit, it wouldn't fit. Henny and Nicole hopped on the tail end of the cart, riding backward. An inch of snow had blanketed the ground overnight. She hoped it didn't get any deeper.

At a cabin, similar to Sarah's but with an add-on, Nicole scooted off the back of the cart and strode toward the door. "Come on in." She opened it.

Henny stepped into the dim interior. Two wide-eyed boys clad in buckskins, twelve and seven, stood huddled together in the corner. They had likely seen Henny, a stranger, coming.

The older one spoke. "Who's that?"

Sarah stepped forward. "This here's my friend

Henny."

Nicole nodded. "She's all right. Come and say howdy."

They stepped forward, dirty from head to toe. Compared to them, Nicole had been nearly pristine yesterday. Had they missed their annual bath this year? *And* last?

The older one straightened. "Howdy."

"Good morning." If it was still morning. Henny wasn't sure.

Nicole pointed from one boy to the other. "That's Rolfy. This other one is Bucky."

The younger one squeaked out a howdy. Then he turned to Nicole, looking her up and down. "What happened to you?"

Nicole beamed. "I had a bath."

"What for? It ain't spring."

"People can take a bath any time of year if they want."

Bucky crinkled up his nose. "Why would anyone want to? Once a year is more than enough." He sniffed the air. "You smell different too. It's not right."

"Unless a person smells as though they've been wrestling a skunk, you wouldn't think it was right. People in town smell real nice. And you will too."

Rolfy furrowed his brow. "You ain't suggesting we go into town, are you?"

"I am. There are a whole bunch of cabins all together. Aunt Henny's offered us a place to stay."

Rolfy folded his arms. "I ain't goin'."

Nicole moved closer to him. "You have to. You both do. We don't have enough food to last us. It'll only be for the winter."

Not if Henny could help it.

Bucky pulled on Rolfy's shirtsleeve. "I am awful hungry."

"I'll hunt and fish and get us all the food we need. We ain't goin' to town."

The boy would prove to be difficult.

Bucky whimpered.

Henny held out an old flour sack. "I brought you

some butter cookies." She rolled down the sides and held it low enough for the younger one to peer inside.

He came closer and licked his lips.

Both boys consumed the cookies in a matter of minutes.

Henny wished she'd brought more substantial food. She hadn't thought they might not have eaten and would be so hungry.

Nicole rummaged in the kitchen area. "Why didn't you cook the beans and make biscuits?"

"We don't like beans, and biscuits are too hard to make."

Nicole shook her head. "Then you deserve to be hungry. Now gather your things. We have Sarah's cart and Aunt Henny's wagon on the other side of the creek."

Rolfy narrowed his eyes but didn't say he wouldn't go this time. A full belly from the cookies must have dampened his resistance.

⁂

Nick sent the boys to crate up the eight chickens with plenty of straw to roost in and burlap to cover the enclosure so they didn't freeze on the way down the mountain. Nick worked inside the cabin, gathering up everything that was personal to her, Grandpa, and the boys, not knowing what they might need over the winter.

Everything of importance fit into one cartload, a locked trunk Nick had never seen inside of, a coffee tin with money, flour tin with important papers and the key to the trunk, the shotgun, the rifle, Grandpa's collection of books including his Bible, a quilt made by a grandma Nick had never met, and a smattering of clothes. The readied chickens were strapped to the top and the milking cow was tied to the back.

Though not nearly the amount of belongings Aunt Henny had, Nick's life had been full and sufficient. Blankets, kitchenware, the meager food supplies, and various things around the place stayed for any trappers or hunters who wandered by needing a roof and food. It could mean the difference between life and death in the winter.

With all the belongings, only room enough for one person remained in the cart, which had been purposely left for Aunt Henny. The rest of them would walk to where the wagon had been left. Aunt Henny tried to talk Sarah into riding—she was, after all, the oldest—but the mountain woman wouldn't budge and claimed Aunt Henny would slow them down with her limp. But Nick suspected Aunt Henny knew, as Sarah did, that the cane-wielding woman wouldn't make it all the way to Sarah's with her bum leg.

With everyone and everything ready, Nick took a long look at the cabin that had been her only home. Would she miss it? She glanced over her shoulder. "You all head down, I'll meet up with you at the wagon. There's something I need to do."

Rolfy scuttled over to her, dragging Bucky with him. "If you're staying, so are we."

"Go on with Sarah and Aunt Henny. I'll be along in a minute."

Rolfy folded his arms. "What if I don't?"

Why was he being so obstinate? This wasn't like him. Sure, he refused to do his chores on occasion and tried to get by with "forgetting" to do his work, but this was different. Something akin to anger flickered in his eyes. Or was that fear?

"Those switches you got last summer are still above the fireplace. Do I need to get them?"

Rolfy stared hard at her for a long moment. "You're mean."

"No, I'm looking out for your best. Like Grandpa always did. He put me in charge. Now go, and don't cause Sarah or Aunt Henny no trouble."

He spun on his heel and stomped away down the trail.

Bucky threw his arms around Nick's waist.

She patted his shoulder. "Go on now. I'll be right behind you."

He ran after his brother, looking over his shoulder.

Aunt Henny waved and gave Nick a nod as Sarah urged the mule forward by a lead rope.

After picking a pair of short fir branches from a tree, Nick strode around behind the cabin to where two graves lay. One a month old. The other nearly two decades.

The older one had a white headstone. She never knew where Grandpa had gotten it. Probably from town. It had her mother's name, birth and death dates, as well as "Beloved daughter and mother." A clump of dead autumn flowers lay at its base. A ring of fist-sized stones with white caps of snow outlined the grave. Grandpa always took meticulous care of Ma's resting place. Nick wished she'd known her, but her mother had never been more than this speck of land, a person Grandpa rarely talked about. She swept the dried flowers away and laid one of the boughs in their place.

She shifted her attention to the freshly turned earth. Its marker a simple wooden cross with Grandpa's name and death date lovingly carved into it. Rolfy had insisted upon doing that. She draped the curved bough over the crossbar of the marker.

"I miss you, Grandpa. I know you can't hear me, but it feels right to speak these things out loud. You're not going to like what I'm doing, but I have no choice. The boys and I are heading into town. Sarah sent me to Aunt Henny. She's been ever so kind. I think you would like her. Now, don't get riled up, but the boys and I are going to spend the winter in Kamola with Aunt Henny. I'll look out for the boys and see to it they don't get themselves into trouble."

Nick rubbed her hands together to fight off the cold. "It's not going to be as easy as I thought to get a husband. I need to dress all different and act different too. I did meet a nice man though. I hope to see him again. I won't be able to return until spring. I'll get you a headstone to match Ma's. I wish you hadn't passed and could move to town with us. I think we might all do fine there." She took a deep breath. "I guess this is good-bye for now."

Something tickled her cheeks. Nick swiped at them, and her fingers came back wet. When had the tears come? She dried her face with her palms.

Then she headed inside the cabin one last time. It

would be months before she could return. She grabbed the pair of switches from the mantel. The plan had been to leave them behind, but if Rolfy had a determination to be contrary, maybe the presence of these twigs would remind him to behave.

Nick caught up to the others as they reached the wagon. The contents were quickly transferred from the cart to the bigger vehicle. No need for a second trip. That was for the best. Rolfy didn't need to get the idea he could stay.

Sarah pointed. "Take this meadow down and through that cluster of trees until you come to the main path. You'll get to town quicker than going by way of my place."

Aunt Henny approached Sarah. "I wish you'd reconsider coming into town."

"My Milton is buried up here. I can't be leaving him after all these years." Sarah climbed onto the seat of the cart. "Best be goin' before you lose the light."

Like Aunt Henny, Nick was reluctant to leave the old woman up here alone, but she doubted there was anything she could say to change her mind. Her stubbornness was likely what had kept her alive all these years.

An exhilaration swept through Nick at the anticipation of getting to experience the town—and for more than a brief visit of one day. But as the space lengthened between her and the only home she'd known, a twinge of guilt swirled inside her over her excitement. She shouldn't be happy to be leaving, should she?

Various trappers and hunters wandering through the area had talked about the towns they visited. Most, like Grandpa, preferred to live outside of them. A few spoke highly of them and could never wait to return to what they called civilization.

Nick determined to like Kamola, at least for as long as she remained there. If she was going to be stuck in town all winter, she might as well experience and learn all she could.

And hopefully see that handsome cowboy.

Four

THE NEXT DAY, NICK DID HER best to remember the order of the layers of clothing that went on before the dress. Lady dressing was complicated. Though she tried, she would need to have Aunt Henny show her again and maybe write it down. Yes, that's what she needed. A little stack of paper to keep notes of everything she wanted to remember how to do and to keep a list of questions to ask Aunt Henny. She peered over her shoulder while trying to tie the bow behind herself but couldn't manage so left the ends dangling. Aunt Henny would need to help her with that as well. She closed her door behind her and went to the boys' room next to hers and knocked.

No answer.

She eased the door open, but no one was there.

Oh, dear.

Rolfy hadn't taken Bucky back up to the mountain during the night, had he?

Her gut twisted. She hurried to the main floor and found Aunt Henny sitting on a chair next to the kitchen entry. The door stood closed. The days before it had always been open.

Aunt Henny looked up from her book and smiled. "Good morning. Breakfast is simple today, biscuits, jam, and hard-boiled eggs." She motioned toward the table.

"Sounds like a right fine meal. But I'm more concerned about the boys. I checked their room and they're missing."

Aunt Henny cocked a thumb toward the closed door. "They are taking a bath."

Relief swept through Nick. "They're bathing? Willingly?"

"Told them they couldn't eat until they were clean. They're pretty hungry, as growing boys usually are. And I wanted them clean before my Friday quilting circle shows up."

"What's a quilting circle?"

"A group of ladies gathers here each week to sew. You'll get to meet them."

Nick looked forward to that. "The only sewing I know is stitching up buckskin."

"We'll teach you. Would you like that?"

"I would. I want to learn everything. I couldn't tie the bow in the back of this dress, and I'm not sure if I got the underclothes on in the right order. I want to write it all down so I can learn which goes on over the other."

"Does everything feel comfortable enough?"

"I suppose."

"Then it's probably fine for now. Turn around, and I'll tie the bow."

Nick did and twisted to peer over her shoulder but couldn't see well enough.

Miss Tibbins came over and rubbed against Nick's skirt. "Looks like she's forgiven me for the terrible smells I brought in on my buckskins."

"Looks like it." Aunt Henny patted Nick's arm. "All done. Get yourself some breakfast."

Nick petted the cat, then sat at the dining room table and put two eggs and a biscuit on her plate.

Aunt Henny reached behind her and knocked on the door. "Are you boys done yet?"

"Almost," Rolfy called through the door.

"Hurry up or Nicole will eat all the food."

"No!" Bucky squealed.

Nick smiled. There was no better motivation than food for an empty stomach. "What are they going to wear? Their buckskins were dirtier than mine, and I doubt you could get them into dresses."

Aunt Henny laughed. "No, not dresses. I washed their summer clothes last night and hung them over the stove to dry."

Bucky burst through the door, scrambled onto a chair, reached for a biscuit, and froze, staring at Nick. "Whatcha wearing, Nick?"

"A dress." Like Aunt Henny, Sarah, and the March

sisters from *Little Women*. She stood and turned around. "Do you like it?"

He shrugged. "I don't know. It looks funny on you. I'm not gonna have to wear one of those, am I?"

"No." Aunt Henny put her book aside and stood next to him. "You'll get used to seeing her in it."

"I won't." Rolfy stood in the kitchen doorway with his arms folded. "What was wrong with buckskins?"

"She's a young lady, and ladies wear dresses."

Bucky's lips flapped as he blew out a breath. "Naw. That's just Nick."

"Her name is Nicole." Aunt Henny twisted the lid off the jam and helped spread some on Bucky's biscuit. "Rolfy, come sit and eat."

Her cousin plopped into a chair.

Nick stared at the food on her plate. How could he not like her dress? Would Mr. Keegan think her out of place in a dress as well?

After breakfast was eaten and the other boarders had left, Aunt Henny patted the back of one of the dining room chairs. "Boys, I'd like you to move these into the parlor for me."

The boys looked from Aunt Henny to Nick.

She waved a hand in their direction. "You heard her. Earn your keep." She picked up one herself and carried it to the other room.

Someone knocked on the door. Aunt Henny answered it and returned with another lady who appeared to be close to Aunt Henny's age. "This is my friend Agnes Martin. Come say hello."

Nick guided the resisting boys in front of her. She held out her hand. "I'm pleased to meet you. I'm Nick."

The woman raised her eyebrows. "Pleased to meet you."

Aunt Henny motioned toward Nick. "This is Miss Nicole Waterby. She and her cousins Rolfy and Bucky will be staying with me over the winter."

Nicole. She needed to start thinking of herself that way and remember to use that name and not Nick.

The woman smiled, causing deeper wrinkles to dent her face. "Why aren't you young men in school?"

School? Nicole had read about that and had wished she could have gone.

Aunt Henny responded. "We thought we'd give them a chance to settle in first."

Mrs. Martin studied the boys. "You two look familiar."

Rolfy scowled. "No, we don't." He grabbed Bucky's arm and ran upstairs.

Nick—cole opened her mouth to call them back, but Aunt Henny gave a little shake of her head. Nicole supposed a bunch of ladies sewing wasn't the place for her cousins.

When other ladies arrived, Aunt Henny introduced Nicole to them by twos and threes as they entered. She repeated their names in her head, but when the next group was introduced the previous ones scattered. She'd never met so many people at once. Would she be able to put any of the names with the faces? One was Lily, another Isabelle, an Adelaide, and someone named Dorthea. But who went with which? Each greeted her with a warm smile. If she didn't talk, no one would know she couldn't remember. She wished she had paper to write them all down on.

Aunt Henny gave her a short lesson on how to sew material for quilt blocks and provided her with a small stack of colorful fabric pieces. Not so different from sewing a patch on a shirt or trousers.

While working in silence, she pictured the first group of ladies who'd arrived and their names, as well as the last group and picked them out of the circle. That made half of them she could remember.

Nicole listened to the ladies around the room as they talked about doing things she had only read about as though they were regular, normal occurrences. But no one spoke of the kinds of things Nicole had done in her daily life. She cleared her throat. "May I ask a question?"

Aunt Henny smiled. "Of course, dear."

"I think I have missed a lot, living up on the mountain *but* learned a lot too. Do none of you hunt, fish, trap, and track?"

Ten pairs of eyes widened, and one older woman

gasped.

Betsy chuckled. "Oh, I'm going to like you." She adjusted her one-year-old son on her lap. "I'm sure more than just me fished when we were young—and I still do on occasion—as for those other things, men do them."

That's what Nicole had figured.

A young woman spoke up. "There is nothing wrong with a woman knowing how to do things a man can do."

Nicole never imagined there was anything wrong with it, but by a few of the reactions, some people obviously did.

The same woman went on. "I may not do some of the things that you have done, but I own a bicycle and enjoy riding it. Which a lot of people think isn't right for a woman, but I don't care."

Nicole didn't know what a bicycle was, but if it wasn't typical for a lady to own or ride one, it must be interesting.

A young woman across the circle caught Nicole's gaze. "I'm so glad you have joined us. I'm Franny. My father owns and runs Waldon's Mercantile."

That made one more she knew. Nicole mentally thanked the young woman for giving her name.

Franny continued. "This is becoming a regular occurrence, having new ladies join our circle. First Lily, and now you. I don't mean to be nosy, but what was it like living in the mountains? It sounds terribly exciting but very lonely. I wouldn't be able to be that far from town and away from people for so long."

"I wasn't alone. Grandpa and my cousins were there." Nicole hadn't known any different.

"But no other women?"

"We visited Sarah Combs a few times a year."

"Is that all? In spite of that, you seem to have turned out all right. Did you make your dress?"

"No. Aunt Henny's letting me borrow it. Until two days ago, I had never put on a dress before."

The same older lady gasped.

Had Nicole said something wrong? "It's all right. I had my buckskins. I sewed them. They are real comfortable. But I do like the dress." It made her feel...feel...more herself.

Another lady spoke. "To have the freedom to wear trousers would be wonderful."

"Isabelle! How unseemly." This from the woman who'd gasped. "You are a married woman. Trousers would be quite inappropriate."

Now, Nicole could remember another name, and with it, the woman's sister came to mind from their introductions. Were trousers truly inappropriate for women? They made sense for the rough mountain work she'd done, but maybe town was different. The sisters in Little Women wore only dresses. But why? "What's wrong with trousers?"

Aunt Henny patted Nicole's arm. "There is nothing wrong with them. They are generally considered men's clothing and dresses are women's."

"Trousers are better for hunting and skinning a deer. You wouldn't want to do those in a dress."

That same woman—whom she now remembered was Mrs. Atwood—gasped again.

"Women don't usually do those kinds of things." Another older woman touched her fingertips right below her throat. "I'm Dorthea. I don't mean to be indelicate, but did no one teach you proper behavior for a young lady?"

"Like manners? Is there a difference? Aren't manners, manners?"

"Yes, but there are certain ways women behave that are different from men. If you are interested in learning them, anyone of us would be happy to instruct you."

The gazes of everyone in the circle were on her, waiting for an answer.

"Yes, I want to know how to be a lady." These women were so generous.

Dorthea gave an encouraging smile. "Now?"

Nicole thought a moment. "I'd like that. I need to learn to be a lady like all of you so I can get me a husband. Aunt Henny says the man is to ask the lady, so I need to know how a lady acts so I can get a man to marry me. I'd appreciate any help you could offer."

Mrs. Atwood fanned herself with her hand.

Aunt Henny spoke for the group. "We would love to."

The silent room erupted in chatter. Betsy jumped to her feet and settled her son on her hip. "This will be fun."

The other younger women around the room set their sewing aside and also stood—Isabelle, Adelaide, Neva, Trudy, and Franny. They proceeded to teach Nicole how to walk and sit and hold a teacup, and what to say and not to say.

"There's a lot to know about being a lady. What if I'm asked a question you haven't taught me about?"

Mrs. Atwood said, "Don't worry about it. No one expects you to learn it all at once."

"I want to. I've learned all your names."

"You can't possibly have," Agnes said.

"But I have. Almost." Nicole went around the room naming all the women, but skipped one promising to come back to her. She pointed to the last lady. "You are either Trudy or Neva. I think you're Trudy." The lady smiled and gave a nod. Nicole returned to the one she'd skipped. "That makes you Neva."

"That's quite amazing," Neva said.

Nicole shrugged. "Not really. You all say each other's names a lot while you talk. I merely listened."

Betsy addressed the group. "If she can learn all our names in a snap, I dare say she can learn to be a lady by day's end." They all agreed.

Nicole liked the idea of being a lady by the end of the day. Then maybe a handsome man, such as Mr. Keegan, would consider courting her like the March sisters in *Little Women*.

Five

NICOLE LOWERED HERSELF TO HER KNEES in front of Grandpa's locked trunk sitting on the floor in the open space between the parlor and the dining room. Saturday had dawned cold and with a thin layer of snow on the ground. Fortunately, Aunt Henny had asked Professor Tunstall and Rolfy to haul it in from the barn after the quilting ladies had left yesterday. The key—though small—weighed heavy in Nicole's hand. She'd found it in the square tin of money Grandpa had stashed under his bed. He'd never let her, or anyone, see inside his trunk. Said there was nothing of interest. It interested Nicole a great deal but prying into Grandpa's personal belongings somehow seemed wrong.

Aunt Henny leaned forward in the chair she'd pulled up near the trunk. "I know this is difficult, but we need to see if there are any documents inside, like a deed to the mountain or bank account or other holdings so you know what you and the boys have. These are your possessions now. If you'd like, I can do it for you."

Nicole considered the older woman's offer. As strange as it was, these *were* her things now. "Thank you. I think I'm ready."

Rolfy and Bucky scurried over and sat silently next to her.

She turned the key in the lock, took a deep breath, and lifted the lid. A musty smell wafted out, prickling her nose.

Grandpa's Bible and *Little Women* sat atop an old quilt. She'd found the novel on Grandpa's shelf of books when she was twelve and had begun to read it. Meg, Jo, Beth, and Amy quickly became her friends. When she prattled on and on about the sisters, Grandpa took the book and returned it to the shelf, saying she didn't need to fill her head with nonsense. She hadn't even gotten halfway through, so she would sneak the book when Grandpa was busy. When Grandpa discovered her reading in the barn, he took it away for good. He'd said he'd burned it, but evidently not. Nicole had longed for that kind of fellowship, imagining herself as an additional March sister. She replayed the scenes she'd read in her head.

She picked it up and ran her hand over the dust jacket. "This belonged to my mother." She opened the cover and held it out to Aunt Henny to see the inscription. "She died when I was young."

"I'm sorry."

Nicole shrugged one shoulder. "I didn't know her." She closed the book. "Grandpa didn't like me reading this. I never really understood why."

"I'm sure he had his reasons."

Nicole lifted out Grandpa's worn Bible. "He would take this out on Sundays and read aloud. We were told never to touch it. He said he didn't want it messed up."

Inside the Holy Book were several old photographs, letters, and newspaper clippings.

She studied a photograph with a gentleman and lady dressed in fine clothes. The young man had Grandpa's eyes, and the round woman wore a lacy dress. On the reverse side, it said *Isaac and Bertha Waterby, 1855*. The back of a baby's likeness read *Maeve Waterby, 1858*. Another was of a young woman who looked a little like Nicole herself. *Maeve age fourteen, 1872*.

She set the Bible and its contents with the novel beside her and removed the quilt. Red embroidery in the corner read, *Bertha Fletcher, 1852*.

Next, she removed a silver brush and comb with intricate designs on them and a baby rattle as well as a tin with additional money. Two calico dresses, a pink and a green. "Can I wear these?" Then she would have dresses of her own.

Aunt Henny took them. "They are pretty worn and stained. Maybe we can take the best parts of both and make you something new. Would you like that?"

"I would." She lifted out the lacy white dress depicted

in the photograph of her grandparents.

"That must have been your grandmother's wedding dress."

Nicole stood and held it up to herself. "Maybe I'll wear this one day." She set it aside.

On the very bottom of the paper-lined trunk sat a stack of letters and papers. "Do you think this is what we're looking for?" Nicole scooped them up and held them out.

"I hope so." Aunt Henny took the bundle.

Bucky gripped the side of the trunk and peeked in. "Ain't there nothing for Rolfy and me?"

Rolfy clasped his brother's shoulder. "No. Now hush up."

Miss Tibbins sauntered over, put her front paws on the top edge, and peered in much the same way her youngest cousin had done. Then she jumped inside and sat.

Bucky waved his hands at the cat. "Shoo. That's Grandpa's trunk."

"It's all right." Nicole petted the cat. "She's not hurting anything."

"But I don't want her in Grandpa's trunk. She doesn't belong there."

She sensed her little cousin was missing Grandpa, so she lifted the cat out and closed the lid. "Is that better?"

Bucky nodded.

Aunt Henny moved to the dining room table with the stack of papers. "Do you mind if I sort through these?"

"I'd like it if you did. I don't know what to look for, and I doubt I'll know what they mean." Nicole sat in the chair beside the older woman. The boys clambered onto chairs as well.

Aunt Henny held up a piece of paper. "I believe I've found a deed of sorts, but I'm not sure how much land it entailed." She made a pile of several papers. "I think we should take these with us to the bank on Monday." She retrieved the Bible and flipped through it. "This might prove useful." She stopped and pointed at the bottom of a page with handwriting on it. "Here it is. Your name and date of birth as well as your mother's and grandparents'.

We'll take this too."

"Thank you so much. I don't know what I would do without you telling me what I need to do."

"I'm glad to help." Aunt Henny turned the page. "And here are Rolfy and Bucky... *Waterby.*" She turned the Bible for the boys to see their names.

Nicole leaned in for a look. "Why don't they have a mother or father listed?"

"I'm not sure, but we'll figure all that out."

Rolfy folded his arms. "Because we ain't got none."

Nicole squinted. That couldn't be right. "You had them at some point."

"Don't matter now." Rolfy stood. "Come on, Bucky." He strutted away.

Bucky followed in his wake. "Why ain't we got no mother or father, Rolfy?"

"We don't need 'em. We had Grandpa." Rolfy's voice broke at the end. "But we ain't even got him now."

Nicole hurt for her cousin. He loved Grandpa as much as she did. "He's sad at Grandpa's passing, but he doesn't want to show it."

"It's hard on a boy to lose the only man in his life."

Losing Grandpa was hard on them all.

On Sunday, Shane sat in the bunkhouse with his ranch hands, his Bible open in front of him. His men weren't of a mind to go to church, but everyone needed God. So it was Shane's responsibility to bring church to them. It had never bothered him until a stray thought the night before wouldn't let him go. Would the buckskin girl be at church? Aunt Henny went, so she would likely take the girl. It would be something to see heads turn her direction. She was sure to set the good townsfolk's tongues to wagging.

Maybe he could plan to go next Sunday. His men wouldn't mind the change. Shane could get inspired by the preacher and hold his Bible reading with his men in the afternoon. Unless, of course, he was invited to stick around. The church sometimes had picnics after the service. But would they in December? Probably too cold, and not with snow on the ground.

Shane's foreman, Handley, cleared his throat. "Are you going to read? Or are we just supposed to stare at you? We do have work we could be gettin' done. For you."

His other men nodded.

"Of course. I was lifting up a silent prayer." Shane rubbed the back of his neck. He must have gotten into some locoweed. How had he allowed a female to completely tangle his thoughts? *Lord, help me concentrate and focus on Your Word and what You'd have me say to these men.*

As he read, his mind replayed the buckskin girl tucking and rolling out of the way of those rearing hooves and then swinging her rifle toward him. Someone with quick reflexes and fast thinking could be a real asset.

He reached the end of the passage and realized he didn't remember reading any of the words, but he knew the selection well enough to pose a question to his men. They all shrugged except Bray, his newest hand. He'd hired the man with the pockmarked face over the summer.

Though he claimed not to be a God-fearing man, he seemed interested enough to ask questions. He screwed up his marred face and pinned Shane with one eye. "If your God is so good and loving, why does He let bad things happen?"

An age-old question. "Because He gave us the freedom to make choices. If He dictated everything to us, that wouldn't be very loving. Love is only truly love if it's given freely. Because we are sinful humans, bad things happen."

Shane flipped to the book of First Samuel and read about the Israelites wanting a king. "God said He would be their King. They wanted a man, so God let them have the one they wanted. Things didn't go well for the Israelite people, but God let them have their choice instead of forcing His decision on them."

Handley grunted. "Having things forced on you stinks."

Shane appreciated his foreman agreeing with him. He sounded as though he spoke from experience.

Bray nodded, not so much in agreement but likely understanding. "Was the man they wanted a good king?"

"Not really. He looked good and looked the part of a king, but he wasn't the leader the people needed."

Handley spit chewing tobacco juice out to the side. "Being a real leader is important. Not some pretender."

What disparaging experiences had jaded Handley? Were they at the hands of Shane's uncle?

Maybe Shane wouldn't sell in the spring but put his faithful foreman in charge for a while and roam the country before making his final decision.

He supposed that was enough for one day and excused his men to their duties. He wished he didn't have any so he could slip into town to see the reaction of people to Miss Waterby. But not today, he'd have to wait until tomorrow. And not to see the buckskin girl. No. He had things to pick up at the mercantile. Things like...like...?

Well, he couldn't think of them right now, but he would. He'd think of a whole list of things.

Six

NICOLE SMOOTHED HER HANDS DOWN HER borrowed yellow dress and turned to Aunt Henny. "Do I look all right? I'm still not sure if I got everything where it should be."

Aunt Henny smiled. "You look lovely."

Nicole touched her hair. "I notice that you and some of the other ladies have your hair all pulled up." She more likely resembled Jo, in *Little Women*, after she had sold her hair. "Mine's not long enough to do that, is it?"

Aunt Henny squinted and studied her. "I don't know. I have a few combs and pins that might hold it up. We could try if you like."

"Yes, please. If it's not too much trouble."

"No trouble at all. It would be my pleasure. Come to my room." Aunt Henny led the way down the hall.

Nicole stopped in the doorway. The bedroom was full of lace and ruffles and things that could break. Miss Tibbins lay curled on the bed with her head upside down, sleeping.

Aunt Henny stopped by a table with drawers and a mirror. "Come on in. You're not going to hurt anything."

Nicole stepped lightly into the room, like she would if she were trying not to crush delicate flowers. "I never knew there were such pretty things in the world." She stopped and pressed her foot up and down on the cushiony carpet. "This is even softer than the one in the other room or upstairs."

Aunt Henny laughed. "I have a weakness for pampering these old feet of mine." She patted the stool in front of her. "Have a seat and face the mirror."

Nicole obeyed. She reached out toward an array of small colored bottles but withdrew her hand before touching any.

Aunt Henny picked up a bulbous pink bottle and

removed the glass stopper. "This is perfume." She took a whiff then held it up to Nicole's nose.

"That's just like a meadow. Is its only purpose for smelling?"

"Sort of." Aunt Henny replaced the stopper, tipped the bottle, then dabbed the stopper on her wrist. "Sniff."

Nicole leaned forward and drew in a deep breath. "Now, *you* smell like a meadow."

"Hold out your arms."

Nicole eagerly obeyed.

Aunt Henny dotted the sweet liquid onto her skin. "And now, *you* smell like a meadow too." She gazed at the bottle a moment. "I've had this a very long time. I haven't worn it in years."

"Thank you for sharing it with me."

"My pleasure." Aunt Henny set the perfume down. "Now, let's see what we can do with your tresses." She pulled a silver brush through Nicole's dark locks.

The bristles felt good on her head. She'd always liked using her mother's brush and comb until Grandpa had hidden them away.

Aunt Henny took a couple of strands of Nicole's hair between her fingers and twisted, added more to it, and twisted again. When she got around to the back, she secured it there, then she did the same twisting to the other side. Aunt Henny coiled both ends together and put a mess of hairpins in it. "How do you like that?"

Nicole's mouth pulled up on the corners. "I look like the other ladies. Not like my cousins at all."

"You most certainly don't." Aunt Henny held up a pair of small, curved white combs. "These combs are both decorative and help hold your hairstyle in place." She tucked one in on each side. "What do you think?"

Nicole turned one way and then the other to see them better. "Is it terrible of me to like them—a lot—when I know Grandpa wouldn't have approved?"

"Not terrible at all. He was merely trying to protect you. I think he might be pleased if he saw you."

Nicole spun around to peer directly at Aunt Henny. "You think so?"

"How could any loving grandfather not be pleased?"

Nicole faced the mirror again. If she didn't know it was herself, she would think the girl in the mirror was a real lady.

She went to the kitchen where Rolfy and Bucky sat eating biscuits with raspberry preserves. Bucky had red smears around his mouth and even on his cheek. "How do I look?"

Both boys swung their heads in her direction, and their eyes widened. Bucky spoke first. "Your hair's funny."

Nicole touched her hair. "Young ladies wear their hair up."

"Oh." He turned back to his biscuit and took another big bite.

Nicole focused on Rolfy. "What do you think?"

"You look strange."

Nicole's shoulders slumped.

Aunt Henny stepped forward. "I think the word you're after is pretty."

Rolfy shrugged and returned to his own biscuit.

Aunt Henny spoke softly into her ear. "Don't mind them. They don't understand. You're beautiful. When they're older, they'll enjoy seeing girls dressed as you are."

Nicole waved toward their plates. "Hurry up and finish. We need to be leaving."

Rolfy shot to his feet. "Are we going back to the cabin?"

Why was her cousin so determined? "I told you we're spending the winter here."

"But I don't want to. I want to go home. I don't like it here."

"You're being rude. Apologize." Nicole hoped she didn't have to pull out the switches as motivation.

He took a long slow breath and then blasted it out. "Sorry."

"Thank you. Now wash up so we can go into town."

Rolfy folded his arms. "I'm not goin'."

"Don't you want to peer in all the shops?"

"Nope."

"Not even the Sweets Shoppe?"

Bucky jumped up and down. "I want to! I do!"

Rolfy nudged him. "No, you don't. He's staying with me."

Bucky's shoulders slumped, and he heaved a sigh. "I'll stay here."

Nicole studied her youngest cousin. "You don't have to." His eyes said he wanted to go, but the pull of his big brother outweighed his own will.

"Everything is new for them and a big adjustment." Aunt Henny placed a hand on Nicole's shoulder. "I think it will be all right if they stay here. We might be a while, and they would be stuck waiting without much to occupy them."

No sense making the boys lollygag around at the bank while she talked to someone there. They could go into town another day. "I'll bring you something sweet." She shifted her gaze to Rolfy. "And something for you too."

Aunt Henny gave the boys instructions about where they were allowed in the house and what they could do. She set out food for later and gave instructions for lunch, in case she and Nicole weren't home in time.

At the bank, Nicole and Aunt Henny sat in padded, leather chairs across the desk from the well-dressed banker, Mr. Mallory.

Aunt Henny leaned forward. "Nicole's grandfather Isaac Waterby recently passed away. I'm given to understand that he might have had some money, and we were wondering if he had an account at this bank?"

"Do you have any kind of proof as to the relationship between Mr. Waterby and this young lady?"

Aunt Henny gave Nicole a nod.

Nicole lifted the Bible from her lap and laid it on the desk. She opened to a page with handwriting on it and pointed. "This is my grandpa's name, my mother's, and mine."

Mr. Mallory studied the writing and gave a nod. "The bank will accept this. Isaac Waterby does—or did have—or rather has an account here. There is an account in his name. I'm also to understand that he had arrangements with an attorney, Bright Thatcher. I'd check with him as well."

"Thank you. We appreciate that."

"Actually, why don't I escort you ladies over to the attorney's office. I can bring this file, and we might be able to take care of all this business at once."

A little something inside Nicole leapt for joy at being called a lady. Like a small piece of her had been missing all these years.

Aunt Henny turned to Nicole. "Would you like that, dear? Mr. Mallory certainly knows more about these things than I do."

If Aunt Henny thought it was a good idea, that was good enough for Nicole. "I would."

"Wonderful." Aunt Henny addressed the banker. "We would greatly appreciate your escort and help. My buggy is out front when you're ready."

Mr. Mallory stood. "I need to give instructions to Jonathan, and I'll be ready."

Aunt Henny got to her feet. "We'll wait for you outside."

Nicole followed the older woman out.

Shane trotted across the street to where Aunt Henny exited the bank with a young woman. "Aunt Henny."

The two stopped and glanced around until they spotted him.

He tipped his hat as he approached. "Howdy, ladies. Aunt Henny, I was wondering if I could stop by your place later and speak with that girl I dropped off the other day."

"Why not speak to her now?" Aunt Henny motioned to the lady next to her. "Shane Keegan, this is Miss Nicole Waterby."

He shifted his gaze to the beautiful lady next to her and stared.

She extended her hand, then retracted it, and made an awkward curtsy. "Pleased to make your acquaintance, Mr. Keegan."

He continued to stare.

He squinted.

He blinked.

She couldn't be the same buckskin-clad girl he met five days ago. Could she?

Aunt Henny chuckled. "Mr. Keegan, unless you're hungry, you're going to catch a few flies."

"Huh?" He shifted his gaze to Aunt Henny.

"Your jaw seems to have come unhinged."

He closed his mouth and focused on the girl again. "You're the one who was in buckskin?"

"I am. I don't think I thanked you well enough for showing me to Aunt Henny's."

He tried to picture this beauty in a dress rolling on the ground to get out of the way of a rearing horse and come up ready to shoot. He shook his head.

Miss Waterby slapped her hand on top of her head. "You aren't going to steal my hat again, are you?"

Definitely, the same girl. "Of course not. You look so different." Beautiful with her dark hair and curious violet eyes.

Aunt Henny cleared her throat. "You wanted to talk to Miss Waterby about something?"

Working on his ranch as a hand? No. He couldn't ask a pretty little filly like her to do that. Wouldn't be right. "I...um..."

Mr. Mallory exited the bank and held the door open. "Mr. Keegan, it's nice to see you. Are you going in?"

Shane shook his head.

Mr. Mallory released the door and addressed the ladies. "You two ready to go?"

Aunt Henny gave a nod. "We are." She turned toward the waiting buggy.

Shane kept his gaze on Nicole. "Are you going with him as well?"

"Yes. He said I need to talk to my grandpa's attorney." She lowered her voice. "I'm not quite sure what that is, but I know it's important."

Shane liked her openness.

"Miss Waterby, are you ready?" Mr. Mallory asked.

"Coming." Nicole spun, causing her skirt to flare out in a feminine swish, as though she were dancing.

Mr. Mallory helped her into the buggy and soon the trio drove away.

Shane stiffened his jaw. Once again Mr. Mallory was escorting a lady Shane was attracted to. How could he compete with a banker? If he were smart, he'd give up right then. He didn't need to be thinking about any female, not when he was going to be moving on. But no one had ever accused him of being smart. And Miss Nicole Waterby was the most intriguing lady he'd ever met.

Maybe he could take the pair of ladies to lunch after their appointment. That should get her out of his system.

Seven

ONCE INSIDE THE ATTORNEY'S OUTER OFFICE, Mr. Mallory said, "You ladies wait here while I speak with Mr. Thatcher. May I take your Bible to him?"

Nicole handed it over and sat with Aunt Henny on a pair of padded chairs in the reception area while Mr. Mallory disappeared through a doorway.

Aunt Henny shifted on the cushion. "What do you think of Mr. Keegan?"

She'd been pleased to see him. The sight of him warmed her insides. If only their meeting hadn't been so short. "He's nice."

"I think he was quite taken with you."

"I'm not sure what you mean. He didn't take anything of mine. Not even my hat."

Aunt Henny chuffed a laugh. "Oh, I don't think he'd do that when you're dressed like a lady. It means, he found you attractive, and he liked what he saw."

"He did?" The thought warmed her all over. "How could you tell with all his sputtering?"

"It's the sputtering that told me."

Nicole delighted in the idea of Mr. Keegan finding her appealing.

"Do you like him as well?"

"He was the only person to be friendly to me when I first came. And he's pleasant on the eyes, doesn't pain mine one bit."

"That he is. He doesn't pain mine either. Should we invite him to supper?"

"I'd like that."

Mr. Mallory stepped out of the attorney's office. "Ladies, please join us."

Nicole stood.

Aunt Henny remained seated. "I'll wait out here for

you."

"You're not coming in?" Nicole's insides twisted.

"How much money one has is a very private matter. I don't want to intrude."

"I don't care if you know. I need you to tell me what to do." Nicole needed her. The older woman had been like a strong hitching rail Nicole could tether herself to. "I would feel better to have your help."

Aunt Henny glanced at Mr. Mallory who gave a nod. "Very well." She stood. "If you would like, I'll come with you. I'd be happy to assist in any way I can."

The trio entered the office. Mr. Mallory introduced the attorney to the ladies then seated Nicole and Aunt Henny in the two chairs opposite Mr. Thatcher's desk. The attorney, who seemed to be close to Aunt Henny's age, resumed his seat.

Mr. Mallory pulled up a third chair next to Nicole.

Mr. Thatcher leaned forward. "I first want to say you have my condolences. I have known Isaac Waterby for many years."

"Then you know about my family. Did my grandpa always live in the mountains?"

"No, he didn't."

Nicole suspected not. He seemed different from the trappers, hunters, and other mountain men who occasionally stopped by their cabin.

"Isaac came west from New York and landed in California in '49 right before the gold rush. He was one of the blessed ones who found his fortune early on and didn't squander it. He married in '55. His daughter, Maeve, was born in '58, and his wife passed a few months later. He stayed in California until the early seventies, saw money in timber and came north and bought a huge portion of forested land. That's when I met him. Maeve must have been about fourteen. He took her everywhere with him. Inseparable, those two. They went into the mountains to survey the timber and to decide where to start their logging business. One day, Isaac came to town distressed. Maeve had disappeared. After a time she returned and had you"—the attorney pointed to Nicole—"and I believe she died within a couple of years."

Nicole knew her mother had died all those years ago. "Do you know who my father is? Grandpa never said."

"I don't. Ike never told me." Mr. Thatcher opened a folder. "This is your grandfather's last will and testament. Do you know what that is?"

Nicole shook her head.

"It's what he wants to happen to his belongings."

"I understand that. But we didn't have anything but the cabin and what's in it. I already have what's important from there."

"Ike had a whole lot more. He has a bank account in New York, as well as one in California, besides the one here in Kamola."

Mr. Mallory nodded. "According to the bank's ledgers, he has moved money to and from each one. I only know the amount in our bank."

Mr. Thatcher nodded. "I can contact the others and get those totals. I believe it's safe to say you are now a wealthy woman."

Nicole wasn't sure exactly what that meant. "All right."

"There are three other beneficiaries mentioned in his will. The first is Sarah Combs, the widow who lives on the mountain."

Nicole was pleased Grandpa left her something. She'd always been a good friend to her and Grandpa and then the boys.

The attorney went on. "She is never to be turned off the property she resides on. When she passes, the land reverts to his other beneficiaries."

Nicole assumed that the farm belonged to Sarah and was glad to hear she wouldn't have to move. She would always have her home. Nicole wouldn't want to be the person to tell Sarah she had to move. She would likely get shot for her efforts.

"The other two are Rudolf Miller and Theodore Miller. He wouldn't tell me who they were, but from the wording, I assume they are children, or at least were, when he changed his will three years ago. Do you know who they are?"

"I guess he must be talking about Rolfy and Bucky, but their second name is Waterby. It's written in his Bible."

He studied the open book on his desk. "I don't see their names."

"They're on the next page."

Mr. Thatcher turned the page. "I see. How old are they?"

"Rolfy's twelve and Bucky's seven."

"And who are they to your grandfather?"

"They are my cousins. They came to live with us about five years ago."

Mr. Thatcher sat silent for a few moments. "Where are they now?"

"At Aunt Henny's boarding house."

"And you are their guardian?"

Nicole darted her gaze to Aunt Henny.

"You look after them."

Nicole focused on Mr. Thatcher again. "Yes. I guard them."

The attorney raised his eyebrows but continued. "Because of their ages, it won't be necessary for them to be present to read the will. He proceeded to read out loud the document in front of him.

Nicole was to be guardian to Rolfy and Bucky until their eighteenth birthdays and to manage their finances until their twenty-fifths. If anyone else were to take guardianship of the boys, they weren't allowed to touch the boys' shares of the mountain, only Nicole would have access. She would hold onto their inheritance until they came of age.

All three children were to have an equal percentage of the mountain as well as money made from it, including the timber. All other properties, holdings, and moneys went to Nicole, his only grandchild. Grandpa's estate was apparently vast, with a shipping business in California. Aunt Henny tried to explain to her what the amount of her wealth meant, but she suspected it would take a while before she fully understood the value of money. Animal pelts, firewood, and necessities for living were much easier to understand, but she would learn.

Nicole let everything settle in. "I don't understand. How can I be his only grandchild? What about Rolfy and Bucky? Who would come and try to take their inheritances?"

"He wouldn't elaborate even when I questioned him on it. I suspected they weren't blood related. He was determined to see to it they have secure futures."

Nicole glanced to Aunt Henny.

The older woman didn't seem surprised by this news and gave a nod. "We'll talk about this later and see if we can figure it all out."

Did Aunt Henny know something?

Both the attorney and Mr. Mallory had Nicole sign various documents. Even though the two men explained everything she was to sign, Aunt Henny helped her understand them.

Mr. Thatcher straightened all the papers. "I'll file these with the courts to make everything official. We'll still need to get the deed to the mountain and various other properties transferred into your name. Did your grandfather have any papers?"

Nicole pulled open the reticule Aunt Henny had loaned her and removed a folded piece of paper. "Is this what you're needing?"

The attorney studied the document. "This is it. This will make the process easier."

"Miss Waterby knows very little about her family. Is there anything else you can tell her about them?"

"I'll tell you what I know. It's not much. Isaac Waterby came here twenty years ago or so from New York by way of the '49 California gold rush. That's why he has bank accounts in all three locations. He wanted to get into timber and build a sawmill. But then the incident with his daughter, Maeve, happened, and he remained in the mountains. Only came into town a few times a year. He went from fine suits in those first meetings to mountain man garb. Like he turned a bit wild. I don't know what went on up there, but the mountain changed him."

Nicole had seen glimpses of the refined man who had worn the suits, and now some of his actions and words she hadn't understood before, made sense. "Thank you."

"I can make some inquiries on your behalf and see if I can locate any relatives in either New York or California if you'd like."

"I would appreciate anything you could find out." How wonderful if she had other family.

This had all been a lot to take in. Her cousins might not be blood related, and she might have kin clear across the country.

"Let's head over to the land office to get this deed transferred. It's right next door. Shall we go now?"

Everyone stood.

She and Aunt Henny seemed to be gathering people everywhere they went.

༄

Stepping out of the attorney's office, Henny swung her cane forward and put it down. She moved along the boardwalk to the office next door. She depended less and less on the use of her cane but still liked to have it for when her leg got tired as well as for balance. It would do her no good to fall and break her other leg.

Across the street stood that man again who'd been outside her boarding house. He held something a little bigger than his hand, which appeared to be about four inches by six, the size of a cabinet card. If so, who was the photograph of? When he noticed her staring back at him, he tucked the card into his breast pocket and hurried away.

Could he be one of the "anyones" in Isaac Waterby's will whom he feared might come for Rolfy and Bucky? Could he be the boys' father? She would keep an extra close eye on the boys and anyone lurking about.

Inside the land office, Mr. Thatcher introduced Nicole to Mr. Jenkins. "She has a land deed we need to get transferred." He held out Mr. Waterby's will and Nicole's copy of the deed.

Mr. Jenkins extended a hand. "Please have a seat, ladies. Sorry, I don't have chairs for everyone. I don't usually have so many people at once."

Henny sat.

Nicole remained standing and offered the other chair to Mr. Thatcher. "You likely need it more than me."

"I'm not so long in the tooth I can't stand. Wouldn't be right for a gentleman to sit and leave a lady on her feet."

"But you're—"

Henny patted Nicole's arm. It would be best if she didn't finish that thought out loud. Everyone knew what she was going to say anyway. "You're not going to convince any of the men to take a seat. Now don't make me be the only one sitting."

Mr. Jenkins remained poised in front of his chair.

Nicole's gaze darted around. She appeared as though she wanted to argue but finally gave in.

After taking his seat, Mr. Jenkins silently read the portion of the will pertaining to the mountain and studied the deed. He got to his feet and opened a cabinet drawer, withdrew a file folder, then he sat, spread it on his desk, and studied it. He stood again and opened another cabinet, withdrew a second folder, and retook his seat, studying it as well.

Henny wanted to scream, *Talk! Let us know what you're doing.*

But the man's every move was in silence, which didn't seem to bother the other two men.

Mr. Jenkins lifted his gaze. "Is there anything in Mr. Waterby's will about his other property?"

Isaac Waterby had other property in the area?

Mr. Thatcher stepped forward and picked up the will. "Nothing specific. The mountain is to belong to all three children equally and everything else goes to his granddaughter, Nicole Waterby."

"That covers the other property, but I'll need some sort of identification for the other two to properly transfer and divide the mountain between the three—when the boys come of age, of course."

"I'm planning to check into Miss Waterby's other relations. I can do so for the boys as well. Then I can draw up the legal documents giving Nicole the rights to do as she wishes with her share while holding the boys' shares in trust until they come of age."

Henny would be inquiring about the boys' previous circumstances as well.

"Good, then I'll make preparations for the deed transfer."

Was no one going to ask what the other property was? Henny stared hard at Nicole, willing her to ask.

The girl widened her eyes in understanding. "Excuse me. Aunt Henny has something she wants to say."

Not what Henny was after, but since she had everyone's attention. "I think Miss Waterby would like to know about the other property."

Nicole sat straighter. "Yes, I would."

Mr. Jenkins' mouth formed an oh. "I'm sorry. I assumed you knew." He rubbed his chin. "He owns—or rather owned a parcel of land on the north end of town. Now, you own it."

The end where Mrs. Kesner and the other society folks lived?

Henny had to ask. She couldn't help herself. "Are there any buildings on it?"

Mr. Jenkins pressed his lips together. "Let me check." He retrieved a large roll of paper and spread it across his desk on top of the papers already there. He tapped the map. "Plot 63." He returned to his cabinet and retrieved another file. "Hmm." He lifted the large map, which extended beyond the edges of his desk, and ducked his head under it. He reappeared with the other two files. He exchanged one folder on the top for the next and the next.

Henny wanted to snatch all the folders and read them herself. Instead, she clasped her hands together. Tightly.

"Plot 63 doesn't appear to have been built upon. He filed plans to build a large, fine house, but construction never began."

Probably because Nicole's mother disappeared. Henny would definitely be having a conversation about all this with Nicole later.

Nicole stood and leaned over the map. "Where is my grandpa's mountain?"

He pointed it out and showed the boundary lines.

"I had no idea he'd owned so much land."

The information surprised Henny as well. Hearing the numbers in the will and seeing the area on the map were very different.

Nicole pointed to the map. "I see the town, but what are all of these?"

"Various ranches." Mr. Jenkins named several. "And this one is the Bristol ranch, now the Keegan ranch." He tapped the map.

Nicole put her fingers on the portion belonging to Mr. Keegan. "He's not so far from the mountain. They touch right here. We're neighbors." She apparently liked that. The girl was sweet on the rancher.

Henny was concerned Nicole had become smitten with the first man she'd met in town. She'd need to keep an eye on that to be certain he was the upstanding gentleman she thought him to be.

Eight

SHANE WAITED UNTIL AUNT HENNY'S BUGGY came to a stop outside the bank before goading Huckleberry forward. Mr. Mallory climbed down and spoke to the ladies, but they didn't get out.

As Shane neared, the banker said, "I should go. I don't want to keep the little lady waiting." He tipped his hat to Shane and ducked inside.

If Mr. Mallory hadn't married Isabelle Atwood, who was this "little lady?" His wife? Someone else? It didn't matter as long as he didn't have his eye on Nicole.

Speaking of which, he tipped his hat to her. "Good day, ladies. I was wondering if I could entice the two of you to join me for lunch at the hotel dining room?"

Nicole beamed at him. "Yes. I'm hungry."

Aunt Henny had opened her mouth to reply but was stopped by Nicole's eager answer. Now, she rolled her eyes.

Shane understood Miss Waterby shouldn't have answered so quickly. Though her swift response was refreshing. No coyness or playing games. He delighted in her eagerness to eat with him. "Is that all right with you, Aunt Henny?"

The older woman's gentle smile told him she appreciated him asking. "That would be lovely. Shall we meet you there?"

"I'll get a table." He galloped away.

After tethering Huckleberry to the hitching rail and securing a table, he waited outside. When they pulled up in Henny's buggy, he helped Nicole down. His hands fit nicely around her waist. Something he could get used to. He set her on the boardwalk. Though he didn't want to let go, he did. He turned to assist Aunt Henny.

She repositioned the reins. "I'm sorry. I'm not going

to be able to join the two of you. I need to go home and see how the boys are getting on. I don't want them to become bored and get into mischief."

Nicole edged toward the buggy. "I forgot about the boys. I should go with you."

"Nonsense. You eat here. We will be fine." Henny shifted her attention to Shane. "You'll see her home safely."

"Yes, ma'am."

"I don't have to caution you on proper manners, do I?"

"No, ma'am. I'll be a gentleman."

"I know you will. If you're not, I'll be talking to my good friend Sheriff Rix about you." She winked.

Shane laughed.

"I'll see you both back at my boardinghouse later." She drove off.

Shane turned to Nicole and pulled open the door. "Shall we go in, Miss Waterby?"

She nodded and entered.

He followed with a strange bounce in his step. He would be spending time with a most intriguing lady. He hadn't been this enlivened over a meal in... Well, he couldn't remember when.

⌒∾⌒

Nicole's innards felt all squirrelly, partly as though they decided to change places and partly like a laugh was itching to burst free.

Shane Keegan pointed. "I have the table by the window saved."

She strolled over to the one he'd indicated and gripped the back of the chair.

Mr. Keegan's hand touched hers as he took hold of the chair as well. "Let me get that for you."

A tingle at his touch skittered along her arm, making her insides even more squirrelly. She was about to tell him she could do it for herself but remembered what the quilting women had said about letting a gentleman seat her. She very much wanted Mr. Keegan to think of her as a lady. She reluctantly removed her hand, waited for him to pull out the chair, and sat the way she had been instructed. "Thank you very kindly."

"My pleasure." After rounding the table, he seated himself across from her. He picked up the heavy paper in front of him and handed her the one on her side of the table. "The menu tells you what foods they are serving."

She gaped at the food listed. "How's a person supposed to eat all this?"

He chuckled. "You pick one of the meat items. Each comes with potatoes, green beans, and bread roll. Then you can have either pie or cake for dessert."

"I don't want to put anyone to any trouble."

"It's no trouble. That's what we're paying them to do. They make us food, and we pay them to do it."

"Isn't that something." Nicole licked her lips. To have someone else cook her whatever she wanted was wonderful.

"You've never been in a restaurant before?"

"Nope." She drank in the delicious smells. "But I'm going to like it."

A woman came and asked them what they would like to eat, then scribbled something on a piece of paper before leaving. Mr. Keegan had seemed surprised she'd ordered steak. Whenever Grandpa returned home from a trip to town with some, she loved it.

Mr. Keegan watched Nicole.

She squinted at him. "Do I have a dirt smudge on my face or something?"

He blinked a few times. "What?"

"You were staring at me as though there was something wrong."

"No. Nothing wrong. I'm just getting used to your transformation. You look very nice."

"Thank you. You look nice too."

He pulled his eyebrows together and a deep crease formed between them. "I'm wearing my work clothes."

"Well, they are nice. They suit you."

"Do they?" A smile played at the corners of his mouth. "May I ask you a personal question?"

"You may."

His frisky smile twitched. "The boys you and Aunt Henny spoke of, who are they?"

"They are my younger cousins, Rolfy and Bucky."

His shoulders relaxed as though he was relieved, then he leaned forward on the table. "I didn't plan for this to be only the two of us, so I don't want you to think I'm courting you or something. Simply friends getting to know each other."

The ladies had told her courting was what a lady and a gentleman did who were going to get married. "What would be wrong with courting?"

His lips parted, and he stared a moment. "Um...we don't know each other well enough to be thinking about courting. It takes time."

"That's what Aunt Henny said. She said I couldn't just ask a man to be my husband. The man has to do the asking. Seems like a lot of waiting for something that might not happen. Wouldn't it save time if both people knew if the other was even interested? Let's say you were interested, but I wasn't. But I'm not saying I'm not"—because inside, she thought she probably was interested, but she didn't think Aunt Henny would approve of her saying so—"then you could say 'so long' and find another lady."

Mr. Keegan's mouth pulled up hard on one side. "You are a refreshing change."

"Change from what?"

"From other ladies. You're different."

What did he mean by that? Wasn't she acting ladylike enough? Hadn't she done everything the ladies told her to do? She reviewed her posture and the position of her hands. She was doing everything as instructed. It must be something else. "How am I different? Don't I have two arms and legs and a head?"

"Not in the way you look—well, yes, partly the way you look—but it's your attitude about things."

"Grandpa would say, 'don't give me that defiant attitude,' or 'don't take that crosswise attitude with me.' So you think my attitude is bad? I'm trying ever so hard to act like a lady."

"There is good attitude and bad attitude."

"So, you think I have a good attitude and other ladies have bad attitudes?" This was confusing.

"Not good or bad, just different. How you view things. Most women wouldn't come right out and talk about courting and how they feel. They would hide it behind a coy smile and keep a man guessing."

That seemed silly. "Why would a lady want to do that? What if the guessing is wrong?"

"Good questions. Control, I suppose? To catch a gentleman off guard."

"Do men like to be caught off guard?" It sounded like a lot of fuss for nothing and time wasting.

"I suppose so."

"Why?"

"Makes a lady interesting if he doesn't always know what to expect."

She would need to ask Aunt Henny about how to do that and how to get a gentleman to ask her to court and be her husband.

The waitress hustled up to their table with plates of food.

Everything tasted wonderful, and Nicole didn't even have to clean the dishes. She was going to like living in town where other people cooked for her and washed the dishes.

After eating, Mr. Keegan escorted her outside. "I'll go rent a buggy to take you home. I'll only be a few minutes."

"No need for that."

"Well then, I can set you upon my horse, and you can ride that way."

"Do all you townsfolk let a horse do all your walking?"

He chuckled. "No. But you're a lady, and ladies don't usually walk places."

"So, because I'm a lady, I shouldn't walk? Then what did the good Lord give me two legs for?"

"I see your point. If you don't mind walking, then neither do I."

"I prefer to stretch my legs. They're getting a mite itchy to be on the move." Nicole wasn't used to not doing so much. On the mountain, there was always work needing to be done.

"Are you sure? It's a few blocks."

"It's not so far. I can almost see it from here. It'll be good on account I ate more than I have in a long time." She slapped her hand on her stomach. Some of these rules about how men and women were supposed to act seemed a little odd. Acting like a woman couldn't walk a short little bit. Like she might break or something.

Mr. Keegan led his horse as they strolled along the edge of the street.

She told him about living on the mountain and some of her cousins' antics and poor decisions.

Once at the boarding house, Nicole found Aunt Henny sitting in the parlor. "Were the boys good for you?"

"Yes. While we were gone, they mended the sagging corral gate, cleaned the horse's stall, and filled the wood box in the kitchen. And when I arrived, they sent me inside, unhitched the buggy, and brushed down the horse. I didn't have to do a thing. I could get used to service like this."

Nicole was glad to hear her cousins had been useful. And they did it all without asking, proving they knew what to do. "Where are they now?"

"They asked to ride the horse after lunch. I told them they could in the grazing field. I hope that was all right."

"Yes, that's fine. I'm going to go check on them."

Mr. Keegan followed her. "Mind if I join you? I'd enjoy meeting the boys who thought they could tangle with a hornets' nest and win."

Maybe she shouldn't have told him that story. "Sure. Come along."

Aunt Henny came as well.

In the field, Rolfy trotted the horse around.

Nicole strode up to the fence where Bucky sat on the top rail.

"Nick! You're back!"

"I am. I hear you helped out."

"I did." He held out his hands. "I got splinters, and Aunt Henny pulled them out just like you. I didn't even cry."

"Good for you. Bucky, this is Mr. Keegan."

Bucky thrust his arm forward. "Howdy."

Mr. Keegan took the tiny hand in his big one and shook it. "Howdy."

Why did Nicole wish it were hers Mr. Keegan was holding? She certainly had some strange thoughts when it came to Shane Keegan.

He pointed toward the field. "How's your brother doing?"

"Swell. He's really good with horses. He let me ride first. Now he's taking his turn."

Rolfy turned the animal and apparently saw Nicole for the first time. He goaded it into a run. As the horse skidded to a stop, Rolfy swung down. "Who are you?"

"Rolfy, that's rude."

"It's all right. He's a young man looking out for his kin." Mr. Keegan held out his hand. "I'm Shane Keegan. I have a ranch outside of town."

Rolfy squinted and eyed him for a moment, then apparently deemed Mr. Keegan all right, relaxed his stance, and shook his hand. "I prefer just straight Rolf."

"Rolf it is. You appear as though you can handle a horse well."

Before Rolfy could answer, Bucky did for him. "He's really good with animals. We all say so, don't we Nick?"

"Yes, we do."

Rolfy squared his shoulders. "Animals are easier to figure out. They always have a reason for what they do. Where's your ranch?"

"About four miles to the northwest of here. Grazing land starts before that."

Her cousin pinned Mr. Keegan with a hard stare. "You need some help out there? I'm a real hard worker."

"Rolfy. No." Nicole couldn't believe her cousin. "We are staying here. Please excuse him."

"I don't want to live in this town. I don't like it."

"How would you know? The farthest you've gone from the house is the barn and this field. You haven't even been in town."

Before Rolfy could spout the retort obviously itching

his tongue, Mr. Keegan spoke. "Hey, boys. Would you bring my horse a bucket of water? He's out front."

"Sure." Rolfy trotted off with Bucky trailing in his wake.

"His name is Huckleberry." Once the boys were out of earshot, Mr. Keegan swung his gaze to her. "I'm not going to get between you and your kin, but Rolf is going to run away if you make him stay here."

Nicole didn't want to lose her cousin. "Why do you say that? You only just met him."

He hesitated for a moment. "It's in his eyes. I see myself in him at that age. Except I had already run away. I have plenty of room out at the ranch, and you can come see him whenever you like. Maybe I can find out what's troubling him. I could always use another hand, and I can pay him."

Nicole shifted her gaze from Mr. Keegan to Aunt Henny.

The older woman nodded. "I agree. The boy has a lot churning on the inside he's not talking about. There won't likely be enough chores around here to keep him out of trouble. He may be more likely to talk to a man."

Mr. Keegan held out his hands. "It's up to you."

Rolfy had been against coming to town from the very start, but she didn't like the idea of him being so far away. "Maybe we could try it and see how it goes?"

"Sounds fair."

"When do you want him?"

"The sooner the better. I can take him with me now if that's all right with you."

A place in Nicole's heart constricted at being separated from either of her cousins, but she believed it to be the best option. If Rolfy was likely to run away anyway, it would be better to know where he was. She took a deep breath to gather her courage. "I best go tell him to pack."

She strode to the front of the house where Huckleberry waited, Mr. Keegan at her side. The boys petted the horse but stopped when she approached.

Rolfy glared at her then leveled his gaze at Mr. Keegan and squared his shoulders. "He drank half the bucket."

"Good. Thank you." Mr. Keegan turned his gaze to Nicole.

No doubt wondering if she was going to tell her cousin her decision. "I've changed my mind. You can stay at Mr. Keegan's ranch. But only for a little while."

Rolfy's face brightened. "Thank you. Bucky too?"

"Yay!" Bucky jumped up and down.

"No. He stays here with me."

"But I'll take care of him. I promise. I always do."

"Go get your things before I change my mind about you going."

Rolfy studied her a moment, probably deciding if he could sway her. "I'm ready. I don't need nothin' but what I got on."

Mr. Keegan shook his head. "If you can't follow orders, I don't think it's a good idea to have you out on my ranch."

"I can follow orders. I'll be right back." He ran for the house.

Bucky ran after him. "Wait for me!"

Tears welled in Nicole's eyes.

Mr. Keegan put his curved finger under her chin and lifted her face. "You're doing the right thing."

A stray drop rolled down her cheek.

"He's going to be fine." He swiped away her tear with his thumb.

A shudder rippled through her at his gentle touch. With him, she believed her cousin would be fine.

A couple of minutes later, the boys bounded out of the house and stopped on the porch. Rolfy knelt in front of his little brother and talked to him in what appeared to be stern words. Bucky nodded, his brown hair flopping to and fro.

Nicole wished she knew what he was saying.

Rolfy hugged his little brother, stood, and trotted off the porch. "I'm ready to go." He turned to Nicole. "The bed is made, and the room straightened."

She studied her cousin, not having realized he was almost the same height as her. When had he grown so tall? He was turning into a young man. "You do everything Mr. Keegan tells you to do."

"I will."

Nicole pulled him into a hug. Why? She didn't know. They'd never really hugged before. "I'm going to miss you."

Surprisingly, he returned her hug. "Keep Bucky safe."

That was a strange request. "I will." She turned to Mr. Keegan. "If he gives you any trouble, send him right back."

"I'll keep him working too hard to get into any trouble. He might beg to return."

"I won't."

Mr. Keegan climbed into his saddle and held out an arm to the boy turning man. Rolfy gripped the rancher's arm and wrist with both his hands and swung up behind him.

As she watched the oldest of her two cousins ride away, she pulled Bucky in front of her with his back to her legs and wrapped her arms around him. "*You* are never going to leave me."

He turned and hugged her. "I won't."

Aunt Henny sat Bucky at the kitchen table with two butter cookies and a tall glass of milk and asked Nicole to sit with her in the parlor. "About what the attorney said about Rolfy and Bucky."

"Why did he say they have a different last name than Grandpa?" Nicole had begun to suspect that maybe there were a lot of things Grandpa had kept from her.

"That's what I wanted to ask you about. What do you remember from when they first came to live with you and your grandfather?"

"Rolfy was seven, the age Bucky is now. He looks a lot like Rolfy did when they arrived. Bucky was just a bit of thing, two, and skinnier than a garter snake. Grandpa said we needed to fatten them up. They seemed scared and huddled together a lot. Rolfy never let Bucky out of his sight and took care of him. He would hide him behind him as though he was protecting him from something. Slowly they stopped being so scared and became ornery, but they are mostly good."

"Did your grandfather ever talk about their parents or how they were related? Like possibly his brother's or sister's grandchildren or from his wife's side of the family?"

Nicole shook her head. "He just said they were my cousins and were living with us now because we were their only family."

"Did they have bruises when they arrived?" Aunt Henny held her with a firm gaze.

"I guess a few. But they get those when they are running around and fall."

"Sarah Combs doesn't believe the boys are blood related to you."

"But Grandpa said they were family." Nicole didn't like thinking they were otherwise.

"I know. I think he was trying to protect them from people who were hurting them, who caused those bruises."

Nicole thought about that. When the boys arrived, they did have a lot of bruises. "People hurt them on purpose?"

"Yes."

Her anger riled. "Then it's good Grandpa got them."

"Yes, and no. If they have family in town, they might want them."

"They can't have them. Do you think that's why Rolfy didn't want to be in town?"

"It makes sense. If they have family who want them, you can't legally keep them."

"But they're kin. I won't let anyone take them away. Not people who might hurt them." The thought twisted her heart.

"I agree. We need to figure out who their family was and if they are still around."

"I won't give them up."

Aunt Henny rested her hand on Nicole's arm. "We'll see what we can legally do to keep that from happening."

"Should I go out to Mr. Keegan's ranch and talk to Rolfy? Find out from him what happened and who he'd lived with before?" Though she just parted from Rolfy, she wouldn't mind seeing him and spending more time with Mr. Keegan.

"If what we suspect is true, I know he'll say Isaac Waterby was his grandfather and deny anything else."

"I'm sure you're right. But I will eventually get him to tell me everything." She wouldn't let up on him until he did.

Aunt Henny laughed. "I have no doubt."

"Tomorrow, we'll talk to the attorney and see what he advises."

Hopefully, he would tell them there had been a mistake, and they were truly related to her. That would also be reason enough to go out to Mr. Keegan's ranch.

As the ranch grew nearer, Huckleberry picked up his pace, no longer plodding. He knew he was heading for home and wanted to get there as fast as he could.

Shane tightened the reins. It would do no good to wear out his horse. Normally, he would let Huckleberry pick his own pace at this point, but not with a second rider.

"Are we almost there?" Rolfy said from behind Shane. That was the fifth time he'd asked.

"Not yet. I can take you back to Kamola if this is too far for you."

"Nope. I'd rather be far away."

What made this boy want to avoid town? Shane assumed he'd lived up in the mountains his whole life. What could have him so scared?

"Do you have visitors out on your ranch?"

"The occasional saddle tramp or trapper."

"Anyone from town?"

Now they were getting somewhere. "People from town only come out on purpose. Someone you're hoping might come?" Or, someone he was hoping didn't.

"Naw. Just wondering. You out here all by yourself?" If this boy were a man, Shane would suspect he had nefarious intentions.

"I have five hands year 'round, now six with Bray, and you make seven." Shane was getting a bit excessive with the number of fulltime, year-round hands he had. "I hire extras for branding, rounding up cattle, and for cattle drives." Not that Shane had done many of those for his own ranch, but he'd participated in plenty for others over the years.

"Oh." The kid sounded disappointed.

"Five of them were with my uncle before he left the ranch to me. I hired the sixth this past summer. They're good men."

The boy didn't respond. Was he contemplating the men? Had he really thought Shane would be running a ranch all on his own? He was young and had lived what seemed to be a secluded life up until now, so he probably didn't know what it took.

"You seem a bit nervous to be coming out here."

"No, sir. Not me. What are the names of your men?"

Though Rolf's question seemed innocuous, Shane sensed he was fishing for information. "Handley's my foreman, Klem, Decker, Tommy Pine, Woods, and Bray is the one I hired six months ago."

"You trust him?"

"Don't know him that well. No reason not to." So far.

"All right. If you trust all your men, then so will I." The reservation in the boy's voice said otherwise.

Huckleberry trotted over the rise where the ranch yard came into view in the distance. He nickered and pranced as though he wanted to run.

Shane gently tugged on the reins. "Easy, boy. I don't want to tucker you out."

Rolf leaned to peer around Shane's shoulder. "That must be your ranch. Your horse knows it and wants to get to the barn."

"He does, but he needs to practice patience. And obey. I can't tolerate animals or people who won't abide by my orders. No way to run a ranch."

"Nope. I can follow orders."

"Good."

Roxy and Pepper trotted over to them as they walked into the yard.

"You aren't afraid of dogs, are you?" Shane should have asked the boy before now.

"Nope. I like 'em."

Bray strode out to meet them. "We expected you sooner."

Shane had expected himself sooner too. "I ran into a few delays." He reached his arm behind him to lower Rolf.

The boy gripped his wrist and dropped to the ground. Pepper and Roxy sniffed him and licked his hands. Rolf petted them in return.

Bray studied the boy. "I can see your delay."

The boy hadn't been nearly the delay Nicole Waterby had caused. But Bray didn't need to know that.

Shane swung down. "Bray, this is Rolf. He's going to be doing some work around here for a while."

Rolf puffed out his chest.

The expression on Bray's pockmarked face said he was doubtful of the boy's abilities.

Shane wasn't sure what the kid could do either, but the boy seemed eager to please.

Bray stuck out his hand. "Welcome to the Keegan ranch, kid."

After a brief hesitation, Rolf shook Bray's hand.

"I'll take care of your horse." Bray grabbed Huckleberry's bridle.

"Thanks." Shane gave a nod. "Where's Handley?"

"He headed out shortly after you with Tommy Pine. They thought they saw smoke from a fire and wanted to see if it was those rustlers that have been spotted a time or two. Woods is riding the range to check on your cattle." Bray led the horse away.

Shane had hoped the rustlers had moved on and wouldn't bother him anymore. So far, he'd lost only a few head of cattle, but if the thieves were still in the area, they would likely return.

"Thanks for introducing me as Rolf and not Rolfy."

"No problem. Come inside, and I'll show you where you'll sleep."

"Ain't I bunking with the other men?"

Other men? Did this boy think himself a man? "It's best if you're in the main house with me. Much more comfortable." Shane preferred the house to bunking in a musty room with several other men snoring. He would miss the house when he sold the place. He wasn't cut out to put down roots and be tethered to one place for very long. It wasn't wise to allow people to get to know him, because in time they would realize he wasn't good enough to be friends with long term. So why had he offered to take the boy on? Because Nicole Waterby had donned a dress? She did look right fetching. Her dark hair had lain in soft waves around her face the first time he'd met her. Today, it had been pulled up, exposing her creamy skin.

"Mr. Keegan?"

That yanked Shane out of his musings and shifted his attention back onto the boy. "What?"

"I asked if you wanted me to leave my belongings on the porch and git to work, or if I should put them in the house?"

"Let's get you settled inside." Shane led the way and hoped he wouldn't regret bringing Rolf.

Nine

As Henny held the reins with one hand, she grasped the collar of Bucky's jacket with the other. "Be careful, or you'll fall out." With Rolfy out at Shane Keegan's ranch, the little boy couldn't stay at the boarding house alone.

"I want to go in every store. Can I? Can I?"

"Not all in one day."

Nicole on Henny's other side wasn't much better, gawking at every place they passed.

The meeting with the attorney had gone well. Nicole hired him to locate and deal with Rolfy and Bucky's suspicious relatives if they were even still around. He would file a request with the courthouse to gain access to any records they might have. It would be best for everyone if the boys' family were no longer around.

Henny wanted to start Bucky in school but thought it would be better to wait until they knew more about his previous family. The time would give Henny a chance to see how much education he already had. Nicole could read and write, but could the boys?

Nicole leaned out the side of the buggy. "What's that place?"

Henny gave a little laugh. "A dressmaker shop. Celeste sews dresses and other clothing for ladies."

Nicole pulled back in. "Would she make me one?"

"If you'd like."

"Do I have enough money to buy one? I appreciate you letting me use this dress, but I'd like to have one of my own."

"I'm sorry we couldn't salvage either of those dresses from the trunk." It warmed Henny's heart to see the girl eager to want feminine things. "You have plenty of money for several dresses."

"I liked the purple one in the window." Nicole leaned

out farther this time to peer at the shop now behind them. "Do you think it would fit me?"

"It can be altered to fit you better than the one you have on." Henny had done her best, but she wasn't a seamstress and had rushed to get it ready for Nicole. She gripped the girl's arm. "Be careful, or you'll fall out."

Nicole righted herself on the seat. "When can we go?"

"Now, if you like. But leaning out of the buggy as you did, isn't ladylike."

Nicole thinned her lips. "I think you told me that before. I just got all excited." She straightened and folded her hands in her lap. "I want you to keep telling me about things I do wrong so I can improve."

It was good Nicole wanted to learn. "I wouldn't say it was exactly wrong. It lacked decorum."

"Decorum. Didn't the quilting ladies say that is good taste and propriety?"

"Yes." Henny turned the buggy around and parked in front of the dressmaker shop.

Nicole jumped down and spun toward Henny. Her face was pinched. "I shouldn't have gotten out that way, should I? Will I ever start thinking like a lady?"

"Give yourself time." Henny set the brake. "When in doubt, always wait before you act. Ladies don't rush."

"What if a bear's chasing you or a raccoon is in the chicken coop?" Nicole proffered a helping hand.

Henny took it to steady herself as she climbed down. "There are always exceptions, but hopefully no bears will wander into town." She glanced up the street and saw that well-dressed gentleman watching her again. Or Nicole? Or Bucky?

When Henny made eye contact with him, he averted his gaze and hurried off. Not this time. She grabbed her cane from the floor of the buggy. "I'll return in a jiffy." She hobbled off.

Nicole kept pace with her. "I thought ladies didn't rush."

"Like I said, exceptions." Henny reached the corner the man had disappeared around, but he was gone. She wished she'd have gotten a better look at him, but he always managed to slip away. It was probably one of those happenstance situations where something appeared one way but was actually nothing.

Bucky swung his head back and forth. "I didn't see no bear."

Aunt Henny faced the boy. "What?"

Bucky held up his hands. "No bear."

Nicole smiled. "Because you were hurrying so, he thought you must have seen a bear."

Henny burst out laughing. "It must have been a sight, seeing me waddle like a duck with its tail feathers on fire. No bear. I thought I saw someone. Let's go look at dresses."

Bucky huffed. "I don't wanta. I want cake."

Nicole crouched. "After I see the dresses, I'll get you something nice."

"Cake?"

"Perhaps. Maybe a new pair of shoes."

At the shop, Nicole opened the door for Henny. "I hope that was all right. There wasn't a man to hold it for us."

"That was exactly right. A younger person should do as you did for…someone older than oneself." Henny'd almost called herself an old person. She didn't feel old, but when she was Nicole's age, she would have thought of a fifty-year-old as not only old, but ancient. My how time tempered one's view.

Mademoiselle Celeste Dumont sat in her receiving area with Mrs. Florence Kesner.

Henny halted Nicole and Bucky inside the door. "The dressmaker is with a customer who is an important person in town. This will be good practice for you in greeting people."

"If she's important, maybe I shouldn't start with her."

"I have every confidence you'll do fine. Remember to address the customer as Mrs. Kesner and the dressmaker as *Mademoiselle* Dumont."

Nicole turned. "She's French?"

"Yes. How did you know?"

"Your use of *Mademoiselle*. Grandpa taught me French."

"He did?"

"Yes. And some Italian. But I like French best. Speaking it and hearing it is like a song."

This girl and her grandfather continued to surprise Henny. Why would a cultured man hide away in the mountains? As Sarah said, what happened with his daughter must have broken him.

Nicole leaned toward Bucky. "You behave yourself. There are things in here that could break. The next shop we go in can be your choice."

"Yeah, but—"

"Shh," Nicole hissed.

Celeste and Florence Kesner rose and crossed to them.

Mrs. Kesner stood equal in height to Henny at five-foot-five inches, but her build was a bit stockier. Though close in age to Sarah Combs, the two women carried themselves very differently. Sarah casual and open. Florence regal and guarded. She had to be in her position.

***

The shorter of the two women stepped forward. Both appeared to be fine ladies who could have stepped out of *Little Women*. "Henny, so good to see you." She turned to Nicole. "Who is this delightful child?"

"Florence, this is Nicole Waterby. She's staying with me for a few months. Nicole, this Mrs. Kesner."

Nicole gave a slight bend of her knees. "Pleased to meet you." Hopefully, she did that right.

Mrs. Kesner studied Nicole. "You aren't related to Isaac Waterby, are you?"

"Yes. He's my grandpa. You know him?"

"Yes. How is Isaac? I haven't seen him in nearly two decades. I told him about the good timberland and thought he'd followed my guidance and purchased some. But he seemed to have vanished."

Nicole remained silent and glanced at Aunt Henny. How was a person supposed to tell another about someone who'd died? Aunt Henny had said to wait before acting. She supposed that went for speaking as well. And after all, there weren't any bears around to rush her.

Thankfully, Aunt Henny spoke up. "He passed away recently."

The woman's expression shifted from pleased to concerned. "I'm so sorry to hear that. You have my condolences."

Nicole found her voice. "Thank you."

"What brings a young lady like yourself to our fair town?"

"I came to get a husband."

Aunt Henny coughed.

Wasn't Nicole supposed to tell people? How else would she find one if she didn't speak up?

Mrs. Kesner, on the other hand, brightened.

The bell over the door jingled, and a young man entered, removed his hat, and gave a nod to Mrs. Kesner.

She waved him over. "Come, Lamar."

The dapper gentleman sauntered over and bowed. "Ladies."

Mrs. Kesner touched the man's sleeve. "This is my grandson, Mr. Lamar Kesner." She waved a hand in the direction of the two older women. "You've met *Mademoiselle* Dumont and my friend Henny before." She settled her attention on Nicole. "This is Henny's charge, Miss Nicole Waterby, granddaughter of Isaac Waterby."

"It's nice to see you again." He dipped his head to each of the older women and turned to Nicole. He took her hand and bowed over it. "Miss Waterby, a pleasure to make your acquaintance." He released her hand.

"Why'd you do that?"

"Do what?"

"Look real close at my hand? Is there something wrong with it?"

His mouth broke into a wide smile. "Your hand is perfect. The gesture is a way of a gentleman greeting a lady." He lowered his voice. "And truth be told, an excuse for a gentleman to hold a beautiful lady's hand." He winked.

"Lamar."

"Yes, Grandmama."

"Don't be impertinent."

"Yes, Grandmama." His mischievous smile stretched wide. "Pardon my boldness."

Nicole hadn't seen anything wrong in what he said, but she did like his playfulness.

Mrs. Kesner focused her steely gray gaze on Bucky. "And who are you, young man?"

He ran his sleeve across his nose while sniffling. "I'm Bucky." He took Mrs. Kesner's hand and leaned over it. "A pleasure to make your acquaintance."

"Bucky!" Nicole squeaked. "Your shirt is not a handkerchief."

"The child is fine. I had a lot worse from this one." Mrs. Kesner motioned toward her grandson.

"Grandmama." The young Mr. Kesner rolled his eyes.

"Don't 'Grandmama' me." Mrs. Kesner waved her hand at her grandson and returned her attention to Nicole. "Henny, you must bring this delightful young lady to my Christmas soirée. Mustn't she, Lamar?" Her eyes twinkled.

Mr. Kesner tucked his grandmother's hand into the crook of his elbow. "Time to go, Grandmama." He angled her toward the door.

Mrs. Kesner smiled. "Do bring her. Celeste, please have my gowns delivered to my home."

"*Oui, Madame* Kesner. I will be happy to."

Nicole wasn't quite sure what to make of that whole exchange, but she wouldn't embarrass Aunt Henny by asking here. Later would be fine.

"And Henny, bring Miss Waterby around for tea on Thursday. I want to get to know her better." Mrs. Kesner and her grandson left with a jingle over the door.

Tea? Nicole had survived this short exchange, but how would she manage an hour or more?

"*Mademoiselle* Waterby, you have made quite an impression on *Madame* Kesner. If she likes you, the whole town will like you."

"She was very nice. I like her too."

Bucky scrunched his nose. "She smelled funny."

Nicole tried not to laugh, but when Aunt Henny and the shopkeeper did, she couldn't help herself.

Mademoiselle Dumont motioned toward a young lady

hovering nearby. "Ruth, would you find this young man a cup of tea and slice of cake, then bring Henny and *Mademoiselle* Waterby some as well."

Bucky eagerly left with the pretty young lady.

Mademoiselle Dumont gazed at Nicole. "Now, about why you have come to me. You have a beauty that is as ageless as time. I do hope you will allow me to dress you."

Nicole spoke in French. "*Oui*, I would like a dress of my own."

Mademoiselle Dumont switched to French. "You speak French? And with almost no accent."

"*Oui*. My grandfather taught me when I was very young."

"We should not be rude to Henny."

Aunt Henny spoke up—and in French as well. "My French is rusty, but I understood what you said."

Mademoiselle Dumont laughed and switched back to English. "But I think it will be best if we all use English."

Aunt Henny nodded. "Agreed."

Mademoiselle Dumont clapped her hands. "Come. Let us see how to dress you."

Nicole followed, a giddiness twirling inside her like the first snow swirling in the air.

The French dressmaker stood Nicole in front of a floor mirror and positioned herself behind her shoulder. "Tell me the kind of outfits you normally wear."

"In the winter, buckskin trousers and over shirt, and in the summer cotton trousers and shirt."

Mademoiselle's eyes widened, and she darted a glance at Aunt Henny.

Aunt Henny nodded. "Very practical for living in the mountains."

Nicole hadn't known before she came to town her attire was all wrong, but she knew now and wanted to change that. "But I've come to get a husband."

"Not in trousers, you won't. We will make you irresistible." She moved all the way behind Nicole and pinched the fabric of the dress at Nicole's shoulders. "Where did this dress come from?"

"Aunt Henny is letting me use it. I like it a lot. I think

it fits me better than the buckskins."

"No doubt, but I think we can do even better." She tipped her head toward Aunt Henny. "No offense."

"None taken. It was the best I could do on the spot. I hastily took it in some."

"It has exquisite fabric but is a couple of decades out of date."

Aunt Henny gave a nod. "That sounds about right."

"I must know a budget."

Nicole glanced at Aunt Henny for the answer, depending on the older woman to tell her what she could afford and couldn't. She really didn't understand yet how to determine the value of money. Aunt Henny and the nice quilting ladies would need to teach her. She could trust those women.

Her new friend cleared her throat. "She can afford a few things but nothing too fancy to start with. A practical dress for every day and one for church to start with. And all the under clothing to go along with them."

"Let's not forget a ball gown for *Madame* Kesner's soirée."

"A ball gown? Like Meg wore in *Little Women*?"

"Better." *Mademoiselle* Dumont smiled at Nicole's reflection. "All the men at the ball will be fighting to get a dance with you. They will wonder where you came from and where you've been hiding."

Nicole shifted her gaze to Aunt Henny. "Will Mr. Keegan be there?"

"I don't know if he's invited."

Nicole's excitement over the party dropped. Did she want to go if he wasn't going to be there?

Mademoiselle Dumont gave a knowing smile. "The handsome rancher has caught your eye. We will make him weak as a newborn kitten in your hands."

"I don't want him weak."

"No. Weak as in he won't be able to say no to you."

Nicole liked that thought. "I like the purple dress in the window."

"You have a good eye. That dress would be *fabuleuse* on you with your hair color and features."

Nicole touched her hair. "I wish it were long like I've

seen on some of the other ladies."

"But you *can* have long hair. Ruth?"

"*Oui, mademoiselle.*" Ruth seemed to always be standing close at hand.

"Would you please bring the darkest hair pieces we have?"

"*Oui, mademoiselle.*" Ruth curtsied and dashed off, returning a moment later with long lengths of hair.

Mademoiselle sifted through the offerings.

"Where do those come from?" Nicole gaped at the wavy locks.

"Women will have their long tresses cut and sell them."

That seemed sad. "If I had long hair, I'd never cut it."

After separating one from the others, the dressmaker held it up to Nicole. "Perfect match." She attached it to her head, letting the ends fall over Nicole's shoulder.

Nicole fingered it. "It makes me look different."

"*Oui.* But don't think long hair will make you more beautiful. You are already *très belle.* No amount of hair will change that."

Aunt Henny stepped up beside her. "You stand taller with it."

Did she?

Aunt Henny spoke to *Mademoiselle* Dumont. "She'll take it."

"Very good. Since the dress you have on is not your own, we shall start with my ready-made collection. A few alterations and they will feel as though they were made for you."

Aunt Henny nodded.

"I think I have the perfect thing for—as Henny would say—Sunday church. With a tuck here and there, we can have it ready for tea on Thursday with *Madame* Kesner. We will start with that one and then a practical everyday frock. And finish with the ball gown that will make Mr. Keegan see only you at the ball."

By the time Nicole and Aunt Henny were ready to leave the dressmaker shop, Nicole had three dresses to be altered as well as another two ordered from scratch and all the under clothing she would need. Two sets!

Also, the re-altered yellow dress from Aunt Henny did fit her much better, and she knew better what to pay attention to in a dress fitting. The subtle changes made were confusing as to why the dress was not out of date anymore. Both ways seemed fine to her.

She'd wanted to order more dresses, but Aunt Henny encouraged her to save those for another time. One of her ordered ones was a riding skirt. She'd never imagined a special skirt for riding a horse. Now, she needed her own horse. Speaking of her own things, she couldn't keep mooching off of Aunt Henny. It was time she paid Aunt Henny rent like the other boarders.

Wearing dresses and being fussed over made Nicole feel like a different person from a week ago. The change felt good. She hoped Mr. Keegan thought so.

Sitting atop Huckleberry, Shane watched the entrance of the dressmaker shop from across the street. Aunt Henny's buggy still sat out front. He'd seen Miss Waterby and Aunt Henny go inside earlier and glanced in through the window.

A dandy gentleman had entered, talked with Miss Waterby and took her hand. Shane's gut had twisted. He shouldn't allow strong feelings for Miss Waterby to develop. He wouldn't. They would stop right now. He would sell his ranch come spring, then leave and not allow himself to get tangled up with a woman again. He could control his emotions.

After witnessing the exchange between Miss Waterby and the dandy, he'd ridden around town aimlessly for two hours intent on heading back out to his ranch, trying to shake Nicole Waterby loose from his sorry excuse for a brain. When would he ever learn not to put any hope in a woman? They weren't for a wandering sort like him.

Yet, here he was waiting for a glimpse of an enchanting young woman. He still couldn't believe her transformation. That was all there was to his fascination with her. Nothing more.

He should leave.

But he didn't.

Why had he allowed Isabelle Atwood to put the thought of him settling down and having a wife and family into his head a couple of months ago? He'd never considered it before and feared the desire would always haunt him now. Once he sold his place in the spring and moved on, he could rid himself of such foolish notions.

Time to skedaddle. But Huckleberry didn't move, which had something to do with the fact Shane hadn't goaded him to go.

He took a deep breath, preparing himself to set Huckleberry into motion toward home.

The dress shop door opened.

Shane's breath caught. Was it Miss Waterby?

Two women he didn't recognize came out onto the boardwalk.

He released his breath.

They went to Aunt Henny's buggy and deposited the packages they carried.

That meant Miss Waterby would be exiting soon. His mouth pulled up on one corner, and Huckleberry plodded across the street. Had the horse known? Or had Shane prodded him without knowing it? Either way, he reached the other side of the street as they stepped out onto the boardwalk. He swung off. "Howdy, Miss Waterby. Aunt Henny."

Nicole's face brightened. Was that because of seeing him? Foolish of him to hope so.

"Good afternoon, Mr. Keegan." As Nicole moved forward, something happened with her feet because she pitched forward.

Shane lurched toward her and caught her as she stumbled off the boardwalk. She fit nicely in his embrace. A hank of long hair draped across his arm. Where had that come from?

She blinked at him with big, violet eyes. "I am so sorry. I didn't hurt you, did I?"

He chuckled. "Not one bit." His heart hammered in his chest.

"*Monsieur* Keegan, how fortunate for *Mademoiselle*

Waterby you were there with your strong arms to catch her. This could have been a disaster." The proprietress smiled at him with a twinkle in her eyes.

Fortunate for him. He didn't want to let go but righted Nicole and released her.

Bucky squeezed between him and Miss Waterby. "Mr. Keegan, where's Rolfy? Is he with you? Is he all right? Indians didn't capture him, did they?"

Spell broken. Shane tousled the boy's hair. "He's fine, and no, he hasn't been captured. I'll let him know you're worried about him."

"I'm not worried. Rolfy can take care of himself. We are going to get me some cake. You want to come?"

Nicole shook her head. "You already had cake."

"Didn't count. You said *you* would get me cake, so I get more."

Shane stifled a laugh. The little mite was a schemer. "Sorry, I can't stay. I have work to do at my ranch." But he didn't want to go. He wanted to stay with Miss Waterby. "Feel free to come out any time. Bucky sounds like he wants to see his brother."

"We'll come out later this week." Miss Waterby turned to Aunt Henny. "Would that be all right?"

Aunt Henny's expression turned thoughtful. "Maybe Saturday would work out. We haven't been home the last couple of days. We have an engagement on Thursday and the quilting ladies are coming over on Friday."

"If this isn't a good week, I'll let Rolf know you might make it out next week."

"That might be better." Aunt Henny turned to Bucky. "Get in the buggy."

Bucky held out his hand to Shane. When Shane gripped the tiny hand in his, the boy put his face real close to their clasped hands. Bucky straightened and released him. "That's what the man did to Nick's hand." The boy bounded off and clambered into the buggy.

Shane desperately wanted to laugh but refrained, until Aunt Henny and the shopkeeper laughed. He joined them as did Miss Waterby. Her lilting laugh warmed his heart.

Ten

NICOLE SWAYED INSIDE THE ENCLOSED, ORNATE carriage Mrs. Kesner had sent for her and Aunt Henny. The seat was so soft, she felt as though she were sitting on a cloud. She rubbed her sweaty palms down the sides of her thighs. She didn't have anything to be nervous about. "I don't think I know enough to have a fancy tea with Mrs. Kesner." Aunt Henny had set up a practice tea that morning and given Nicole a quick lesson.

Also, she had advised against having Bucky come on this outing and took him to stay at someone else's home.

Aunt Henny gave her a reassuring smile. "You'll do fine. If being yourself will make Mrs. Kesner not like you, then who should you be?"

"I don't know. I fear I'll say something wrong. I don't know all the right things to do."

"I'm sure you'll do fine."

"No, I won't. I said all the wrong things to Mr. Keegan at lunch on Monday." Nicole plucked at the folds of her skirt. "I talked about Grandpa's money and asked him about courting. I now know I shouldn't have."

"If you stay away from subjects like courting, money, politics, and religion, you should be fine. You are a pleasant person with a good heart."

"Thank you. But what's wrong with talking about God?"

"Some people believe differently and don't like it when others don't share their views."

"Are you saying not everyone believes in God?"

"Sadly they don't."

People had some strange notions. "I understand about the courting, money and not talking about God, but what's the politics?"

"People are even more fierce about their political

views. Anything to do with government and how the country and the town is run. Basically, anything in town or that has to do with the town."

"That sounds as though it encompasses a whole lot of things." Nicole was sure to say something wrong. "Maybe I shouldn't talk at all."

"Don't start thinking you have to stay silent and can't have a mind of your own. Think of these things as ways of being considerate to others. The weather is usually a safe subject. Compliment her on her home but nothing that suggests to her wealth. Say something like, 'What a nice home you have.' 'This is a beautiful teacup.' 'Your dress is pretty.' And ask her questions about herself. People love to talk about themselves."

"So, don't talk about anything of meaning?"

Aunt Henny laughed. "That sounds about right."

Though that seemed simple enough, Nicole hoped she didn't accidentally talk about something she shouldn't.

The carriage came to a stop. Nicole shifted forward to get out and help her companion.

Aunt Henny put her hand on Nicole's arm. "Let the footman help us."

"But I can..."

"I know, but it's proper for a lady to let someone else assist her when someone is available. It would insult our hostess to refuse her graciousness."

Nicole didn't want to insult anyone.

The carriage door opened. A man dressed in a black suit stood in the opening and unfolded the set of carpeted steps and proffered his hand.

Nicole glanced at Aunt Henny who gave a nod, so she put her hand in the man's and got out. He released her and did the same for Aunt Henny.

Aunt Henny wrapped her arm around Nicole's as the man led the way up the stairs to the front door. "I shouldn't have been so vain and left my cane at home. You'll steady me, won't you?"

"Of course." Nicole would feel more grounded attached to Aunt Henny.

"I have a confession. I'm a bit nervous too. I've only

been in the Kesner mansion twice. Once for a reception after Mr. Kesner's funeral. And again last year with Professor Lumbard—one of my boarders—for a party to celebrate the opening of the teachers' college."

"I'm glad to know I'm not the only flustered one." That made Nicole's spirit settle a little easier and comforted her.

"I have found Mrs. Kesner to only be kind, but all that money intimidates me."

"Are people with money usually mean?"

"Some can be. They like to lord their good fortune over others. Please don't turn into one of those."

"Why would I?"

"Because of your— Never mind. I don't know if it would be possible for you to change that much."

"I want to change. I'm trying ever so hard to be a lady. I want people to like me."

"The changes you're talking about are on the outside and are fine. I'm talking about on the inside—the kind of person you are and how you treat others."

"Grandpa taught me to be gracious to everyone who passed through our property, regardless of their disposition or cleanliness. He said that's what God would want, and we could be entertaining an angel from God and not know it."

"Then you should have nothing to worry about."

The tall carved arched door swung open. The man who had helped them out of the carriage and led them up the outdoor steps stopped and remained there while another man in a black suit welcomed them inside.

A thick round rug on a shiny floor greeted Nicole's feet.

"I'll announce you." The man walked away.

When Nicole started to follow, Aunt Henny touched her arm. "We wait here."

Nicole sensed there were even more things to know when one was wealthy. "Learning all the rules to being a lady is hard enough. I'm glad I'm not wealthy to have to learn those ones too."

Aunt Henny chuffed out a breath.

"Are you all right?"

"Yes. We need to have a long talk about money. In particular, yours."

Nicole didn't understand how a piece of paper with numbers on it could be worth more than a tanned deer hide. So much to learn. "I thought you said Mrs. Kesner's husband died. Didn't he answer the door?"

"No. That was the butler."

Nicole recalled a butler in *Little Women*. Not at the March house but at others. So much to know. She would need to read the book from the beginning and see what she could learn from it about being a lady and how to act.

The butler returned. "Lady Kesner will receive you in the drawing room. Right this way."

Nicole let Aunt Henny enter ahead of her so she could copy what the older woman did. How was she supposed to address a person with servants? Lady Kesner as the butler had used? Or Mrs. Kesner as she had been introduced at the dressmaker's shop?

Mrs. Kesner's grandson stood and held his hand out to his grandmother.

Smiling and taking his offered assistance, Mrs. Kesner rose to her feet. "Henny, I'm so pleased you've come and brought Miss Waterby. You remember my grandson."

"Florence, it's so good to see you." Aunt Henny turned to the handsome young man. "Lamar. You're looking fit."

"Thank you, Miss Henny."

"You remember my friend Miss Nicole Waterby."

What should Nicole do now? How should she address these two? How would the March sisters do it? She would pretend to be Meg. "Mrs. Kesner, thank you for inviting me into your home." Nicole turned to her grandson. "Mr. Kesner, I'm pleased to meet you again." It felt right to use their surnames.

He took her hand and bowed over it. "I assure you, the pleasure is mine. And do call me Lamar."

"Lamar! That is inappropriate. We don't know the young lady well enough."

Lamar winked at Nicole. "Yes, Grandmama."

Lamar, or rather *Mr.* Kesner, had a mischievous side. "I don't mind if he uses my given name." Nicole would prefer it. Miss Waterby was a mouthful. She'd always been Nick, so getting used to one new name—Nicole—was enough.

Mrs. Kesner gave Nicole a tolerant smile. "I do mind. My grandson will behave like a proper gentleman even if it kills me. And I think it might. Now, let's all sit before I faint."

Nicole stepped closer to Mrs. Kesner. "Are you feeling poorly? We can leave if you are."

Mrs. Kesner's face split into a wide grin. "You are refreshing. I feel fine, my dear. 'Before I faint' is an expression one uses when one wants to do something promptly." She lowered herself into the chair she'd been in before.

Aunt Henny sat on the settee, and Nicole joined her. Lastly, Lamar Kesner retook his seat.

Nicole had never felt such soft furniture and would have sunk into it if she hadn't recently been taught to keep her back straight. The corset thing helped with that.

Mrs. Kesner poured tea for everyone.

Nicole listened as Aunt Henny and Mrs. Kesner chitchatted.

Aunt Henny was skillful at talking about trivial things while appearing to be interested in everything the other woman said. She acted a little different here, as though she belonged. She seemed to have visited many times, but she'd said she hadn't. Maybe it was something a town dweller knew naturally.

Mrs. Kesner turned her attention on Nicole. "I hadn't anticipated you to be so quiet, my dear."

Oh, no. Nicole would be expected to hold a conversation and not say the wrong things. *Don't say anything important.* "Your dress is lovely."

"Thank you." The woman gave her a charitable nod. "Your dress is lovely as well. Is it one of *Mademoiselle Dumont's* creations?"

"It is." One's attire had been an appropriate topic. "I bought two other dresses and ordered two more. One of the dresses is a beautiful ball gown for your party—soirée. Aunt Henny said I could have bought a dozen more, but I should wait."

Aunt Henny cleared her throat, and Mrs. Kesner's mouth pulled into a gentle smile.

Oh, dear. Nicole must have said something wrong or divulged too much, but she wasn't sure what.

What she really wanted to know about was her grandpa, but Aunt Henny hadn't approved the topic, and Nicole couldn't exactly ask her. It had nothing to do with courting, God, or politics, and she wouldn't mention money, so it should be all right. "Mrs. Kesner, at the dressmaker shop, you said you knew my grandpa. Would you tell me about him?"

"I met Isaac, Gene Tuttle, and my Henry at my coming-out soirée. While Isaac and Gene battled each other for my attention, Henry silently won my heart. Gene had been a sore loser and broke friendship with us, but Isaac and Henry remained friends."

This woman had known Nicole's grandpa from a long time ago. "Was that in New York?"

"Yes."

"Does my grandpa still have family there?"

"Let me think. His parents—your great-grandparents—have long since passed away. His three brothers—all older—are gone. None were favored with children who outlived them. The only one I don't know about is Beatrice. She ran off with a man her parents didn't approve of. As far as I know, no one in the family ever heard from her again."

So, if Nicole had any relatives, they were nowhere to be found.

Mrs. Kesner took a sip of tea. "That's all so very depressing. Let's move on to happier thoughts. I am pleased the two of you will be at my Christmas soirée."

Nicole wanted to know more but doubted there was much more the woman knew. "I've never been to a Christmas soirée. What goes on at one?" She hoped her question wasn't considered rude or out of place.

"There will be food, dancing, games, and of course, mistletoe." The older woman gave her a knowing smile.

"Mistletoe?"

Mrs. Kesner's eyes widened in glee. "You'll like mistletoe. It's for the young in love. It's a greenery with white berries that is hung from above, usually in a doorway. When a couple finds themselves under it, they must kiss and then take a berry. When all the berries are gone, the romantic power of the sprig is as well, so make haste and see to it you wander under it with a special gentleman before all the berries are gone." She glanced at her grandson then turned to Aunt Henny. "This girl's education has been seriously neglected. We must work together to make her presentable."

Nicole pictured herself standing under the plant with Shane Keegan and smiled. "Is Mr. Keegan coming to your soirée?"

"The rancher?" Mrs. Kesner glanced at Aunt Henny who gave a little nod. "It's not the sort of event suitable for a rancher. He would find it not to his liking. I would be remiss in my duties as hostess to inflict that upon such a man."

That was too bad. Nicole had hoped to have his friendly face there. Maybe she wouldn't go. She would ask Aunt Henny later about it.

"I assume you have at least been taught to waltz. Do you know any other dances?"

"No, ma'am. I don't know waltz. I've never danced."

"Oh, dear. This will never do." Mrs. Kesner picked up a small hand bell on the table next to her and jiggled it. It made a tiny tinkling sound.

The woman appeared mildly upset. Had Nicole said something wrong?

A second later, a maid in a black dress and white apron appeared and curtsied. "Yes, ma'am."

"Have Rogers set up the gramophone in the ballroom."

"Yes, ma'am." The maid scurried out.

Mrs. Kesner turned to her grandson. "We must teach her to waltz."

"What if she doesn't want to learn?"

"Nonsense. All proper young ladies want to waltz." Mrs. Kesner stood.

Lamar shot to his feet.

Was it appropriate for her to think of him in such a manner? He'd asked her to use his given name.

Their hostess led the small group, like chicks following behind a mama quail, into an enormous empty room. The ceiling went up to the second story with dangling crystal lights. Long narrow windows framed with heavy red drapes stood at the ready to one side. The floor of crisscrossed wood gleamed like glass.

Along one wall sat a stray table with a strange contraption on it. The butler and another man hovered over it, appearing to be perplexed as they studied the odd machine. Lamar joined them and tinkered as well.

Mrs. Kesner became annoyed and huffed. "What is the delay?" She marched over to the trio of men, leaving Nicole and Aunt Henny near the door they had entered.

Nicole leaned closer to Aunt Henny. "Why isn't there anything in here but that table and a few chairs scattered along the walls?"

"This is called a ballroom and used for entertaining large numbers of guests and for dancing. It's mostly empty to accommodate a lot of people."

"She expects enough people at her soirée to fill this whole place?"

"Not fill it completely. There needs to be space for people to move about and for all the ladies' full dresses."

"Like the one I bought at the dress shop?" She couldn't wait to wear it. Aunt Henny had said it wouldn't be suitable for anything but a big party like the one Mrs. Kesner was having.

"Exactly like the one you bought."

"Well, that would cut down on the number of people who could fit in here considerably."

"Yes, it does."

"With so much space, why wouldn't it be appropriate to invite Mr. Keegan? What wouldn't he like?" Certainly, he'd want to dance in this spectacular room with its gold-gilded columns, sparkling lights, luxurious drapes to keep out any winter draft, and a floor so shiny she could almost see herself looking back at her.

"She assumes he wouldn't be comfortable dressing

up and making light conversation with people he doesn't know."

"Well, maybe I won't like it either, but I do want to wear that beautiful purple dress." If Mrs. Kesner's party was the only place Nicole could wear it, then she'd go.

"People with excessive money expect other people with excessive money to attend their functions. Otherwise, their feelings are hurt, and they might exclude a person from other society events."

"There is so much to know. I'm sure to do or say something to get Mrs. Kesner to exclude me."

"You have the advantage of a family connection. She knew your grandfather and because she and her family liked him, they like you."

"That seems a silly reason to like someone."

"Yes, it does, but that's the way people are regardless of your social status."

"I'm going to have to go to this soirée whether I want to or not." She wanted to go, but she didn't like feeling as though she had no choice.

"I think you will enjoy it. Don't pass judgment before you've experienced something."

"You're right."

"Don't think of it as something you *have* to do, but rather that you are doing a favor for a family friend. How would your grandfather want you to treat one of his friends?"

"With kindness and respect."

"When it's all over, if you didn't like it, you don't have to go to another one. But you will be making an informed decision."

"And I do want to wear the purple dress."

"That gown is lovely, and you looked breathtaking in it."

A scratching sound followed by music echoed throughout the empty room.

Nicole glanced around. Where was it coming from? None of the men held instruments. Was the box making the sounds?

"Ah, success!" Mrs. Kesner strolled toward Nicole and Aunt Henny. "Come sit with me, Henny."

Nicole followed them.

When Mrs. Kesner turned and sat, she waved her hands at Nicole. "Not you, my dear. You must learn to dance."

Nicole pivoted.

Lamar stood a couple of feet from her. He bent at the waist and held out his hand. "May I have this dance?"

Nicole assumed she was supposed to take his hand, so she placed hers in his. "I would be ever so pleased to do so."

His eyebrow rose. He led her to the middle of the room, showed her where to put her hands and which foot to step with first. After making a couple of squares with their feet, the music stopped but the crackling continued.

Lamar remained in place. "That wasn't so bad, was it?"

How might one of the March sisters answer that question? "It was ever so much fun." She'd expected it to be harder.

Mrs. Kesner gave directions from her seat next to Aunt Henny. "Rogers, start the cylinder over please."

The music began again, and Nicole concentrated on the steps. She made a few good rotations and thought she was doing well, but then her feet tangled around themselves or went in the wrong direction and invariably his foot ended up under hers. "I'm so sorry." She tried to step away from him to avoid injuring him any further.

He held her in place. "You're doing fine."

"I don't think your feet would agree."

"What happened to the charming lady I met in the dressmaker shop?"

She shifted her gaze from her shoes to his face. "What do you mean?"

"You're more formal now."

"I'm trying ever so hard to act like a proper lady."

"I much prefer the version from the shop."

"You do?"

His smile consoled her. "Indeed. She was a lady I could have a real conversation with."

She glanced at her hostess, knowing she wouldn't

approve. "What other kind of conversations are there?"

"Ones where people talk about banal things and don't say what they really mean."

Did he mean talking about things that didn't really matter? "Aunt Henny said there were certain subjects I shouldn't talk about."

"Ah." He tilted his head back for a moment. "Money, politics, and religion. The usual."

"And courting."

He pinned her with his gray gaze. "You wish to talk about courting?"

"I'm not supposed to."

"People can have real conversations without talking about any of those subjects. Tell me about Mr. Keegan. I know he's a rancher. How did you meet him?"

"It was my first time in town, and no one would talk to me so I could find Aunt Henny. Except Mr. Keegan. He was ever so nice and took me to her."

"I can't imagine anyone ignoring a beauty like you."

"I think it was on account I was dressed like a boy in buckskins and all that trail dust I was wearing. I didn't know ladies wore dresses."

"Ah. I see. Had I been one of the first to see you, I definitely would have spoken to you regardless of your attire."

"That's very kind of you."

The music ceased, but the crackling once again continued.

Mrs. Kesner clapped. "Marvelous. You are a natural. So graceful."

Lamar stilled. "You did it."

"Did what?"

"Waltzed."

"I did?"

Lamar wrapped her hand around his arm and escorted her across the room. "When you stopped trying so hard and let me lead, you had no trouble."

Shane sat on Aunt Henny's porch steps, rolling a coin

over his fingers and practiced what he was going to say. A calico cat watched his every move from a few feet away on the porch.

"Do you know where Nicole and Aunt Henny are?" He was a knucklehead for coming at all. "You probably think I'm touched in the head for running into town to wait for a girl I hardly know. There is something special about this one."

The calico continued to study him.

"It's not as though I need to report on Rolf, but it had seemed like a good reason to see her—and Bucky." Would Nicole accept his flimsy excuse? He was more of a knucklehead for talking to a cat.

An ornate carriage rolled up the street and stopped in front of the boarding house. A dandy-dressed man on the rear of the contraption hopped down and opened the carriage door.

Aunt Henny stepped down in fancier duds than he'd ever seen her wear.

Shane stood, pocketed his coin, and headed along the walk.

Nicole disembarked next in an expensive-looking velvet cape with an elaborate pink gown peeking out the bottom that shimmered in the sunlight. She wore that hairpiece she'd purchased the other day. She didn't need it to be beautiful. He opened the gate as the carriage drove away.

Aunt Henny passed through first and spoke in a low voice. "You're going to catch flies again, Mr. Keegan."

He snapped his mouth shut.

Nicole's smile for him caused his knees to go weak. "Mr. Keegan, I'm so glad to see you."

He was glad to see her as well.

Aunt Henny called over her shoulder. "Nicole, invite your young man inside."

Was Shane her young man? And she his lady?

Miss Waterby's face brightened even more. "Yes, do come in."

"All right." He strode up the walk with her, entered, and stood in the parlor.

"I'll be in the kitchen if you need me." Aunt Henny

walked away.

Shane pointed to the settee. "Do you want to sit?"

"Thank you." Miss Waterby sat, appearing to struggle with the full dress so as not to become engulfed in it.

Shane joined her. Was that proper? He wasn't sure, but if she didn't object, he would stay there. "I came to let you know Rolf is doing well out on my ranch. The men call him Kid."

"I'm glad. I do miss him. Bucky misses him something fierce."

"He talks about the two of you a lot. He doesn't say so, but I can tell he misses you too." Shane wasn't sure what else to say. His reason for coming had been weak to begin with and now it was exhausted.

Miss Waterby tilted her head and gave him a quizzical look. "Lamar said he prefers a lady to be less formal. Do you feel the same way?"

Who was this man spending enough time with Nicole to be using first names? "Who is Lamar?"

"Mrs. Kesner's grandson."

Shane choked on his intake of air. "You're using his first name?"

"Yes. He told me to. His grandmother chided him for it, but he insisted."

Shane just bet *Lamar* insisted. What else would he *insist* upon? Who was Shane to stand on formality then? "Then you must call me Shane."

"I like using people's given name, Shane. It's so much more friendly. And I want you to call me Nick—I mean Nicole."

"Thank you, Nicole. Did you always go by Nick before you came to town? I notice that's what Rolf calls you."

"I did. Is it a boy's name?"

"Generally."

"I think it suits me when I'm wearing my buckskins, but not when I'm wearing a dress."

"No one would mistake you for a boy dressed as you are."

"Thank you, but you didn't answer my question, though I think I might know the answer."

Shane scrambled his thoughts back to when she

asked a question, but he couldn't remember it. After she'd spoken about a man in such a familiar way by using his first name, everything else stamped out of his head. "Do you mind repeating your question?"

"Do you prefer a lady to be less formal? I think you do, and that's why you asked me to use your given name."

He definitely wanted things with Nicole more casual and friendly. "I'm not cut out for all those fancy trappings, so yes, I prefer things less rigid."

"I like being a lady and all, but it's wearing trying to remember all the rules. I'm always afraid of saying or doing something wrong."

"People do like their rules."

"Did you know that the boys and I might have nearly as much money as Mrs. Kesner?"

Shane did choke on the incoming air now. He coughed several times.

Nicole slapped him on the back. "Are you all right?"

Shane had thought himself out of his league trying to court Isabelle, Nicole was even farther out of reach. Good thing he'd be leaving come spring. But leaving Nicole behind bothered him more than losing Isabelle. Isabelle had been an elusive dream. Nicole had seemed somehow attainable. Evidently not. When would Shane learn not to set his hopes on the wrong women? When would he learn not to set his hopes on *any* woman at all?

Eleven

THE FOLLOWING DAY, FRIDAY, HENNY SAT in the parlor with the other quilting ladies. She was proud of how Nicole had practiced piecing blocks together for the past week as Henny had instructed her to. Not only was she getting better, but she said she enjoyed creating something out of what would have otherwise been useless scraps.

After tea at Mrs. Kesner's the day before, Nicole had talked Henny into stopping in at the mercantile to buy a small length of every fabric they had. Even some ill-suited for a quilt. Nicole wanted her quilt to have as many different colors and fabrics as she could. If she used half of what she bought, she would achieve her goal.

The conversation around the circle lulled as it often did from time to time. It would pick up again momentarily.

Franny lowered her work to her lap. "I can't stand it any longer. Is it true, Nicole? Did you have tea with Mrs. Kesner?"

How had the news swept through town so quickly? They had been over there only yesterday afternoon, less than twenty-four hours. Some tidbits traveled faster than others. When the information had to do with Mrs. Kesner or her grandson, lightning would have a hard time keeping up. One of the perils of being wealthy, a person had no secrets. Henny didn't miss that.

Nicole smiled. "I did. She was very nice."

Trudy jumped in. "Tell us all about it."

"Don't leave anything out," Franny said.

"We want to hear it all," Betsy said.

If these young ladies only knew what it was really like to be someone like Mrs. Kesner with all eyes on them, judging everything they did, they wouldn't be so eager to want to be like her. The Kesners, no doubt, had troubles like everyone else. Money didn't make anyone immune.

"We had tea." Nicole, on the other hand, didn't revere wealth like the others. She saw Mrs. Kesner as merely another person.

Henny prayed the girl never lost her innocence or fell into the many pitfall's wealth had to offer. Too hard to climb out of.

Nicole smiled brightly. "Then she wanted me to learn to dance for her Christmas soirée. I had never danced before, so she had Lamar teach me."

"Lamar? As in her grandson, Lamar?"

Nicole nodded.

"What was he like?"

Nicole shrugged. "He was taller than me and had brown hair."

"We know that. Was he nice?"

"Or witty? I bet he was witty."

"And charming."

To these young ladies, Lamar Kesner was equivalent to a crown prince.

"What was it like being in his arms, dancing?"

"Did you want to swoon?"

Nicole glanced from one lady to another as they pelted her with questions. "Swoon?"

Henny had to laugh to herself. Nicole was far from the swooning type.

"Faint."

"Why would I *want* to faint?"

"Because he's so handsome and has all that money."

Nicole frowned. Bless her heart for not understanding the silliness of these young ladies.

Marguerite stared at Nicole. "*You* had tea with Mrs. Kesner?"

"Yes, Mother," Adelaide said. "Haven't you been paying attention?"

Marguerite's mouth pulled into a stiff smile. "Well, you must come to our home for tea then. Tomorrow. I'll have it all arranged."

Henny wanted to say no. She couldn't believe

Marguerite was going to gush all over Nicole now that the rumor mill had confirmed her wealth and the girl had been entertained by Florence Kesner. Actually, she could believe it. "I'm afraid Saturday won't work."

"Monday, then. I won't take no."

Henny knew she wouldn't. "I'll let you know after church on Sunday if that will work. Nicole has business to attend to."

Marguerite smiled. "Sunday! What a grand idea. After church, we'll have you over for afternoon tea."

It seemed to be all settled. "Sunday would be lovely. We look forward to it."

Henny supposed Nicole would be receiving more invitations as word got around about who she was and that Mrs. Kesner had entertained her.

Once all the ladies had left, Henny turned to Nicole. "I'm sorry for agreeing to another social engagement without talking to you about it first, but some people you just can't say no to."

"That's all right. I enjoyed myself at Mrs. Kesner's."

She might not think the same of tea with Marguerite. "We'll have to take Bucky with us." Marguerite wasn't going to like that, but she would cope.

"He can behave when he wants to. I'll talk to him."

Henny wasn't sure how to broach the next topic. She knew what others expected, but would Nicole understand. "About tea with Marguerite. The dress you wore to Mrs. Kesner's will suffice, but people like the Kesners and the Atwoods expect other people like themselves to wear different clothes than they wore to other functions. It's sort of a breach of etiquette."

Nicole twisted her mouth around. "I can't wear the same dress? Should I wear the purple ball gown?"

"No. That would be entirely unsuited and a grievous faux pas."

"Why?"

"Certain attire is appropriate for certain occasions. A fancy gown for a fancy party. An afternoon dress for tea. An everyday dress for work around the house."

"I never knew there were so many kinds of clothes. Simpler to wear buckskins for everything."

"That it would be." *Henny, now you've done it.* She'd wanted the girl to dress and behave like a lady, and now that Nicole had all that money, she needed to behave appropriately for her new station. "As I said, the dress you wore will be fine, but—now that people know who you are—you might want to consider ordering more outfits."

Nicole's eyes brightened. "At *Mademoiselle Dumont's?*"

"Yes."

"There were several other dresses I liked, but I don't know if Grandpa would want me spending all his money on dresses. It's not as though the dress got worn out with only one use."

Though Nicole seemed naïve in some ways, her judgment and thoughtfulness of others seemed like a fine, aged wine. How had Henny slipped so easily into old ways of thinking? "You're right. Your dress has plenty of use in it. If people don't like that, then it's their problem."

∞

Though the next day was brisk, Nicole enjoyed the walk to the mercantile.

Bucky hopped about, darting from a twig to a rock to peer up a tree at a chattering squirrel and back to another rock. He seemed to not have a care in the world, unlike Rolfy who hadn't wanted to leave the boarding house.

Nicole halted. But he'd eagerly agreed to go out to Shane's ranch to work. So, it wasn't that he wanted to stay at Aunt Henny's, but that he didn't want to go into town in particular.

"Whatcha doing, Nick? Why'd you stop?"

Nicole shifted her focus to Bucky swinging from the lowest branch of a tree ahead. "I was just thinking." She set her feet into motion again.

"Why?"

She caught up to him. "Why was I thinking?"

"Yah."

"Everybody thinks. Even you."

He plopped the three inches to the ground and bounced next to her. "Not if I can help it. Thinking hurts my brains."

"You're thinking right now or you couldn't talk."

"Uh-uh. The words just come out. I could talk and talk and talk and not do one lick of thinking."

That was probably how it seemed to a seven-year-old. Would it do any good to explain to him that thinking happened lickety-split? That a person didn't have to be aware of thinking to *be* thinking? Let him believe life was as simple as he viewed it.

Nicole stopped on the boardwalk a few feet from the mercantile. She pointed toward the entrance. "See how that man is holding the door open for the lady?"

Bucky nodded.

"That's because he's a gentleman. You need to learn to be a gentleman."

"All right."

At the entrance, he pulled the door open and hopped inside.

"Bucky?"

He spun around. "What?"

"I thought you were going to hold the door for me."

"Why?"

"I'm a lady."

Bucky guffawed. "Naw, you're just Nick." He spun around and pranced farther into the store.

Shane would have held the door for her. He had when he'd taken her to lunch. He'd treated her like a lady even before she knew how a lady should be treated. Nicole would have to work on Bucky. She entered.

Bucky strolled around the mercantile wide-eyed. He'd never seen so many things in one place. Neither had Nicole the first time she'd come.

Nicole picked out a pair of trousers and a shirt for both Bucky and Rolfy. She couldn't do much about new shoes for Rolfy, but she could get Bucky a pair.

Her cousin scuttled over and motioned for her to bend lower.

He whispered in her ear, "I don't like that man."

Nicole glanced up to find an older man with a stern expression, staring at Bucky. He wore a rumpled work shirt and a long, scraggly beard. She refocused on Bucky. "Ignore him. Let's pick out some candy."

"Yummy!"

Nicole peered over her shoulder from time to time at the man. He had no qualms about openly staring at Bucky.

Mr. Waldon crossed over to the man. "Sir, if you're not going to buy anything, I need to ask you to leave."

The man groused and left.

Relief swept through Nicole. Bucky didn't seem to notice and had apparently forgotten about him.

Mr. Waldon gave Nicole a nod. She nodded in return. It was nice of him to look out for her and Bucky.

In addition to the clothes and three different kinds of candy, she bought her little cousin a small, wooden horse. For Rolfy, she purchased a pocketknife and candy as well. When she went out to Shane's ranch, she would give them to him. Probably next week.

She paid for her purchases, grateful Aunt Henny had insisted she take more than a few coins with her. After tying the laces of Bucky's new shoes together, she hung them around his neck.

"Whatcha do that for?"

"So you can easily carry them."

Bucky took them off and held them out. "I don't want to carry them. You carry them."

"If you don't take them, then you can't have your horse and candy."

He quickly draped the shoes around his neck.

She handed him his parcel of goodies, while she took both bundles of clothes for each of the boys as well as Rolfy's candy and gift. She hugged her older cousin's belongings. She couldn't wait to see him. She missed him.

With his toy horse tucked under his arm, Bucky opened the door and stopped, facing a woman on the other side of the threshold. "Are you a lady?"

The woman smiled. "I am."

Bucky stepped aside, holding the door.

The woman entered.

Then he trotted out and along the boardwalk without Nicole.

So, it wasn't that he hadn't understood about ladies and gentlemen, but that he didn't see Nicole as a lady. She shook her head and exited.

Bucky reversed direction and hustled up to her like a scared rabbit.

The frowzy man who'd watched Bucky inside the store approached. "You look familiar. What's your name, boy?"

Her little cousin pressed into her thigh.

"Come over here, boy. Let me get a good look at you." He squinted.

Nicole stepped between the man and Bucky. "Leave my cousin be. I'm sure you don't know him."

Bucky peeked around Nicole's skirt.

"He looks a lot like someone I once knew, but he'd be older." He jabbed a finger toward Bucky. "Are you that little runt who was with him?"

Bucky ducked out of sight behind her.

Nicole put her free hand around behind her and onto Bucky's shoulder, then took a step backward, moving her cousin with her. She spoke in a stern voice. "Leave us be."

"You're a sassy little thing but purdy." He gave her a dirty-toothed grin that stretched his cracked lips.

She took another retreating step, understanding why Grandpa had cautioned her to stay away from some men.

A red-haired man hopped up onto the boardwalk. "Is this man bothering you?"

"Yes, he is." Nicole was grateful to the stranger for coming to her aid.

The red-haired man rested his hand on the handle of his gun. "The lady would like you to leave her alone."

The shabby man narrowed his eyes at Bucky peering around her skirt but backed away. He touched the brim of his well-used hat with sweat stains around the crown. "Be seeing you."

If she'd had her rifle, she could have scared him off.

But Aunt Henny had told her a lady didn't walk around town toting a gun. Didn't see why not. Men seemed to do it. She wasn't quite sure why there were some rules for men and others for women. If it was good for men to carry guns, why not women too? It was going to take her a long time to figure out all these rules.

Nicole turned toward the red-haired man. "Thank you so much."

He tipped his clean, crisp hat. "You're welcome, miss. I'm Ian O'Gillis, at your service."

"I'm Nicole Waterby. If I had my rifle, I could have scared him off myself."

His eyes widened. "So where is it?"

"Aunt Henny said ladies don't carry around guns like men do. Not if I'm going to find myself a husband."

"Nicole Waterby, you say?"

"Yes."

"And who's the little one hiding behind you?"

"My cousin." She twisted to peer at Bucky. "Come on out and say good day to this nice gentleman."

Bucky shook his head. He held his new shoes by the laces in one hand as though he might swing them around.

"That's all right." Mr. O'Gillis inclined his head. "He seems a little shy."

"He's not normally like this." What had gotten into him? Probably still scared from the other man.

"You're the young lady who lived up in the mountains, aren't you? Your grandfather owns the mountain."

"Yes. I had no idea. He had wanted to cut and sell the timber."

"I know a little something about lumber operations. If you need any help, I could do that."

"How kind of you to offer." Now why couldn't she have met him when she first came to Kamola? Because she'd met Shane.

"I'm happy to help you in any way I can. A pretty little lady like yourself shouldn't have to trouble herself with a huge burden like that all alone."

Mr. O'Gillis was so thoughtful. And he didn't even

steal her hat.

"May I buy you a cup of coffee and a slice of pie, and one for the boy."

Bucky shook his head so hard, he almost knocked Nicole off balance.

The man's mouth curved into a smile that didn't reach his eyes.

Grandpa always told her to be wary of people when they smiled in such a way.

"Maybe another time." Mr. O'Gillis must have sensed her reluctance too.

"Maybe." But she thought not. "We need to be getting home."

Bucky took the cue and yanked on her arm, pulling her away.

Once out of earshot, Nicole slowed her cousin. "Why did you act so strangely with those two men? I understand the first one, but Mr. O'Gillis seemed nice."

Bucky pressed his lips together.

Nicole stopped and crouched in front of him. "What is it? Has Rolfy told you something again he wants you to keep secret?"

Bucky shook his head, then nodded, then resumed shaking it.

"Tell me or, I'll take your candy away."

Bucky eyed his bag of sweets then tucked it close to his chest. "He didn't say it was 'xactly a secret."

"Go on."

Her cousin huffed out a breath. "He sayed if someone showed any interest in me or think they knowed me, I was to get away from them. But I couldn't leave you behind, so I hided."

He thought he'd been protecting her? How cute.

"I see. Did he say who this person might be?"

Bucky shook his head. "And I didn't like Mr. O'Gillis. He has what Grandpa would call 'shifty eyes.'" Poking out his bottom lip, Bucky squinted and rolled his eyes back and forth.

Interesting. Grandpa's will had said if anyone else besides her took guardianship of the boys, they couldn't touch their mountain inheritance. Sarah had told Aunt

Henny she didn't think the boys were blood related. And she remembered when the boys arrived how scared they both had been. Was that first man related to them? She hoped not. And what about Mr. O'Gillis? She would have to tell Aunt Henny about this.

Shane strolled up to her, scattering all her worries. "Hey, kid."

"Shane!" Bucky dropped his shoes on the boardwalk but held tight to his candy and horse and lifted his arms.

Shane scooped him up. "How about some pie?"

"Yes!" Bucky turned to Nicole. "Please, Nick, can we? My belly's hollow and talkin' to me. It's sayin', 'Feed me now!'"

Quite the change from Mr. O'Gillis's invitation. Had Shane seen her exchange with him? She hoped not. Since Bucky was the one with qualms and he had none with Shane, neither did Nicole. "We would love to." And she would delight in spending time with him.

Shane opened the door to the White Hotel for Nicole and Bucky. What was he doing here? He'd never spent this much time in town before. Not any town. Not since he was fourteen, bought a nag of a horse, and rode west out of Detroit. Not even when he thought he was interested in Isabelle. He could count on one hand the number of times he'd eaten at the White Hotel dining room in the past year and still have fingers to spare. This would be the second time this week. Something must be wrong with him.

The muscle under his left eye began to twitch. *Rat-a-tat-tat.*

He growled to himself. Not again. He hated it when this happened. So distracting. He rubbed the spot, but it didn't give up its beat. He would ignore it. He hadn't had this problem since he'd had lunch with Isabelle. It must be time to move on. Cut and run.

While Bucky scrambled onto a chair, Shane held one out for Nicole. The scent of her hair wafted around him. Flowers. How could she have been the same tomboy in buckskin?

"Bucky settled in his seat. "Why'd you do that? Nick can move her own chair."

Shane set her packages on the extra seat and sat. "Because *Nicole* is a lady, and a gentleman holds out a chair for a lady." He hoped Nicole thought of him as a gentleman. Not that he was much of one. Though not genteel bred, he did have some manners.

Bucky pursed his lips and squinted at his cousin. "Are you sure?"

He gazed at Nicole. "Very sure."

Rat-a-tat.

Ignore it.

Bucky heaved a sigh. "I guess that means I'm gonna have to open doors for her everywhere. It's a lot of work to be a gentleman."

Nicole laughed, soft and soothing.

Shane wanted to hear it more. He ruffled the boy's hair. "Yep. That's what it means."

Tat-tat.

Good. It was slowing down.

Nicole shifted in her seat. "How is Rolfy? Does he want to come back?"

"He's doing good. He's a little restless and wanting more responsibility than I'm willing to give him so soon. He needs to prove himself."

"He's always itching to do more than he's able. So, you're teaching him patience. That's good."

Patience wasn't what Shane had in mind. More like protecting the boy from himself. Eagerness could easily be carelessness, which could get him injured.

The waitress came and took their order of two rhubarb and one blueberry pie, one coffee, and two cherry sodas. She promptly returned with their food and drinks.

Nicole took a huge chunk off the point of her rhubarb pie and put it into her mouth.

Shane smiled to himself. Nicole wasn't like any other woman he'd met. Though beautiful and dressed like a proper lady, she likely had the ability to match him in a shooting contest.

She took a sip of cherry soda and set down her glass. "I'm surprised you're in town again. I thought you had a lot of work out on your ranch. Not that I'm not glad you're here—I am—I'm just surprised. A nice surprise."

Shane was surprised too.

Rat-a-tat-tat.

"I needed to come in to check for any mail." What a feeble excuse. He rarely got mail. Hopefully, Nicole didn't notice his flimsy explanation.

Rat-a-tat-tat-tat.

He wiggled his face around to try to get the twitching to stop.

Nicole leaned forward. "Is something wrong?"

"It's nothing. An itch under my eye." He scratched the place with one finger, but it made no difference. His best bet was to ignore it. Distract himself. He turned to the boy. "What have you been up to?"

Bucky struggled to contain his huge mouthful of blueberry pie. He did his best to keep his lips sealed, but a drizzle of purple juice oozed out each corner.

Nicole held out her hand. "Don't you dare speak with all that in your mouth." She retrieved his napkin and wiped at the boy's face. "You don't have to put it all in at once."

Shane wanted to laugh but feared berries and crust might fly across the table at him. He took a bite of his own tart rhubarb pie.

Bucky swallowed hard. "My mouth isn't as big as I thought it was." He looked from Nicole to Shane. "Nothin'."

Why had he said that? "Nothing what?"

He took a swig of cherry soda and set his glass down. "I've been up to nothin'." He took another bite of pie, smaller this time.

It was probably best if he didn't bother Bucky again while he tried to eat. Shane shifted his attention to Nicole again, and his breath caught at her purple-blue eyes gazing intently at him. Full of intelligence and mirth.

He should look away but wanted to stare into those violet depths forever.

Rat-a-tat-tat.

Twleve

WHEN THE CHURCH SERVICE ENDED THE next day, Nicole received a pleasant surprise. Against the rear wall stood Shane and her cousin. Rolfy pressed into the corner with his chin tucked to his chest. She searched for a quick path around the other people, who moved too slowly, but there was none.

Bucky caught sight of his brother. "Rolfy!" He dodged to and fro, trying to figure out which direction would be fastest. He dropped to his stomach and scooted under the pews.

"Bucky!" That was *not* an option for her. She slipped between two pews and shimmied her way to the other end near the wall. Fewer people clustered in the side aisle.

Shane's mouth broke into its one-sided smile.

Her mouth automatically returned the gesture. She didn't care if he thought her silly and unladylike. Her cousin was more important. And anything to cause Shane's face to be happy was well worth it. But now wasn't the time to be staring at him.

Bucky popped up at the back of the room and threw himself at his brother.

The people on the outside aisle scooted between the pews to the middle.

Nicole reached her quarry. "Rolfy, I've missed you." She gave him a quick hug whether he liked it or not. She hadn't been able to go out to Shane's ranch yet. "Are you ready to come back?"

Her cousin raised his head to reveal a black and purple bruise on his cheek.

"Mercy snakes!" Bucky jumped up and down. "I want a bruise like that. You are so lucky."

Rolfy gave his little brother a cheeky grin, then

grimaced.

Boys. Even when living on the mountain, she'd found it peculiar how they could be proud of their injuries. Nicole had always done her best to avoid such afflictions. She turned a questioning gaze on Shane. "What happened?"

"Rolf, tell your cousin what you did to earn yourself that temporary brand on your face."

"Wasn't nothing. Just in the corral with a bronco the men were trying to break. It rammed me, and I landed against the fence. It's not so bad."

Nicole narrowed her eyes at Shane.

He nudged Rolfy's foot with the toe of his boot. "Tell her why you were in the corral."

Her cousin's shoulders rose and fell with his deep intake of breath, and he lowered his gaze. "I wasn't s'posed to be there. Mr. Keegan told me not to go in the corral without him. The other men had gone to do their chores."

"You disobeyed? What were you thinking?"

He lifted his head. "I wanted to prove I could handle the horses as well as any of the other men."

"But you can't, because you are only a boy."

He squared his shoulders. "Am not. I'm almost a man."

"Almost but you're not. *You* are coming straight back to the boarding house with me."

"No! I like being out on the ranch. I wanted to show Mr. Keegan I was as tough as any cowboy when he returned from town yesterday."

Nicole shifted a hard gaze to Shane. She wanted to be angry with him but found she couldn't. It wasn't the handsome rancher's fault her cousin had a thick head and wasn't born with any sense.

Shane held Nicole's gaze. Her deep purple-blue eyes piercing him. Sweat prickled his upper lip. He'd wanted to hide the fact Rolf had gotten hurt. But if she came out to his ranch during the week and saw the boy's bruise, she'd likely be madder than a nest of disturbed rattlers at him.

Any blood there had been from the small cut on his lip was cleaned up before Shane had returned. Good thing, because he didn't handle human blood well. He could butcher a chicken, skin a rabbit, and gut a fish, but he couldn't stomach blood from a person. Not since he was eight, and there was all that blood. Even thinking about it gathered under Rolf's skin made him shudder.

Besides confessing the boy's injury, Shane had planned to come to church today to be able to see her. He hadn't seen her since the last time he was in town. Just yesterday. He smiled to himself. That was before her cousin had decided to prove his manhood. Yep, the boy was a lot like him. Problem was, at his age, the perception of what made a man was twisted around backward.

Nicole returned her focus to her cousin, giving Shane a chance to breathe. "Remember what Mr. Keegan said about not following orders?"

"I know. He said he'd give me another chance, but you got to decide. Please let me stay out on the ranch. I promise to do everything he says. Promise."

Yes, let him stay so you'll have a reason to come out to see me. Shane jerked his head to the side toward the boys. "You two go outside while I talk to Miss Waterby."

Rolf scrunched up his face. "Miss what? It's just Nick."

No, she wasn't just Nick. She was so much more. "Go."

Rolf and Bucky skedaddled out.

Nicole held Shane's gaze. "I'm sorry he's been trouble for you."

One of his eyebrows shot up. *She* was apologizing? "You're sorry? I figure I'm the one who needs to apologize. I had told the men to have one of them keep Rolf in their sights when I'm away from the ranch. I should have kept a closer eye on him." *Not spend so much time in town.*

"He's real good at slipping around unseen when he wants something."

Not how Shane thought this would go. "Regardless, I'd like him to stay out on my ranch. Other than his unfortunate encounter with the bronco, he's been good and works hard." The prospect of Nicole visiting occasionally was well worth the small wage he paid the boy.

"Even though he can be a handful at times, I do miss him."

But?

"But I think it might be good for him to be working more like a man. I'll let him stay on one condition—you call me Nicole. Hadn't we settled the issue of names?"

"With what happened to Rolf and being in front of the boys, I figured I should use your proper name."

She put one hand on her hip. "Nicole is my proper name. Now, I need to talk to him about something else before I let him go with you."

This conversation didn't go in any of the directions he'd imagined. All of his rehearsed words to convince her to his way of thinking had been cast aside. "Anything I should know about?"

"I'll let you know after I speak with him."

He poked out his elbow. "Can I walk you out?"

"I'd like that." She hooked her hand around his arm, and a shiver danced up to his shoulder and down to his fingertips.

Nicole wasn't like any woman he'd ever met. He suspected he could spend a lifetime and still be surprised by her.

○∾⊃

Even though Nicole had told Aunt Henny to go ahead home without her, the older woman said she didn't mind waiting and sat in her buggy.

Shane took Bucky for a ride on his horse to give Nicole and Rolfy some privacy to talk.

Rolfy appeared on the edge of tears. "You're going to make me come with you, aren't you?"

"Depends on if you tell me the truth."

"I already did. I won't disobey him again. Promise."

"Not about that. About your family."

Rolfy opened his mouth, but she held up her hand to stop him. "Before you try to convince me Grandpa was your real grandpa, I know he wasn't. Your true name is Rudolf Miller and Bucky is Theodore Miller. How did Grandpa come to bring the two of you to the mountain?"

Rolfy set his jaw, and his breathing became shallow.

She would wait him out. Truth was, she would rather have him out of reach on the ranch. Almost asked Shane if Bucky could go as well.

Rolfy blew out a breath. "When our pa died, Ma had to take us all to live with her kin. She didn't want to. Said it would only be temporary until she could find us something better. Her brothers treated us something awful. Ma got real sick and died. Bucky wasn't even a year old yet. Our uncles made me do all the work they could and when I couldn't, beat me and Bucky too, just for crying."

Her poor cousins, to be treated so awfully.

"I taught Bucky not to cry. To stay as quiet as a clump of dirt."

No wonder Bucky hadn't spoken and made very little noise when he'd arrived on the mountain.

"I'd hide him and sneak him food. Ray got all fired up mad. I thought he was going to kill Bucky for wetting his diaper, so I took Bucky and ran away. We scuttled under the steps of the boardwalk in town. I planned for us to stay until night and then go as far away as we could."

"How? You were only seven. Where did you think you could go?"

"Anywhere would have been better. A man saw us hiding. I was afraid he'd rat us out, but he stood in front of the opening. When Ray comed by and asked him if he'd seen us, the man said he had. That two little boys went scurrying up the street. Ray run off, and the man grabbed Bucky and put him in the tail end of his cart and then me. He threw a blanket over us and drove out of town."

"Grandpa."

Rolfy nodded. "He saved us and treated us like real family. Like Ma and Pa before they died. You ain't going to send us back to them, are you?"

A tear rolled down each of Nicole's cheeks, and she shook her head. "I'm glad Grandpa got you."

"Me too."

"There is a problem though. A man in town recognized Bucky."

"How? He's not at all like he was when we ran away."

Neither of them were. "I believe the man thought Bucky was you."

"I never reckoned with Bucky looking like me." Rolfy's eyes widened enough to pop right out of his head. "You gotta let him come out to the ranch. You just gotta."

"I don't think the ranch is a good place for him. I'll keep him at the boarding house. Aunt Henny is helping me to try to keep you both. Make you legally mine."

"You can do that?"

"The attorney says it's possible and will help us to make it so."

Rolfy threw his arms around her. "I'll come to Aunt Henny's if you want me to."

"Do you truly like working on Mr. Keegan's ranch?"

"I do."

"Then I think that's where you should be for the time being, but you mind him. I don't want you getting hurt again."

"I will. I promise."

Well, now she understood why Rolfy fought being in town. He'd been afraid his blood kin would come for him.

She and Rolfy walked in the direction Shane rode with Bucky seated in front of him. Her littlest cousin didn't seem to have any ill effects from before Grandpa got him.

A thought flew in her head. Both Rolfy and Bucky needed a man in their lives. They'd always revered Grandpa, and now, both were naturally drawn to the rancher. But then, she was as well.

Shane trotted Huckleberry over and lowered Bucky to the ground and swung down himself. "Is everything settled?"

"Now, I need to talk to you."

Shane addressed Rolfy. "You want to ride Bucky

around for a few minutes?"

"Yes, sir."

He helped the boys onto Huckleberry and faced Nicole with a worried expression. She told him about Rolfy and Bucky's family, in case anyone came out to his ranch searching for them.

His face changed from nervous to concerned and a little angry. "Yesterday? Before or after I saw you?"

"A little bit before."

"Why didn't you say anything?"

Why? Because once Nicole saw Shane, the other two men vanished from her thoughts. "I needed to talk to Rolfy about it first." She wouldn't blame Shane if he turned her cousin away. "I'll understand if you don't want the trouble. I can keep Rolfy at the boarding house with me."

"On the contrary. The ranch is exactly where he should be. No one will know he's out there. Bucky too. I can protect them. You should come as well."

How touching that he so willingly wanted to protect her and her cousins. "Bucky and I will remain at Aunt Henny's, but I'd rest easier if Rolfy was out with you."

Shane locked his gaze with hers and spoke in earnest. "I could protect Bucky and you as well."

"No one's after me, and I can protect Bucky."

"I don't doubt that." A grin tugged at his mouth. "I've seen you with a rifle. I only want to help."

"I appreciate your offer, and you are helping by taking on Rolfy."

"If you change your mind, you and Bucky are welcome to come anytime. You and the boys could have the main house, and I would stay with my hands in the bunkhouse."

A part of her wanted to accept his offer. She wouldn't mind seeing him every day, but she needed to stay in town—at least for the time being. "I'll keep that in mind if the need should arise. Knowing Rolfy is safe will ease my worry tremendously."

"I think you should know, he prefers Rolf."

He would always be Rolfy to her. One of the scared little boys Grandpa rescued.

Shane waved the boys over. He lifted Bucky off. Her other cousin swung his leg over the horse's head and jumped to the ground.

"Don't look so worried." Nicole smiled and tried to ruffle Rolfy's hair, but he ducked out of the way. "You can stay at the ranch providing you obey and earn your keep."

Rolfy beamed. "I will."

"If I had known you were going to be here today, I would have brought the things Bucky and I bought for you."

Shane perked up. "I can bring him into town tomorrow."

She appreciated his eagerness. "I'd like to come out to the ranch to see where he's staying. Besides, in light of the stranger, Rolfy probably won't want to ever venture into Kamola."

Rolfy shook his head, agreeing he didn't want anything to do with town. "But you'll keep Bucky safe."

"I will. If I think he's in any kind of danger, I'll bring him right out to the ranch." When she turned to Shane, his mouth quirked up on one side, causing her heart to leap, and she hesitated.

"Did you need something else?"

She blinked several times and drew in a deep breath to retrieve her thoughts.

"Are you batting your eyelashes at me?"

"What?" Then she realized what she was doing and forced her eyes to remain open. "No. I'm sorry. My eyes... Nothing." She stared at his chin to keep the rest of his face from distracting her. "Would it be all right if Bucky and I come out tomorrow? If I can borrow Aunt Henny's buggy."

"I look forward to it." Shane touched the brim of his hat and rode off with Rolfy.

Nicole watched them go before heading for Aunt Henny's buggy with Bucky.

Later that afternoon, Nicole stood with Aunt Henny and Bucky on the Atwoods' porch. "I'm sorry for making us late."

"We're fine. Marguerite will be pleased you didn't

cancel."

"Don't you mean *we*?"

"It's you she wants at tea. I'm merely your chaperone."

A maid opened the door. "Good afternoon, Aunt Henny." She shifted her focus to Nicole. "You must be Miss Waterby the missus has talked so much about. I'm Sissy. Come in."

Nicole stepped inside. "I'm pleased to meet you."

"And who is this handsome young man?" Sissy closed the door.

"This is my cousin Bucky."

Bucky squared his shoulders. "I got new clothes and got all dressed up."

"You look spiffy. A right fine gentleman."

Nicole gazed at the maid. "Would it be out of place for you to call me by my first name?"

"It would be, miss."

Nicole didn't think she liked some of these formalities. "Let's say whenever you call me Miss Waterby, I'll pretend you're really calling me Nicole."

Sissy smiled wide. "I'm going to like you. Follow me." She slid open a pair of doors that disappeared right into the walls. "Your guests have arrived with a gentleman escort."

Nicole peered at the slot the door had settled into. Wasn't that something. They simply vanished.

Aunt Henny tapped Nicole's arm, and Nicole shifted her attention to Mrs. Atwood.

Their hostess stood. "Come in."

Her daughters, Isabelle and Adelaide, both smiled and nodded their greetings as to not interrupt their mother.

Mrs. Atwood leaned toward Bucky. "I'm sure Molly has some cookies in the kitchen. Would you like some?"

Bucky flopped his head about. "Would I ever."

Mrs. Atwood straightened. "Sissy, would you show this young gentleman to the kitchen."

Why was Mrs. Atwood acting strange? It wasn't that she wasn't generally a nice person, but she seemed to be trying too hard.

Bucky trotted off with Sissy.

Mrs. Atwood beamed at Nicole. "He's such a fine young man. Shall we sit?"

After Nicole joined Aunt Henny on the settee, their hostess sat.

Isabelle shifted in her chair. "I'm so happy we have the chance to have you all to ourselves. It's so hard to get to know someone when all the ladies are chattering."

Adelaide nodded. "I agree. You must have led such an exciting life. Did you truly track and hunt?"

"Adelaide, honestly." Mrs. Atwood pinned her daughter with a glare. "I don't think it's appropriate conversation for ladies."

"Well it should be."

Mrs. Atwood glared at her daughter. "But it simply is not."

Out of the corner of her eye, Nicole could see Aunt Henny trying to stifle a laugh.

"Then what is appropriate conversation?" Adelaide's bottom lip protruded slightly.

"Lady things." Mrs. Atwood retrieved the china teapot on the serving table and poured light brown liquid into a white porcelain teacup with delicate roses painted on it. "Things that ladies do."

Since Nicole had never done what their hostess would consider lady things, she had nothing to talk about.

Mrs. Atwood handed the first cup to Nicole. "Help yourself to the sugar and cream." Then she handed one to Aunt Henny, and one to each of her daughters before preparing one for herself. After that, she offered around the plate of pastries. Mrs. Kesner had served tea in the same order. And both had poured for everyone. Why did one person have to do all the work? Why couldn't Nicole, and the others, serve themselves?

Nicole would have to ask Aunt Henny if they did the same things on purpose, or if it was happenstance.

The other four ladies conversed about the latest fashions from New York and socials, marriages, and newborn babies. It was obvious Adelaide was expecting a child, but no one mentioned her coming little one. Was that on purpose? Or something ladies didn't talk about?

Not knowing what she could talk about, she nibbled on her pastry.

Mrs. Atwood addressed Nicole directly. "You've been so quiet, dear. Tell us something you like to do."

"You wouldn't be interested." The woman had already told Nicole so.

"Of course, we would. Wouldn't we, ladies?"

Her daughters nodded.

Maybe she wanted to know after all. "Last fall when I was tracking a deer to shoot for meat for the winter, a mountain lion—"

"Oh, my!" Mrs. Atwood grimaced and parted her lips as though she had more to say.

Aunt Henny held up her hand to their hostess who closed her mouth. "You asked and told her you were interested. I, for one, am fascinated to know what happened."

Isabelle and Adelaide nodded eagerly.

Mrs. Atwood apparently realized she was outnumbered, shifted in her seat, and lifted her cup to her lips.

Isabelle leaned forward. "A mountain lion what?"

Should Nicole continue? Aunt Henny nodded, so she did. "A mountain lion crept up on me from the side. I caught sight of her right before she leapt."

Mrs. Atwood gasped.

But Nicole continued. "I swung around with my shotgun at the ready and barely clipped her in the shoulder."

Adelaide's eyes were wide with curiosity. "Did you kill it?"

"Naw. She ran off."

"You didn't go after it and make sure it was dead?"

"I could see she was a nursing mother. She had cubs."

"But wouldn't it be better if they all died? Fewer of those menaces to wander into town."

Why did people want to kill everything they didn't understand? The meat wouldn't be good to eat. "She was simply doing what comes natural to her. Trying to feed her young. If we killed all the mountain lions, then the coons, rabbits, and rodents would overrun us. Do you want your kitchen full of mice and rats?"

Adelaide's mouth formed a little oh shape. "I never thought of it that way."

Isabelle stared with wide eyes. "Did you get the deer?"

"Not that day, but four days later I did."

Aunt Henny put two lumps of sugar in her tea. "Mrs. Kesner enjoyed that one and your description of the buck."

Mrs. Atwood sat forward. "You told Lady Kesner lurid hunting stories?"

Aunt Henny's mouth twitched in a small smile.

Nicole nodded. "She asked me to tell them. Her late husband hunted, and she loved hearing his stories. She said it made her feel closer to him to hear mine."

Mrs. Atwood licked her lips and swallowed. "Then please, regale us with your tales."

So, because Mrs. Kesner listened to Nicole's hunting stories, now Mrs. Atwood was interested? Townsfolk were a peculiar lot.

What would Shane think of her hunting? Would he think her too unladylike? Should she try to change her ways?

Could she live with a husband who wouldn't let her hunt?

Thirteen

ON MONDAY MORNING, HENNY LEANED HER cane against the bedside table in little Bucky's room. She mainly used it for balance and stability when traveling the stairs. And for peace of mind. She was too old to fall again and break something. No need to repeat that kind of pain or strife.

She folded down the blue and gray star quilt. Time to switch out the sheets on all her boarders' beds. Though cold, it was a nice enough day to hang the quilts on the line to air out. Her patrons would appreciate fresh bedding. Once the quilt was in a tidy bundle, she set it on the chair at the desk facing the window.

A person stood across the street. She pushed the curtains aside to get a better view. The same well-dressed young gentleman she'd seen before seemed to be studying her house again. But why? No coincidence he appeared right around the time Nicole and her "cousins" arrived. What was the man's interest in them? But they weren't even here now. So, why was he?

Nicole had taken Bucky out to visit Rolfy at Shane's ranch. So, was the man watching them or Henny? But again, why watch any of them? He could easily know Nicole and the boys were staying with her. And word had gotten around town that the beautiful young lady had inherited a tidy sum.

She was going to find out what he wanted once and for all. She spun around and exited the room, clomped down the stairs with a death grip on the railing. She'd been in too much of a hurry and left her cane in the boy's room. No time to return for it now. She flung open the front door.

A startled Saul Hammond stood before her, hand poised to knock.

She peered around him, but the man had

disappeared. "Did you see him?"

"Good day to you too." Saul doffed his hat, revealing a full head of graying hair.

"Yes, good day." Henny shimmied around her friend and to the edge of the porch where she could gander down the street. No one. "Where did he go?"

"I'm jealous you're looking for another man." He thinned his lips in a playful gesture.

Henny planted her hands on her hips and huffed out a breath. "You are not amusing. A man was standing over there a moment ago. You must have seen him."

"Sorry, I didn't. I had my sights set on your house and didn't pay attention to much else. But I can see this has upset you. He's probably searching for a place to stay. You do run the best boarding house in town."

Henny faced her friend. "Then why didn't he come to the door and knock? Why run away again?" She didn't expect answers and moved past him back inside.

Saul followed her. "He's been here before?"

"He has." Henny thrust her arms through the sleeves of a hip-length walking jacket. "The same day Nicole arrived." She swung a wool shawl around her shoulders to ward off the December cold. "That can't be a coincidence." She pinned on her hat. "Never approaches to talk or rent a room or anything."

"Where are you going?"

"After him. Maybe I can catch up and find out what he wants. I can't tell if he's watching me or them, but he's watching."

Saul stood in her open doorway, blocking her exit. "I can't let you race off alone after a stranger."

"You're welcome to tag along."

"*Tag* along?"

"Saul, you're a dear friend, but you can't stop me. I'll simply go out my kitchen door. And he's getting away."

He heaved a breath of what seemed like resignation. "Where's your cane?"

Henny glanced around. "I left it upstairs. I don't need it."

He folded his arms. "You may not need it at first, but if you plan to run after a phantom, your leg is going to get tired. I'm not interested in getting a tongue lashing from my son's new wife if you get hurt. Where is it? I'll fetch it."

Henny didn't have time for this. The man was getting away. She snatched a parasol from the umbrella stand and pointed with it. "Let's go."

Saul threw up his hands and closed the door behind them. "Which way did he go?"

Henny marched along her front walk. "I didn't see. He was standing there, and when I came downstairs, he was gone."

Saul opened the gate. "I came from over there and didn't pass anyone, so he couldn't have gone that way. The fellow likely headed into town." He closed the gate behind her.

"I agree."

He took her hand and wrapped it around his forearm. "If you're not going to use that fancy umbrella, hold on to me. That flimsy contraption is more kinds of useless than I can count."

Saul was sweet and a cherished friend for twenty years, ever since she'd arrived in Kamola. Henny had been friends with his wife before she passed away a few years ago. Had watched his son grow into a fine man. His granddaughters almost felt like her own.

She squeezed his arm. "Thank you for coming with me and not thinking I'm touched in the head."

"Oh, I'm thinking it. I'm just not saying it." Saul chuckled.

Henny laughed too. "I must seem like a person possessed."

"A little." He patted her hand on his arm. "We'll find this man and get everything sorted out. I wish you had told me about him before."

"There hasn't been a chance. I haven't seen you in a couple of weeks."

"That's my fault—or rather my granddaughters'. Most of the children at school came down with a nasty illness, and we've been passing it around the house."

"I heard. I planned to stop by, but Nicole arrived, and I've been busy helping her."

"I'm glad you didn't come over. I'd hate for you to catch whatever we had."

"I'm glad all of you are better."

"Me too. I've regained my appetite." He patted his stomach with both hands. "Held down food for the past three days, so I think I'm cured."

As they approached the first businesses in town, Saul inclined his head toward the various people strolling around. "Do you see him?"

Henny studied each person on foot, on horseback, and in buggies. Those she knew, she let her gaze skim past, as well as the ladies and cowboys. She focused on the well-dressed gentlemen, which were few. "I don't see him." Where could he have gone in such a hurry? An idea popped into her head, and she marched faster, slightly pulling Saul along with her.

"What's the rush? Do you see him?"

"No, but I think I know where to find him." At the corner, Henny stepped off the boardwalk.

"Where?"

"The White Hotel. I don't think he's a local, so he's probably staying there."

Saul stopped short. "Oh no, Henny. You know nothing about this man. You're not going to hunt him down at a *hotel*."

"I'm only going to inquire at the desk. I know Grant, and he likes me." She gave Saul a sweet innocent smile.

"Don't look at me like that. He's not going to tell you anything."

"He might." She had recently been a witness at the young man's wedding. "Are you coming with me or not?"

He heaved a sigh and continued along the street. "You are a headstrong woman."

"You knew as much before now. If it bothers you so much, why be my friend?"

"I know. It doesn't bother me...most of the time, only when I feel you could be heading into a trouble which could be avoided."

She figured as much. "I do appreciate you trying to look out for me."

"And just so you know, I happen to like headstrong

women. No fear of them wilting at the first sign of difficulty. But it can also get them—you—into a pickle of a predicament."

On the next block, Saul held open the door to the White Hotel. "After you."

"Thank you." She headed straight for the desk. "Hello, Grant. How is married life? Is Isabelle doing well?" It wouldn't hurt to remind him she had helped him get the young lady he loved. They had married right in her parlor.

"Being married is good. Real good." A flush crept up his neck and bled into his cheeks. "Isabelle is doing really well."

If she didn't change the subject, he was going to resemble a beet. "I'm hoping you can help me. A man came to my boarding house." The truth. If Grant inferred anything from what she said, it wasn't her fault. "I didn't get his name. Could you see if he's in your registry? He was about six-foot one or two, brown hair, and dressed real nice, charcoal-gray suit."

The color subsided from Grant's face and a slight smile tugged at his mouth. "Aunt Henny, I can't tell you that."

"Why not? A simple name is all I need."

"Mr. Howard doesn't allow us to give out customers' information."

Time to be frank. "Here's how it is. This man has shown up at my boarding house twice at a distance, and I've seen him other times in town watching me or Nicole. I want to make sure he isn't out to cause any problems for her."

Saul jumped in. "You've seen him multiple times, other than outside your place? You didn't tell me that."

Now she'd made him worry. "He always walked away. He doesn't want to talk to me, and I want to know why."

Grant leaned forward against the desk. "You should talk to Sheriff Rix. He's the only one I can let see the registry—or one of the deputies on his behalf."

Saul straightened. "Excellent idea, Grant. We'll take our leave and let you return to your work." He hooked his hand around Henny's elbow. "Come on, Henny. Edric is the one to help us."

Henny didn't want to get Grant in trouble with his boss and let Saul guide her outside. "Us? Are you in on this with me now?" Strangely, his touch reassured her.

"I have to, in order to keep you safe."

"I really don't think I'm in any danger." But Saul's concern warmed her heart. "He doesn't carry himself like a miscreant and dresses like a decent fellow."

"A moment ago, you were bothered he might cause problems for Miss Waterby. Which is it? Dangerous or decent?"

"I-I don't know." She had no evidence for either. "Both. He seems as though he could be decent, but it would be prudent to make sure. I only want to know one way or the other. Then I'll know what course of action to take."

"My son will find this man and figure out what he's up to. It's his job. I don't know why you didn't go to him in the first place or come to me."

Probably would have been the logical thing to do. "I've been busy helping Nicole sort her affairs and learn to be a lady. When I saw the man, yet again, I decided to find out once and for all what he was about."

This time, it was Saul in a hurry. He headed straight for Edric's office.

Henny didn't mind, even though her leg was beginning to protest at so much exertion. She was anxious to get to the bottom of this. If anyone would know who this stranger in town was, it would be their sheriff.

But it was his deputy Montana who sat behind the desk. The young man stood when she entered. "Howdy, Aunt Henny. Mr. Hammond. What can I do for you two?"

"Is Edric around?"

The deputy shifted his gaze from Henny to Saul and back and forth. He obviously felt the need to speak to the man, but it had been Henny who had addressed him. He finally settled on studying the space in between them. "He went out. The mayor needed him. Maybe I can help you."

She preferred to speak with Edric, but the sheriff had

hired good deputies. "I've seen a stranger in town several times now who seems to have been watching the young lady and her cousins who are staying with me. I was wondering if the sheriff could find out who he is."

Montana sat again and removed a piece of paper and pencil from one of the desk drawers. He touched the tip of the pencil to his tongue. "Can you give me a description?" He glanced up, noticed she remained on her feet, and shot to his feet, knocking his chair against the wall. "You want to sit or something?"

Henny struggled not to laugh at his discomfort and sat. "Thank you."

Apparently unconcerned about whether Saul stood or not, Montana retook his seat and poised his pencil over the paper. "I'm ready."

"He appeared to be in his mid-to-upper twenties. Well dressed. His suit likely came from back East. He might have stood over six feet tall."

"That's pretty tall. Are you sure?"

"I only ever saw him from a distance. What's an average height?" Henny was terrible at judging heights, distances, and other such measurements.

"Five seven or eight."

"Is that how tall you are?"

"I'm five ten."

"Maybe your height? Maybe less?"

"What kind of a build did he have?"

"Not husky or thin. He had brown hair. I wasn't close enough to see the color of his eyes."

"Brown hair, you say. Most common color. Like the sheriff's? Or like yours? Or lighter? Or darker?"

"I suppose similar to mine without the gray, but he was wearing a hat." An all too common color. Her description wasn't going to do anyone any good.

"Anything else you can think of? Anything distinguishing?"

"I haven't gotten a good look at him."

"You saw him outside your boarding house? Where else?"

Henny described in detail the various times she saw the stranger.

The deputy shifted his gaze to Saul. "Do you have anything to add?"

Saul shook his head. "I didn't see the man."

"But you were at Aunt Henny's when he was outside, weren't you?"

"I guess so, but I didn't see him."

Montana's gaze darted to Henny and returned to Saul. "I see."

Oh, bother. She wasn't a doddering old woman or hallucinating. The man *had* been there. Even if no one believed her. "Mr. Montana, have you seen this man around town?"

"It's just Montana. Can't say I have." The deputy stared at his paper. "It's not much to go on, but I'll pass this information on to Sheriff Rix when he returns." He gave Saul a surreptitious nod.

It didn't matter. The young man had written down the information, and Edric would believe her. "Thank you." Henny stood.

The deputy shot to his feet. "My pleasure, ma'am."

"Would you ask Edric to stop by my house on his way home?" Then she could gauge what the deputy told him and if he took her seriously or not.

"Sure will. And don't you be fretting. Probably nothing more than someone new in town or passing through, and you happened to see him a couple of times. Probably nothing. Nothing at all."

Henny could believe that if the man hadn't scurried away each time.

"In all likelihood, he's simply after a room to rent."

The same thing Henny had thought the first time. "Then why dash off?"

"I don't know."

Another deputy entered and held the door open. "Are you heading out?"

Saul nodded. "Yes, Sammy. Thank you."

Henny limped out, leaning more on her parasol than she liked. She hadn't done this much walking all at once since before she'd broken her leg in the early summer.

"Your injury's bothering you. This is why I insisted upon your cane. Or in this case, an umbrella. Wait here."

He ducked back into the sheriff's office.

She lifted her walking instrument. *It's a parasol.* There was a difference, but it didn't really matter.

He returned. "We can take Sammy's horse."

"What if he needs it?"

"They have Montana's, and I'll return it posthaste. Let me help you." He took her parasol and assisted her into the saddle then tapped her shoe. "Move your foot."

"You're riding too? I thought you were merely being chivalrous." Teasing aside, Henny removed her foot from the stirrup.

Saul gripped the saddle horn and cantle and swung up behind her. "I'm not old, but I'm not a spring chicken either." He reached around her and grabbed the reins. "Besides, I don't want you to get some fool idea in your head of where to find this man and take off without me."

She liked Saul's arms around her, even if innocently so. A tingle danced across her skin, and her heart thrummed in a manner it hadn't done in a couple of decades. She longed to lean into him and enjoy his presence. Sadly, decorum dictated she keep some space between them. "Tongues will wag about us riding like this."

"So, let them wag. I've lived too many years to worry about such nonsense. Would you mind if they did?"

No. And yes. "I don't like people gossiping about my friends."

"We're friends, are we?" His question had a touch of hurt in it.

"Of course, we are, Saul Hammond." That was all.

He harrumphed and put the horse into motion.

All they ever could be.

Fourteen

LATER THAT SAME MORNING, SHANE GLANCED at the clock on the mantelshelf in his uncle's house. *Wait.* This was Shane's house. He still had a hard time thinking of a permanent place as his. *His* clock on *his* mantelshelf in *his* house read half past nine. Nicole could arrive soon, depending on when she headed out. And providing nothing else cropped up to keep her from coming today. He'd seen her only yesterday, still something inside him longed to see her again. Needed to see her. He would try once more to convince her to stay at his ranch.

He strode outside. Two branches, several feet in length, lay in the yard between the house and the barn. How long had they been there? How had he not noticed them before? How could he have let his place get in such disarray? He grabbed the two limbs by each of the large ends and dragged them over to the woodpile to be chopped later. A good chore for Rolf.

He scrutinized his yard with new eyes. A bucket sat by the corral where the men and Rolf had congregated. A pitchfork rested against the side of the weathered barn, and a wheelbarrow looked as though it had wandered out into the yard on its own and stopped part way to its destination. Had he and his men always been this slipshod, leaving things about? What would a lady think of this mess? Nicole's grandfather had probably kept things tidy. He didn't want her to believe him sloppy.

Shane strode toward the ranch hands. "What are you doing standing around? Clean things up."

Handley swung his gaze to him. "Clean up what?"

"The wheelbarrow, pitchfork, and bucket for starters." Shane pointed to each item in turn.

His foreman glanced about. "We were using them."

"If you're done, put them away."

"You heard the boss." Handley motioned to the men. "Let's get back to work. Kid, put the wheelbarrow away. Bray, the pitchfork. Decker, the bucket. Klem, the horse blankets. Tommy Pine, the mucking shovel. Woods...find something."

All the men ambled at a pace slightly faster than if they stood still. Only Rolf scampered like a jackrabbit and disappeared into the barn.

Shane hadn't noticed the shovel or blankets. How could he not have noticed how careless they had all become?

Handley moseyed over to Shane. "What's got you all riled up?"

"I'm not riled up."

"You are. You know we always put the tools and such away, in time."

So, Shane was a little ruffled. "Rolf's cousin, Miss Waterby, is on her way." He hoped. "I don't want her to think her cousin has fallen in with bad company."

His foreman chuckled. "You let a woman vex you?"

Shane guessed he had.

Handley strolled away. "You are a sorry wretch."

If Nicole gazed at him with her violet eyes, he'd consider himself a fortunate wretch indeed. If he wanted *his* place cleaned up for a woman or any other reason, that was his prerogative.

At an undistinguishable sound, Shane spun around. He closed his eyes and listened. Hoof beats and traces. She was here. "Rolf!"

The boy barreled out of the barn and stood next to him. "Yes, sir."

Shane pointed as the buggy crested the hill still a quarter of a mile off. "They're here."

Bucky bounced on the buggy seat. Nicole seemed to be talking to him. Shane doubted any words would contain the excited boy. Who would guess that the brothers had seen each other only yesterday?

Roxy and Pepper raced out to greet the new arrivals.

Bucky stood in the buggy and waved his arms. "Rolfy!"

"Bucky!"

Nicole reached for her youngest cousin. "Sit down. You'll fall. What are you doing? Don't get out! You know better. This isn't a two-wheeled cart. You could get caught under the wheel!"

As Bucky clambered over the side, preparing to jump to the ground, Nicole hauled back on the reins, stopping the conveyance.

Bucky landed with a thump and ran headlong toward his brother, the dogs running beside him.

The boys hugged and smiled. The pair was fortunate to have each other, as well as having Nicole and her grandfather. Shane'd had no one. Alone to fend for himself. How different things would have been if he'd had someone to look after him or to look after.

Nicole rolled the buggy to a stop near Shane. "He could have killed himself."

"But he didn't, thanks to you." He stepped closer. "Let me help you down."

Nicole set the brake and reached for his hand.

Instead of taking hers, he gripped her waist. "Put your hands on my shoulders." When she did, he lifted her to the ground. He held her a little longer than necessary and spoke in a low voice. "Don't call your cousin Rolfy. Call him Rolf so the men don't tease him."

"What does it matter what I call him if they called him Kid?"

"They do, but that won't stop them from teasing him. Let him have the dignity of a man."

"All right." She gazed at him a long time with her violet eyes.

One of his men whooped.

Shane moved away, clearing his throat. He was likely the one who would get teased. He studied her blue skirt that stopped short of her ankles. "This is a different outfit."

She spun in a circle. "It's a riding skirt. Do you like it?"

"I do." But he guessed that anything would be fetching on her. "Do you plan to go riding today?"

"I'm hoping you have a horse I can purchase."

"I need all mine, but I have a neighbor who breeds

horses. He's sure to have one to your liking. We'll go after dinner."

Nicole gave Rolf a bundle of clothes with sweets and a pocket knife on top. She squinted at his bruised cheek and sighed but didn't make a fuss. Good. Less for the men to tease the kid about.

After introducing each of his men, Shane followed along as Rolf took his brother and Nicole on a tour of the ranch, at least the buildings in the yard, and told them all the things he did around the place. Rolf seemed happy and content there.

Gunshots went off nearby. His men keeping their skills sharp. Or were they taking advantage of Shane being preoccupied with Nicole?

Nicole glanced around. "What was that?"

"The men like to do some target practice."

"Why?"

"Never know when those skills will come in handy."

"Who's the best?" Rolf asked.

"They're all good shots." Shane liked to think of himself as the best of the lot, but Handley and Bray were close.

Rolf turned around and walked backward. "Can I shoot?"

Nicole nodded. "I don't see why not."

Bucky jumped up and down. "I want to shoot too."

"Not by yourself."

Soon, they all collected at a place beside the house where a snaggletooth tree stood in the distance. From its branches hung various items, tin cans, hunks of wood, strips of fabric, old cutlery, a tin plate with several holes in it already, and a broken tea cup. All designed for target practice.

Each of the men took several shots as well as Rolf and Bucky, hitting something at least once.

In light of her encounter in town with Rolf and Bucky's relatives, it would be a good idea for Nicole to practice with a weapon smaller than her rifle as well. Shane held out his revolver—handle first—to her. "Your turn."

She took the weapon and turned it over in her

hands. "I've never shot one of these."

Shane smiled inwardly. "I'll teach you." He put it in her hand the proper way and showed her how to hold it, cock the hammer, and aim. Then he moved around behind her and lifted her arm toward the target. She smelled of flowers of some sort. He closed his eyes to clear his head. "Aim for the board on the far left. It's heavy and doesn't move in the wind as much."

Though he didn't want to, he stepped away from her. She glanced over at him.

He gave her a nod. "You can do this."

She nodded back, raised the gun toward the target, and pulled the trigger as though she'd done it a hundred times before.

The men laughed, and Handley said, "Sorry, darling. Nice try."

Nicole shot again and again, missing each time. "Oh, fiddlesticks." She stomped her foot. "How's a person supposed to hit a plum thing with such a short barrel?"

Shane struggled not to laugh. She was adorable. "It takes practice." He held out his hand. "Let me reload it for you."

She slapped the revolver into his palm. "Bucky, would you get Grandpa's rifle out of the buggy?"

Bucky raced off and returned more slowly with the long weapon cradled in his arms.

Nicole took the Winchester, checked the chamber, and cocked the rifle.

The ranch hands snickered, and Handley said, "That's a lot of gun for such a little lady. It's got quite a kick."

She turned to them with a smile. "Yes, it does."

Shane pictured his first meeting with the buckskin-clad girl and suspected his men wouldn't be laughing right soon. Nicole was apt to hit something with that weapon. Even if not her intended target.

Nicole studied the tree then glanced at the ranch hands. "What would you like me to hit?"

Handley inclined his head. "Darlin', you can try to hit anything you like. Even the trunk of the tree."

Shane stepped closer. "The wood pieces are the

easiest to hit."

"What else?"

Did she seriously think she could hit something smaller? "The plate is next easiest, but you need to account for any wind. There's usually a slight breeze coming down the mountain."

She pointed with the rifle. "What's that on the right, up high?"

"The blue neckerchief?" Not an easy target.

"Above that."

Shane squinted. "The teacup?"

The men snickered.

He wanted to throttle them all.

Nicole tilted her head. "Looks more like a half of a teacup."

"It's only been hit once." By Shane himself. "It would be best to stick with one of the bigger targets."

She huffed out a breath. "Very well." She planted the butt of the rifle squarely against her shoulder.

At least she knew how to hold the weapon.

Surprisingly, his men didn't heckle her. Were they as eager to see if she hit anything as he was?

Nicole drew in a slow breath and let it out.

Take your time. Shane stood slightly behind her so he could both see the targets and catch her when the kick knocked her backward. He smiled at the prospect of having her in his arms.

She squeezed the trigger and hit the largest plank of wood. Though she jerked a little, the recoil didn't topple her.

Too bad. His arms still wanted her in them.

Bucky and Rolf cheered.

She cocked the lever, expelling the spent shell while allowing the next bullet into the barrel, and shot again, hitting the tin plate. *Tink.* Cocked the lever, shot, hit the tin can. *Tink.* Then a ladle twirling in the breeze. *Tink.* She clipped the rope holding the flapping blue neckerchief, sending it fluttering to the ground. And then the teacup shattered into bits. Nicole lowered the rifle.

The men appeared stunned. Handley pushed back his hat, spit tobacco juice onto the ground, and cursed.

The others cursed as well. Not quite admiring but not angry.

"I'll have none of that kind of talk around a lady."

"Ain't no lady can shoot like that."

A special kind of lady could.

And she had.

After the noon meal, Nicole sat on the wagon seat next to Shane, resisting the urge to lean in to him. The quilting ladies had told her something like that wouldn't be socially acceptable. If not for Rolf and Bucky in the back, she might give in to the temptation.

"Jasper breeds good horses. We'll find you a fine one. I purchased a couple from him last summer. If he still has Peppermint, I think she would be a decent choice for you."

Unfortunately, the trip ended too soon, and Shane lifted Nicole to the ground.

Two men strode out of the barn and gave Shane a friendly greeting. He in turn introduced her to Jasper Whittier and Guy Jones.

"Whittier? Neva's husband?"

The man's mouth broke into a wide smile. "Yes, ma'am."

"I know her from the quilting circle."

"My wife too." The other man thumbed himself in the chest. "Betsy's mine." He pointed to Mr. Whittier. "And Jasper's sister."

"I had no idea." Nicole hadn't gotten a chance to get to know the ladies very well yet.

"They have both spoken very highly of you. Pleased to make your acquaintance."

Footsteps approached from behind them, and soon Betsy and Neva joined them.

Nicole could see the resemblance between the siblings, Betsy and Mr. Whittier.

Betsy planted her hands on her hips and glared at Guy Jones. "Where is our son? You were supposed to keep an eye on him."

"He's fine, woman. Fell asleep in the hay." He put his arm around his wife's shoulders. "Stop your clucking."

Betsy swatted him. "I'll cluck all I like." She turned to Nicole. "Come in and have a cup of tea."

"We don't really have the time. I came to buy a horse." She was anxious to meet the livestock.

Shane inclined his head to Jasper. "You still have Peppermint? I think she'll suit Miss Waterby."

The whole group headed into the barn.

Nicole trailed along at the end. A beautiful black horse with a long forelock poked its head over the half door of its stall, eyeing her as though it had something on its mind. She walked up to it. It snorted an intimate breath into her face and pawed at the ground. Her heart quickened, and she reached out to pet it.

Suddenly, she was yanked backward, and Mr. Jones hissed in her ear. "Queenie can be unpredictable."

The horse neighed a warning and glared at the man. He released her. "She needs a firm hand."

Betsy joined them. "You mean only a man can handle her." She stroked the black horse's nose. "Queenie is just particular about who rides her. Personally, I think she prefers a woman's touch."

As Nicole moved with the group down the way, Queenie watched her with a perceptive gaze.

Mr. Whittier walked a stout chestnut-colored horse out into the open space between the rows of stalls. "Peppermint is a quarter horse. She has a gentle disposition and will pull a buggy fine." Not a particularly tall horse with a burst of white on her forehead and one white sock.

Nicole stroked the nose. "I want a horse I can ride."

"She's saddle broke and can be ridden too."

The gentleness in the horse's eyes almost made her look sad.

Betsy went over to Peppermint and hugged her around the neck. "This is the sweetest, gentlest horse you will ever find. She has a heart of gold." She turned to Nicole. "But she's not right for you." She faced Mr. Whittier. "Brother, Nicole needs a more spirited horse. I think Bear might suit her better."

Bucky petted the horse's nose. "Nick, get Peppermint. Please. I love her."

The horse put its head over her youngest cousin's shoulder and pulled him closer.

Bucky laughed. "See. She loves me too."

Betsy leaned closer to Nicole. "Peppermint will hug anyone who gets close enough."

Nicole turned to Shane. "What do you think? You know more about horses than me." The reason she'd wanted him to help her. Well, maybe not the only reason. Though Shane was near, Nicole ached to be closer to him and brush against his arm as she'd done in the wagon. But that wouldn't likely be socially acceptable. She looked forward to the trip back to his ranch where they could sit close and it not be frowned upon.

Shane stroked the horse's shoulder. "Peppermint will never give you a moment's trouble, that's for sure."

He thought she could only handle a horse docile enough for a seven-year-old. That was disappointing.

"But I reluctantly must agree with Mrs. Jones. You'll likely be happier with a more spirited mount. But not a horse as difficult as Queenie."

"No!" Bucky wailed. "I want Peppermint."

She patted her cousin's shoulder. "Let's see what else they have."

"I don't want another horse. I'm staying with Peppermint. I'm never ever leaving her."

He would once his stomach started howling for its next meal.

Mr. Whittier tossed the horse's lead rope over a railing. "She won't go anywhere." He led them back the way they'd come to a stall diagonal to Queenie's and opened the half door.

The golden-tan animal pranced in place and tossed its head, causing its black forelock and mane to whiffle. He sported four black socks of varying heights.

Mr. Whittier walked him out. "Bear is a good sturdy Mustang. He can be a little muleheaded, but he'll obey you. He's a good cattle horse, but I don't suspect you'll be around cattle much. If you are, he's not going to spook."

Shane ran his hand down the horse's side. "I almost bought Bear this past summer."

"Why didn't you?" If there was something wrong with the animal, Nicole didn't want him either.

"Sometimes a rider picks the horse, and other times the horse picks the rider. Huckleberry chose me. When a horse wants you as its rider, they are more apt to respond to your commands. I've been very happy with Huckleberry."

Mr. Jones appeared with a saddle. "Let's saddle them both and see who you fancy."

"Good idea." Shane nodded.

From behind Nicole, Queenie blew a snort. She glanced at the beautiful animal who had intelligence in her eyes.

As they walked out of the barn with the two saddled horses, Queenie neighed.

Bucky jumped up and down. "Can I ride Peppermint? Can I? Can I?"

Shane ruffled the boy's hair. "Let your cousin ride first, then you can have a turn."

Nicole rode Peppermint around the fenced field without one little problem. At the same time, Rolf rode Bear. Then she took a turn on the mustang while Bucky rode the docile quarter horse. Though the horse obeyed her, Bear did seem more spirited.

Next, Shane rode Bear but not like she or Rolf had done. He raced the mustang across the field, having him cut right and left after imaginary cows. He returned and swung to the ground. "Good horse flesh. I still like him."

"You think this is a good choice for me?"

"I think you'll be happy with him."

Nicole turned to Mr. Whittier. "I'll take him."

From atop the chestnut quarter horse, Bucky whined. "What about Peppermint?"

The slightly smaller mare did seem to suit her cousin. And after all, her inheritance was partly theirs too. "We'll take Peppermint as well."

Rolf huffed out a breath. "He gets a horse? What about me? I'm older. I'm the one who should get a horse."

Why shouldn't they both have their own?

"Fine. Bear can be yours." A fitting animal for working on Shane's cattle ranch. But that left Nicole without a horse for herself, and she faced the pair of breeders. "And I'll take Queenie."

Mr. Whittier's eyes widened. "You haven't even ridden her."

Shane touched her arm. "Queenie might be too much for you. Maybe in time."

"You said if a horse picks a rider, they are more apt to obey that rider. I believe Queenie was trying to choose me." And Nicole wanted the strong beauty.

"How do you know?"

"She looked at me."

Shane raised one dark eyebrow. "She *looked* at you?"

"It's *how* she looked at me. I can't explain it. She was trying to get my attention from the start. I felt something from her."

Mr. Jones heaved a sigh. "I'll saddle her up so you can give her a try. We wouldn't feel right selling you an animal without you riding it first."

A few minutes later, Queenie pranced out to the meadow and right up to Nicole. The large mare nudged her side.

Nicole laughed and fished the sugar lump from her skirt pocket. Aunt Henny had insisted she bring the sweet for whatever one she decided upon so the animal would know to come home with her new owner. She held her hand out with the sugar, and Queenie took it with velvety lips.

Shane stood next to her. "Do you want me to ride her first to see how she does?"

"No. I'd like to ride her." This was already her horse, and she climbed up.

Mr. Whittier held onto the bridle. "Keep a firm grip on the reins. Don't let her get away from you. You are in control, not the horse."

Shane mounted Bear. "I'll be right beside you."

For some reason, Nicole wasn't as concerned as the men. She knew she should be but wasn't. She walked the mare first then trotted. This was the one. She returned to where the others stood. "I'll take her."

Mr. Whittier and Mr. Jones shifted their wide-eyed gazes to Shane.

Shane laughed. "The horse seems to like her. If she wants Queenie, I can't stop her."

His laugh warmed her inside. Nicole paid the men what she had with her—only anticipating purchasing one horse—and promised to make arrangements with the bank to deposit the rest into their account.

All three animals were unsaddled, and their halter ropes tied to the back of Shane's wagon.

Shane drove away from the horse ranch. "I'll come into town tomorrow and help you find the right saddles for all three animals."

"I'm meeting with Mr. Thatcher to learn what he found out about Rolf and Bucky's family. Then I have to go to Mrs. Kesner's and learn more dancing for her Christmas Eve soirée."

Shane narrowed his eyes. "I suppose *Lamar Kesner* will be your partner for that."

"You could come and be my partner." What a great idea.

"I doubt I'm invited to such a function."

No, he hadn't been. Too bad.

"How about Wednesday for picking out saddles?"

"That would be lovely." Wednesday couldn't come soon enough. One downfall to having her own horse was that she wouldn't have an excuse to ride next to him in the wagon anymore. Even though she liked dress shopping, saddle hunting with Shane held more appeal.

Could a trip to the preacher be far behind?

Fifteen

THE NEXT DAY, HENNY SAT WITH Nicole across the desk from Mr. Thatcher again. Bucky remained in the outer office with the secretary.

The lawyer's grim expression disquieted Henny's soul. "The Sewells, Rudolf and Theodore's relations, might prove to be difficult. At first, they seemed agreeable to relinquishing rights to the boys. But Mr. Sewell senior, the boys' grandfather, suspects there might be money in this for him, though I don't believe he truly wants the pair. He did seem most interested in the older one. Thinks he could get some work out of him."

Nicole leaned forward. "I won't let him take them."

The lawyer's features relaxed. "I'm glad to hear that. I think these people can be bought for little money if we angle this right."

"I'll pay any amount to keep Rolf and Bucky from them."

Mr. Thatcher leaned forward. "Don't tell *anyone* outside this office that. Keep your eagerness to yourself. If the Sewells find out, you could lose everything to them. Including Rudolf and Theodore."

Henny couldn't believe this conversation. "Are you suggesting Miss Waterby buy her cousins like property?"

Mr. Thatcher took a deep breath. "Sort of, but not strictly speaking."

Nicole turned to Henny. "I don't mind. They mean more to me than any amount of money."

"That's beside the point. People are not things to be bought and sold."

Mr. Thatcher cleared his throat. "If I may say something, I think I can ease your objections."

Henny gave a small nod. How could he make the selling and buying of those two precious children less objectionable?

"I agree, the boys are *not* property. If I thought that was how Miss Waterby viewed them, I'd petition the courts to have them removed from *her* custody. I'm suggesting we compensate the Sewells in exchange for them relinquishing their rights to Rudolf and Theodore. Miss Waterby wouldn't be buying their rights to the pair but encouraging them to sign a document, giving up any future claim to them. A legal transaction to protect two innocents. The money is only to make them more agreeable to the idea."

Henny both liked the way this lawyer thought and didn't like it. Lawyers could be sneaky. When they were sneaky in favor of good people, she liked it. But when they weren't...

Mr. Thatcher went on. "This is not the only option. We can certainly take the Sewells to court and fight them for custody. I think you would have a very good chance of winning, but it would take time and money. Likely more money than negotiating with them out of court. I assume you don't want to put the boys through that."

Nicole shook her head. "You're right. I don't."

"I can step out and let the two of you discuss this."

"No need. Offer them money."

Mr. Thatcher looked at Henny.

"I'll support Nicole in whatever she wants to do. *And* I think it will probably be best. Let the boys put their minds to rest sooner than later."

"I think you've made a wise decision. I'll try to set up a meeting with the Sewells for the day after tomorrow, Thursday." The lawyer stood and held out his hand.

Nicole stood and shook it.

Henny shook his hand as well.

Out in the reception area, Bucky sat on the receptionist's desk with chocolate on his face.

The lady smiled guiltily. "I hope you don't mind. He's such a darling. Quite a charmer, this one." She held up the box of candies. "You want one?"

Nicole took one, but Henny waved the box away. She already had more of a middle than she liked. Lying around with her broken leg this past summer had made her corsets and clothes a bit snug.

In the buggy once more, Henny drove to the sheriff's office and stopped. "I want to talk to Edric. It will only take a minute or two. Do you mind? We have time before we are expected at the Kesners."

"Not at all. Do you want us to wait here?"

Bucky bounced on the padded seat. "I want to see a jail cell. Can I?"

Henny laughed at the boy's enthusiasm. He tugged at her heart. "I don't mind if the two of you come in." After climbing down, she glanced both ways on the street to see if the stranger happened to be around. Not this time.

Inside, the sheriff stood from behind his desk. "Aunt Henny, I was going to come see you."

"Edric, this is Nicole Waterby. She and her cousins are staying with me through the winter." Hopefully longer. "Well, Nicole and Bucky are staying with me presently. Rolf is out at Mr. Keegan's ranch. They were neighbors to Sarah Combs."

"Nice to meet you. Have a seat." He motioned toward the two chairs. "I didn't know Sarah had any neighbors."

Henny sat. "I didn't either until a few weeks ago. It's all a tragic story."

Bucky stared at the cells. "Can I go inside where the bad guys are held?"

Edric smiled. "Sure."

Bucky entered the far cell and pressed his face against the bars, peering through them and making faces.

Edric focused on Henny. "Montana showed me the description you gave him." He narrowed his gaze. "And *my father* gave me an earful. Anything else you remember?"

Henny shook her head. "The only thing that stood out was he seemed to be watching me. And I have no idea who he is." She lowered her voice to keep her words from Bucky's young ears. "I don't know if his interest lies with me or Nicole and the boys."

Edric addressed Nicole. "Have you seen him too?"

"Once, but only as he was disappearing around a

corner. I couldn't give you a description or recognize him."

"I went to the hotel and asked. There were seven men registered matching your description. It could have probably fit a lot more men."

Henny sighed. "I know. Half the men in town could answer to that description. Even you."

"I spoke to six of the seven. I don't think any of them were following you. There were a couple of other men who checked out recently. Also, there is the possibility the man you've seen is staying at one of the other boarding houses in town or has a room above one of the many saloons."

"This is an impossible task. Next time I see him, I'll catch him."

Edric gave her a hard stare. "No. You won't. I'll keep asking around and speak to any strangers I see no matter how nicely they are dressed. Let me do my job. If anything happened to you, my father would tan my hide."

Henny laughed. "I won't do anything ill-considered."

"Why doesn't that set my mind at ease?"

Bucky tromped up to Edric. "Do you have shackles?"

Edric smiled. "I do."

"Can I try them on?"

Edric pulled them out of his bottom desk drawer and fit them around the boy's wrists. Then he put on a serious face. "Why aren't you in school, young man?"

"I don't have to go to school because mean people are looking for me. And Rolfy."

Edric jerked his gaze back to Henny. "Mean people? Who?"

"That's another matter altogether. The boys' family before they came to live with Nicole and her grandfather. Their lawyer is working on it."

"I had candy at the lawyer place." Bucky still had a trace of chocolate on his chin.

Edric smiled at the boy then focused on Henny. "Do you think the man you've seen has anything to do with their kin?"

"I don't know." She wasn't sure if she should hope

for that or not. Maybe they would find out on Thursday.

"Aunt Henny," Edric shook his head, "how is it you manage to find the most trouble?"

It did seem that way lately. "I can't help it if the Lord has brought people in need to me. It's all going to work out. Don't worry about a thing."

"It's my job to worry."

"I'm done with these." Bucky slipped his small hands out and let the shackles clatter to the desk.

Nicole laughed first, then Henny joined in, and finally Edric.

Sixteen

ON WEDNESDAY MORNING, NICOLE STOOD IN the kitchen with Bucky and Aunt Henny. She couldn't wait to see Shane and go shop for a saddle.

Clad in an apron over his clothes, Bucky held up the oatmeal-stirring spoon. "I don't like cooking."

Aunt Henny waggled her index finger at him. "'Thou shalt not tell a lie.'"

"Huh?"

Nicole struggled not to laugh.

Aunt Henny put her hands on her hips. "You liked cooking when it was only the two of us. I've seen you smiling. Why do you now say you don't like it?"

Bucky shrugged. "I don't know. I just don't."

Time for Nicole to intervene. "Because Rolf says he shouldn't like cooking because he's a boy. Cooking is woman's work." She tousled Bucky's hair. "Isn't that right?"

"I don't want to turn into a girl like Nick did."

Nicole couldn't hold it in any longer and laughed. "I'm sorry. Liking to cook isn't going to turn you into a girl. I was already a girl."

"But Grandpa always called us all the boys."

"He was trying to protect me. I don't need that kind of protection anymore. You are a boy and will always stay a boy. Cooking or not."

Aunt Henny sat in one of the chairs and motioned Bucky over. "There are many world-renowned chefs who are men. Most of the fanciest restaurants have men as their head chefs."

Bucky's eyes widened. "Really? You're not playing a fiddling tune because you think I want to hear it, are you?"

One of Grandpa's favorite sayings. Nicole missed

him.

Aunt Henny shook her head. "I'm not playing a fiddling tune. I don't even know how to play the fiddle. A long time ago, I learned to play the piano."

"Gosh. How do you know which keys to play? There are more of them than feathers on a chicken."

Aunt Henny laughed. "It takes practice. The same as cooking. If you like to cook, you shouldn't let anyone tell you not to do it."

A knock sounded on the door.

Nicole jerked her gaze in that direction. Shane. Her lips pulled up, and she scooped the long hair from her hairpiece over her shoulder.

"Don't keep him waiting, child."

Bucky darted out of the room toward the front of the house and the door. "Mr. Keegan's here!"

Aunt Henny shook her head. "Nicole, I meant for you to go to the door."

"That's all right. It gives me a chance to ask you something. Would it be all right for Bucky to stay with you?"

"Of course. May I ask why?"

"I don't want that man to see him again. Mr. Thatcher said his family might cause trouble." And it would give Nicole some time alone with Shane.

"I doubt you would run into him again, but I would love to have Bucky with me. I miss having Lily's son in my home and enjoy having Bucky and you staying with me. He is so adorable and full of life."

The older woman was cut off from saying more by Bucky's peals of laughter.

Shane entered the kitchen with Bucky flung over his shoulder. "Has anyone seen Bucky? I was looking for him, but I can't find him."

"I'm right here." Bucky kicked his legs.

Shane froze. "Did you hear something? Was that him?"

"Yes, it's me. I'm on your shoulder." Her cousin squealed.

It warmed Nicole's heart to see the two playfully interacting. She pointed at her cousin's squirming body.

Shane lifted Bucky to the ground and feigned surprise. "There you are."

"Yup." Bucky turned to Nicole. "See, I told you he was here."

Nicole tore her gaze from the handsome rancher. "You certainly did. You are going to stay here and make something delicious with Aunt Henny while Shane and I take our horses to get saddles."

Bucky's eyes widened. "I'm going too."

"I think it's best if you stay here."

Bucky shook his head hard. "I have to go. I have to protect you."

Shane ruffled Bucky's hair. "Don't worry about that. I'll protect her."

Nicole planted her hands on her hips. "I think I can protect myself."

Bucky sized up Shane and then Nicole, then stomped his foot. "If Peppermint is going, I'm going. She cain't go nowhere without me."

Nicole regarded Aunt Henny. "What do you think?"

"I think the two of you will be fine with Mr. Keegan."

Nicole supposed Bucky would be safe, and they wouldn't likely see that man again. "All right. Get your shoes and coat."

"Be right back." Her cousin dashed off.

Shane cleared his throat. "I have to ask. Can you really afford three horses and now saddles and tack for them?"

"I can." Nicole glanced at Aunt Henny for confirmation.

Shane shrugged. "Then I'll help you find the best deal I can and see to it they are fitted properly. I'll go out to the barn and get Peppermint and Queenie."

"I'll come with you."

"Me too." Bucky stood in the doorway with his shoes in one hand and coat in the other.

Nicole heaved a sigh. "You have to put those on before you can go outside." She turned to Shane. "We'll be out in a few minutes."

"I'll get the horses and meet you out front." He left through the kitchen door.

Nicole wiggled Bucky's new Brogans onto his feet. Her cousin squirmed the whole time, antsy to get going. He shoved one arm into a coat sleeve and rushed for the door. Nicole gripped his collar. "You aren't going outside until your coat is all the way on and buttoned. It's cold out there."

"I won't be cold."

"Frost is covering everything. Put it on right or stay here." She plopped his hat onto his head.

He heaved a sigh, wrestled his other arm in, and buttoned it—crooked—then shot out the door.

"Put on your mittens!" Nicole threw her hands into the air then shut the door. "He won't think wearing his winter clothing an inconvenience if he catches a cold."

Aunt Henny shook her head. "Children his age think they are impervious to illness. They can't quite connect cold weather with coming down with an illness."

"I forgot something upstairs. Let me know if you want me to get anything for you while I'm in town. I'll be right back."

In her room, Nicole donned the short jacket which matched her blue riding skirt. Then she retrieved her rifle and scabbard from the wardrobe. After loading it, she slung the strap over her shoulder and head, letting the weapon rest comfortably on her back. At the front door, she called to Aunt Henny, "Did you think of anything you need me to get while I'm out?" She swung on her hip-length cape but had a challenge getting it to sit over the stock of the rifle.

"What are you doing?"

Nicole spun around to face Aunt Henny. "I can't get this cape to fit right."

Aunt Henny removed Nicole's cape and lifted the occupied scabbard off and set it aside. Then she settled the cape around Nicole's shoulders. "It fits beautifully."

"What about my rifle?" Nicole pointed to the weapon leaning against the staircase.

"That stays here."

"Why? Shane is carrying a revolver. Wouldn't it be better if I had a gun, also? Bucky would be safer."

"Ladies don't wander around town toting a gun, and certainly not one that large. Shane will look out for you and Bucky. You'll both be safe."

Nicole didn't like the two-sided standard.

"There is a handsome young rancher waiting for you."

"Very well." Nicole pinned on a narrow-brimmed hat and tugged on her soft-leather gloves. Then she caught Aunt Henny smiling at her. "What? Did I do something wrong?"

"Nothing at all. You put on those things as though you've been dressing this way your whole life. You learn quickly."

Nicole's mouth tugged up on the corners. "Thank you." She felt more comfortable in her lady clothes all the time. "I don't know how long we will be. I thought I'd treat Shane to dinner for helping us."

"I think that's a fine idea. I won't expect you to return until this afternoon. Enjoy yourselves."

Nicole headed out the front door.

Shane and Bucky stood on the street side of the fence with only three horses, two without saddles.

Nicole strode down the front walk and out through the gate. "Where's Bear?"

Though she'd spoken to Shane because he was supposed to bring Bear from his ranch with him, Bucky jumped in. "Shane found a saddle and bridle at his ranch, and it fits Bear *per*fectly."

Shane gave a nod. "It was in the tack that came with the ranch."

"Thank you. How much do I owe you?"

"Nothing." He held up a hand. "It's part of Rolf's pay."

"That's very kind of you."

He gave his crooked smile that made her insides prance. "Oh, I'll make him earn it."

She wanted to gaze into his blue eyes. Did he ever think about kissing her? She leaned toward him as though being pulled by an unseen force.

Bucky stepped between them and tilted his head to gaze up at them. "How are we supposed to ride without saddles?"

Shane chuckled and glanced away. "We walk them by their lead ropes."

Bucky scrunched up his face. "Nope. I want to ride. Peppermint wants me to ride."

Shane grabbed Bucky under the arms and swung him onto his horse's bare back.

Her cousin hugged Peppermint's neck. "I love you."

The handsome rancher shifted his attention to Nicole, and her insides shuddered with excitement. "Do you want to ride as well?"

"Do you think it would be wise to ride Queenie without a saddle?"

"I meant Huckleberry."

A smile pulled at her mouth. "With you?"

He returned a smile. "As enticing as that prospect is, it wouldn't be good for your reputation."

Nicole squished her eyebrows together. "I don't understand why?"

"I don't really understand either, but there are people who believe it's not appropriate for a lady to ride on a horse with a man who is not her relation."

Every time she thought she knew everything about being a lady, something new popped up. "If you're walking, so will I."

He jutted out his elbow.

"Is there something wrong with your arm?"

He chuckled again. "You are refreshing. I'm trying to be a gentleman and offer my arm to escort you."

That's right. The quilting ladies told her about such things. "Thank you, kind sir." She hooked her hand around his strong forearm, and a giddiness twirled around inside her.

After a successful morning finding tack for both horses and a delightful dinner with Nicole and Bucky, Shane left the pair at the bank to take care of some business while he retrieved the horses. He hoped Nicole wasn't financially overextending herself. She had little to no experience handling money. Aunt Henny had assured him she had enough. Just because she owned a mountain, didn't mean she had funds without selling it off.

Shane had gathered the trio of horses from the livery where their shoes and hooves had all been checked. Now, he walked toward the bank, leading the horses by their reins. Instead of plodding behind him like Huckleberry and Queenie, Peppermint strolled right up next to him with his nose in Shane's face, whiskers tickling his cheek.

"Mr. Keegan?" A voice reached him from the far side of the horse. "Mr. Shane Keegan?"

Shane halted Peppermint to get a better view of a dandy on an all-white stallion. No good conversation could start with a stranger knowing who Shane was. "Do I know you?" He didn't like the superior position the man had on him, being atop his horse.

Mercifully, the dandy swung down and stood at Shane's same height of six feet and one. "I'm Lamar Kesner." He extended his hand. "I'm pleased to meet you."

So, this was the famed Lamar Kesner, heir to the Kesner dynasty. Shane didn't want to return pleasantries with a man who had danced with Nicole and was probably vying for her affections. Shane shook the man's hand. "I'm glad to meet you as well." He sized up his competition.

"Miss Nicole Waterby has mentioned you."

"As she has you, Mr. Kesner."

"Please call me Lamar."

Shane gritted his teeth. "We don't exactly associate with the same sort of people. I think it's best if I stick with Mr. Kesner."

"As you wish, Mr. Keegan. Nicole speaks highly of you."

Shane liked the sound of that.

"I've been teaching her to dance for my grandmama's Christmas soirée."

Shane *didn't* like the sound of that. Didn't like to picture Nicole in this man's arms—any man's arms, but his own. But what could he do? "How kind of you." Or more likely, he was taking advantage of the opportunity.

Mr. Kesner stroked Queenie's neck. "She's a beauty. You want to sell her?"

"Nope. Not for sale."

Queenie sidestepped and whinnied. Shane gripped the reins tighter in case the mare decided to bolt.

"She's spirited." Mr. Kesner chuckled. "Like a young lady we both know."

"Yes, she is. And so is her horse."

The dandy faced and studied him. "Nicole seems taken with you—which I can't claim to understand. We'll see whom she favors Christmas Eve."

"I won't be going to your grandmother's little party."

"You must. I'll see what I can do about that but make no promises." Mr. Kesner stepped into the stirrup and swung up onto his stallion.

"Don't do me any favors." Shane would never fit in at such an event. He didn't have the appropriate clothes and would never go to that kind of fancy shindig.

"I'm a sporting man. No fun winning if there's no competition." He gave a nod. "Until Christmas Eve." He goaded his horse into a trot.

Nope. Shane wasn't going. He didn't have a fancy suit to wear nor know how to dance. He continued walking along the street toward the bank, leading the horses.

When he got close, Nicole and Bucky stepped out of the door. A man pushed away from the building and stood in their path. Nicole tucked Bucky behind her skirt.

Shane tried to trot to hurry and get to her, but independent Queenie refused to do anything more than plod along.

The man spit chewing tobacco out of the side of his mouth and pointed a finger in her face. "I knows who you are, and I know'd who the little runt is. He don't belong to you." He jabbed a finger to his own chest. "He belongs to me."

Shane tossed all three horses' reins over the hitching rail and bounded onto the boardwalk, putting himself in between the man and Nicole. "Move along, mister."

"These here United States is a free country, and I'll stand wherevers I like."

Shane felt a slight tug on his holster and reached for his hip a moment too late. His Colt was gone.

Nicole aimed his revolver at the man. "Leave us alone."

Did she really just take his gun?

She took his gun.

She *took* his gun!

Didn't she know it was unwise to touch a man's gun without permission? And she took it! But he couldn't exactly wrestle it away from her during this encounter.

At least her hand wasn't shaking. But shooting a man—even someone like this—was very different from shooting at targets or food for the table.

"I'd do as she says. She's a crack shot." Maybe not with a revolver, but at this distance, no one would miss.

The man jabbed his finger in the air. "You ain't heard the last of me, missy." He spit again and strode off.

When the man was a good distance away and no fear of him returning, Shane swung around and held out his hand. "May I have my gun?"

Nicole returned it to him. "This is why I wanted to bring my rifle."

Shane holstered his Colt. "You were going to bring your rifle?"

Nicole huffed out a breath. "Aunt Henny wouldn't let me. Said ladies don't carry guns."

"She's right." He pointed with his thumb over his shoulder. "Is he the same man you encountered before?"

"No. The other one was younger." She planted her hands at her narrow waist. "And Aunt Henny isn't right. If I can't tote around my rifle, then I'll get a gun with a short barrel like yours."

She wanted a Colt? There probably wasn't anything he could say to deter her. "Let's get something to fit in your little bag."

She lifted the velvet item dangling on matching cords. "It's a reticule."

Ridiculous was more like it, but it could hold a small

weapon. Shane peered around Nicole to Bucky. "You all right, kid?"

The boy nodded with large motions. "Can I get a gun too?"

Shane was about to tell him no, but Nicole beat him to it. "You don't need one."

Bucky pushed out his bottom lip and folded his arms.

They rode their horses to the mercantile and tethered them outside.

Shane held the door for the pair.

Franny Waldon's expression brightened, and she came around the counter and hugged Nicole. "Are you getting some things for Aunt Henny?"

Shane wouldn't mind holding Nicole.

"No. I offered, but she didn't need anything. I want to buy a gun." She turned and pointed at Shane. "Like his"—she held her little bag aloft—"but to go in here."

"Not a Colt. It wouldn't be the right weapon for her and wouldn't fit in her bag. Or any revolver. I think a pocket pistol."

Franny gave Shane a stern look and looped her arm around Nicole's. "I have no doubt you could handle any gun you want, but I agree. A smaller weapon will fit more easily in your pocket."

Nicole patted her hip. "I would like to be able to carry it in my pocket. Much better than a reticule."

Mr. Waldon, Franny's father, showed her several.

She settled on a double shot model and slipped it into her skirt pocket. She allowed Bucky a slingshot. He reluctantly agreed.

Though Shane would still keep her and the boys safe when he was around, he was relieved Nicole now had the means to protect herself if need be.

But watch out ne'er-do-wells, the lady has a gun.

Seventeen

ON THURSDAY MORNING, NICOLE SAT NEXT to Shane in the buggy on the way to the courthouse, grateful to have him there. Aunt Henny sat on his other side. The older woman had been a godsend. Nicole couldn't have managed without her.

Today, Nicole would meet with the Sewells, the day she would hopefully get permanent custody of Rolf and Bucky and adopt them. Bucky had been left with the sheriff's wife, and Rolf was blessedly out on Shane's ranch. Neither one needed to be with the people who had mistreated them. She was glad they were safely away from the day's event.

Shane hauled back on the reins, stopping in front of the brick courthouse that stood strong and imposing. Rolf and Bucky's future would be decided today. Nicole's too. If she lost her cousins, she would have a very different life than if she could keep them. She prayed once again the Lord would see fit to have her cousins remain with her. Shane helped her and Aunt Henny out of the buggy and secured it.

Nicole smoothed her hands down her green walking suit and patted her skirt pocket where her miniature pistol rested. "Do I look all right?"

While Shane merely gazed at her, Aunt Henny spoke. "You look lovely." She tapped Shane in his midsection with the back of her hand. "Doesn't she look lovely?"

Shane cleared his throat. "Yes, ma'am."

His crooked smile sent Nicole's insides to fluttering. She took a calming breath. "I want them to think I'm a capable person."

"You *are* a capable person." Aunt Henny touched her chest below her throat. "I have a peace in my soul all is going to turn out well."

"You do?"

Aunt Henny nodded. "Of course, and God has us all in His hands."

Her confidence calmed some of Nicole's nerves.

Shane poked out his elbows on both sides. "Are you ladies ready?"

Nicole remembered this time and tucked her gloved hand into the crook of his arm. Aunt Henny did the same on his other side. A small part of Nicole wished she had Shane all to herself.

A short, thin cowboy leaned against a tree with his hat pulled low, covering his face, and his arms crossed. Something oddly familiar about him gnawed at her. She glanced at one of the horses tethered to the hitching rail. Bear? She studied the man again. Rolf? She marched over and snatched his hat. "What are you doing here? You're supposed to be safely on Shane's ranch."

He swiped his hat back. "I had to come. I need to see 'em."

"I don't think it's a good idea for you to be in the same room with those people." They might take a gander at him and decide to keep him.

Rolf shook his head. "No. I don't want to be close. I only want a glimpse when they leave."

Shane joined the pair. "He could wait in the hall."

Nicole faced him. "I don't want him anywhere near them."

"I think he needs this." The rancher's expression turned compassionate.

Aunt Henny nodded. "I agree. It will give him a sense that this part of his life is really over."

"And what if it's not. What if they are allowed to take the boys?" Tears pricked Nicole's eyes.

Rolf pushed away from the tree. "I won't let those awful people hurt Bucky ever again. I'll take him and ride far away from here. Far, far away."

Shane spoke abruptly. "No, you won't. You'll always have one eye peering over your shoulder. You'll never have peace."

Nicole contemplated Rolf's plan. It could work. The three of them had horses and a bank account full of money. Head south to California and warmer weather. Then after the winter, decide where they wanted to go. Perhaps Europe. But what about Shane? Would he go with them? She shifted her attention to him.

He stared at her. "Don't you agree?"

Nicole realized Shane and Aunt Henny must have continued to try to persuade Rolf. "We'll discuss your plan after the meeting, if we need to."

Shane's expression turned perplexed. "What? You can't condone this."

Condone it she did and was puzzling out the details. "When Rolf didn't want to stay in town, you convinced me to let him go to your ranch so he wouldn't run away. If his relatives are unreasonable, he will be even more determined to run away. And *with* Bucky. It would be better if I went with them."

Rolf gave her a big grin and a nod.

Shane widened his beautiful blue eyes. Eyes that made Nicole want to capitulate, but she couldn't. Rolf and Bucky depended on her. Shane jammed a finger in the air. "Aunt Henny, talk some sense into these two."

The older woman gave a slight grimace. "In my experience, running away isn't always a bad choice. Sometimes it's necessary."

Shane threw his hands in the air. "Since when am I the voice of reason?"

Aunt Henny patted his arm. "You've always been a reasonable man. Let's see how things go and make a decision then."

Nicole's skin prickled all over as she entered the courthouse. She prayed the Sewells wouldn't be too difficult and would relinquish the boys without a fuss. She didn't want to have to run away. Her nerves eased with having Shane at her side. Rolf shuffled along behind them. She hadn't wanted him here, but since he was, she would keep him safe. He didn't need to face these contemptible people. And she certainly didn't want them to say anything disparaging to him.

Mr. Thatcher waited inside and approached. "Good morning."

Nicole hoped it was. She introduced Shane and Rolf.

"But Rolf's going to wait in the hall."

The attorney gave a nod. "I think that's best. The Sewells are already here and waiting." He motioned the group to walk with him, so Nicole fell into step beside him while the others followed. "Miss Waterby, while we are in the room negotiating, don't say anything to these people. Speak only to me. The most important thing for you to remember is I work for you, so everything I say and do is to benefit you and the boys. Sometimes, I might say something that sounds as though I'm on their side, but it's merely to lower their defenses. I can't have you contradict anything I say, because that might give them the upper hand. Do you understand?"

Grandpa had taught Nicole to keep quiet when new people visited their cabin. "I do. I'll give every last cent of Grandpa's money to keep Rolf and Bucky safe."

"Like I said before, don't let anyone know that." Mr. Thatcher turned to Shane. "And you?"

"I'm here to make sure no one hurts Nicole or Aunt Henny, and now Rolf too." Shane rested his palm on the handle of his revolver.

"If you can't control yourself, you will be sent out of the room. Am I clear?"

"Yes, sir. If they don't cause any trouble, then neither will I."

At a closed door, the attorney pointed to a place farther along the hall. "Rolf, if you wait over there, they likely won't glance in this direction when they leave."

Rolf nodded and went to the place indicated.

Mr. Thatcher opened the door to the meeting room where six men sat at a long table. Four on the far side, one at the head of the table, and the last a little behind him near his left elbow.

The man at the head of the table stood and stretched out his arm. "I'm Leopold Peabody, the court's arbitrator."

Mr. Thatcher shook his hand.

The man continued. "I'll be overseeing these proceedings. I won't interfere, merely ensuring everything goes smoothly." He motioned toward the man to his left who furiously wrote on his pad of paper. "This is Stanley

Cross, the court secretary who will write everything that is said here, which is the reason he has remained seated. He's not being impolite, merely doing his job."

Mr. Peabody indicated the four men seated on the other side of the table. "These are the Sewells. The senior Mr. Sewell and his three sons."

Nicole fingered the petite weapon in her pocket, glad Shane had suggested one so small.

The senior Mr. Sewell appeared to be about the oldest person Nicole had ever seen. He'd also been the one she'd pulled Shane's gun on yesterday. The eldest of the three sons sneered at Nicole, the first of the Sewell men she had encountered. The youngest of the four, who wore a dispassionate expression, had started to stand, but the middle brother put a hand on his shoulder.

So, only one of the Sewells had enough manners to stand in the presence of a lady. Nicole brightened. Had she just thought like a lady without being prompted? There was hope for her yet.

Mr. Thatcher motioned toward Nicole. "This is my client Miss Waterby, her friend Miss Henny, and their bodyguard Mr. Keegan."

Mr. Peabody motioned to the vacant chairs at the table. "Please take a seat."

Mr. Thatcher held out a chair for Nicole, then sat himself. Shane held one for Aunt Henny.

Shane waved away the offer of a chair. "I'll stand over here out of the way."

Nicole gave him a questioning glance. Shane gave a slow nod, and she realized he probably chose that spot to have a better vantage point.

Mr. Peabody clasped his hands on the table. "Shall we proceed?"

Mr. Thatcher nodded. "Miss Waterby wishes custody of Rudolf and Theodore Miller."

The oldest Sewell, Rolf and Bucky's grandfather, grunted. "Those boys are kin, and we want 'em."

The youngest son shook his head slightly. Was that because he didn't think the grandfather really wanted them? The young man didn't seem quite happy with the situation.

"They are family to Miss Waterby as well. Theodore, the younger one, has only known the Waterbys as family."

"He's still kin. Old enough to work. Every pair of hands is important on a farm. We've lost five years of help."

Nicole opened her mouth to tell Mr. Sewell he was a mean old man but closed it again. When the boys had arrived, Rolf, at age seven, could barely start taking responsibility with small chores. Mostly he took care of Bucky and kept him away from harm. And Bucky could do no chores at age two. Mr. Sewell didn't love the boys at all, didn't want family, only free workers.

The attorney continued. "Miss Waterby understands your loss."

No, Miss Waterby does not.

"Anticipating this, I've taken the liberty to draw up some figures." Mr. Thatcher removed a sheet of paper from a folder in front of him. "At age seven, the older boy wouldn't have been able to do much work that could translate into a monetary amount."

The eldest Mr. Sewell leaned forward. "He's got Sewell blood in him. He can work young and work hard."

Mr. Thatcher removed his spectacles. "You aren't suggesting you were overworking a seven-year-old, are you? Such practices are frowned upon."

"Oh, no-no-no." Mr. Sewell shifted back in his chair. "We would never do that."

Nicole didn't believe him.

"I'm glad to hear." Mr. Thatcher replaced his spectacles. "That means you have lost only five years' worth of work from him. The first year his contribution would have been minimal and increasing the amount he could work each year—before and after school and during the summer—times the amount he could earn. Now the younger one, who is currently seven, would only now be at an age where he could make any real difference. So, there is no earning potential lost. We have been very generous with these figures." He handed the page across the table to the Mr. Sewell senior. "Do those figures seem fair?"

Mr. Sewell grinned. "Real fair."

How much was Mr. Thatcher offering them? He hadn't shown her the figures. She hadn't even known he was going to make such calculations. But he worked for her, and she needed to trust him.

"I'm glad you agree." Mr. Thatcher removed a second paper from the folder. "To feed and clothe two growing boys, who would eat more and more food each year, and to keep a roof over their heads. As well as the added burden of caring for a two-year-old. That is a full-time task." He studied the paper and shook his head. "My, it's expensive to raise children. Oh, dear. It appears as though it cost more to care for the boys than they could have earned. Here are the figures."

Nicole wanted to squeal for joy. She had a higher respect for the attorney. She would have kept offering the Sewells money until they agreed to let her keep the boys.

Mr. Sewell snatched the offered page. "That cain't be right."

"I'm afraid it is. We were quite conservative with those numbers. It appears you owe Miss Waterby a tidy sum for caring for your grandsons for five years."

Mr. Sewell sputtered. "I won't pay her or anyone else one cent for my own kin."

Mr. Thatcher folded his hands on the table, inclining forward. "Miss Waterby is willing to compensate you with a modest amount."

"Keep talking."

"The ratio between each boy's earning potential and how much it will cost to feed, clothe, and keep a roof over their heads, you'll be fortunate if you break even." The attorney handed over another piece of paper.

Mr. Sewell grumbled at the figures.

"We can offer twenty dollars compensation for each boy."

That seemed too low to Nicole, but then she didn't have a good handle on the value of money.

The father jabbed a finger in her direction. "She's got more money than that."

"That doesn't mean she's willing to part with it. The boys have become a burden to her."

They hadn't, but she liked that the Sewells thought they might be.

Mr. Sewell narrowed his eyes. "Fifty."

Mr. Thatcher put his mouth near Nicole's ear. "Nod."

Instead, Nicole whispered in his ear. "Pretend I'm displeased with the offer."

He whispered again, "Shrewd and not to be trifled with."

Nicole responded with a gentle nod.

Mr. Thatcher again faced her opponents. "Very well. Fifty for the pair."

Mr. Sewell shot to his feet and slapped the table. "Fifty each! Not a penny less."

Shane rushed to Nicole's side.

Nicole's mouth tugged into a smile at Shane coming to her aid. She put up a hand to hopefully keep him from shooting anyone. No good would come from this getting out of control.

Mr. Peabody pinned Mr. Sewell with a glare. "Resume your seat, sir."

The man did.

Shane retreated a step.

Mr. Thatcher cleared his throat. "Miss Waterby will agree to fifty apiece provided each of the Sewells give up all rights to Rudolf and Theodore Miller immediately and into the future."

Nicole huffed out a breath of feigned displeasure. She could play along to help bolster her attorney's words.

The Sewells glowered.

"Unless of course you are willing to reimburse Miss Waterby for her expenditures over the past five years?"

Mr. Sewell curled his lips into a snarl. "One hundred dollars for each boy. Not a penny less."

"A moment ago, you were going to accept fifty."

"I changed my mind."

Nicole suspected he would keep changing his mind. She pushed away from the table and stood. "I've had enough." She spun around and headed for the door. She hoped she was making a wise move.

Shane opened it.

"Where's she going?" Mr. Sewell asked.

Chair legs scraped the floor. "I'll talk to her." Mr. Thatcher met her in the hallway and left the door open.

"Miss Waterby?"

Nicole stopped and faced the attorney.

He leaned close and whispered. "You think this will get them to stop dithering around?"

Nicole whispered also. "I'm hoping so, or this could go on all day." She lowered her voice even more. "I thought I wouldn't mind giving them all the money, but they don't deserve even a penny. But I won't risk Rolf and Bucky."

"Wait right here and appear inconvenienced. I think they'll sign if they think you're about to leave." He spun around.

Shane put his mouth next to Nicole's ear. "They seem nervous."

A shiver went through her at his nearness. "They should be. I'm about to pull out my pocket pistol."

"You brought it with you?"

"Of course. I take it everywhere." She resisted the urge to glance at Rolf but could see him out of the corner of her eye.

Mr. Thatcher returned to the table. "I've convinced Miss Waterby to agree to the one hundred apiece." He leaned forward and lowered his voice. "But I don't know if I can get any more out of her. She's about to leave."

"Th-that's fine. We'll sign."

Nicole peered over Mr. Thatcher's shoulder as he wrote in the dollar amount of compensation on a prewritten document and slid it across the table. "You all must sign this, then we'll get you the money."

The Sewells all greedily signed.

Mr. Thatcher turned in his chair. "Miss Waterby, this requires your signature as well."

She returned to the table but didn't sit. She signed the document and the bank promissory note.

Mr. Thatcher handed over the slip of paper. "Take this to the Kamola Valley Bank, and they will give you the cash."

The oldest son stretched out his hand, and the elder Mr. Sewell slapped it. "Git your paws off that. I'm takin' the money." He studied the paper.

Mr. Thatcher put his folder into his satchel, stood, and offered Aunt Henny a hand.

Aunt Henny joined Nicole and Shane in the hall.

The attorney shook the arbitrator's hand. "I'm pleased there was little for you to do." He exited into the hall as well.

Mr. Sewell folded the note, scuttled around the table, and left the room. His oldest son swaggered out behind him.

Nicole and those with her, stepped in line to form a wall in front of Rolf so his relatives wouldn't see him.

The old man sneered. "Best not tighten those purse strings just yet, missy." He strode away followed by his two older sons.

What had he meant by that? Was he going to try for more money at another time?

The youngest Sewell lagged behind and stopped next to Nicole. "They are better off with you." He glanced over his shoulder at his family traipsing down the hall, then strolled after them.

Nicole sensed the young man hadn't faired any better than her cousins at the hands of his family.

"They have no legal rights any longer." Mr. Thatcher patted his satchel. "I'll file these and get the necessary papers drafted for you to adopt Rudolf and Theodore Miller. Once approved, the boys will be permanent members of your family."

"For good?"

"Yes. I'll let you know when I hear anything." Mr. Thatcher strode away.

"I can't believe we did it." Nicole turned and hugged the closest person. Shane. He returned her hug. She wanted to stay in his strong arms, but the quilting ladies wouldn't approve, so she released him. Then she hugged Aunt Henny. Once the Sewells disappeared down the hall, she turned to Rolf and hugged him. "We did it!" She couldn't believe how giddy she felt.

Shane gifted her with his one-sided smile. "*You* did it. You were great in there."

"You think so? I was so nervous. And angry."

"Couldn't tell. You seemed unflappable."

She wanted to stay right there in his gaze.

Rolf shuffled his feet. "Can we go tell Bucky?"

"Of course." She hooked her arm around Shane's and pressed into his side, more than the quilting ladies said was appropriate. She didn't care.

Eighteen

HENNY WALKED INTO HER PARLOR WITH a tray of hot chocolate for Bucky and Nicole. She wished Rolf were here as well to enjoy Christmas traditions. She set the tray on the serving table in front of the settee.

Nicole and Bucky sat stringing popcorn and cranberries to decorate the evergreen boughs on the fireplace mantel. Though they had described decorating their cabin with fir and pine branches, pinecones, and holly sprigs, they hadn't experienced other decorating traditions and treats. Bucky's string was pitifully short. The boy had eaten more of the popcorn than stringing it, but that was one of the most enjoyable things for a child.

Henny planned to make sure they experienced a few of the things they'd missed out on so far. She put one mug of the steaming beverage on the table closest to Bucky. "This is too hot to drink, so keep working until it cools." *Or keep eating the popcorn.*

Bucky disregarded her advice and tossed his popcorn and cranberry string aside, knelt on the floor in front of his cup, and stared into it.

"I said it's hot. Be careful." Henny shook her head. Little boys thought nothing could hurt them. She took the third one and sat on the settee next to Miss Tibbins and stroked the calico's fur.

Nicole gingerly picked up her hot chocolate and inhaled deeply. "It smells delicious. What is it?"

Henny blew on her beverage. "Have you never had hot chocolate before?" She had assumed their grandfather would have at least given them this.

Nicole shook her head.

Bucky did the same. "But I'm going to love it."

"You are both in for a treat." She took a tentative sip and burned her tongue. She set her cup down. "It's still a little too hot to drink. Let's string some more popcorn while we wait."

Nicole set hers down and went back to work. "One year, Grandpa and I strung big and small pinecones on a cord and hung it along the hearth with Christmas stockings."

The little boy remained on the floor, staring into his cup, likely willing it to cool. Henny loved seeing him enjoy so many new experiences. It also made her heart ache at all she'd missed out on in her own life. Best not to dwell on things of the past she couldn't change.

Though she enjoyed this time introducing these two to new activities, she really needed to shut herself in her room to finish remaking her dress for the soirée. She knew if she'd said something, Nicole would have purchased a beautiful gown for her. A waste of money for one short evening. Henny had a few perfectly good dresses to choose from—though a couple of decades out of date. Since she wasn't as thin as she'd been in her younger days, she took two of them and was creating a contemporary style. She'd studied a few of Celeste Dumont's drawings in her fashion book and dresses in the shop. The gown needed to hold up for only one evening, so if she took a few shortcuts it wouldn't matter.

Someone knocked on the door.

Bucky shot to his feet. "Maybe that's Rolf!"

Henny tilted her head to peer out the window to see who had come to visit, or if she had a prospective new boarder four days before Christmas. Saul stood on her porch with a pine tree. Her stomach constricted. What was he up to? "It's not Rolf."

She hadn't had a Christmas tree since Winston. The image of him presenting her with their first Christmas tree jumped to her mind. No. She mustn't think of such things. No good could come of it.

Henny stood and headed toward the door as Bucky returned to his spot, watching his hot chocolate. She met Saul in the entryway as he pulled the tree behind him. Henny's heart and head warred with each other. She didn't want a tree, and the fact he got her one without asking, upset her. But on the other side, it had been so sweet and thoughtful of him. No sense in denying the children a Christmas tree because such things held sorrowful memories for her.

She put her hands on her hips in a playful gesture. "Saul Hammond, what have you gone and done?"

He smiled sheepishly. "I know you don't normally put up a tree, but I thought with the children being here, it might be nice."

Yes, Nicole and Bucky deserved to experience a decorated tree. "I don't have anything to put on it, but we are making popcorn strings. We can hang them on the tree instead of the mantel. We'll need to make a lot more. Maybe I can purchase some red ribbon at Waldon's."

"I brought a few things. They are in a crate outside." Saul carried the tree all the way into the house and set it up in the corner on a wooden stand he'd apparently created.

While Henny and Nicole helped get it positioned, Bucky dragged the crate from the porch into the entry.

Saul hoisted the crate and took it into the parlor, setting it on a chair. "These were the things Barbara and I had. Even though Edric had his own decorations, I could never get rid of them. Now, I know why." He removed a cloth angel dressed in white. "They were meant for you." He put it on top of the tree.

Though so sweet, was it a good idea for Henny to accept things that had been Saul's late wife's?

Saul retrieved a sprig of greenery. "I thought this would go nicely in a doorway."

Henny snatched the mistletoe and hustled into the dining room, glancing over her shoulder into the parlor where Nicole and Bucky were. "No. It won't go nicely. Have you been touched in the head?"

Saul's expression turned wounded.

She shook the twig at him. "I have a beautiful young lady under my roof and two professors who are bachelors. Not a good idea."

Realization of the situation dawned on his face. He tucked the greenery into his pocket. "I'm sorry. I wasn't thinking."

"No harm done. It will be better served at your home

where there is a newly wedded couple."

"As always, Henny, you are right."

She wasn't always right. There were plenty of times she was very wrong. Though she tried not to repeat the same mistakes too often. She and Saul returned to the parlor.

Bucky pulled a small quilted star ornament from the crate and hung it on a limb. "I never knowed a tree to be inside before."

While Nicole and Bucky continued to hang the ornaments, Saul took Henny aside. "I thought having a tree would make you happy, but you seem sad. Sorrowful memories?"

She nodded. Haunting memories of bygone Christmases threatened to surface. She shoved them to the dark recesses of her mind where they had come from before they could ruin the day. "Dwelling on the past never did anyone any good."

"I'm sorry. I should have asked first."

"No. I want Nicole and the boys to experience everything the holiday has to offer. Thank you. This was very kind and thoughtful of you."

"I hate to have upset you."

"Nonsense. Having the children here would have stirred up old memories eventually. Time to create new ones."

"That's one of the many things I admire about you, Henny. You make the best of whatever life throws at you. You think of others and choose to do good."

A survival skill, she supposed.

Saul lowered his voice. "Shane Keegan is outside and wants to talk to you, but he doesn't want the young lady to know. Is everything all right between them?"

"As far as I know it's fine. What does he want?"

"He wouldn't tell me. He's waiting in your barn."

Henny poked her head into the parlor. "I need to go out and check on something. I'm sure your hot chocolate is cool enough to drink. I'll be right back." Henny put on her coat and followed Saul out.

Shane waited in the tack room inside the barn. When he heard someone enter, he peeked his head out. Saul Hammond and Aunt Henny. "Is it just the two of you?"

"Yes." Aunt Henny squinted at him as he stepped into view. "What's going on?"

He retrieved the envelope from his inside duster pocket and gave it to her. "Do you know anything about this?"

Aunt Henny removed the gilded card with raised lettering and opened it. She lifted her wide-eyed gaze to him. "You've been invited to the Kesner soirée?"

Mr. Hammond let out a whistle.

"Did you have something to do with this?" Shane knew most people would be thrilled, but he wasn't.

"No, but this is an honor."

Not to him. "I don't want this *honor*." He walked a few paces away from them.

"I understood Florence Kesner didn't intend to invite you, but since she has, you should go."

Aunt Henny knew he wasn't wanted at this event?

He turned around and headed back. "Why would you know she wasn't inviting me? And how did I end up on the guest list?" He wasn't sure which was worse. Not being invited. Or being invited. Both were bad.

"I thought she wasn't because she said so when Nicole and I were at her home for tea. How you ended up on the list, I don't know. Since you are, Nicole will be thrilled you'll be there. I can't wait to tell her."

"No! You can't." He paced away again. He wanted to flee the barn—no, the state. If he left now, maybe he could get over the pass before more snow fell in the mountains. "I'm not going. I can't."

"Of course, you can. I promise you'll have a good time."

Shane wouldn't. "This must be Lamar Kesner's doing." He'd said he'd see Shane Christmas Eve. This must be what he'd meant. Shane never imagined the dandy to make good on his threat. "That scoundrel."

"I've never heard anyone refer to the young Mr. Kesner in such a way. He is a fine gentleman."

The man was cunning. Shane strode back to the older woman. "He did this to humiliate me. He wants to make a fool out of me in front of Nicole so he can go after her." Ingenious plan. Something Shane might have thought of if the roles were reversed.

"And how is inviting you to a party going to do all that?"

Shane rubbed the back of his neck. "I don't know how to dance."

Aunt Henny smiled. "Is that the only thing stopping you? Come inside, and I'll teach you."

"I don't want Nicole to know. I don't want her to expect me at that party and then not show up."

Aunt Henny narrowed her eyes. "I can send Nicole and Bucky on an errand, and it will be our little secret."

Shane walked a few steps. Maybe that could work. Then he retraced his path. "What if she returns while I'm...I'm *dancing*? No, I don't think I can risk that."

Aunt Henny huffed out a puff of white air. "Don't be absurd."

Mr. Hammond cleared his throat. "May I make a suggestion?"

Shane stopped his pacing. "Please do." Mr. Hammond was a man. He understood. He would get Shane out of this.

"I'll tell Nicole and Bucky I need Henny's help for a couple of hours, then we can go to my house and teach you to dance there."

Not what Shane had in mind. "You expect me to learn in a couple of hours? Christmas Eve is in three days. No. You're supposed to get me out of this."

Aunt Henny touched his arm. "Saul has a fine plan. You can learn. You are a highly motivated young man."

He scrunched his eyebrows together. "What makes you think that?"

She propped her hands on her hips. "You want to impress a certain young lady, and you don't want one of the other many, *many* gentlemen at the party to steal her away. So, you'll learn to dance, and you'll go to the party."

Not only Lamar Kesner, but a whole town of men vying for Nicole's attention. Did Shane even stand a chance? He heaved a sigh. "Tell me what to do."

Mr. Hammond slapped him on the shoulder. "Good man. Hitch up Henny's buggy, we'll make our excuses, and meet you back out here."

It didn't take long before Shane, atop Huckleberry, trailed behind the buggy.

A short time later, he stood in Sheriff Rix's living room. The elder Mr. Hammond, the sheriff's father, played a meandering tune on a harmonica. Mrs. Hammond, the sheriff's new wife, stood in front of Shane with her left hand on his shoulder and her right held aloft. Holding Lily Hammond in his arms could end very badly for Shane. "I don't think this is a good idea."

Mr. Hammond stopped. "You have to practice if you're going to learn."

Though the sheriff wasn't here, his three wide-eyed children were there to bear witness to their father of all Shane's transgressions. "But this is the sheriff's wife."

Mrs. Hammond offered him a gentle smile. "My husband isn't going to do anything to you. We have five incorruptible, trustworthy chaperones."

Aunt Henny waved her hand at Shane. "You asked for my help. Now, take Lily in your arms as we instructed you."

Shane drew in a deep breath and cautiously put one arm behind Mrs. Hammond but didn't actually touch her.

Mrs. Hammond reached around and pressed his palm to her back. "I won't know where you are guiding me if I can't feel the subtle shift in your hand."

Shane put the fingers of his free hand to his throat. "If your husband comes home and catches us, I'll hang for sure." He swallowed hard. Being on the wrong side of the law was never a good feeling.

Mrs. Hammond offered him a gentle smile. "That would never happen."

Aunt Henny shook her head. "Stop fretting. Edric probably won't come home, so you have nothing to worry about. Besides, he's a reasonable man."

Shane stepped away from Mrs. Hammond and gaped at Aunt Henny. "Probably won't? Stop fretting? Reasonable?" What man could possibly be reasonable with another man dancing with his wife? He would hang for sure.

Aunt Henny narrowed her eyes. "If you don't want to learn to waltz, then don't. Nicole will have plenty of men willing to have her in *their* arms and sweep her around the room to romantic tunes."

Shane growled under his breath. "You are going to drive me to my grave." He retook his place in front of Mrs. Hammond and rested one hand on her back and held out his other. She put hers in his. He wished it were Nicole in front of him. Yes, Nicole. Risking his neck to learn to waltz would be worth it to have Nicole standing right where Mrs. Hammond was.

Two hours later, Shane had managed to learn to waltz—more or less. But the schottische had a hopping thing he didn't care for, and the quadrille had people changing partners. He didn't want to be handing Nicole off to anyone. The waltz had a slow rhythm his body could move to.

The sheriff's three children danced in their own little circle, giggling. At least, they were enjoying themselves and were better at learning the dances.

More than Shane could say for himself. "Can we practice the waltz again?"

"Of course," Mrs. Hammond said, and her father-in-law changed tunes.

Aunt Henny perked up. "In all this excitement over teaching you these dances, I forgot to ask. Do you have proper attire for this soirée? A formal evening suit?"

Mr. Hammond stopped playing.

Shane supposed he couldn't pretend he didn't hear. "Unfortunately, I do. When the fancy man showed up at the ranch and delivered the invitation, he also left a big box with one of those dandy costumes."

Aunt Henny brightened. "How kind of whomever is responsible for the invitation to think of your attire. Does it fit well?"

Shane shrugged. "I don't know."

Aunt Henny took a controlled breath. "Haven't you tried it on?"

"I had no plan to go to this thing, so there was no point." He still wasn't sure he would.

"You need to bring it into town tomorrow and put it on so I can make sure it fits you properly."

"That's too much fuss. If it doesn't fit, I'll have a good excuse not to go."

Aunt Henny tilted her head. "And if it does fit?"

He hoped it didn't. "I'll think about going."

Sheriff Rix strode in through the kitchen. "What's going on here?"

Shane jerked away from Mrs. Hammond, bumped into a side table, steadied the tottering lamp on it, before stumbling over the arm of a large cowhide chair and landing in it sideways.

The sheriff laughed and appeared as though he was about to say something to Shane when his little girls squealed and launched at him.

Mrs. Hammond went over to her husband with two of the three children in his arms. "Oh my, is it time to prepare supper already?"

"I'm early. Don't worry about it." He glanced at the people around the room.

Aunt Henny motioned toward Shane. "Mr. Keegan has been invited to the Kesners' Christmas Soirée. Your father and I, with the help of your lovely wife, have been teaching him to dance."

Shane wished she hadn't singled him out. He must look like a grounded fish, the way he struggled out of the chair.

"I see. I hope you learned what you need to know. That party is in a few days."

"I have." Even if Shane hadn't, he wouldn't risk another lesson. "I should be going."

Sheriff Rix inclined his head toward Shane. "I'll walk you out. I need to talk to you."

Shane swallowed hard.

Aunt Henny stood from where she sat on the settee. "I should be going as well."

The elder Mr. Hammond set his harmonica aside. "Do you want me to take you?"

"That's not necessary. It's my buggy. I don't want you to have to walk home in the cold and approaching darkness. I can manage."

It would be well after dark before Shane arrived back at his ranch. He held the door for Aunt Henny, walked out with her, and assisted her into her vehicle. "Thank you for helping me."

"My pleasure." She patted his hand. "Don't you fret about Edric. He's not upset with you."

"I'm not so sure about that." What else could the man want to talk to him about but dancing with his wife?

"And you have to go to the soirée."

If it could be only him and Nicole, he wouldn't hesitate. "I'll think about it."

The sheriff's voice came from behind Shane. "You have a good evening, Aunt Henny."

Shane's insides tensed, and he sidestepped as he turned to cover his edginess.

The sheriff put his hand on the side of the buggy. "Have you seen that man again?"

Aunt Henny shook her head. "Not since I last saw you. And the sense I'm being watched has gone away. It was probably all merely a happenstance."

"I'm still going to keep a look out, and you stay vigilant."

"I will." Aunt Henny drove away.

Shane felt twice as vulnerable now that he was alone with Sheriff Rix. He should climb on Huckleberry and race off before the sheriff could stop him. Then he'd keep riding. But what about Nicole? Could he truly leave her behind? He straightened his shoulders, bracing for what was to come.

The sheriff faced him. "Thanks for waiting." His eyebrows pulled together. "You seem tense. Like you're going to your own hanging."

Yup. That was about right. "I was only trying to learn to dance for that silly party at the Kesners'. Nothing more."

"You had some good teachers." The sheriff clasped him on the shoulder. "Relax. I'm not out here to talk about that. But you should go to the 'silly party'."

Shane wanted to relax but couldn't. "Why?"

"Because Aunt Henny said you should, for starters. She's a smart woman. I'd heed her advice. Secondly, this party is a big deal and an honor you shouldn't slight. And most importantly, a certain young lady will be there. Don't disappoint your sweetheart." The sheriff winked.

Shane could only dream that Nicole was indeed his sweetheart. "If not my dancing lesson, then what did you want to talk to me about?"

"The cattle rustlers. Have you seen any of them? Or have any more of your herd gone missing?"

Shane breathed easier. A much better topic. "I haven't seen the rustlers, but my hands tell me a few more heifers are missing. Since I haven't seen anyone or noticed any unaccounted-for tracks, I'm wondering if the animals wandered off or got caught in a ravine." But his horse sense told him otherwise.

"Not likely. Four other ranchers are missing a few head each. I think these bandits are hoping we will all assume the cattle have wandered off and not go searching for them." The sheriff held out his hand. "Let me know if you see or hear anything, or if any more of your herd goes missing."

Shane shook the man's hand. "I will." But when he tried to let go, the sheriff held on.

"Go to the party. Don't let my wife's effort go to waste." He released Shane, spun around, and strolled back inside his house.

Shane stood frozen in place and after a moment drew in a much-needed breath. Well, that sounded like an order. Now, he had to either go to the party or leave the state.

Tonight.

And never see Nicole again.

Nineteen

NICOLE GAZED AT HERSELF IN THE vanity mirror in an upstairs room at the Kesners'. This whole Christmas event seemed unreal, like floating in a dream. She expected to wake to find herself back at the mountain cabin in buckskins.

Aunt Henny patted Nicole's arm. "I hope you don't mind Mrs. Kesner taking over. All this frivolity is fine, but don't let it go to your head. This is important to Mrs. Kesner. She really is trying to help. This will be a night for you to remember always."

"I appreciate all she's doing. And I appreciate even more everything you've done for me. I would be at a loss without you."

Mrs. Kesner had intercepted Nicole's gown from the dressmaker's shop, having it sent here. She'd said Nicole shouldn't dress before she arrived, or her gown would get wrinkled. Aunt Henny had worn her gown over, and it seemed fine.

Mrs. Kesner had decided her annual Christmas soirée would double as Nicole's "coming out." She said she was doing all this to fulfill her duty as a family friend to Nicole's grandfather. Though it had been explained to Nicole, she didn't really understand the purpose of a "coming out" or much care. She was merely excited to wear her beautiful purple gown with the lace and ruffles.

Nicole ran her hand across the edge of the vanity and touched the delicate glass bottles. She wanted to get one of these small tables, with a mirror and padded stool, used to do one's hair and get ready for whatever the occasion.

Mrs. Kesner's maid Hazel fussed over Nicole, pulling her real hair up then attaching her matching hairpiece. The maid was an older woman but not quite as old as

Aunt Henny. Hazel had curled the hairpiece so soft ringlets cascaded over Nicole's shoulders. Mrs. Kesner wanted Nicole to look perfect. No one could actually be perfect.

Except maybe Shane.

He had perfect eyes the color of blue meadow flowers. He had a perfect crooked smile. Some might see that as an imperfection, but on his face, it couldn't be more perfect. He had a perfect... Well, a perfect everything, laugh, gait, smell, disposition. And he didn't seem to mind she wasn't quite a lady.

Nicole sensed Mrs. Kesner trying to steer Lamar and her together. Lamar was kind, but she could tell the difference between the two men. With Lamar, it was like he saw her as a wounded bird needing help. Though compassionate and pleasant, he wasn't a good choice in the long run.

Shane, on the other hand, didn't seem false or like he was fulfilling some sort of duty. His actions were real. No subterfuge.

She sat in her undergarments and a dressing robe while the maid finished fussing with her hair. Mrs. Kesner had tried to talk Nicole into having her hair all pulled up in a fancy concoction of curls, but Nicole loved her long hairpiece and the way it brushed her shoulders, so she wanted it to hang long. In the end, Nicole got her way.

Mrs. Kesner swept into the room and over to Nicole. "Breathtaking, simply breathtaking."

Nicole swiveled on the stool to face the kindly woman. "I don't even have my dress on yet."

Her hostess waved her hand. "A dress never makes a lady beautiful. A lady makes the dress beautiful." She squinted at Nicole's head. "Are you sure I can't convince you to wear your hair up? It would be very stylish."

"I like it down and long."

Mrs. Kesner smiled. "Then that is how you shall wear it, because if you feel beautiful, you will be more poised. The guests have all arrived. Hazel will help you into your gown now. When she lets me know you are ready, I'll introduce you. You'll appear at the top of the stairs, pause for ten seconds, then make your way to the bottom slowly, like I taught you last week. There will be distinguished guests in the foyer. At the foot of the staircase, Lamar will meet you and escort you into the ballroom where you'll be introduced there as well. The orchestra will begin. You and Lamar will dance the first waltz, in the beginning alone, then others will join in. Lamar will give you your dance card."

Nicole repeated the instructions in her head to memorize them. Gown. Stairs. Pause. Go down. Lamar. Dance. She glanced up to ask the woman a question, but she was gone. Nicole faced Aunt Henny. "What's a dance card?"

Mrs. Kesner peered back in through the doorway. "Come, Henny. You need to be at my side when I introduce Miss Waterby."

Aunt Henny's mouth hung open, and she scooted out the door. "I'll see you downstairs and explain anything you need me to. Your grandfather would be so proud of you." She disappeared.

Nicole wasn't sure Grandpa would be proud of her. He'd always tried to hide who she was, and from everything Nicole had gathered, this "coming out" was all about being a girl. But the Lord had made her this way, and she would honor that. A peace swirled inside her. She believed Grandpa would understand.

Hazel flounced out Nicole's purple gown on the floor, all spread out with the hole in the middle. She motioned Nicole over. "Step inside, and I'll pull it up. This way your hair doesn't get spoiled."

Nicole did as instructed.

Hazel guided the dress over her hips and to her torso. "To answer your question, a dance card is where you write gentlemen's names so they can save various dances with you."

Nicole tucked her arms through the gauzy holes. There weren't really sleeves but filmy things that dipped off her shoulders. "Nobody knows me. Who would want to dance with me?"

The maid adjusted the sleeve things. "Miss, you will be the belle of the ball. This is your night, and every gentleman here—young and old—will want the privilege of a dance or even a partial. Those who are fortunate to be your partner, will have something to boast about."

"That seems ridiculous. I'm no different or better than anyone else. God made us all in His image."

Hazel moved around behind her and tightened the lacings. "Ridiculous or not, it is the way of things. For tonight, you are like royalty. Exhale all your breath, and don't take another until I tell you."

Nicole expelled the air from her lungs.

The maid tightened the lacings. "All done. You can breathe now."

Nicole drew in air but not as much as she would like. "I think it's too tight."

"It will loosen some as your body adjusts to it and the fabric stretches. If it's not a bit snug to begin with, it will become too loose later. There aren't proper sleeves to hold up all this fabric. The bodice has to do that."

That made sense—sort of. Though she loved this dress, she could see the benefit of her old buckskins. She actually missed them at times.

The maid turned her to face the mirror.

Nicole couldn't believe the vision in the looking glass. She put her hands on her abdomen, not yet convinced it wasn't too tight. If she could just draw one deep breath. But it did feel better than a moment ago and it did support her torso. Her buckskins never did that.

Hazel held the loop of a purple feather fan out for Nicole to slip her hand through. "Your fan has many purposes."

Nicole spread it out and waved it in front of her face. "To cool me off. But I doubt I'll get overheated on a winter's day."

"You will, milady. All that dancing will warm you. You can put it in front of your face to conceal your expression. When you are tired of smiling, you can hide behind it. There is a whole language of the fan, but that is too much for tonight. One more use, you can slap a gentleman's hand if he gets too fresh with you."

"Fresh?"

The maid looked at her squarely. "How do I put this?

If a gentleman behaves in a way you don't like, whop him with it."

Nicole wasn't quite sure what the maid was getting at, but she would keep it in mind.

"If you are unsure about anything, you can ask Mr. Kesner. Her ladyship told him to stay close at hand." Hazel moved to the door and grasped the knob. "One more thing. In various places around the ballroom and main floor are hanging balls of mistletoe. Make note of where they are right off, that way you can be sure to avoid them with certain men and steer others artfully under them."

"Why should I avoid mistletoe?"

"If a lady and gentleman find themselves under it, they must kiss. So, you might want to avoid it with certain men."

Nicole did understand. The only man she wanted to be under the mistletoe with was Shane.

"Are you ready, miss?"

Nicole drew in her deepest breath yet since donning the gown. Either her body was indeed adjusting to the dress, or she was getting used to the snug fit.

The maid opened the door a crack and gave a nod to someone outside. She turned back to Nicole. "It will only be a few minutes now."

Before long, Hazel opened the door wide. "They are ready for you, miss. Mr. Kesner will be waiting at the foot of the stairs. If you can't bear the others, focus on him alone."

Nicole nodded. She wished it was Shane who would be waiting for her, but he hadn't been invited. That some people were deemed good enough to invite and others weren't, perplexed her.

At the top of the stairs, she stopped and stared. People crowded the foyer with more peering up from doorways. They all gazed at her. Expecting something from her. She wasn't sure how she felt about all this attention. Even though she knew better, she sought out Shane's face.

"Miss?" A soft voice said from the side of her.

Nicole turned to the voice. Hazel stood out of sight

pressed against the wall, presumably so the multitude below couldn't see her.

The maid motioned upward at both sides of her mouth. "Smile, find Mr. Kesner, and make your way down to him. He will help you from there. You will do fine."

Nicole nodded, faced the hushed crowd, and forced a smile. Lamar stood where expected and gave her a nod. She took a deep breath and hurried down toward him.

Mrs. Kesner closed her eyes and tightened her face.

Nicole slowed. One step at a time.

Lamar offered her his arm, and she tucked her hand in the crook of his elbow.

He handed her an ivory embossed card with a red tassel on it. "I took the liberty to see to it your dance card was full so you wouldn't have to bother yourself with that."

How thoughtful of him.

Even more people lingered in the ballroom. How could they all possibly be interested in her? She was nothing more than a simple girl from the mountains.

Lamar guided her into the throng of people waiting there.

But no Shane.

Twenty

SHANE HAD FORGOTTEN TO BREATHE AS Nicole had floated down the stairs in her purple dress like an ethereal dream, vivid yet unreal. He'd hidden himself behind as many people as he could opposite the ballroom entrance. He'd wanted to rush to the foot of the staircase to meet her but held back.

Even though she'd put on a smile at the top of the stairs, he could tell she was nervous. He wanted to whisk her away and protect her from the gawking stares. But she had all the help she needed in Lamar Kesner, and he had seemed to soothe her nerves.

Then she drifted away on Lamar's arm as she retreated into the ballroom.

Shane should leave.

"Mr. Keegan." Aunt Henny strolled over to him.

He was caught. No leaving now.

"I'm so glad you decided to come."

"That makes one of us. I think I should skedaddle before anyone else notices me."

"No, you don't." She looped her arm around his. "You went to all that trouble to learn to waltz and put on this suit—which fits you quite well, by the way. You can't leave. Nicole will be so pleased you came."

"I think she'll do just fine with Mr. Kesner."

"Fine? Yes. But you would make her happy and this evening more special. Her dance card is going to fill up rather quickly, so ensure you get your name down to secure a dance or two with her."

He hadn't decided if he was going to stay or not but nodded anyway.

A male servant in a black suit approached. "Miss Henny?"

"Yes."

"Mrs. Kesner wishes your presence."

Aunt Henny tightened her grip on Shane. "Escort me in?"

Crafty old lady. "I'd love to." He wanted to part from her inside the arched entryway, but she wouldn't release him, so he took her all the way to Mrs. Kesner.

When they reached her, Aunt Henny patted his arm. "Mrs. Kesner, this is Mr. Shane Keegan."

The hostess studied him a moment. "You're the rancher."

He wasn't sure how to take that. She didn't sound condescending. "One of many."

She gave a gentle smile. "But the only one our lovely Miss Waterby speaks of. I'm pleased you came. Make sure you secure a dance with the belle of our soirée. Now, I must steal Henny from you. Come along, dear." She strolled away.

Aunt Henny appeared torn and shook a finger at Shane. "Don't you dare sneak out, or I'll send the sheriff after you." She followed in Mrs. Kesner's wake.

Shane maneuvered to the edge of the ballroom and tucked himself into a corner.

Nicole glided around the floor in Lamar Kesner's arms. The tune ended and another man took Kesner's place as Nicole's partner. Then another man and another.

"How did you slip in without me noticing?"

Shane jerked around to face Lamar Kesner. He could have gone all evening without seeing the man up close. "Not very observant?" He had nearly been seen by the popinjay several times but had managed to avoid detection. Until now.

"You're a sneaky one." He surveyed Shane from head to toe. "The suit fits well enough."

That had caught Shane off guard. He'd expected—or rather hoped—it would be ill-fitting or atrocious in some way. Then he would have had an excuse not to come, and he would have had a better idea of what kind of man Mr. Kesner was. For now, the man's actions served only to confuse Shane. Or were they meant to disarm him? He tugged on the lapels. "I'm surprised it fits."

"You have Mademoiselle Dumont to thank for that. She has a very good eye."

Shane had met the dress shop owner a time or two, to hold a door for her or talk while waiting at the mercantile.

Mr. Kesner faced the throng of swirling couples. "The next dance with Miss Waterby is mine."

Of course, it is.

"Once we've gone around the room, tap me on the shoulder, indicating you wish to cut in, and I'll step aside."

Shane narrowed his eyes. "Why?"

"So you may dance with her."

Not what Shane meant. "Why are you being nice to me? I'm your rival for her affections. What are you up to?"

"Miss Waterby isn't like other young ladies who want to find a wealthy man to marry regardless of her feelings toward him—or his toward her. She leads with her emotions. I won't have a chance with her until she has gotten you washed out of her thoughts and heart. She will hold on to the misguided feelings she believes she has for you. She has no experience with affairs of the heart. When she tires of you, I'll be waiting."

Shane didn't like picturing that. "What if she doesn't tire of me? What if I win?"

"Then I will bow out like a gentleman."

Shane did a double take. "Why would you do that?"

"I wouldn't want a wife who would always be pining for another man."

"You want a wife to worship you."

Kesner chuckled. "I wouldn't say that, but I would like to hold her heart. Miss Waterby belongs here." He stretched out his hands. "Surrounded by beautiful things. When she realizes that, she *will* tire of you."

Did Kesner know where Nicole came from? That she arrived in town in dusty buckskins and trail dirt? That she was agile enough to get out of the way of a rearing horse? That she could shoot better than most men? That she could track and hunt? That she likely feared nothing? That her hair wasn't long at all but cropped short to a little above her shoulders? That she was more comfortable with a gun in her hand than a feathery fan? Kesner wouldn't be so interested in her if he knew all the unladylike things she had done. Shane could inform this dandy and put an end to this rivalry here and now. But he wouldn't betray Nicole by spilling all her secrets. "You know she lived in the mountains?" That was already common knowledge.

"I know. She won't be returning to that place. Being an old family friend with her grandfather, my grandmama intends to see to it she experiences all she missed out on growing up. That she has all the finer things in life." Kesner held his hands out. "And who wouldn't want all this?" He strolled away.

Shane wouldn't. To him, all these things were trappings to tie a man down. Much like his ranch had done to him. Could he learn to be a part of all this for Nicole? Unlike with Isabelle Atwood, for Nicole he would consider it.

He bristled when Kesner took Nicole in his arms. Nicole smiled at Shane's rival. As the pair approached, Shane stepped into the dancing couples and tapped Kesner's shoulder. Hopefully, the man wasn't setting Shane up for embarrassment, and hopefully, Nicole would be pleased he was there.

Kesner stopped and stepped aside.

Shane let out a sigh of relief.

Nicole's smile brightened. "You came!"

His knees weakened. *Even more beautiful up close.* He held up his arms. "May I have this dance?"

"Of course." She put her hand in his.

Fortunately, the tune was a waltz. Shane would be able to manage. He moved her around the floor. "You look beautiful."

"Thank you. And you look quite dashing."

Thanks to Kesner.

"Your hair is lovely that way."

Nicole pulled the locks over her shoulder. "It's a hairpiece, but I'm growing my hair long. Do you like long hair?"

A smile pulled at his mouth. "I do. Very much."

"I do too."

"I hope you have saved me a dance or two on your card."

Nicole's dark eyebrows pulled together. "I don't know. Lamar filled it up for me so I wouldn't have to."

Which meant this was likely the only dance Shane would be getting unless he cut in again.

Nicole stopped in the middle of the twirling throng and opened the ivory card dangling from her wrist. "Oh, no. They're all taken except for the last one."

Shane peered at the contents of the card. Every fourth dance or so the same name, Lamar Kesner. The schemer had insured he would monopolize Nicole this evening. Once again, Shane admired him for his cunning.

She took the small pencil that hung from the card and scrawled Shane's name in for the last dance. "I'll ask Lamar if I can change some of these names. I'm sure that would be all right."

"I think you are supposed to dance with a variety of men. This is your night after all. I wouldn't want to deprive anyone." In reality, he wanted to deprive them all, but Nicole deserved to have this grand night with all the attention on her.

"If it's truly my night, shouldn't I get to choose whom I spend it with?"

"One would think so, but from Mrs. Kesner's speech, I'm not so sure." The wealthy had their own set of rules of right and wrong.

"Well, Lamar doesn't need so many dances with me." She crossed out the next two instances of his name and wrote in Shane's.

Kesner wasn't going to like that.

Dancers had begun to stare as they moved around Shane and Nicole.

Shane took Nicole into his arms and moved to the music. "You can do that later." He didn't want her to be disgraced for what people might consider inappropriate behavior.

The tune ended and another man swept her away. Shane's gut tightened, and he made his way to the edge of the room.

"Kesner waited for him. "What happened out there?"

"She didn't like some of the names on her card. She put mine in place of yours for your next two."

"As it should be. I put my name down for several dances so she could have that option."

How chivalrous of him. Or conniving. Nicole wouldn't have known she could change his name. Even though that was what she'd done. He liked a woman who had a mind of her own and could stand up for herself. No wilting hot-house flower for him.

It took too long before Shane's turn with Nicole came up again, but he met her on the floor. The tune changed to a dance he hadn't learned. "Do you mind if we sit this out and have a cup of punch?"

Nicole let out a sigh. "I would love that. It's been one partner after another."

He held out his elbow to her, and she wrapped her hand around his arm. He might not get to hold her this way, but he wouldn't embarrass himself or have to watch her dance with Kesner again, and he'd allow her a much-needed rest. He escorted her toward the refreshment tables.

"Hold it, you two."

Shane turned to face Aunt Henny.

She crooked her finger.

What had he done now? He guided Nicole over.

Nicole squeezed his arm. "Look, Aunt Henny. Shane came after all."

"I see that." The older woman gave a sly smile.

Shane dipped his head. "Ma'am, I hope you're having a good evening."

Aunt Henny put her hands on her hips. "Ma'am? Just for that, I might not help you out."

Help him?

Someone nearby motioned up. "You're under the mistletoe. You must kiss."

Shane tilted his head to see the ball of greenery, ribbons, and white berries above him and Nicole. He returned his gaze to Nicole. "I didn't do this on purpose."

She smiled sweetly. "I know." She continued to gaze

up at him as though waiting.

He had thought about kissing her before and now was his chance. Not only was it expected, but Nicole seemed amenable.

"Am I supposed to kiss you? Or do you kiss me? No one told me how this goes."

He stepped closer and put his hands on her waist.

"I'll kiss you." He leaned closer, giving her the chance to realize what was about to happen and pull away. He wished so many eyes weren't on them. He'd rather have done this some place private. But better in public than not at all. He pressed his lips to her soft, warm ones.

She sighed into him and wrapped her arms around his neck.

He could get lost in this kiss but knew he shouldn't. A second longer, then he inched away from her lips.

Her eyes remained closed for a moment before her long, black lashes fluttered.

Cheers rose around them, and someone called, "Pluck a berry."

Shane grabbed one and moved Nicole off to the side. "Next."

Another couple hurried under the mistletoe.

Aunt Henny winked at him.

He smiled back. He would have to do something nice for her in return. With a few steps to the side and behind the crowd, he slipped out of the room with the most exquisite lady at the party next to him. The adjoining room, also large, held various seating, some occupied, some not, and additional refreshment tables. He found a vacant padded bench for Nicole. "Have a seat, and I'll get you a cup of punch."

Nicole held out the sides of her dress. "I'm not sure I'm allowed."

"It'll be fine. Better than falling over from exhaustion." Too much fuss over a dress. Clothing should be functional.

She sat and sighed.

When he turned around to retrieve drinks for them, a male servant held out a tray. "Beverage, sir, for you and your lady?"

"Thank you." Shane took two cups of punch and handed one to Nicole.

She drained hers in one go. "I didn't realize how thirsty I was."

He traded cups with her. "You have been on the move all evening."

The same servant took the empty one from him and replaced it with a full one.

Maybe he could get used to service like this.

Nicole took another sip, set her punch on the side table next to the bench, and opened her dance card. "I put your name in for every other one of Lamar's after the next one of course. I didn't think I should replace him every time. He is the host after all, and he has been ever so kind."

Shane just bet. The man was cunning, that was for sure.

"There isn't anyone else I can cross off. Some of these men are supposed to be very important, and I don't want to offend anyone. Certainly not the Kesners after their kindness to me."

Nicole managed a perfect blend of confident and capable mixed with innocence and sweetness. She treated the wealthy and the servants with the same level of respect. She really didn't understand class differences. Everyone was equal in her eyes. Refreshing.

After a couple of minutes, a red-haired man approached and held out his hand. "I believe this dance is mine."

Nicole opened her card. "Are you Ian O'Gillis?"

"I am. We met in town one day."

"That's right." She seemed reluctant but put her hand in Ian's and stood. As the pair walked away, she cast a glance over her shoulder at Shane.

He wanted to follow them and steal Nicole away from Mr. O'Gillis. But that would only serve to prove Kesner right that Shane didn't belong there. He should stay in this room until his turn to dance with her again, so he wouldn't have to see other men holding her. But he found himself making his way to the ballroom.

An older gentleman near him spoke as though he

and Shane had been in a long dialogue. "She is a rare beauty."

Only one person he could be talking about. "Rare indeed." And not only her beauty but rare in many ways.

The man went on. "She will be the most sought-after woman in the Pacific Northwest when she returns."

Nicole was leaving? "Returns from where?"

"Mrs. Kesner is sending her to the finest finishing school back East, then a year-long tour of Europe. The young lady will likely return as someone's wife, and if Mrs. Kesner has anything to say about it, the lucky gentleman will be her own grandson."

Two years away? Europe? Shane's gut twisted. "How do you know this?"

"Mrs. Kesner, herself, told me."

No wonder Kesner wasn't worried about having Shane at this party. He would soon be gallivanting on the other side of the world with her, far from Shane. No doubt wooing her with everything money could buy and proposing to her with a diamond the size of a walnut. The man had appeared benevolent in his action, but in reality, was setting Shane up for a worse fall.

Later in the evening, Shane held Nicole in his arms for the fifth time, each making him feel worse. Nicole went on about the beautiful surroundings and how wonderful everything was. She fit here as though she'd been raised in luxury.

He, on the other hand, would never fit in. This wasn't the place for him.

Nicole would no doubt be a big hit in Europe, men fawning all over her. If she didn't accept Kesner's proposal, there would be plenty of other wealthy men vying for her hand.

She may have come down from the mountain in buckskins and dirt, but she belonged in beautiful ball gowns surrounded by fancy things. A world he had no business being in. A world he would never be a part of.

Kesner was right. Eventually, Nicole would realize Shane didn't belong in all this opulence.

The tune ended, and he handed her off to the next man then backed off the floor, keeping her in his sight.

"Good-bye, mountain girl. Good-bye, Nicole. Good-bye, the soon-to-be-Mrs. Lamar Kesner." He turned and walked out the front door.

The crisp winter air slapped him in the face, restoring some sense to his addled brain. Maybe he could winter in Montana. He'd heard he had a cousin of some sort there. Though he'd never met him, they were family.

A footman stood at the ready. "May I send for your carriage, sir?"

He huffed a humorless laugh. Sir? He'd been a fool to come. "No carriage. Just my horse."

"I'll have it saddled and brought around. You can wait inside where it's warm."

"I'd prefer to do it myself." Better than standing around waiting. He pointed. "The barn's that way?" He strode off the stoop or whatever rich people called it.

"The stables. Yes, sir. But-but—"

Shane waved a hand over his head. "I'll find it. Thank you."

In the barn—stable—Shane had a time convincing the hands there that he would saddle his own horse. He threw Huckleberry's blanket over his horse's back then the saddle.

"You're leaving? The soirée isn't over yet."

Shane paused a moment before turning to face Kesner. "I think it's best."

"What did you tell Miss Waterby?"

"Nothing."

"Nothing? You can't do that."

"Yet, I am." Shane fed the front saddle strap under Huckleberry's chest. Did Kesner even know how to properly saddle a horse? Or did one of his many servants do that for him?

"Running out on her like this will break her heart."

He cinched the strap tight. "I doubt that." Nicole was the strongest woman he'd ever met. Fearless. Needed no one, least of all him.

"She's smitten with you. We don't always choose whom we love. The heart wants what the heart wants."

But Nicole was better off without Shane. "The heart

doesn't always know what's best or get what it wants." His certainly didn't. He secured the bucking strap. "This little exercise of yours was to show me that I don't fit into this stuffy world of yours and Nicole does. You win."

"Win? If you walk away like this, I may win the lady, but I'll never have her heart. If you care about her at all, you won't do this to her."

It was because he cared, he was walking away so she could have the life she deserved. He fitted the bit and bridle.

"If you are going to give up on her, you have to let her know. You can't end it like this. She needs to be the one to end things with you. She's not the kind of person who can move on otherwise."

"Tell her whatever you like to make it easier for her and for you." Shane led Huckleberry out of the stable.

"Are you daft?" Kesner followed. "No. You're a coward."

That rankled. "I'm no coward. I'm just not skilled in these games of the heart you polite society people play." He had been daft to think he ever stood a chance. And Kesner knew it. Shane would head for Montana as soon as he could. Or maybe south to the sunshine.

Shane swung up into his saddle. "Have a good time in Europe." He rode away, leaving his heart behind. Nicole would be better off for this.

Twenty-One

SOMETIME AFTER MIDNIGHT, HENNY SHOOED NICOLE up the stairs of her boarding house and followed. She didn't know how either of them were still standing. "You've had a long night."

"I want to check on the boys." Nicole cracked open the door to the room next to hers, where Bucky and Rolf shared the bed. Rolf had come that afternoon to stay with Bucky while Henny and Nicole were out, and also to be here in the morning for Christmas.

Once in Nicole's room, the girl held up her hand. A string of amethysts glimmered from her wrist. "Did you see the bracelet Lamar gave me?"

Mercy. It had started. Men trying to buy her attention. Henny proceeded to unlace the back of Nicole's purple gown, a confection she would likely never wear again. "It's very pretty. But don't mistake gifts for true affection."

Nicole twisted to peer over her shoulder. "What do you mean?"

How to caution her without dampening her pleasure? The bracelet was not an indicator whether Mr. Kesner's feelings for her were real or not. "Sometimes, when a man gives a lady a gift, the lady can mistake the expensiveness of the gift with how much the gentleman cares about her."

"Lamar said it was nothing, just some little stones on a chain. But I think they are pretty."

Henny stepped around and faced the girl. "Those are not 'just some little stones.' Those are amethysts and the chain is solid silver. That is an expensive piece of jewelry. Granted he could have given you diamonds and gold, but nonetheless, by giving you this, he's telling you and everyone else he's interested in you. He'll likely ask to court you."

"I thought he was merely being nice." Nicole fingered the gems.

"He might have been, but he also might have been claiming his territory. You'll have to see how he behaves in the future."

Nicole unclasped the bracelet. "What should I do?" She placed it on the top of the bureau. "Should I get him a gift in return?"

"No, that would give him the wrong impression." The girl probably shouldn't have accepted the gift, but since she had... "I can speak with Mrs. Kesner and see if I can determine his motivation." This poor girl had been thrust into a segment of society she was ill-prepared for, which could be ruthless. In Henny's zeal to turn this mountain hermit into a lady, she may have done Nicole a disservice.

Nicole heaved a huge, contented-sounding sigh. "Aunt Henny, this was a perfectly perfect evening. I could have kept dancing and dancing. I didn't want to stop, at least not when I was with Shane."

Henny was pleased Nicole had a nice time. "Mr. Keegan is a good man."

The girl spoke in a wistful voice. "When a man kisses you, is it always like that? So wonderful?"

Ah, the feeling of first being in love was like nothing else. Henny's thoughts threatened to drift to the past, but she stopped them. No good could come of it. "When you're in love, it can be like that a lot, but not always."

Nicole's eyes widened. "Do you think I'm in love?"

"I believe so." And Henny hoped as much. Though the Kesner boy was a fine young man, she hoped Nicole ended up with Mr. Keegan. He was a balanced, levelheaded man who wouldn't be chasing after the next fashionable trend from Europe. She believed he could give Nicole more than seeing the world, expensive jewelry, and beautiful things. He could be the kind of husband she truly needed. One who could sincerely love her. "You have all the signs."

"It feels simply marvelous. I never want it to stop. I feel as though I could fly."

Though Henny had wanted Nicole to enjoy being a lady, she worried the girl liked the wealthy lifestyle a little too much. She hoped Nicole didn't get caught up in society's entanglements—the darker side of things. There were many who would take advantage of her naivety. After Christmas, she would caution the girl. Good thing Nicole had a sensible man like Shane vying for her affections. "Let's get you out of this dress and into bed." Henny shimmied the dress down over the petticoats to the floor. "Step out."

Nicole did and touched her lips. "They tingled when he kissed me."

Definitely in love.

Henny hung the gown on a hanger in the wardrobe and steered the girl to her bed. "Put on your night dress and finish getting ready for bed."

"I wish Shane didn't have to leave the soirée so early. I saved the last dance for him."

"I know." Henny wondered what had happened to the young man. One minute, he had Nicole in his arms, then in the change of partners, Shane Keegan disappeared. Strange. Had Mr. Kesner had anything to do with that? She hoped nothing bad happened to the rancher.

"Merry Christmas, Aunt Henny."

"Merry Christmas." Henny went downstairs to her room. The girl might not sleep at all tonight. Henny remembered that feeling. Like nothing could stop her, nothing could hurt her.

And then it did.

She prayed Nicole never felt the stabbing pain of a broken heart. It changed a person.

◦◦◦

Nicole jerked awake to Bucky jumping on her bed.

"Wake up, Nick! Wake up! It's Christmas!"

She hadn't been asleep long enough for it to be morning. She groaned and plopped the pillow over her head.

Bucky tugged at the pillow. "Come on, Nick, come on!"

Suddenly, the bouncing and pulling stopped as though someone had plucked her cousin off the bed.

"Bucky, leave Nick alone." Rolf's footsteps retreated out of her room, and the door closed.

Bucky's voice carried through the barrier. "But we can't open presents until she comes."

The footsteps trailed down the stairs along with their muffled voices.

Blessed peace. She snuggled deeper into the warm quilts.

Her eyes popped open. Shane. He would be coming today. No longer tired, she threw off the covers. She had to be ready when he arrived.

Dressing in a hurry, she wished she had some of the mistletoe from the soirée last night. Her lips still remembered his touch.

She pinned on her hair piece and hustled down to the parlor and then the kitchen, where Aunt Henny had made a feast of flapjacks, eggs, bacon, fried potatoes, and applesauce.

After breakfast, Aunt Henny gave each of them the end of a string. A blue strip of fabric tied to the end of one for Rolf, red for Bucky, and purple for Nicole. "I tied the cloth on so I could remember which one belonged to who. Follow your string to find your present from me." The strings were twisted around each other and looped through and around furniture.

The boys took off, untangling their strings from the other two, climbing under and over things in the path.

Nicole held up her string end. "You didn't have to do this. You've already done so much for us, and you tell me we have plenty of money."

"You do dear, but not only have you and the boys missed out on a few things, I have as well. This was no trouble. The excitement on their faces fills me with joy." She pointed. "Now go find your gift."

Nicole followed her string. This was exciting, not knowing what was on the other end. Her search would be easier than Rolf's and Bucky's because the strands had already been untangled.

Bucky squealed and ran up to Nicole with a fistful of

string in one hand and a red wooden top and a peppermint stick in the other. "Look what I got."

Miss Tibbins trailed behind him, attacking the dragging string.

"Go tell Aunt Henny thank you."

He ran off to the other room, and the calico followed.

Nicole continued to follow her string.

Rolf moseyed up to her, holding out a bolo tie and a peppermint stick. "Make sure you thank her."

"I will. If you don't want to go through all this trouble, you could go straight to the front hall."

"Thank you, but this is fun. I want to follow the string to see where it takes me."

Rolf strolled off.

Nicole rolled up her cording as she moved through the house until she ended up by the front door. She, too, received a peppermint stick and a pearl-tipped hatpin.

She found Aunt Henny and hugged her. "Thank you. This is beautiful."

"I'm glad you like it. My mother gave that to me."

"Oh." Nicole held it out to the older woman. "I can't take it then." She might not have grown up with such heirlooms, but she knew that the few things of Grandpa's she had were treasures to her. "This has to hold special meaning for you."

"It does, as do you." Aunt Henny pushed Nicole's hand away. "I want you to have it. You and the boys have filled a missing place in me I didn't even realize was there. Thank you."

Nicole tucked the hatpin close to her chest. "You are special to me too. I couldn't have managed without you. I'm still trying to figure things out, but I'm not scared like when I first came down from the mountain not knowing what to do. I will treasure this always."

The only thing that would make this day more perfect would be to see Shane walk through the front door.

Determined to get as far away from Nicole and her fancy new lifestyle as he could, Shane pressed his bedroll behind the cantle on the back of his saddle and tied it down. His two collies watching him from a bed of straw.

Handley entered the barn. "Where are you off to? I thought you were going to town to see your gal, but you appear to be preparing to leave for a spell."

Shane didn't want to get into his comings and goings with his foreman. "I have a few ideas about where my missing cattle could be. I'm going to head out for a couple of days and see if I can bring them in before winter settles in hard." Or he might keep going once he got on the trail, then send word that he wouldn't return until spring.

His foreman's eyebrows knit together. "But it's Christmas. Don't you want to visit your gal?"

He did, but he wasn't going to.

Kesner's smug face came to mind, and his taunting words crashing over him. *Running out on her like this will break her heart. You can't end it like this.*

She would be better off without Shane. She belonged in Kesner's lavish world.

"If you wait until tomorrow, I can go with you. Two sets of peepers would be better than one."

Shane didn't want anyone tagging along. It would limit his options. What could he say to make it not sound as though he was making excuses? "Tomorrow then." He loosened Huckleberry's girth strap and removed the saddle.

"Aren't you going into town to see your gal?"

"Naw. Too much to do around here." Shane returned Huckleberry to his stall and then strode across the yard and into the house.

He half expected to see Rolf there. He'd gotten used to the boy being around, but Rolf had gone into town the day before to spend Christmas with his brother and cousin. He wouldn't return until tomorrow or the next day. That's why he needed to leave today.

Maybe he should go back out and saddle his horse again. It would be better if he left before the boy returned. Less questions.

He kicked at the leg of an overstuffed rawhide chair. He was a coward. He didn't want to face Nicole or her cousin. He wanted to slip away without anyone noticing. But Handley had caught him. Why did the foreman care? Why not simply let Shane go search for his missing cattle? Did Handley suspect Shane might not return?

At a knock on the door, Shane grunted. He didn't want to talk to anyone right now but opened the door anyway.

Bray stood on his stoop. "Boss, I heard you might be heading out tomorrow to search for the stray livestock. I'd like to go with you."

Was everyone going to go? How was Shane supposed to slip away unnoticed if everyone came? "I'll think about it."

Ranching had been easier when he'd been a simple hand. There were aspects of owning his own land and cattle which appealed to him, but all of this kept him tied down. He had responsibilities and couldn't up and leave whenever he wanted.

And he needed to leave before he had to witness Nicole on Lamar's arm, smiling up at him. That image rankled.

He shouldn't have kissed her. Never experiencing her soft lips or holding her in his arms again would haunt him the rest of his life.

He kicked the chair a second time and grimaced.

⁂

Around noon, Job Lumbard, one of Aunt Henny's two regular boarders, ambled down the stairs. Nicole liked the older college professor, and his distinguished white hair and beard reminded her of Grandpa. The other younger boarder, Professor Tunstall, had taken a train two days ago, heading home to his parents for Christmas.

The professor focused on Nicole sitting on the settee.

"Your young man stopped by yesterday. Did you open his present?"

Nicole straightened. "Present?"

"I put it on the tree." He strode over and plucked a bundle of fabric the size of a small book off a branch and handed it to Nicole.

She gazed at the purple calico tied with a leather cord the color of her buckskins. She glanced up to say something to Aunt Henny and found four pairs of eyes staring at her.

Bucky spoke for the group. "Aren't you gonna open it?"

"I don't know." Nicole sought out Aunt Henny. "I didn't think to get him anything."

"I'm sure he won't mind. I bet a smile from you is all he needs."

Bucky sat next to her. "Do you want me to untie it for you? I think it could be in a pretty tight knot."

It wasn't in a knot at all but a nice bow. "I think I'll wait until Shane gets here to open it."

"Come on, Nick." Her younger cousin tilted his head at an exaggerated angle, almost like when a cat sleeps. "I wanna see what it is."

Rolf stood, leaning against the parlor's doorframe from the front entry. "I know what it is. I saw him making them."

Bucky leapt to his feet. "What is it, Rolfy? Tell me, tell me."

Shane had made her something? That piqued her curiosity, and she didn't want to wait to see what he'd made. She glanced at Aunt Henny who gave a nod, so she pulled on the leather cord.

Bucky plopped onto the settee again next to her.

She unfolded the cloth. In the calico lay a pair of wooden hair combs carved with flowers and waxed to a shine.

Bucky sighed. "Those aren't any fun." He jumped up and then plopped onto the floor with his top and spun it.

Aunt Henny sat next to her and picked up one of the combs. "These are lovely. I never realized Mr. Keegan had such a talent. A lot of time went into these. He must care a great deal about you."

Nicole couldn't take her eyes off the delicate flowers. The surface was smooth as a stream-worn stone. "Would you put them in my hair?"

"Of course."

Shane would get to see her in them as soon as he arrived.

Nicole spent most of the afternoon sitting sideways on the settee with her hands stacked together and her chin perched atop them, staring out the window. Shane should have been here long before now. Had something happened to him?

A teacup clinked, and Aunt Henny spoke. "I brought you some hot chocolate."

"Thank you."

"I'm sure he's fine. There are many things which could have come up on a ranch to keep him there. He'll come into town in the next few days."

But Nicole wanted him to come now. She missed him and wanted to see him today. She laughed to herself. She sounded like Bucky impatient for sweets.

Twenty-Two

IN FRONT OF AUNT HENNY'S BOARDING house the following morning, Nicole sat atop Queenie, Bucky atop Peppermint, and Rolf on Bear. She and Bucky were on their way to the mercantile to get a present for Shane. Why Shane hadn't come into town yesterday still confused her. He'd said he would. Something must have come up on his ranch.

Rolf's horse stepped anxiously, shifting around sideways, so he walked Bear in a circle to face Nicole. "I'll let Shane know you'll be out later."

"Don't tell him. I want it to be a surprise. Why don't you come to the mercantile with us, then we can all ride out together?"

Rolf shook his head. "I need to get to the ranch. Chores to attend to."

"You don't have to worry. The Sewells won't be at the mercantile." At least, she hoped they didn't run into those awful people.

"It's not that. I know I've only been away a couple of days, but I miss it. I love being on the ranch. I can't explain it."

Nicole thought she understood. She hadn't known how much she wanted to be a lady until she experienced it. "Go, but don't tell him."

"I won't." He turned his horse and trotted off.

For a few moments, Nicole watched her cousin riding away. He'd grown up in the short time he'd been on Shane's ranch. Not a man yet, but further on his way than when they lived in the cabin on the mountain. She turned to Bucky. "You ready?"

"Yup." He tapped his heels against Peppermint's sides, and the chestnut plodded into motion.

Without being prompted, Queenie took off after the

other horse and didn't slow until she was a nose length ahead.

At the mercantile, Nicole showed Bucky how to tether his horse. Not that the quarter horse would go anywhere, even if she wasn't secured. It was a good habit to get into for future mounts.

Inside, Franny greeted them. "Did you have a good Christmas?"

"Yes. It was wonderful." Except for Shane not showing up. "Did you have a nice one too?"

"We did. I got some blue pin-striped taffeta that I can't wait to make into a new Sunday dress."

Nicole wished she knew how to sew clothes. Maybe Aunt Henny would teach her. She had said that Nicole and her cousins had filled a missing place in her. But when would the older woman grow tired of taking care of Nicole? She had her own life and responsibilities before Nicole showed up on her doorstep. She would talk to Aunt Henny and ask her what she should do. Nicole trusted her to be honest.

Franny's words pulled Nicole back to the present. "Can I help you find something?"

Nicole focused on the glass case of the counter. "I'm looking for a gift."

"Who for?"

Nicole bit her bottom lip to contain her smile.

Franny's eyes twinkled. "A certain handsome rancher?"

Nicole nodded and turned her head. "He made me these beautiful hair combs."

Franny gasped. "Oh, that man is sweet on you."

Nicole hoped so. Her lips tingled thinking about his kiss.

"You're blushing."

Nicole glanced over her shoulder to locate Bucky, finding him gazing in wonder at a shelf full of wooden toys. She turned back to Franny. "The other night, at the soirée, he kissed me under the mistletoe."

"I'm jealous. I wish I had a sweetheart to kiss me." Franny reached under the glass counter and retrieved a tray of jewelry. She picked up a gold pocket watch. "He would like this."

Nicole took the cold piece in her hand. She released the catch, and the cover popped open. A slight ticking came from it.

She tried to picture Shane pulling this out of his pocket to see the time. She couldn't and made another unsuccessful attempt. Lamar's face popped into her head. This would better fit him. She pictured the purple bracelet he'd given her. Aunt Henny had said it would probably be best not to reciprocate with a gift. She handed the watch back. "This won't do."

Franny showed her another watch and a pair of cuff links as well as a few other items around the store. "You are picky."

Was she? Nothing seemed to fit for Shane. "When would he use those things?" They were sort of like the purple bracelet Lamar had given her. She didn't know when she would wear something so impractical again.

"Well then, what would he use? You could get him something for his day to day work. What do ranchers do all day?"

Nicole thought a minute, and Grandpa came to mind. She pictured him out hunting with his rifle. That was it. She would give Shane Grandpa's scabbard. "Thank you, Franny. You've been a big help. We'll take the candy Bucky picked out." She paid for the sweets and left with her cousin.

Outside, an older couple stood nearby, gazing at Bucky. The woman stepped forward. "See, I told you he looks like Joseph did at that age."

The gentleman with her took the woman's arm. "Not here. You'll scare the boy."

"But..."

"In time, Caroline. We'll do this properly."

Who were these people?

Nicole knew she should hustle Bucky away but found herself rooted in place. There was something familiar about the man. His eyes and the shape of his brow.

The gentleman gave her a nod. "Sorry to have bothered you, miss." He ushered the woman away.

One of Bucky's cheeks rounded as the boy shoved the candy to the side of his mouth. "Who was that, Nick?"

"I have no idea. We better get home. Aunt Henny will have food on the table for us."

At the boarding house, Aunt Henny came out of the kitchen, wiping her hands on a towel. "I'm glad you've returned. Dinner is ready."

Bucky peered up at her. "People seed me."

Aunt Henny shifted her attention to Nicole. "What people? Not those terrible Sewells?"

Nicole shook her head. "These were different ones. A man and lady about your age. They were dressed nice like you. The woman thought Bucky looked like someone else, and the man seemed familiar to me, but I'm sure I've never seen him before."

"I wouldn't worry about it. They were probably mistaken."

After the noon meal, Nicole went out to the barn where some of the items from the cabin had been stored. If she hurried, she still had time to go out to Shane's. She delved into the pile and spotted what she was after. Grandpa's rifle scabbard, leather with tooling, silver studs, and fringe. Shane would like this.

Bucky raced into the barn. "Nick, come quick."

Her stomach flipped, and she stood. "What is it? Is Aunt Henny all right?"

"Yup. A carriage comed for us."

Nicole's stomach settled to normal. Nothing was wrong. "What carriage?"

"A thatchy one." Bucky ran toward the house.

A thatchy carriage? What was he talking about? Nicole hurried to the house.

Aunt Henny stood in the front entry with a man in a black suit. "Mr. Thatcher has sent for you. It's probably about the adoption."

That's what Bucky meant by a thatchy carriage.

The man dipped his head. "I'll wait for you all outside." He left.

Aunt Henny closed the door. "I recommend changing out of your riding skirt and into one of your dresses, and

Bucky should wear his nicer clothes."

An hour later, Nicole eagerly sat in Mr. Thatcher's office, even with the twisting in the pit of her stomach. Aunt Henny sat in the chair next to her, and Bucky sat on the floor with a tablet of paper and a pencil, drawing.

The attorney handed over a document. "Mr. Jenkins sent this over. It's the deed to the mountain. It now legally belongs to you and the boys."

Pleased, Nicole took it, but it wasn't what she'd been hoping for this visit. "I thought perhaps you had news about the adoption."

Mr. Thatcher cleared his throat. "I'm afraid there has been a little snag in completing that."

"Do those horrible people want more money?"

"It's not them. It's the grandparents on their father's side. Five years ago, after the boys' father passed away and when they learned the mother had also passed away, Mr. and Mrs. Miller filed for and were awarded custody of Rudolf and Theodore. By the time they came to retrieve them, the boys had disappeared. The Millers are in town and want to see their grandsons."

Nicole stared in disbelief. She tried to make sense of what Mr. Thatcher said as well as what she knew about her cousins. That must have been the woman who'd recognized Bucky—or thought she had. And the boys had disappeared because Grandpa took them to protect them from the Sewells. If he had known there were good people to care for them, he never would have done it. But since he had, Nicole couldn't imagine not having them in her life. "Are they kind people?"

"I believe so."

She hoped not so she could keep her cousins. "Why did they come now?"

"Because we filed for custody."

Her heart dropped into her stomach like a hot coal. "What if I don't want to give them up?"

Mr. Thatcher heaved a sigh. "You won't have a choice. You can, of course, fight for custody, but I wouldn't recommend it. You wouldn't likely win."

The coal in her stomach burned. "Why not? I'm the only family they know." Her throat began to close up at the thought of losing her cousins.

"You are a young, unwed woman and aren't blood related. They are a husband and wife who are related and already have established custody."

"But the boys don't know them."

Bucky climbed into her lap. "I don't want to go no place but with you."

Nicole wrapped her arms around him. She had forgotten her cousin was present in the room.

Mr. Thatcher folded his hands atop the file in front of him. "Where is Rudolf?"

"He's out on Shane's ranch. Why?"

"I need you to bring him into town. I'll set up an appointment with the Millers to meet the boys tomorrow afternoon."

The coal blazed hotter. "So soon?"

"If they want, they can legally take their grandsons right now."

The breath froze in Nicole's chest. She was going to lose Rolf and Bucky. She wanted to run away with them.

Mr. Thatcher removed his spectacles. "I could put them off another day but no more. Thursday, one o'clock."

Aunt Henny, who had remained quiet, patted Nicole's hand. "I know this is hard." She had a catch in her voice as she spoke. "Bring the boys and see how things go. Rolf might remember his grandparents and can tell you what he thinks of them."

No. Nicole wanted to return to the cabin with her cousins where no one could find them. But someone *could* find them. Aunt Henny and Sarah knew where the cabin was. Sarah wouldn't help anyone find them, but Aunt Henny would because it would be the right thing to do.

Maybe when the Millers saw she and the boys were kin in the ways that mattered most and that she could take care of them, they would allow her cousins to stay with her. Or maybe, Nicole would fight for custody. Or she could pay them money like she did with the Sewells.

The following morning, Shane rode away from his ranch. Bitter cold air bit at his exposed skin. Yesterday would have been a better day to leave. Three of his hands trailed behind.

His foreman's horse trotted up next to him.

Shane wasn't in the mood for idle chatter.

Handley pointed ahead. "Why south?" His question came out on a white puff of air. "Better grazing land to the north. If I were a bovine wandering off, that's the direction I'd head."

Because south would get Shane out of snowy weather sooner. He was already risking getting caught in storms, leaving so late in the year. Almost next year. "I reckon you're right. But if I was a cattle rustler with a small herd, I'd head south to warmer weather."

"I see. Why not east? There's more grazing land that'a way."

Because Shane wanted to escape to the south. "This way, I'd have water all the way along the Yakima River for the cattle. Why don't we split up? You take east, and I'll go south." Shane hauled back on his reins, and the other two stopped behind them. He turned in his saddle. "Which direction do each of you want to go? West and north aren't spoken for yet."

Bray scrubbed his hand across his mouth. "I don't think it's a good idea for any of us to go it alone. Weather could turn. We should at least go in pairs."

Why did his new hand have to be practical? "Bray and I'll head south. You two take east." Or one of the other directions. Shane didn't care. He was getting antsy to leave this place. The longer he lingered, the harder the pull on his heart to turn around.

Handley pressed his lips together and shook his head. "Klem and I know the area better than either of you. One of us should be in each pair. I'll go south with you, boss."

Shane would have rather had Bray. He was the quiet sort. "Let's go then." He nudged Huckleberry into motion.

He would keep an eye out for a place down the trail to split off from Handley and keep on riding.

Nicole deserved more than he could offer her. She fit well into Kesner's world. She should have beautiful dresses, fancy things, and expensive trips to Europe. He shouldn't hold her back.

He recalled the kiss. Sweet and tender. He'd longed for more, having to temper his impulse to hold her in his arms forever. She'd smelled of sweet flowers.

Stop it, Shane. This will do you no good.

He needed to ditch his foreman and be on his way. The longer he delayed the harder it would be. She deserved better than a saddle tramp.

The image of their first meeting tickled a smile to his lips. The way she'd tucked and rolled and came up ready to shoot. Her irritation at him for taking her hat. She'd been like a prickly thistle. Barbs on the outside protecting the delicate purple flower within. And then she bloomed into an unimaginable beauty, never to be put in her plain shell again. Forever changed. A part of him wished she'd stayed in that husk of her buckskins. Then maybe he could stay and try to woo her.

Shane, you're gonna drive yourself crazy.

He'd met a lot of nice women and kissed quite a few of them. But none caused his chest to ache or made him nauseous when he left. Not even Clementine who he'd fancied himself in love with at age seventeen. He could take 'em or leave 'em. Didn't think twice about them once he was gone. Even Isabelle.

But Nicole was different than the whole lot. He'd do more than think twice about her in the coming days, weeks, and months. But leaving was the best thing he could do for her. Because he loved her, he wouldn't tie her down to ranch life. It wouldn't be right. She needed to be free to become the woman God intended her to be.

A couple of miles up the trail, Shane stopped and tilted his head. "What do you think? That dell could be the sort of place rustlers would hide cattle."

Handley shrugged. "I wouldn't. Too many ways for the cattle to wander off. I'll go check it out. Be right back." He goaded his horse forward.

Shane stared after his foreman. That had been too easy. He waited for Handley to disappear around a bend, and then he turned Huckleberry and nudged him into motion.

Would Handley or his other men even miss him? They had been running the ranch fine for the months between his uncle's passing and Shane arriving. But he should send a telegram to them once he was away. For now, they would assume he was following the trail of his missing cattle and wait for his return. It could be a week or so before they started to worry.

Nicole ducked and rolled into his mind. His chest tightened. Though he would long for her the rest of his life—and miss her cousins—she would likely think of him for only a short time and then forget all about him. He would write separate letters to her and her cousins to let them know he was fine.

But he would never be fine again.

He had to be strong and do this for Nicole's good.

By the time his foreman returned, Shane would be gone. Doubling back, he could take the other ravine that cut through a pass. He knew the area better than Handley realized. Up and over the ridge. To the left, Nicole. To the right, freedom.

At least freedom for her.

He would always be her prisoner.

Twenty-Three

THURSDAY MORNING, NICOLE RODE OUT TO Shane's ranch. She hadn't figured a way out of the boys meeting their grandparents. Shane's two collies wagged their tails as they ran up to greet her.

Rolf stood in the middle of the corral, encouraging Bear to run in a circle around him.

She rode up to the fence, with the dogs trotting alongside, and dismounted. Pepper, the black and white one, rolled to his back. The tri-colored, Roxy, gazed up at Nicole, waiting to be petted.

Nicole crouched and scratched both dogs behind the ears.

Rolf strolled over, leading his horse by a rope. "Shane's not here. He, Handley, Bray, and Klem took off the day after Christmas before I got here. They're searching for the missing cattle."

Disappointing to not see Shane, but it was just as well. In her worry, she'd forgotten his gift. Besides, Shane wasn't the reason for her visit. "I need you to come into town with me."

"Why?"

"Your grandparents have shown up."

"I thought you got to keep us. I don't want to have anything to do with those people."

"Not the Sewells. Your father's parents, the Millers."

Rolf knit his eyebrows together, and a mild recognition changed his expression. "Our grandparents?"

"You remember them?"

"A little."

"Are they good people?"

"I don't remember much of them. They were mostly gone. They went to another country to tell people about God or something."

"It turns out they have legal custody of you and Bucky. We saw them in town two days ago and the woman said Bucky looked like someone named Joseph."

"Our father. I don't really know them. They have custody? Does that mean we have to go with them?"

Nicole reluctantly nodded.

"What if we don't want to?" Rolf folded his arms. "I ain't living in another country. I'm staying here and so is Bucky."

Nicole was glad to hear that. "I see that we have three options. Fight in court for custody, which Mr. Thatcher says we would probably lose. Offer them money like with the Sewells. Or...you and Bucky go with them." That coal in the pit of her stomach flamed back to life.

"Or you, me, and Bucky climb on our horses, ride away, and keep on going so no one can find us."

Not even Shane? She would want *him* to find her. She tried to squelch the selfish thought. There was more at stake than her personal happiness. "We can't do that. It wouldn't be right. What about school? You and Bucky are supposed to start in a week." She wouldn't tell Rolf that riding off had crossed her mind more than once.

"Grandpa gave me all the schooling I need. Do I have to meet them?"

Nicole's heart hurt for her cousin. "I'm afraid so."

He coiled the rope around his hand, uncoiled it and coiled it again. "I'll meet them if I have to—but I'm not going to another country with them and neither is Bucky. He's staying with me. I've always looked after him."

"To at least meet them would be the right thing to do." Even if she disliked the idea as much as Rolf. "Saddle up, and let's go. The meeting is set for one p.m."

※

Nicole stepped out of Aunt Henny's buggy in front of the courthouse. She smoothed her hands down the sides of her walking suit. She'd wanted to stay in her riding skirt and arrive atop Queenie, but Aunt Henny advised her against her small act of rebellion. She needed to make the best impression possible so these people didn't take the boys immediately.

Leaning against the hitching rail, Shane gave her a nod.

Her breath caught at the sight of him. A dance fluttered inside her. He came. She bit back a delighted squeal. "I thought you were searching for your missing cows."

"I returned shortly after you and Rolf left the ranch and heard about this little meeting. I couldn't let you go in there without your bodyguard."

Though his words were friendly, there was something off about him. Or perhaps there was something off with her. All her nerves were a jitter. "Thank you. I appreciate you being here."

Rolf strolled up. "You'll tell 'em I have a job with you, so they won't take me away, won't you?"

Shane put his hand on Rolf's shoulder. "As much as you want to be a man, you *are* still a boy. If they decide they want to take care of you and Bucky, I doubt there is much I can do about it. But if they are anything like your other kin, I got your back."

Rolf smiled and moseyed up the walk toward the courthouse steps with Bucky.

Bucky had chattered ever since Rolf arrived in the late morning, telling Rolf how he wasn't afraid of the new kin like he was the other ones. He didn't know why, he just wasn't.

Shane gestured toward the front of the building. "Shall we go inside?" He didn't offer her his arm but walked beside her.

Inside, Franny Waldon, Isabelle Dawson, Trudy MacVay, and Agnes Martin waited. Some of the quilting circle ladies. Franny stepped forward. "We drew straws to see who would get to come and be here for you. Trudy, myself, and Adelaide—Isabelle's sister—won, but Adelaide was feeling peaked with the baby on the way and all, so Isabelle came instead. She wanted to anyway."

These women, she'd only known for a month and a half, all wanted to support her? She never would have imagined. She glanced at Mrs. Martin's pinched face. Her usual expression that made her seem as though she were unhappy wherever she happened to find herself. Evidently, not eager to have *won.*

Mrs. Martin raised her eyebrows. "I don't draw straws."

Franny fluttered her hand. "Agnes said it wouldn't matter what she drew, she was coming."

So, the older woman had wanted to be here after all. That touched Nicole. Living up on the mountain, she never imagined having so many friends.

Aunt Henny cleared her throat. "We should get to the meeting room."

Nicole hesitated.

Shane leveled his gaze on her. "It's going to be fine. I won't let anyone who might hurt those boys take them."

"Thank you." With some of her reluctance assuaged, she followed the others.

Mr. Thatcher stood outside the meeting room. He extended his hand to Rolf. "Nice to see you again, Rudolf Miller." He shook the boy's hand and then Bucky's. "The Millers are inside with the court reporter. Would you boys wait out here while the adults talk for a few minutes? Then we'll come and get you."

Rolf nodded and took Bucky to a bench and sat. Nicole hoped they didn't run off.

Mr. Thatcher opened the door.

Nicole took a deep breath to brace herself before entering.

The older couple from outside the mercantile sat on the far side of the table. They appeared to be perfectly normal, nice people. But Grandpa always said appearances could deceive a person.

Mr. Thatcher made the introductions around the room, and Nicole shook both of the Millers' hands.

Mrs. Miller kept tilting one way and then the other to look around Nicole's entourage. "I thought the boys were coming. They were supposed to be here."

"I asked them to wait in the hall. Miss Waterby has some concerns about you taking custody of Rudolf and Theodore."

"We only want our grandsons." She tapped the folder in front of her. "We have all our paperwork."

Agnes Martin stepped forward. "Where were you when those boys needed you?"

Nicole wanted to know that too and was grateful for Mrs. Martin asking what was in Nicole's heart.

Mr. Miller spoke this time. "We were in South America when we learned of our son's death. We came home as soon as we could, but it takes months. Claudia, our daughter-in-law, had returned to her family home with the boys. By the time we reached Kamola, she had passed as well. The Sewells wouldn't let us see our grandsons, so we sued for custody. All the terrible things Claudia had told us about her kin, we knew we didn't want our grandsons to stay with them. When we got custody, they told us the boys were gone, disappeared."

That must have been when Grandpa found the two frightened boys and brought them up to the mountain.

Mr. Miller continued. "We feared the worst. When we were notified someone else had requested custody, we came as fast as we could. We were afraid it was those terrible people. We're glad it wasn't them, and it was you." He turned a compassionate gaze on Nicole.

Agnes Martin folded her arms. "You know you can't touch their inheritance. Miss Waterby has control of that until they come of age."

"We don't know anything about an inheritance. We just want our grandsons. It broke our hearts when they were gone."

It was breaking Nicole's heart now.

Seemingly satisfied, Agnes Martin retreated.

Mrs. Miller gazed expectantly. "If you've heard enough, we'd like to see the boys."

Nicole's insides flipped, and she wanted to say no. Reluctantly, she stood and approached the door, suddenly feeling as though she were wading through several feet of snow. Masking her emotions before opening the door, she motioned her cousins inside.

Rolf and Bucky eased into the room as though a swarm of bees were buzzing around. Rolf's eyes brightened. "Gram? Poppy?"

Mrs. Miller clutched her hands to her chest. "He remembers us." Tentatively, she held open her arms, tears in her eyes.

Rolf stepped forward and allowed the woman to hug him. "I didn't before, but I think I'm remembering some stuff. You made cookies with cinnamon on top."

"Old Time Cinnamon Jumbos. They were your favorite."

Nicole glanced between Rolf and his grandfather. They had the same eyes. That was why the man had seemed familiar to her.

Mrs. Miller held an arm out to Bucky. Rolf motioned him over and nodded that it was all right. Bucky joined the trio. They were family, and Nicole was not.

She would lose her only kin. She scooted out into the hall. An oak log settled on her chest, threatening to press all the breath from her body.

Shane followed. "Are you all right?"

Her vision blurred, and she shook her head. "They are good people. As much as I want to keep my cousins, they belong to the Millers. Wait, they aren't my cousins. We aren't even blood related." She squeezed her eyes shut, and the tears rolled down her cheeks.

He pulled a folded blue bandana from his hip pocket and dabbed at her face.

Though sweet of him, she really wanted him to gather her in his arms. "I've lost them."

"Think of it this way. When you go to finishing school and Europe, they will have family to take care of them."

"Go where?" She'd heard of finishing school from Little Women and the quilting circle ladies. "Why do you think I'm going anywhere?"

"I thought Mrs. Kesner was sending you to finishing school before taking you to Europe for a year."

"She is? This is the first I've heard of it."

"That's what someone said at her Christmas party. It seemed all set. You can learn everything about being a lady like you've wanted to. You should consider it."

She did want to be a proper lady. "Where is the finishing school? Is it part of the normal college here in town?"

Shane shook his head. "I think it's back East somewhere."

Was Shane trying to get rid of her? "So far—"

The door to the meeting room burst open, and Bucky ran headlong into her and wrapped his arms around her waist. "I won't go, Nick! I won't!"

Nicole crouched to his level. "Go where?"

"Away from you. I won't do it." He threw his arms around her neck, and she held him tight, every bit as willing to keep him as he was to stay. "They can't make me."

Nicole shifted her gaze to the crowd pouring out of the meeting room.

Rolf stood in front of the group. "They want us to move to the other side of the mountains with them. I told them I can't, that I have a job." He cast a pleading glance at Shane.

Mr. Miller scooted to the edge of the crowd with his wife. "We didn't mean to scare the boy."

Mrs. Miller clasped her hands in front of her chest again. "We have a sweet little place in Olympia. Plenty of room for two energetic boys to run around in."

Mr. Miller nodded. "We bought it when we filed for custody five years ago so our grandsons would have a home to live in. We kept it in the hopes of one day finding them."

As Nicole straightened, she picked up Bucky and settled him on her hip. *My, he's getting big.* Would they really take her cousins so far away? She didn't want to let either of them go. She held onto Bucky as tightly as he was holding on to her.

Aunt Henny stood beside Nicole, and the rest of the quilting circle shuffled behind her. "I think it's going to take time for the boys to get used to you and the idea of change. Why don't you come to my boarding house so we can all get to know each other better?"

Mrs. Miller nodded. "We would like that."

Nicole didn't want to but nodded anyway. She glanced around.

Shane was gone.

Twenty-Four

NICOLE WATCHED ROLF AND BUCKY INTERACTING with their grandparents and warming up to them. Not only did the Millers come for the afternoon and stayed for supper, Aunt Henny invited them to rent a room at her boarding house so they could spend more time with the boys. She had consulted Nicole first. Nicole saw no point in saying no. These people could take her cousins at any time—and eventually they would.

The following day, Mr. Miller left early and returned shortly before noon. He gave his wife a nod, and she smiled back at him.

Something was brewing between those two. Were they planning to skip town without delay? Nicole wasn't ready to lose the boys completely. Would they take them without warning? She prayed not.

After dinner, Mrs. Miller talked Bucky and Rolf into showing her their horses. Rolf gave a backward glance as though he, too, realized the Millers were up to something.

Mr. Miller cleared his throat. "I would like to speak to you, Miss Waterby. If that's all right."

Aunt Henny stood from where she'd been sitting on the settee. "I'll leave you two to talk."

Nicole stood as well. "Don't go." Whatever the man had to say to her, she wanted Aunt Henny there for support and help if she needed it. She still knew too little about living in a town and interacting with so many people. It was all overwhelming at times.

Aunt Henny resumed her seat. "Of course, dear."

Nicole sat as well and folded her hands in her lap.

Mr. Miller took a seat in a wingback chair across the tea table. "We wanted to speak to you first before saying anything to the boys. We understand you're concerned about us, and that our grandsons have a life here. Theodore is very attached to you."

Nicole's throat tightened. She noticed he'd purposefully used *our grandsons*.

"The missus and I talked about it, and I sent a telegram to a man who has wanted to buy our home in Olympia. We've agreed to sell to him and have decided to get a small place here in Kamola. We know it's going to take little Theodore time to get used to us. The boys have been through enough, and we want to make this as easy as possible on them."

Nicole stared in confusion. Why did these people have to be so nice and considerate? If they were mean in some way, she could justify trying to get custody from them. Mr. Thatcher was right about her never being given custody of her cousins with grandparents like these. "You would move here?"

"Of course. Is it all right with you if we tell them today? Or would you rather be the one to let them know?"

"I...I don't understand." Could they truly value her opinion? "Why would you ask me? You are the ones who have custody."

Mr. Thatcher had cautioned her to be careful about what she said and to not do anything the Millers could perceive as threatening their position with the boys. The Millers could take her cousins without notice and refuse to allow her to see them.

"You know them better. You are sort of like family to them."

Sort of like? She *was* family.

But she wasn't. She swallowed around a lump in her throat.

Her thoughts and emotions jumbled together in a confused chaos. She had a hard time pinning one thing or another down. She was grateful her cousins were going to stay, but at the same time, anger roiled around inside her at these people for coming at all. Anger with herself for trying to get custody in the first place, alerting the Millers and causing them to come. But then the Sewells would have taken Rolf and Bucky. Most of the time, she just felt like crying. She would not do that in front of the Millers.

Aunt Henny put her hand on Nicole's arm. "Dear? Isn't it wonderful they are staying? And it's kind of them to ask you. What would you like to do?"

Nicole focused on Mr. Miller. "You can tell them." She stood and hurried up the stairs.

A few minutes later, a light knock sounded on her door, and Aunt Henny's voice filtered through. "May I come in?"

"Yes." Nicole sat up.

Aunt Henny entered. "Oh, sweetie, don't cry." She eased onto the edge of the bed, pulled an embroidered hankie from the cuff of her blouse, and wiped Nicole's tears. "This is good to have them stay in town. It was very considerate of them to ask you."

"But why bother? They have custody and will eventually take them away. And I'll be alone. I lost Grandpa, and now I'm losing Rolf and Bucky."

"You aren't losing them. They're staying in town. You can see them whenever you like."

"It won't be the same." Her cousins would have a whole other life without her.

"What about Mr. Keegan? He's taken with you."

Nicole had hoped so but had obviously been deceiving herself. "He was acting strange yesterday at the courthouse and then disappeared without a word. He left the Christmas soirée the same way. No good-bye. I think he only kissed me because of the mistletoe. He must not have really wanted to."

Aunt Henny uttered a soft chuckle. "He wanted to. He came all the way into town when he heard you were meeting with the boys' grandparents. He didn't have to do that. He did so to protect you and them. He did it because he cares about you."

"You think so?"

"I do."

Nicole's spirits buoyed.

"Do you think you can wipe away the rest of those tears and come downstairs?"

"Why?"

"The Millers would like you present when they tell the boys. They feel it would go better, and Bucky wouldn't be so afraid. They are being very considerate."

Nicole pushed out her bottom lip a little. "I know, and I hate them for it."

"Why?"

"Because I don't want to like them."

"But you do?"

Nicole nodded. Why did the boys get to have good relatives while Nicole had none at all?

"Will you come down? For the boys?"

"I'll be there in a few minutes." It was the least she could do to help her cousins adjust to their new life. A life without her.

Aunt Henny left, and Nicole pulled herself together. Grandpa would have told her to stop sniveling and shape up. She was a Waterby, and a Waterby had backbone. No room for feeling sorry for herself. Deep down, she was happy for her cousins to have kin who would love them and treat them well. She splashed cool water on her face from the pitcher on the washstand, took a deep breath, and headed down.

At the bottom of the stairs, Bucky grabbed her hand. "Come on, Nick." He pulled her over to the settee and squished in-between her and Aunt Henny.

She sensed her poor little cousin was insecure. He could probably tell that things were changing for him. She gave him a side hug. "The Mill— Your grandparents have some news for you."

Mr. Miller cleared his throat. "We realize Kamola is your home." He shifted his gaze between Bucky on the settee and Rolf leaning in the doorway between the entry and the parlor. "So, we have decided to move to Kamola."

Rolf straightened, pushing off the doorframe. "You are?"

The prospect of leaving had bothered Rolf more than he let on, but Nicole could tell.

Mrs. Miller nodded. "Yes. We are selling our house in Olympia and will buy one here. Would you like that?"

Rolf nodded. "Then I can still work on Shane's ranch."

The boys' grandmother widened her eyes. "You wouldn't need to work."

"I want to."

The Millers exchanged looks, and Mr. Miller said, "All right. It's good for a man to work, but we'll expect you to attend school as well."

Rolf stood a little taller, no doubt at being referred to as a man. "I will."

Mrs. Miller focused on Bucky. "And what do you think about us getting a house in town for the four of us?"

"Can Nick come too?"

"Um...I...don't know." Mrs. Miller glanced at her husband then to Nicole and returned her gaze to Bucky. "I don't know if there will be room. We won't be able to afford a big place."

Bucky squished his mouth from one side to the other, his thinking face. "I don't think so." He jumped off the settee, crossed to Rolf, and reached up to put his little hand on his big brother's shoulder. "I'm gonna work on Shane's ranch with Rolf. And Nick's gonna come too. We'll all live there."

The Millers exchanged glances again.

Nicole tilted her head. "I can't live on Shane's ranch." Maybe someday she would though. She hoped so. If Aunt Henny was right about the way he felt about her.

"Why not? You can do ranching stuff."

"Because I'm a girl." Nicole sought out Aunt Henny for help in explaining the situation.

Aunt Henny patted Bucky's hand. "It's not proper for a lady to live on a ranch with men who aren't her relatives."

Bucky heaved a big sigh. "I don't like you being a lady. You can't do a lot of stuff you *can* do. It's no fun at all. Stop being a lady, Nick."

She chuckled. "I can't, and I don't want to." She tried to picture herself with Shane strolling arm in arm through town. Her wearing buckskins and carrying a rifle. People would cross the road to get away from her like they'd done when she first arrived. He wouldn't be romantically interested in a woman like that, acting like a wild man. She'd be an embarrassment to him. Maybe she would go to a finishing school. Maybe Aunt Henny knew of one closer. Or maybe the quilting circle ladies would teach her all about being a proper lady. They seemed to know a lot. Then maybe Shane wouldn't distance himself from her and disappear.

As the week rolled by, Bucky grew more comfortable with his grandparents and even agreed to live with them. A snowstorm had kept Rolf in town for half of that time. Truth be told, the storm hadn't been that bad. He'd been out in worse up on the mountain. It was good he willingly agreed to spend time with his grandparents.

The Millers had fallen into a routine at the boarding house, helping Aunt Henny. Mrs. Miller in the kitchen and around the house, and Mr. Miller outside and fixing little things around the place. Mr. Hammond, the man who was sweet on Aunt Henny, had even gotten chummy with Mr. Miller. Everyone fit.

Except Nicole.

She slipped out to the barn and knelt in front of the trunk that held Grandpa's possessions from the cabin. She pulled out his Bible. "I miss you, Grandpa." She wished she'd never left the mountain. But if she hadn't, she never would have met Shane.

She wandered over to Queenie's stall. Tied to the post with twine was a folded piece of paper. She untied it and unfolded it.

Nicole,

She glanced to the bottom of the page, and her heart fluttered at seeing Shane's name. She sat on a bale of hay and read.

I'm sorry for leaving the Christmas party so abruptly and for leaving the courthouse without saying goodbye.

You deserve all the best. You should go to all the fancy parties you can.

So, to not repeat my previous mistake, I'll say goodbye.

What? Good-bye? Why?

You deserve all the best things in life, finishing school, a tour of Europe, fancy parties, and a dozen beautiful dresses. Lamar can give you all those things. I can't. I won't hold you back.

He wasn't holding her back. He'd set her free.

I'm heading out. I've stayed in one place far too long. I'm itching to roam the rest of the country. My foreman and hands can look after my ranch until I decide what to do with it.

She blinked at her blurry vision so she could finish the letter. But her eyes wouldn't cooperate. Aunt Henny had been so sure he liked her. Nicole never should have gotten her hopes up. Why couldn't Shane have taken her with him to see the country?

Shane didn't want her. He was leaving. Probably already left.

She would leave too. She had nothing to keep her in Kamola now. The boys had a family that didn't include her, and Shane didn't want her. Life had been simpler up on the mountain.

Maybe she would go off to the fancy school back East Mrs. Kesner wanted her to attend. She always wondered what Europe and the rest of the world were like.

But she didn't want any of it. She was nothing more than a simple girl from the mountain. She had been foolish to think she could be a lady. She dug through her things and found her buckskins. This was her true self. She would return to Grandpa's cabin and live alone like Sarah Combs did.

Twenty-Five

SHANE STOOD IN HUCKLEBERRY'S STALL BRUSHING his coat. He had nearly everything ready. He'd stashed his bedroll and saddle bags along his intended route, and he had two stashes of food tied up in trees.

And he'd delivered the letter to Nicole. She wouldn't likely discover it until this evening when she checked on the animals for the night. He would send word to his hands that he wouldn't be returning. Until then, they would assume he was out searching for his cattle. He would send a letter to Rolf explaining things the best he could. The only thing left to do was choose the right moment to slip away unnoticed. It had to be today. The skies had cleared for a few days and melted the snow.

The last time he'd tried to escape, his plan had been foiled by Handley tracking him up the ravine he'd taken. The problem was, Handley paid too close attention to his duties as a foreman.

He'd thought about giving his hands an excuse like he was going to check on fences or something, but it always seemed as though one or more of them wanted to go with him. When had they all turned into sissies?

Rolf he could understand, still being a boy. And since he'd returned three days ago, he'd been at Shane's side more than usual. He might prove to be the toughest to give the slip to. The boy kept asking when Shane planned to go into town to visit Nicole. He didn't. If he did, he might lose his nerve. Using the excuse of visiting Nicole had been a viable option that wasn't likely to provoke any of his men to want to tag along. But with Rolf back, going on and on about his grandparents, he might want to accompany him. Then how would Shane get out of seeing Nicole? He couldn't risk it.

Thud-thud-thud. Someone ran into the barn. What

was the hurry?

"Shane!"

Rolf. The boy sounded panicked. Shane stepped out of the stall. "Right here. What's wrong?"

The boy crossed to him and bent over with heaving breaths. "I...heard...them."

"Give yourself a moment to catch your breath. Slow, deep breaths. Then tell me what you heard."

"Taking...the cattle."

Shane stretched his eyes wide. "The rustlers?"

Rolf nodded. "Handley..." The boy still struggled for breath.

"Handley heard them too?"

He shook his head. "Handley...rustler."

What was the boy saying?

Rolf gulped in two deep breaths. "Handley is the rustler." He heaved air in and out. "And your other hands."

"What?"

"They've been stealing your cattle and from other ranchers. They are planning to leave with all the cows and heifers they've gathered."

Handley? "But he was my uncle's faithful foreman. He's been with this ranch for fifteen years or more. Why would he steal from it?"

Click.

At the sound of a revolver cocking, Shane spun around with his palm on the handle of his Colt.

Handley held his revolver pointed at Shane. "Easy there, boss. Take your gun out nice and gentle and toss it away."

Shane had no choice but to do as ordered. "Handley? You're part of the rustling ring?"

"Not rustlers." Handley snarled. "Just taking what's rightfully mine."

"Why are you doing this?"

"Because I got nothin'. I worked my tail off for your uncle. I put my sweat and blood into this land and the cattle for over *fifteen* years." Handley's voice grew louder and more bitter. "I was like a son to Bristol. He owed me this ranch. Was going to give it to me too. Then he finds out about a nephew he never met, had someone hunt you down, and gives you everything. He didn't even know you. You were nothing to him."

Shane had to be something to the man, or he wouldn't have left him the ranch. "I was his kin."

Handley spit on the ground. "This ranch should have been mine. If I can't have the land too, I'll have to settle for the cattle."

"You won't get away with this."

"I got a buyer lined up. Once I have the money in hand, I can head in any direction I please." He twisted his head and spoke over his shoulder. "Klem, tie 'em up."

At least he didn't plan on killing them.

Yet.

The stout man bound Shane first, hands behind his back, and then Rolf. The poor boy's hands shook so bad, Klem had a little bit of a hard time.

"Let the boy go. He's not part of this."

"So he can go running to the sheriff? No, thanks."

Shane glanced about. He didn't see Pepper or Roxy. "Where are my dogs?"

"I took care of them." Handley waved his gun. "Get in the stall."

Shane cocked his head to the side and spoke to Rolf. "You go in first, Kid." He wanted to be between his foreman's revolver and the boy.

Rolf scurried in.

Shane backed up into the stall. Huckleberry stepped around nervously.

"Sit," Handley barked.

Rolf moved around behind Huckleberry and sat in the far corner. The poor boy must be terrified.

Shane went down on his knees and then sat. "There's no place you can go the law and I can't find you." He would hunt Handley and the others down and make sure they rotted in jail.

Handley crouched in front of Shane. "I don't have anything personal against you, but I'm gettin' my due." He retrieved Shane's Colt from the straw covered floor and stood.

If Shane got out of this alive, he would see to it the

man got his due and it wouldn't be cattle.

"Stay out of our way until we're gone, and we can all be happy." His foreman left the stall and kicked the door closed. "Gather the others and saddle all the horses. We don't want them coming after us if they get loose."

As their footsteps faded away, Shane twisted his wrists to see if there was enough give in the rope to get free. "Kid?"

No answer.

Shane prayed the boy wasn't crying. "Rolf?"

From between Huckleberry's legs, he saw Rolf stand.

The boy walked around the horse, the rope dangling from one hand and a smirk on his face. Not a trace of his earlier fear.

Shane raised his eyebrows and whispered, "How did you get loose?"

Rolf kept his voice low as well. "A trick a traveling trapper taught me." He knelt behind Shane and worked at the knot. "If I fist my hands and make them shake, I can keep my wrists farther apart. He thinks he's tying me tight, but he's not. That, and most of the ranch hands think I'm a child and a nitwit. They don't expect much out of me, so I gave them what they expected."

Amazing. He had fooled Shane. "Remind me never to underestimate you. Now, when we get out of the barn, go east and then south toward town, and bring the sheriff."

"What are you going to do?"

"Stop Handley and the others." How he was going to do that, Shane hadn't a clue.

When the stall door jerked open, Shane spun around.

Decker cursed and drew his gun. "Handley! We got a problem!"

Shane lifted his hands.

Handley appeared in the doorway and shook his head. "Don't make me regret not putting a bullet in you." He removed his revolver. "On your knees."

Shane lowered to one and then the other.

Rolf knelt as well.

"Not you, Kid. You're coming with us."

"No! Leave him out of this."

"I need him to make sure you don't cause trouble." Handley shifted his attention to Rolf. "Give me the ropes."

Shane hoped he hadn't made things worse for the boy.

Rolf stood and tossed them at the foreman's feet. "Oops. Missed."

"You're a cocky one, Kid." Handley scooped up the rope. "Now get Huckleberry's lead and bring him out here."

"You're stealing my horse and taking the boy? You know you'll hang for all of this."

"I won't hang if they don't catch me."

Shane prayed Rolf remained safe. He was a good kid. And Nicole would be heartbroken if anything happened to him.

∞

Once in her buckskins, Nicole saddled Queenie. Hopefully she could get to Sarah's by dark.

"Nicole? Are you out here?"

Aunt Henny. She didn't want to talk to her. Or anyone. Nicole wanted to disappear without a fuss. Like Shane had done. She sighed. "I'm in Queenie's stall."

Aunt Henny appeared in the doorway. "Mercy. What are you up to?"

"I'm going up to the cabin for the rest of the winter."

"Why? What about your cousins?"

"They don't need me. They have a real family now."

"That's not true. You will always be family to them."

But Nicole never really had been family to them. Grandpa had stolen those boys. No matter how hard she continued to blink, her vision didn't improve.

Aunt Henny sat on the same hay bale Nicole had a little bit ago. "Come sit and tell me what this is really about."

Nicole fished Shane's letter out of her saddle bag and handed it over. "You were wrong. He doesn't care about me." She remained standing.

Without a word, Aunt Henny read. When she had

finished, she looked up with a smile.

How could his letter make her happy?

Nicole blinked, waiting for the older woman to say something. "See?"

"I do. Probably more clearly than you. Do you want to know what I get from this letter?"

"Yes."

Aunt Henny patted the bale next to her. "Sit."

Nicole did.

"I see a man who cares about you so much, he's willing to let you go to fulfill your dreams. A man who doesn't feel worthy of you. A man whose heart is breaking to let you go."

Nicole snatched the letter back. "Where does it say all that?"

"Between the lines."

Nicole frantically read to find the meanings the older woman found in it.

"He's freeing you to be with Lamar Kesner."

Blinking, Nicole lifted her gaze. "But I don't want to be with him."

"I know. What is it about Mr. Keegan that you like?"

What was there not to like? "He was the first person to be kind to me when I arrived, scared and alone. I could tell right off he was a good person even though he kept taking my hat. He didn't laugh at me when I spoke of things I shouldn't have. But when he did laugh, it tickled my insides and woke up my heart. He wanted to protect me and my cousins from the Sewells. He took Rolf in to keep him from running away. There are so many things. Oh, and he's pleasing to look at."

"That he is. If you feel this way about him, shouldn't you tell him before you run away? I think he feels the same way about you."

"I hoped he did, and then he left this letter. He doesn't care about me. He wants me to go away to finishing school and Europe."

"No. He wants you to be happy. He thinks finishing school and Europe will make you happy."

"They won't."

"But Shane will?"

Nicole nodded. "I think so."

"Then you need to find out before you both go riding off and miss your chance at happiness with each other."

"What if he doesn't feel the same?"

"Wouldn't you rather know the truth? You'll be able to make a better decision then."

"How did you get so smart?"

"By learning from a *lot* of mistakes."

If Aunt Henny was right, Shane could be preparing to leave right now. Nicole jumped to her feet and snatched Queenie's reins.

"What are you doing?"

Nicole led her horse outside. "I need to hurry so I don't miss him before he rides off."

"In your buckskins? At least change into your riding skirt."

Nicole slipped her foot into the stirrup and swung up. "I don't want to take the time. What if he's preparing to leave right now?"

Aunt Henny sighed. "Be careful. I'll keep a supper plate warm for you."

Nicole goaded her horse into a gallop.

Twenty-Six

SHANE'S RANCH STRETCHED OUT BEFORE NICOLE, eerily quiet. Pepper and Roxy didn't come out to greet her. No hands in the yard or corral. No Rolf. No anyone. Maybe the hands were out following the tracks of the rustlers. Rolf and Shane were probably in the barn.

She swung down and smoothed her hands along the sides of her buckskins. She wished she'd taken Aunt Henny's advice and worn her riding skirt. Or something better. She liked the split skirt, the best of both trousers and a dress.

Barking came from inside the house. What were Pepper and Roxy doing in there? Shane didn't let them inside. Working dogs belonged outside.

As she straightened, someone grabbed her from behind, pinning her arms to her sides and clamping a hand over her mouth. Her stomach jumped to her throat. She kicked and wriggled but it did no good. His grip was too tight.

The man hissed in her ear. "Keep real quiet." He hurriedly hauled her around the side of the house and to the back.

She continued to struggle. This must have been what Grandpa had been so afraid of. A man carting her off. She wouldn't go without a fight.

He stopped, tightened his grip, and gave her a shake. "Settle down if you want to see that man of yours alive."

Shane? Was this man threatening Shane? Her cooperation for his life?

"That's better. Now, I'm going to remove my hand and release you. Don't be screaming or running off."

His hand loosened incrementally.

Her stomach recoiled at what he planned to do to her. Dare she scream?

"That's good." He removed his hand all the way and turned her to face him.

Bray, the pockmarked man? He'd been so kind to both her and Rolf.

"They got Keegan and your cousin in the barn."

"They? The rustlers?" This man wasn't trying to hurt her but to keep her out of harm's way and help his boss. Her fear shifted from herself to Rolfy and Shane, her insides twisting one way and then another.

"Turns out the rustlers were closer to home than Keegan realized. Handley and the other hands."

"His own men?"

Bray nodded. "Handley tried to get me to join them, but I wouldn't. Even though I've only been working for Keegan a few months, he's been good to me. I need you to go to town and bring the sheriff. I'll keep an eye on things here. If they leave, I'll follow them."

Leave her cousin and Shane when they were in trouble? Never. "I'm not going anywhere until Shane and Rolfy are safe."

"I can't be looking out for you too."

"I can take care of myself."

The pockmarked man narrowed his eyes. "Is there nothin' I can say to convince you to go?"

She planted her hands on her hips and shook her head. "Not while my cousin and Shane are in danger."

Bray heaved a sigh. "Fine. But do as I say."

She would consider that. "Only if what you say makes sense."

"Women are vexing."

She flashed him a smile. "Thank you. Now, let's free your boss and Rolf."

He gazed up to the top of the house. "I was going to climb up on the roof and wound each of them as they came out of the barn." He patted the revolver strapped to his hip.

"I like your plan. If you can help me get up to the lower branch of that fir tree, I can shimmy up and be out of sight. They won't be expecting someone there."

"You want to climb a tree? But you're a girl."

"I've climbed trees before. No one would suspect

anyone to be up there." True, she'd not climbed a tree in a long time, but she would manage.

"If this works and we get Keegan out of this mess, he'll probably kill me for letting you go up in a tree."

"No, he won't." But that depended on whether his letter held the truth or if Aunt Henny was right about reading between the lines.

"Fire me at the very least."

"You save his hide, and he'll make you foreman. Let's stop yammering and get to climbing."

"You got a gun or anything?"

"My rifle's on my horse. I'll go get it." She started striding for the side of the house when Bray grabbed her arm.

"Too risky. Someone might see you. I only got my revolver."

Remembering her own handgun, she retrieved the derringer Shane had chosen for her from the top of her knee-high moccasins.

Bray stared at the small weapon.

"I know it's not much, but it's all I have." It was designed for close up. How would she hit anything at this distance?

"It's better than nothing."

But not much better. She wished she could get her rifle but agreed it was too risky.

Bray peered around the side of the house. "No one's in the yard. Wait here." He hustled over to the tree in question and ducked behind the trunk. After glancing toward the barn, he waved her over.

She scuttled as fast as she could and glanced up. The lowest limb was higher than she realized.

He lowered to one knee and patted the one that was level. "Step here and then up onto my shoulders."

"You want me to stand on your shoulders?"

He nodded. "Steady yourself with the trunk, and I'll stand. You shouldn't have any trouble reaching where you need to."

She tucked her derringer back into the top of her moccasin boot, put her foot on his horizontal thigh, and paused. "Do you think Handley and the others will hurt

Rolfy and Shane?"

"It's hard to say. It depends on how desperate they are. Now hurry, before someone comes."

She pushed off the ground and put one foot and then the other on his shoulders. Would he be able to stand with all her weight?

As though she weren't even there, he stood.

She scrambled onto the branch. Grateful now for her buckskins, she moved up the tree, branch after branch and found a spot where the limbs parted enough for her to clearly see the opening of the barn.

Decker exited the barn and headed for Queenie in front of the house. He scanned the area as though searching for the horse's rider and headed around the side of the building. She willed Bray to hurry. She wanted to call out to him to warn him, but then she would reveal herself. He wasn't fast enough.

Decker pointed his gun at Bray and cocked it. "Come on down."

Bray stilled and jumped to the ground.

Decker wiggled his gun. "Take out your Colt real easy and throw it away."

The man obliged, tossing it near the base of the tree Nicole was in.

"Bray, Handley was afraid you'd muck things up. He thought sending you to town would have taken care of you long enough for us to get away."

Nicole might be able to hit him at this distance but was in an awkward position. She couldn't reach her derringer without making her presence known. It was best if she remained still and hidden.

Decker pointed toward Nicole's horse. "Whose horse is that?"

"Mine."

"That ain't yours. Not the one you left here on."

"I borrowed it. Mine went lame. The reason I had to return so soon."

Nicole prayed the ranch hand didn't notice the stirrups were cinched too short for the tall man.

"So you came back and decided to climb on the roof?"

Bray shrugged.

"Grab the reins. We can always use another horse. We're taking her to the barn. I'll tie you up with the others."

Bray took the reins, but Queenie wouldn't have it. She tossed her head and reared, pulling the leather strips from Bray's grasp. Once free, the black horse ran away.

Nicole prayed Queenie didn't go far.

The two men continued their pursuit toward the barn.

Queenie pranced up the road, down the hill to the side of it, and returned toward the house, stopping near the tree Nicole sat perched in. Her horse proved to be more of a blessing every day.

It was up to Nicole to free them all. She had two shots in her derringer. If all the other hands were in on the rustling, her two bullets wouldn't be nearly enough. She wished she could get down and nab the revolver Bray had tossed in her direction. But then how would she get back up again? Her rifle would be better. She willed Queenie to come a bit closer. The horse remained pulling at the grass.

The hand named Klem came out of the barn and strolled over to where Queenie grazed. "Hey, boss!"

Flattening her ears against her head, Queenie gave a warning snort and pawed the ground.

Handley appeared in the barn doorway. "Come on! We're almost ready in here."

"Isn't this that horse Keegan's sweetheart bought?"

Handley cursed. "Find her!" The foreman disappeared back into the barn.

There went her element of surprise. She aimed her derringer at Klem. Dirt sprayed wide to his left. She missed. This bitty thing wasn't worth much. She shot again but closer to his feet. Out of ammo.

He ducked and backed up. "Where'd those come from?"

While the man scrambled, Nicole jumped from the bottom branch, tucked, rolled, snatched Bray's Colt, rolled to her stomach, aimed, and winged Klem in his shooting arm. She couldn't believe she hit something with a short-barreled gun.

He dropped his weapon and clasped the wound.

"Don't move, or I'll shoot you again."

Klem cursed.

"Look out!" came from deep within the barn a second before a shot rang out and grass erupted near her left shoulder.

She rolled back behind the tree.

Several more shots ricocheted around the tree. Then hoofbeats of multiple horses took off at a fast speed. Nicole waited for the racing animals to fade into the distance before venturing to move from behind the trunk. She inched out cautiously to make sure none of the rustlers had stayed behind. No one remained in sight. When no more bullets flew in her direction, she figured they had all gone—including the injured one—and raced for the barn. "Rolfy? Shane? Bray?"

"In here." Shane's voice came from one of the stalls.

She rushed over and opened the door.

Shane and Bray lay in the straw in the empty stall tied together. She knelt beside them and quickly untied the ropes.

Once freed, Shane wrapped his arms around Nicole. "Are you all right?"

She liked the feel of being in his arms and smiled up at him. "I'm fine." *Very fine.* "How about you?"

"I'm alive, thanks to you. I saw you do your tuck and roll. I'll never grow tired of seeing that."

She scanned the stall. "Where's Rolfy?"

"Handley took him out the back. Says he knows who he belongs to. Gonna get a reward."

Nicole's insides twisted, and her eyes burned with tears. "Poor, Rolfy. He must be so scared."

"He's a smart boy. He's stronger than you think. I won't rest until I get him back."

Neither would Nicole.

Shane shook Bray's hand. "Thank you for being loyal."

"Before you and me come to the ranch, they were already here and loyal to each other."

"And your loyalties lie with me?"

"I'm here, ain't I? I had my suspicions about the others but not enough to bring to you, boss."

Shane gave a nod as though he understood. "They took all the horses so we can't follow them."

Bray thumbed over his shoulder. "My horse is tied up in the trees."

"Queenie's in the yard."

"Perfect. Nicole, you ride into town. Tell the sheriff what's gone on here and have him bring some men. Bray and I will double up and ride to the nearest ranch to borrow another horse."

Nicole glared at him. He didn't really expect her to ride *away* from danger? Not when her kin was in trouble.

"We'll find Rolf. I promise."

"He may not be blood kin, but he's family just the same. I'm going after my cousin. You two men can do what you want."

Bray lowered his head and shook it. "You ain't gonna talk her into nothin' she don't want to do."

Shane heaved a sigh. "I know. I thought it was worth a try. I heard one of the hands say something about heading south. If we cut over to Turner's ranch, he'll loan us a horse." He grabbed his Colt from where Handley had discarded it in the barn and holstered it.

At Nicole's mount, Shane gripped a stirrup strap and lowered the stirrup. "I'm taking the reins. I know the way. Turner knows me." He rounded the other side of the horse and did the same there. "If he sees you first, he'll think something's up. So I'm taking the reins."

Nicole raised an eyebrow. He was babbling. How cute. She would tease him about it, but now wasn't the time. "Well, don't stand there jabbering, climb on up so I can too."

His serious expression turned quizzical, but he swung up and held out his hand for her to climb up behind him.

She did so and wrapped her arms around his waist, leaning into him. Not that she couldn't take care of herself, but he made her feel safe.

Twenty-Seven

SHANE RODE TOWARD TURNER'S RANCH AT a slower pace than he'd like. He didn't want to tire Queenie with two riders. They may have a long haul before they caught up with Handley's gang. He couldn't believe he'd been so blind to his foreman's animosity, but the man had always called him boss, almost emphasizing it. Shane had foolishly believed it had been to solidify Shane's position to the other hands.

If it weren't for the rustlers gaining a lead on him, he'd go even slower to keep Nicole close to him like this, with her arms wrapped around him. He should tell her she didn't need to hold on to him to stay atop the horse, but he wouldn't. She probably hadn't seen his letter and read it, or else she wouldn't be holding on to him this way. She wouldn't have risked her life to save his.

"Did you mean all those things you said in your letter?"

He swallowed hard. She had read it. "Let's talk about it later."

"Aunt Henny thinks you meant different things than what you wrote on the page. I thought your letter meant you didn't care for me."

Oh, he cared for her all right. More than he should.

"But Aunt Henny thinks you do care for me by saying you don't. She said it was between the lines, but I couldn't see anything there."

No, she wouldn't. She hadn't spent her life trying to interpret people's motives and words to figure out what they actually meant. Whether a person's, "Sure I'll help you," was true, or they really intended to plant a knife between your shoulder blades the minute you turned around. He'd grown careless and had gotten stabbed in the back.

There had been so much he'd wanted to say to her but held his tongue.

"Is it because of my buckskins? I can be more of a lady. I can try harder and go to one of those finishing schools."

"You're fine as you are, but I want you to become every bit the lady you want to be. If you feel you need more schooling, I'd never keep you from that."

"I don't think I could be fancy like Mrs. Kesner, but I'd do all right being like Aunt Henny. I'm not ready to part with my buckskins, though. They serve a certain purpose. Like climbing a tree. I wouldn't want to do that in a dress."

He smiled at the memory of her dropping out of the tree to the ground. He hadn't been the only one surprised at her presence. He'd been fortunate enough to be poised in the stall with the door open to have a direct line of sight out through the main big entrance.

"Or riding to rescue Rolfy. My riding skirt would be all right, but my buckskins are probably better. I wouldn't want to wear them all the time like I used to because I really like wearing dresses, but wearing fancy gowns all the time is tiring. There are so many things I can't do. And I had to be so careful in that Christmas soirée getup. Too much fuss over a single outfit. Do you know that those dresses take another person to get a body into them? What good are beautiful clothes if I can't even dress myself?"

That did seem silly. He had never realized rich people's clothes were so difficult to put on.

"Did Rolfy tell you that the Millers are going to move to Kamola?"

"He did." Shane had been glad to hear that. He liked the kid.

"They plan to buy a house here for them and the boys. I suppose that's good."

He heard the sadness in her voice at not being included in the new arrangements. But it would free her to travel the world. He should stop her prattling, but he liked listening to her voice, a salve for his battered soul. He loved her too much to keep her from her destiny.

Good thing she sat behind him or he would kiss her, and that would undo his resolve to leave.

"I suppose I'll stay at Aunt Henny's...until I have—until I figure out someplace else to go. If I had someplace or someone to go to, I could leave the woman in peace. She's been ever so kind to me and the boys, but I can't live in her boarding house forever. I'll have to go somewhere else. I liked dancing with you at Mrs. Kesner's party."

Shane sensed those were all hints for him. Kamola was the one place he'd felt as though he belonged. Ever. The one place he wanted to stay. But if he remained, he would ruin her life, rob her of a future of fine dresses, a future of fancy balls, and a future of trips to Europe and around the world. He would not allow her to be deprived of who she could become because of him. "I can't stay, Nicole."

She didn't respond. She didn't move. Her breathing didn't change.

Had she heard him? He'd kept his voice low because he didn't want Bray to overhear. "Nicole?"

Nothing.

"Nicole, did you hear me?"

"You could stay if you wanted to." She had heard.

"I can't. I'm a wanderer." His chest ached. "A saddle tramp leading a life alone on the trail." He'd been a loner from a young age. He'd had no one to look out for him but himself. His heart ached to stay put for a change. He'd wandered in search of a place to belong. He didn't want to wander anymore, but he'd have to a little longer for her sake. Until he found a new place to belong.

"Take me with you. Rolfy and Bucky have their grandparents. I'm like you. I have no one."

She wasn't like him. She'd had her grandfather to count on, and she'd always have her cousins.

"I can't. The trail is no place for a lady."

"I'm no lady. Just look how I'm dressed."

"Buckskins can't disguise who you truly are."

"I'll never be a lady." She removed her arms from around his waist and pushed away from his back.

His chest tightened, and his throat closed. He didn't

want to do this, but he needed to be strong. She was naive and had too little experience in the world to know what was best for her. Shane was *not* what was best for her.

He wanted her to yell and rail at him. But she sat mutely behind him. There, but not there.

Once at Turner's, Shane stopped Queenie and hopped down. His neighbor was more than happy to loan him a horse and saddled it for him.

His neighbor had also lost cattle to the rustlers. "I can't believe it was Bristol's men—and now yours. I've known them all for years. I wish I had hands to send with you, but they are out on various tasks. One of which is looking for my missing cows. But I can ride along with you."

Turner *would* make the numbers a little more even, but Shane needed him elsewhere. "What would help more is if you would go into town and inform the sheriff. I believe the rustlers went south. You and the sheriff can catch up to us."

"Good idea."

Nicole swiveled her head toward Turner. "Tell Aunt Henny I won't be home for supper."

Turner gave a nod and raced off.

Now that they each had their own mount, they could travel faster. He had no fear Nicole couldn't keep up, or that she would slow them down. But he did miss having her close with her arms around him. He missed that a lot.

Three against five. And the rustlers had Rolf as a hostage. Not great odds, but not bad either. He was a good shot and had no doubt Nicole could hold her own and wasn't reckless either. He remembered her words from their first meeting, *Grandpa said move fast or die.*

He wished the sheriff would rendezvous with them before they found Handley and the others to even the odds or tip them in his favor.

Bray was the only wild card in this whole thing. If he was indeed on Shane's side, that was good, though he didn't know how the man would handle himself in a stressful situation. And there was the chance that the man would betray him and be loyal to Handley. In that case, the odds stunk. Six to two with a traitor close at hand. He hoped Bray was as trustworthy as he claimed, or Shane and Nicole could be heading straight into a trap.

Even though it was only mid-afternoon, the sun hung low in the winter sky. A shadow across the trail caught Nicole's attention. She reined in and swung down. The hoof tracks they'd been following shifted direction.

Shane and Bray dismounted as well and studied the ground.

Nicole touched one of the impressions. "The horses turned left and headed that way."

Shane chuckled.

Was he laughing at her? If not for Rolfy's safety, she would have parted ways from him at Turner's place. "Don't you believe me?"

"I believe you." Shane pointed. "That's the same dell I told Handley rustlers might hide some stolen cattle in. He dismissed the idea but checked it out anyway, knowing the cattle were there, right where he'd put them. He played me the fool, with all the aces up his sleeve. He must have had a good laugh at my ignorance."

Nicole glanced toward the dell, pushing aside the pain of Shane's rejection. Somewhere in that direction her cousin sat afraid.

"How far ahead do you think they are?" Shane asked.

"It's hard to say. I don't hear any voices traveling this way to us, so far enough to not be heard." She removed her rifle scabbard from her saddle and strapped it to her back. "To be safe, we should leave the horses here." She looped Queenie's reins over a tree branch. "I'll go on ahead. You two follow at a safe distance. When I locate them, I'll double back to let you know where they are."

Shane seemed to choke on his breath. "You aren't the one who is going first and certainly not alone." He tethered his horse as well.

Nicole held out her moccasined foot. "These are

quieter than your boots. I *am* going."

Shane stared wide-eyed and glanced at Bray.

The other man shrugged. "She makes sense. I think she can handle herself. She's not a prissy lady afraid to get dirty."

No, Nicole wasn't a lady at all. That saddened her. "Don't forget to stay at a safe distance." She headed toward the dell.

In a loud whisper, Shane called after her. "Nicole. Stop."

She continued on, ignoring his protest. She was the logical choice to be the one to traverse ahead with her soft moccasins. Nicole had played this game of sneaking up on her cousins all the time. She always won, by not only be the quietest but also by anticipating their moves. Bucky was the easiest to best, but Rolfy had been improving and was getting harder to creep up on, as well as being stealthier in his approaches.

Soon, she heard the slight crunch of footfalls on the ground coming from behind her. She kept silently moving forward. After a few minutes, muted voices ahead reached her. She spun around and hurried as silently as possible to where Shane and Bray were.

When she stepped out in front of Shane, he opened his mouth and sucked in a startled breath. She slapped her hand over his mouth to keep him from giving away their approach.

Bray stopped behind him.

Shane took her hand in both of his and spoke softly. "You startled me."

The feel of his hands surrounding hers sent a shiver along her spine. "That's because I'm noiseless." Hopefully, when this was all over, she'd have a chance to convince him she could be enough of a lady for him. Though this current situation contradicted that. No lady would slip through the woods in moccasins. Shane wouldn't want her. Not after witnessing her today.

"Did you find them?"

She returned her focus to the task at hand. "I heard faint voices ahead. I turned around to let you know to make sure they didn't hear us."

"So you don't know exactly where they are?"

"They shouldn't be far. I don't even know if it's them."

Shane scowled. "It's gotta be them. Lead the way."

The rustlers' camp came into view near sunset. She hid behind an outcropping of rocks with Shane and Bray. Rolfy sat at the base of a scraggly tree with his hands tied around behind it. He must be so scared. She wanted to run to her cousin, but all that would accomplish would be to get herself caught.

Once all the rustlers were accounted for and the horses located, Shane waved her and Bray back the way they had come.

After dark would be the best time to make their move.

Shane laid out the plan. Bray would knock out the guard closest to them. Shane would circle around and untether the rustlers' horses to cause a distraction, and Nicole would sneak up behind Rolfy, freeing him and then waiting for the commotion of the loose horses.

Shane pinned Nicole with his gaze. "I need to know you are going to follow this plan. I need to know I can count on you to be where I expect you to be when I expect you to be there. No deciding to do something different because you thought of it."

"Your plan seems sound. I'll follow it." The first thing she cared about was her cousin's safety, then she would help with the rest of the plan. Which was how Shane had laid it out.

They each headed off to get into position.

Nicole slipped silently to a boulder near her cousin and waited for the right moment to steal behind him and cut his ropes. The lowing of cattle came from nearby. She made a soft animal call to alert Rolfy to her presence so he wouldn't be surprised when she surfaced behind him. Her cousin nodded his head. He had heard. Now, all she needed to do was wait.

Woods scrubbed his hand across his bewhiskered mouth. "I say we drive the cattle south right now. Keegan's been long loose by now. What if he's coming this way?"

Handley shook his head. "Too hard to keep track of the whole herd in the dark. We'll lose too many. Keegan doesn't know which direction we went. By the time he goes into town, whines to the sheriff, and picks a direction, it'll be too dark for him to find his own backside let alone us. We'll be out of here at dawn, and he will never catch us."

Nicole wanted to laugh. Not only had they caught up to Handley and the others, but they planned to best them before they had their supper.

At present, one man guarded the way they had come, which Bray was to render unconscious. Another man stood guard near the rustlers' horses, which Shane was going to take care of. That left Handley, Woods, and Tommy Pine here by the fire.

Handley and Woods milled about the camp, apparently getting ready to cook their grub. Tommy Pine squatted by the small ring of rocks, adding wood to the fire. Handley called him over with a mundane order, which resulted in Woods joining them to see what the fuss was about.

This left Nicole free to slither up behind her cousin and cut the rope. "Don't move. Pretend you're still bound."

Rolfy nodded.

The men circled the fire, warming their hands and trapping Nicole in her spot behind her cousin. In the waning light, if she didn't move, they might not see her with her buckskins blending into the ground and shadows. Another reason to be grateful to be wearing them. She lay as still as possible and prayed no one came over to check on Rolfy. It shouldn't be long before Shane made his move.

Handley drew his gun and looked around. "Something ain't right."

The other two men drew their weapons as well. "What is it, boss?" one of them asked.

"Doesn't feel right. You two go check on Decker and Klem."

Oh, dear. She willed Shane to get this rescue moving, before both he and Bray were each outnumbered two to one.

As though he heard her thoughts, the horses galloped through the camp, cutting Woods off from the other two.

Nicole jumped to her feet, helped Rolfy stand, and pulled him out of harm's way.

Then everything seemed to happen at once.

Woods swung his gun around toward Nicole and Rolfy. She pushed her cousin behind the boulder and dove after him as the man got off a shot. She grabbed Rolfy's shoulders and inspected for a wound. "Did you get hit?"

He swatted her hands away. "No. I'm fine."

Relieved, Nicole removed her rifle from the scabbard on her back and peered out around the boulder.

A cacophony of chaos ensued. Men swinging fists at one another. A horse rearing. And another gunshot.

Nicole couldn't tell who had fired or at whom. Between the waning light and the dust being kicked about into the air, she dared not take a shot, lest she hit Shane or Bray.

From behind her, she heard, "Drop your rifle, mister."

She spun around to find Woods holding Rolfy in front of him, pointing his revolver at her. Her heart sank. She had been foolish not to pay attention to the vulnerability of someone coming around the boulder.

"I said drop it."

Nicole had no choice. She bent, laying her rifle on the ground.

"Now, step away from it."

She did.

The ruckus behind her in the camp seemed to have calmed. Who had prevailed? Shane? Or the rustlers?

Then suddenly Woods raised his hands and let go of Rolfy.

Shane, standing behind the man, took his gun. "You two all right?"

Relief swept through Nicole. "We're fine."

Shane guided Woods over to the center of camp. Rolfy retrieved Nicole's rifle, and the pair of them followed.

The firelight illuminated Bray holding Tommy Pine on the ground, tying his hands behind him.

Handley lay unconscious—hopefully not dead—on the other side of the fire.

Then he moved.

He lifted his head.

Shifted his arm around.

And aimed his gun at Shane.

Could Nicole get to him in time to stop him?

Doubtful.

And she had no gun.

So she lunged.

Bang!

Twenty-Eight

SHANE JERKED TOWARD THE SUDDEN MOVEMENT to his right as the shot rang out.

Nicole slammed into him.

He snapped his arms around her collapsing body and sank to the ground with her. "Nicole?"

Dancing firelight flickered off the liquid oozing through the hole in her buckskin shirt on the upper left side of her chest. Though the red color could be from the firelight, his brain told him it was blood. But not just any blood, human blood. Nicole's blood.

His surroundings dimmed. A locomotive roared through his head. His chest ached.

Don't do it, Shane. Don't let this get to you. Not now.

He pushed the debilitating feelings aside and forced himself to press his hand to the wound.

Things returned to focus, and Nicole was speaking, but her words were garbled to him. He focused, and they became clearer.

"Rolfy, don't do it. Rolfy, don't do it. Rolfy, don't do it."

He shifted his attention. The boy stood with one foot on the back of Handley's neck and had the rifle barrel pressed to the man's head.

No! The boy didn't want to cross that line of taking a human life. Shane opened his mouth and told the boy not to do it. But did the words actually come out?

Bray had wrestled Tommy Pine to the ground and was binding his hands behind him. The pockmarked-faced man stood and crossed over to Rolf. "You don't want to do that, Kid."

"He shot Nick." Rolf's voice wavered from tears. "He doesn't deserve to live."

Bray inched his hand toward the rifle. "That may be,

but let the law take care of that." Bray wrapped his fingers around the weapon and eased it away from Rolf. "Now, tie him up."

Once Rolf was done, Bray knelt in front of Shane. "How bad is it?"

Embarrassed that he didn't know, Shane glanced away, not willing to look at the wound and risk passing out. He would be no good to Nicole if he did that. He hated this weakness in himself, but Nicole needed him. "I'm not sure. She was talking." That had to be good. Right?

Nicole lay still with her eyes closed, but her chest rose and fell in shallow breaths. She rested on his thighs and against his chest.

Bray pointed to Shane's hand pressed to her injured shoulder. "Can I take a gander?"

Shane didn't want to think what lay beneath but removed his hand. Blood oozed, and his insides betrayed him again with the roaring train and dimming vision. His chest tightened in pain.

Pull yourself together, Shane. Nicole needs you.

He did the best he could to not think of it as human blood—as Nicole's blood—to clear his vision and to silence the noise inside him.

"I need to get a better look." Bray slipped the tip of his knife into the hole in the buckskin. With the leather pulled away from her skin, the oozing to the outside stopped. "Hold her still." He cut a slit and then ripped it the rest of the way with his fingers. Red liquid oozed onto an already blood-stained undergarment. Bray tore that one as well.

Rolf stood over them, staring in horror.

Bray studied the wound. "Did the bullet go through?"

Shane shook his head. "I don't know." He struggled to hold himself together...but he must.

Bray slipped his hand around behind. "I feel blood, so the bullet isn't lodged inside. Good."

Was it? Now, she had two holes in her...leaking blood.

"Give me your bandanas." The ranch hand spoke to both Shane and Rolf and removed his own. He folded two of the pieces of cloth to a clean area, pressed one to the front and one to the back, and tied the third one around Nicole's armpit to keep the other two in place, more or less. "We need to get her to a doctor."

Yes, a doctor. "Help me stand with her."

Bray held out his hands. "I can take her."

"No, I will." He wanted to keep her close.

"All right." Bray motioned to Rolf. "You get that side, Kid."

Shane adjusted Nicole into his arms, and Bray and Rolf helped him to stand.

"The horses are all down the trail." Bray angled Shane toward a boulder. "Sit here, and I'll get one."

Shane shook his head. "She can't wait. I need to get her to the doctor as quickly as possible." He took a couple of feeble steps. His legs as weak as a newborn baby's.

Rolf trotted a few steps. "I'll run ahead while you walk and bring back a horse and meet you along the way." The boy took off down the trail and disappeared into the night.

Yes, that would be the fastest.

"Are you going to be all right if I lag behind to secure these fools to a tree and catch up to you?"

"We'll be fine." Though Shane felt weak all over, he put one foot in front of the other. Focusing on his steps rather than the bl—

Don't think about that, Shane. Think only of getting her to the doctor. Lord, protect Nicole and keep her alive.

His body gained strength. He appreciated Bray making sure the rustlers didn't get away.

He didn't know how far he'd gone when Rolf came running up leading Bray's horse, the mount borrowed from Turner, and Queenie. "Some of the loose horses stopped by the ones you had tethered."

The black horse hurried up to Shane, sniffed Nicole, and flapped its ears, agitated. Did Nicole's horse sense her life draining away?

Bray caught up to them as well. He and Rolf helped Shane up onto Queenie with Nicole. Rolf mounted Turner's horse.

Bray remained on the ground. "If you two can handle things, I'm going to round up the rustlers and walk them out."

"We'll be fine." Shane tapped his heels on Queenie's sides, and the horse trotted into motion.

At the entrance to the dell, Turner, the sheriff, and a few other men stood with a couple of the loose horses. The sheriff stepped forward. "Is everyone all right?"

"Nicole has been shot. I need to get her to a doctor. Bray is up the trail. He has the rustlers. He could use some help."

The sheriff and his men headed off, and Shane and Rolf continued on their way.

Shane checked Nicole's breathing every couple of minutes and prayed in between.

Once close to town, Shane said, "Hurry on ahead, find the doctor, and have him meet us at Aunt Henny's." He didn't want to risk riding to the other side of town to the doctor's clinic.

Without a word, Rolf goaded his horse into a gallop.

With the boy gone, the roaring train inside Shane's head picked up speed, and the pain in his chest stabbed. He hadn't realized how comforting it had been to have another person with him. It wouldn't be long now before Aunt Henny would be at hand to help him. "We're almost there, Nicole. Hold on a little longer."

He stopped in front of the boarding house. Lights still glowed downstairs. He shifted his weight to dismount. When Nicole moaned, he froze. What if he dropped her in his weakened state? Blood had bothered him from a young age but never this bad. But then, he didn't usually see someone he loved bleeding.

So, if he shouldn't dismount, he needed to get the attention of the people inside. He drew his Colt to shoot into the air, but that might startle Nicole and definitely scare those inside. He holstered it. If there wasn't a fence, he'd ride right up to the porch.

Only one option left. "Aunt Henny!" He hoped he was loud enough to be heard. He yelled over and over until the curtain in the parlor momentarily pulled aside.

The front door opened, and Aunt Henny's silhouette

stood in the framed opening. "Mr. Keegan? Is that you?"

"Yes. I need help. It's Nicole."

The older woman pulled her shawl tighter, hastened down the steps, and out the front gate. Behind her came three of her boarders, the Millers and Professor Tunstall. Aunt Henny reached them. "What happened?"

"She's been shot. Rolf went to get the doctor."

"Mercy. Let's get her inside. You can tell me how this came about later."

The professor and Mr. Miller moved to the front of the pack, and Shane eased Nicole down into their arms. With Aunt Henny's direction, they carried Nicole into the house.

Only Mrs. Miller remained. "Aren't you coming?"

Shane swung down, and when his feet hit the ground, his knees buckled, but thanks to his grip on the saddle horn, he didn't collapse to the ground.

Mrs. Miller put her arm around Shane. "Are you all right?"

"I don't do well with human blood."

"A lot of people don't." She took Queenie's reins and draped them over the fence.

"Don't tell anyone."

"I won't." She guided him toward the gate opening. "Let's get you into the house."

"I'm not usually this bad." He straightened to support himself but let her keep her arm around his waist just in case.

"It's understandable. You care a great deal for Nicole."

He did. He shouldn't have let himself fall so completely for her. It would make leaving that much harder.

Once inside, voices came from the back room.

Mrs. Miller helped him out of his coat and hung it on the coat tree bench. When she swung around to face him, she gasped. "You're bleeding."

Shane glanced down at the red stain in the middle of his chest and shook his head. "That's Nicole's." His head buzzed and grew light.

The woman grasped his arm and moved him to a

chair in the parlor.

He sat. He was tired. His body ached. His chest felt as though a stampeding herd had trampled across it. The roaring in his head had quieted to a distant train.

Mrs. Miller knelt in front of him. "Let me take a little look." She drew in a quick breath. "You've been shot too."

He stared at the red on his shirt. That meant this blood wasn't Nicole's. Good. The lights in the room dimmed to blackness.

Twenty-Nine

THE PAIN PIERCED NICOLE'S CHEST LIKE nothing she'd felt before. It hurt to breathe. It hurt to move. It hurt to lie still.

"Are you hurting?" came a female voice from beside her.

Nicole nodded, or at least thought she had. She forced one eye open.

Mrs. Miller sat next to the bed, holding a spoon and pouring liquid from a brown bottle into it. "This is laudanum. It will help."

Nicole lifted her head, winced, and dropped back onto the pillow. "I can't."

"That's all right." The woman who was stealing her cousins slipped her hand behind Nicole's head and lifted it. The pain wasn't as bad with her help. "Open your mouth and let the medicine slide down your throat."

Nicole did, then her head lowered. She blinked several times to get her eyes to stay open. A lamp burned low on the bedside table, and the window revealed the inky black of night. The room was not her own. "Where am I?"

"Henny's bedroom."

Yes, she remembered now from the couple of times she'd come in here. "Why are you helping me?"

"Because you're family." The woman motioned to the other side of the room.

On the floor, wrapped in quilts, lay Rolf and Bucky bundled together, sleeping.

"Henny tried to get them to sleep in their own room, but they wanted—no, needed—to be close to you."

In a ladder-back chair, Shane half-lay, stretched out with his legs straight and crossed at the ankles, his arms folded, and his hat pulled over his eyes. How could anyone sleep like that?

"He's been here the whole time."

"So, he's all right?"

"You are quite the hero. You saved his life. The bullet you took went clean through and lodged between two of his ribs over his heart." The older woman patted her chest. "It would have killed him."

Nicole smiled to herself. Shane was alive, and Rolfy was safe. That was all that mattered.

"Rolf told us all about what you did, not only in saving Mr. Keegan, but rescuing our grandson." The older woman put her hand tenderly on Nicole's arm. "Though we came for our grandsons, we want to get to know you as well. You are kin to our boys, so you are kin to us. We want to be *your* grandparents too. You're too old to officially adopt, but we'd liked to unofficially, if you'll have us. We're looking for a house big enough for all five of us. Would you like that?"

They wanted her as part of their family? "I would."

Mrs. Miller smiled wide and squeezed Nicole's arm. "Now that we have that all settled, I'll let your young man know you're awake."

"No, don't."

"Why not?"

"I don't want him to leave." She wanted to watch him sleep. She may need to let him go, but not yet.

As the pain diminished a little at a time, the medicine lassoed her consciousness and dragged it down to sleepiness. She fought to keep her eyes open and on Shane, lest he disappear.

─────

Shane shifted in the chair. His back ached. His head ached. His chest ached. The laudanum must have worn off. He rubbed his chest and winced. The two stitches the doctor had put in hurt as much as the bullet hole. He wrenched his eyes open.

Predawn light tinted the sky.

Rolf and Bucky remained asleep on the floor.

Nicole lay still under the covers. Mrs. Miller sat in a

chair with her head resting on her folded arms on the bed.

Shane stood and crossed to where Nicole slept soundly.

Mrs. Miller lifted her head. She kept her voice low. "You're awake. How are you feeling?"

Shane whispered back, "I'm fine. How's Nicole?"

"She woke up a couple of hours ago. I gave her laudanum, and she's sleeping peacefully now."

"So, she's going to be all right?"

"She'll be fine."

Good. Shane moved toward the door.

"You aren't leaving, are you?"

If he didn't while he still had the courage, he might lose his nerve. "I kind of need to."

"Oh, I understand. I'll see you when you return."

Let the woman believe she knew his reason for leaving. He gave a nod and slipped from the room.

He tiptoed out into the hall. He would go straight to the barn. Someone had likely brought Huckleberry with the other loose horses from the rustlers' camp and stabled at least his horse last night after Rolf arrived with the doctor.

"Where are you sneaking off to?" came a whispered voice.

Shane lifted his gaze.

Aunt Henny stood a few feet down the hallway, holding a laden tray, blocking his escape route.

He pressed himself against the wall so she could go past. "I don't want to keep you."

"If you think you can steal away and leave that young lady, think again."

His eyebrows twitched. "Why would you think that?"

"A certain letter you wrote her."

That's right, she'd read that. "I'm no good at goodbyes. She's better off without me."

Aunt Henny hoisted the tray at him.

Shane instinctively took it.

"In the parlor. Now, young man."

He gulped. That tone was never good. "Yes, ma'am." He followed in her wake.

Aunt Henny sat on the settee and tilted her head toward the serving table.

He set the tray down. Could he still escape? Better not try. He sat.

"She is *not* better off without you. You're not leaving this house until Nicole wakes up and the two of you talk. Having someone leave without a word is one of the worst things to endure. All the questions and wondering if you could have done something different. The not knowing."

"It'll be easier this way."

"Maybe for you, but not for her. That girl fell hard for you from that first day you brought her here. When she read your letter, she packed her things and was prepared to live as a hermit the rest of her life up on the mountain in a little cabin." She paused and leveled her gaze at him. "All alone."

That's not what he wanted. "You need to encourage her to stay in town. She needs someone like Lamar Kesner who can give her fancy dresses, present her at elegant balls, and take her to Europe and around the world. I can't give her any of that."

"All those things mean nothing without the person you love to share them with. She literally took a bullet for you. If she hadn't, you would be dead. Is this any way to thank her, by sneaking off?"

"No, ma'am."

"Would you truly sentence her to live the rest of her life with a broken heart?"

"She'll soon forget about me with men like Kesner to sweep her off her feet."

"Mr. Kesner is no match for Nicole. She would spend her life trying to change to please the Kesners and society people. She would try and try because that's what she believes she needs to do to be accepted, and she'd be completely miserable. You see who she truly is and love her for it, not in spite of it."

Shane sighed, his chest aching on the inside as well as out. "I'm not good enough for her. She'll realize that sooner or later."

"Sooner or later, you'll realize leaving her would be the biggest mistake of your life." Aunt Henny folded her arms. "If you choose to be a plum fool and leave, you're going to tell her exactly why. If you don't, you'll wish that bullet had killed you."

"You think Nicole would come after me?"

Aunt Henny pointed to herself. "No. I'll be the one hunting you down if you hurt her like that."

Shane swallowed hard. He believed her.

Nicole woke again to a stabbing pain in her chest, but not quite as bad as last time. She blinked her eyes open to bright sunlight streaming in through the window. Miss Tibbins lay in a patch of sunshine on the floor.

Rolf and Bucky were gone, not even the quilts remained as evidence to their previous presence.

The ladder-back chair sat empty. A new pain stabbed inside her chest.

Shane was gone.

Her eyes filled with tears and overflowed in hot rivers down her temples. The ache inside her proved to be more difficult to bear than the wounds on the outside.

He didn't even say goodbye.

When a floorboard creaked in the hallway, she turned her head in that direction as that was all the movement she could muster.

One Bucky-height eye peered in through the partially cracked door and blinked.

Then Rolf's hushed voice. "Bucky, get away from there."

"I think Nick's awake." Bucky pushed the door open and tiptoed in an exaggerated manner.

"I can see you." Nicole grimaced. How could talking hurt so much?

Bucky grinned and picked up his pace. As he was about to leap for the bed, Rolf nabbed him, lifting him off the ground and held him under one arm. "You can't be on the bed. She's hurt." Rolf gazed forlornly at her. "You're going to be all right, aren't you?"

"Yes." Her outward wound would heal, but her heart might never.

Her older cousin continued. "We talked about it, Bucky and me, and we decided to stay with you. We don't care what the lawyers or anyone says. No one can make us live anywhere else."

Bucky nodded from where he dangled from Rolf's arm at his brother's side. The boy's hair flopped around. He needed a haircut.

The Millers obviously hadn't told the boys yet about their new plan. She wouldn't spoil their surprise. Or get her cousins' hopes up if the Millers changed their minds. But she would love to have the boys live with her. "Your grandparents love you very much." She could see that clearly.

"Don't matter."

"We can talk about it later. Is Shane still here?" She hoped so.

Bucky lifted his head. "Nope. He left."

Rolf frowned at his brother and jiggled him. "I think he was coming back."

Nicole doubted that. His letter had been pretty clear. "I need another dose of medicine. Would you tell Aunt Henny or Mrs. Miller?"

Rolf turned to leave with Bucky still tucked under his arm. He hesitated at the doorway. "I'm sure he's coming back."

She didn't want to think about that right now. Soon voices filtered from the other first-floor rooms, but no one came to give her something for her pain. What was taking so long?

The bedside table held the bottle and spoon Mrs. Miller had used during the night. Maybe she could reach it. She steeled herself for the pain she knew was to come with moving. She stretched her arm out and reached back, holding her breath—like that did any real good against the pain—and fingered the bottle. Once in her grasp, she brought it quickly to her chest and hugged it there, then exhaled.

A short respite then the spoon. She didn't relish the thought of reaching for it. Maybe she could drink straight from the bottle. She removed the cork stopper and brought it to her lips.

"Whoa, there." Shane rushed into the room and snatched the bottle and cork from her.

"What are you doing here?" Was it really him? Or was she delirious from the pain?

He sat in the chair beside the bed. "I'd hoped you'd be a bit happier to see me."

"Oh, I am. Bucky said you'd left." Dare she hope he was real?

"Only to run an errand." He retrieved the spoon. "Now, you didn't already swallow any of this, did you?"

She shook her head.

He measured out the liquid.

"I don't want it." She didn't want to sleep again and risk him leaving. Better to suffer with the stabbing sensation.

"Yes, you do. You're in considerable pain." He angled the utensil closer to her face. "Take this, or I won't tell you the two surprises I have for you."

"Promise you won't leave the minute I fall asleep."

His voice took on a compassionate tone. "I won't. Now, take this."

She still wanted to refuse, but the pain was tiring, so she opened her mouth and took the bitter liquid. "Mrs. Miller said you were shot. Are you all right?"

He corked the bottle and placed it on the table with the spoon. "Nothing more than a scratch thanks to you."

"I'd do it again."

"I believe you."

She stretched out her hand. "I'm glad you're here."

He took it in his warm, strong one. "I'm glad I'm here too. Aren't you going to ask me what the surprises are?"

"I don't care as long as you're here."

He gifted her with his lopsided smile. "I think you'll care about these. The first one is contingent on the second one. I've spoken to William and Caroline Miller. They've agreed to come live out on my ranch with the boys rather than buying a house in town."

Rolf would love that, and so would Bucky. "What's the catch?"

Keeping her hand in his, Shane slid off the chair and knelt. He lifted his free hand that held a silver band with a small purple stone. "Will you spend the rest of your life with me?"

She wanted to say yes but hesitated. "I'm not going to finishing school, so I'll never be a proper lady."

"You are the perfect amount of a lady for me. When I first saw you and you ducked out of the way of that rearing horse, I was in awe of you. Then when I discovered you were a girl, I started falling in love with you. I knew I shouldn't. I knew I wasn't good enough, but I couldn't help myself. I'm no fine gentleman like Mr. Kesner, but I do love you and want to spend the rest of my life making you happy."

"I don't want a fancy man. I only ever wanted you. And you are the finest gentleman I know."

"Can I take that as a yes?"

"Yes!"

After slipping the ring onto her finger, he leaned over and kissed her fully on the lips.

She was home with him. It had been as though she had been in a perpetual state of falling since Grandpa died, and Shane had been her solid ground. He was the stabilizing force the Lord had provided from the moment she'd come to Kamola.

Epilogue

April 1894

AT THE KEEGAN RANCH, NICOLE STOOD by the corral with Caroline Miller, watching the men repair the roof of the newly built, three-bedroom cabin for the boys and their grandparents. They had been living in it for a week now, ever since Nicole and Shane's wedding. But yesterday's rain had tested the structure and shown its weaknesses.

Bray and one of the newly hired hands sat straddled on the ridgepole of the cabin, removing shingles, tarring beneath them, and putting on new ones. Shane stood safely on the ground at a chopping block with ax in hand, cutting new wooden slabs.

William Miller supervised Bucky to make sure he remained out of harm's way. The boy took the fresh-cut planks and put them in the bucket on a rope and pulley, where Rolf hoisted them up to the men on the roof.

Nicole pointed toward the cabin. "If it wasn't for this dress, I could go up there and help if they'd let me."

Caroline smiled. "If the women did everything, the men would feel useless."

Nicole didn't want any of them to feel that way. "Time for them to take a break. I'll go get refreshments."

"Do you want some help?"

"I think I can get it all. Stay here in case the men need anything." Nicole went into the ranch house and loaded a tray with a pitcher of cold tea, a pot of hot coffee, glasses, mugs, and a bowl of muffins.

Bucky ran into the kitchen. "Look at what I did." He waved a shingle in the air.

Taking it, Nicole turned the thin slice of wood over. "You made this?"

"Shane started it, but I had to finish it for him. He

couldn't do it. It was a tough one."

So kind of Shane to let Bucky help.

"Very nice." She returned his handiwork. "Would you open the door for me so I can carry this out?"

He swung around and then back. "Oops. I leaved it open."

"*Left* it open." She picked up the laden tray, heavier than she'd expected. "Well then, you can close it after me." She headed out the door.

Shane swung the ax down on a block of wood. He'd become proficient at chopping shingles.

Nicole could watch him all day. Instead, she crossed to the sawhorse table with tools and wood on it where William and Caroline Miller stood, and set the tray down. Nicole tilted back to see beyond the brim of her straw hat up to the men on the roof. "I brought coffee, tea, and muffins."

"Coming down," Bray called.

The recent hire fumbled with the hammer in his hand. The tool slipped from his grasp and slid down the roof. It headed straight for where Nicole's new husband stood, setting the next piece of wood on the chopping block.

As Bray called, "Look out below!" Nicole charged toward Shane, knocking him over and rolling on the ground with him.

His arms latched around her. When they stopped, he lay on his back with Nicole on top of him, her hat askew.

The hammer thudded to the ground right where he'd been standing.

Shane yanked off her hat.

"Hey!" She slapped the top of her head but was too late to stop him.

"You all right?"

"I'm fine, but that hammer would have clonked you on the head."

"*Move fast or die*, like your grandfather always said?"

"Yep."

He offered her his lopsided smile. "So, once again, I owe you my life."

"At this rate, you may be in debt to me forever."

His voice came out raspy. "I already am."
Her heartbeat sprinted into a gallop. When he sounded like that, her knees went weak. Good thing she wasn't standing. "May I have my hat back?"
He replaced it at the same time he pulled her head closer and kissed her.
She loved being married to him. He and the Lord completed her. She loved the feel of his soft lips and longed to deepen their kiss until their very souls touched.
Bucky's head peeked under the wide brim. "Whatcha doin', Nick?"
She broke off the kiss and laughed.
Shane tapped the boy's hat. "I'll explain the allure of fair maidens to you when you're older. Now, go away. I'm kissing my wife." He pulled Nicole back in for another kiss.
Ah, she had the best life. A husband. Her cousins. And the Millers as an extended family. More than she'd imagined when she'd come into town last fall, toting a gun and intent on snagging a husband.

Author Note

The Damsel's Intent, the third in The Quilting Circle series, was a blast to write. After becoming smitten with Shane Keegan in book two, I knew I needed to find him his perfect match and write his tale of love. In strolled Nicole "Nick" Waterby wearing buckskins and toting a gun. I delighted in getting to know this naïve, yet capable young lady. Nicole is among my favorite characters I've created.

I enjoyed exploring how much Nicole would change to get her man and how much she would stay the same. Her transformation consisted mostly of her outward appearance; her inner lady, who had been suppressed her whole life, had a chance to bloom. Inside, she remained the same sweet girl who had come down from the mountain.

Early on in writing this story, I found the image of the models who are on the cover and used them as my inspiration. They are perfect. Not only because of Nicole's great expression showing her intent to get her man, but because her dress is *purple!* I *love* purple, and this dress is *sooooo* beautiful with its gossamer ruffles and lace. I want this dress. I would come up with a reason to wear it a few times a year. Or I might simply waltz around my house in it feeling like a princess.

As a romantic at heart, I love seeing two deserving people find that extra-special someone—even if they are merely figments of my imagination. I hope you enjoyed reading Nicole and Shane's story as much as I did writing it.

In book four of The Quilting Circle series—along with a new couples' romance—I plan to explore Aunt Henny's mysterious past. Why won't this woman tell anyone her last name? It was a little bit of a battle, but I got the information out of her.

Happy Reading!

Mary

☺

If you enjoyed *The Damsel's Intent*, or any of the Quilting Circle series books, I'd love it if you'd consider posting a review on Amazon, Christianbook.com, Goodreads.com, BarnesandNoble.com, BookBub.com or anywhere else books are sold or reviewed. Reviews are a tremendous help to authors! Thank you for anything you can do.

I'd love to connect with you. Readers can find me at:

FaceBook: Mary Davis READERS Group – www.facebook.com/groups/132969074007619/

Blog: marydavis1.blogspot.com

Subscribe to my Newsletter:
marydavisbooks.us17.list-manage.com/subscribe?u=cbe8a2ec4ef27cfcf51813f02&id=82ad258f06

Amazon: www.amazon.com/Mary-Davis/e/B00JKRBJKE

GoodReads:
www.goodreads.com/author/show/8126829.Mary_Davis

BookBub:
www.bookbub.com/profile/mary-davis?list=author_books

DISCUSSION QUESTIONS

1. What was your favorite quote/passage? Why did this stand out and how could you use it in your own life?

2. Which character did you relate to the most, and what was it about them that you connected with? To what extent do they remind you of yourself or someone you know? Do you empathize with the characters? What fears do they each harbor? Have you personally had to deal with similar fears? If so, what helped you overcome?

3. Describe the dynamics between Nicole and her grandpa, Nicole and her "cousins", Nicole and Shane, Shane and Rolf & Bucky. How do the characters change, grow, or evolve throughout the course of the story?

4. Once in town, Nicole embraced her feminine side but still held onto her mountain roots and skills. Her grandpa lived in fear because of his losses and what happened to his daughter, so he raised Nicole—for the most part—as a boy. Would you ever raise a girl as a boy to protect her from harm? How does the Bible verse that it's not good for man, or a person, to be alone play into this?

5. What are the major conflicts in the story? What events in the story stand out for you as memorable? What main ideas—themes—does the author explore? How are they relevant for your life? Do you believe that Christian fiction can actually impact lives, and if so, how?

6. If Nicole had chosen Lamar instead of Shane, what would her "happily ever after" have looked like? Where do you image Shane would have gone, and what would he be doing? Do you know someone who had to choose between two different people to marry? What ramifications can happen if the wrong one is chosen?

7. Did any parts of the book make you uncomfortable? If so, why did you feel that way? Did this lead to a new understanding or awareness of some aspect of your life you might not have thought about before? Has this novel changed you or broadened your perspective?

8. What do you think will be your lasting impression of the book and why? Did the issues that were raised touch or impact you in any way? Would you recommend it to a friend, and if so, why? Can you see yourself reading it again?

9. On several occasions, Aunt Henny saw a man watching—or so she thinks. Do you believe the man she saw was truly watching her or the children? If so, was he watching Nicole? Or the boys? Or Aunt Henny? Who do you think he was? Friend or foe?

Now—A Sneak Peek At

THE DEBUTANTE'S SECRET

The Quilting Circle Book 4
Coming August 1, 2021

One

Central Washington State, Spring 1894

GENEVIÈVE MARSEILLE PEERED THROUGH THE GRIMY train window. This couldn't be right. This couldn't be Kamola, her destination. It was bigger than most of the frontier towns the train had passed through, but not nearly as large as she had imagined or hoped. And nothing like her beloved Paris.

Several dusty cowboy-looking men mingled on the platform. Or were they outlaws? She blinked and blinked again. Was that an *Indian*? She knew the West was lawless and wild, but this was worse than she'd imagined.

A grubby old cowboy on the platform turned to her window, smiled with dirty teeth, and winked at her.

She inhaled sharply and jerked away from the glass.

Her breaths came in short gasps. She had been fortunate enough to have procured a private sleeping compartment. Scarcely enough room for one to turn around in, but better than being forced to mingle with all the other passengers. She didn't do well in crowds of strangers for long periods.

At the knock, she turned around.

Julius, a black porter, slid open the door, his salt and pepper hair proceeding his broad smile. "Miss Marseille, your trunk has been deposited on the platform with your other luggage, and arrangements have been made to have them delivered to the White Hotel. Are you ready to disembark?"

Geneviève shook her head and lowered herself to the bench. "I do not think I can do this."

The kindly porter, who had been a help and comfort to her during her trip, stepped inside but only barely. He understood propriety. "Sure you can, Miss Marseille. You've been around the world, and now you've traveled clean across this country all by yourself."

"But the people look...scary." That sounded silly, but they did. She had no experience outside of polite society, those who were cultured and well educated. "I do not know how to talk to such individuals."

"They's just like you and me. You talk to me just fine. You just don't know them yet. I've traveled from one side of this country to the other many times as a train porter, and you know what I noticed?"

Geneviève shook her head. "What?"

"People is pretty much the same everywhere. And a lot of them are scared, just like you, when they get to a new place."

"You think so?"

"I know so. You come for a purpose. It'd be a shame to not see it through."

She *had* come for a purpose. To prove her brother wrong and to put an end to that charlatan woman who would try to steal any of her family's money. She drew in a deep breath and stood. "You are right, Julius. I can do this." But her insides weren't convinced yet.

"There you go, Miss Marseille. I know'd you could do

it."

What would she do here without the porter? *Grand-mère* would have a fit at Geneviève for being so familiar with a servant. Maybe she was right, but the man had been indispensable. Everything about Geneviève's trip would have given *Grand-mère* the vapors. Traveling alone. Her destination. Her purpose in coming. But if she'd told anyone her plans or brought even a lady's maid, someone would have stopped her. Geneviève had to talk her brother out of his absurd plan.

Julius stepped out of the compartment doorway and aside in the corridor.

She retrieved her reticule and looped the drawstring handles over her gloved wrist. "I wish you could come with me."

He smiled. "You be just fine."

"*Merci beaucoup.*" She straightened her shoulders and headed toward the exit. Rallying her courage, she descended the stairs, ignored the cold April wind nipping at her cheeks, and strode with confidence along the platform. Her progress halted abruptly.

Something had caught hold of her shoe, so she glanced back. Her heel wedged in a knothole and wouldn't pull free. Tugging only managed to release her foot from her shoe. She hopped in a circle to view the trouble.

A ruffian in a brown leather vest and brown hat, not a gentleman's hat or attire, descended on her position. *Oh, dear.* Would she die here and now? What should she do? Run with only one shoe? Scream? Instead, she held her breath. She never should have come.

When he scooped her up into his arms, a squeak escaped her. How dare this man take such liberties, and without even asking? Was he kidnapping her? Would anyone stop him? No one seemed to take notice or care. Would they if she screamed? Was this how men thought they should get a wife out in the untamed West? Well, she wasn't going without a fuss.

Before she could do or say anything, he deposited her on a wooden bench and retrieved her wayward shoe. Upon returning, he knelt in front of her and pointed toward her foot. "May I, ma'am?"

The cowboy had kind brown eyes and an engaging smile. Without thinking about proper etiquette, she poked her stocking foot out from under her skirt.

And like Cinderella in the fairy tale, he slipped her shoe back on. It was no glass slipper and this ruffian was no Prince Charming, but still... "*Merci beaucoup, Monsieur*—I mean thank you, sir."

He tipped his hat. "My pleasure, ma'am. Deputy Montana at your service."

"Deputy?" Her gaze homed in on his tin star. "Why you are not a ruffian at all. You are in law enforcement."

He chuckled, deep and warm. "You thought me a ruffian? Much obliged."

Julius hurried over. "You ah right, Miss Marseille?"

She kept her gaze on the deputy. "I will be fine, Julius. *Merci.*"

The porter nodded and returned to the train.

The deputy nodded to the porter as well then turned back to her. "I can tell you are new in town. May I escort you to the White Hotel?"

"How did you know where I am staying?"

"Being decked out as you are, I wouldn't imagine you'd be staying in one of the less reputable establishments. That doesn't mean you aren't staying with family, friends, or acquaintances, but if you were, someone would have come to meet you at the train station. So, the most obvious choice is the White Hotel. Personally, I'd choose Aunt Henny's instead."

"I do not believe it would be appropriate for me to stay with your aunt."

"She's not my aunt. She's no one's aunt. She's just Aunt Henny to everyone."

What a strange notion. "I do have reservations at the White Hotel, and my trunk is being delivered. I would appreciate an escort."

He poked out his elbow. "I'm at your service, Miss Marseille."

Did he expect her to take hold of him? "I appreciate your offer, but a lady does not accept a gentleman's arm whom she is not related to or acquainted with for some time. It would be highly inappropriate. People would think me a woman of loose morals."

Deputy Montana rubbed his hand across his jaw. "Why's that? I've already held you in my arms."

Geneviève sputtered. "That was not by choice. A lady does not go around holding on to whatever man asks her to."

"I guess out here, those kinds of rules got dumped alongside the trail way back, out of necessity. You let me know what your fancy rules are, and I'll abide by them."

The man didn't seem put-off or offended or judgmental of her. Merely accepting. She expected such courteous behavior from well-bred men of her station but had experienced the opposite from people of a lower station. Quite refreshing.

⊙∕⊃

Montana reached the end of the platform and descended the steps. He turned and held out his hand. "In case you need it to steady yourself. I'll leave that to you."

He should cut this fancy lady free. No future in helping her or spending any time with her. But something in her shocked expression when he'd scooped her up in his arms had lassoed him. He hadn't thought at all, simply saw her in need and acted. He'd expected to get slapped—and hard—once he set her on the bench, but he hadn't. Then the lilting tone of her French accent had done the rest.

Something about her made him want to walk her to the hotel. Once there, it would likely be the last he'd see of her. Might as well enjoy her company for the few minutes he had it.

She placed her gloved hand lightly on his as she glided down the steps. How did refined ladies look so graceful when taking stairs? He just tromped up and down them.

Her butterfly touch sent a warm shiver skittering to his core. Her outfit had so many parts, it was hard to tell where one thing ended and the next started. The long skirt went clear to the ground but didn't quite touch it.

The shorter skirt—if that's what it was—hung over that. A jacket, with sleeves so wide she would need to turn sideways to get through a doorway was next. Her shirt peeked out in a wad of white ruffles. Not to mention other drapey and hanging things, tassels and fringes and such, here and there. To top it all off, a hat sat atop her blond hair at an angle that should cause it to tumble off, but it didn't, and a feather, the same blue as her dress, shot out from it. Her attire should be a confusing mess, but it all worked together to frame this beauty perfectly. No sooner had her feet landed on the ground than she broke the contact.

What could he do to get her to touch him again like that? Maybe there would be a puddle or two to dodge between there and the hotel. But the weather had been dry as of late.

On the street side of the train station, Miss Marseille glanced about. "Do you have a conveyance here at the depot?"

"Conveyance?"

"A means of transportation."

"Just Cletus." He moseyed over to his horse.

She stroked Cletus's jowl. "He is a fine steed."

"I can boost you into the saddle if you like."

She stared wide-eyed at him. "Pardon? That is not a sidesaddle. It is wholly inappropriate for a lady."

He'd seen plenty of ladies out West ride astride. He supposed her extra fancy getup wouldn't allow for it. "The hotel's not far. I could go to the livery and bring back a buggy, but we could walk to the hotel quicker'n that would take."

She remained silent a moment, presumably contemplating her options. "Very well, proceed. I could do with a bit of exercise after being cramped on a train for a week."

He checked to see no wagons were barreling down the middle of the road and motioned. "It's safe to cross."

She seemed to be carefully tiptoeing to the other side.

He'd never noticed how many droppings were in the street before. Had he, he would have chosen a less troublesome place to cross. He pointed. "Careful. There's one over there."

"*Merci.*"

Montana breathed easier once on the opposite boardwalk. "What brings you to Kamola?"

"My brother is here in town."

"Then why didn't he come for you at the train station?" Montana might not be fancy bred, but he knew enough to meet a female relation. Wasn't right to leave her to find her own way.

"My visit is impromptu."

"You should have told him so he could meet you. What if some scoundrel had happened upon you?"

"Like someone lifting me off my feet on the train platform?"

"So, I'm a ruffian and a scoundrel?" Though not in the true sense of the words. Bad people preyed on women alone. "Promise me you'll contact your brother right away and let him know you're in town."

"I will. He is staying at the hotel, which you said was not far."

"It's up yonder."

"Mr. Montana, your American dictionary defines *not far* differently than mine. That distance has come and gone." She removed a handkerchief from her little bag hanging on her wrist and waved it about to emphasize her point.

One side of his mouth hitched up. "I could carry you if you're too tired." And he had offered to put her atop his horse or get a buggy. Both of which she had rejected.

"I will manage." She stepped off one boardwalk and onto the next.

He did the same. "You can call me just Montana."

"No one is *just* their name. Everyone has some sort of a title."

"Most call me plain Montana. I like it that way."

"Well, you must have a title."

"Why?"

"Using one's title shows a sign of respect and honor to a person."

"Is this another one of your fancy rules?"

She gave a nod and held out one hand palm up. "So, either mister"—she held out her other hand— "or deputy."

"I'm no mister."

"Then Deputy Montana it is."

It didn't matter what she called him. Once he saw her to the hotel, she wouldn't be calling him anything. She would go her way, and he his. "Here it is." He pulled open the hotel's front door and watched to see if her voluminous sleeves touched the doorframe.

She turned slightly toward him. *"Merci."* At the same moment she spoke, her leading shoulder cleared the entrance, a shift and a step, and she was inside.

Impressive. She made the action appear natural and unintentional. But he suspected it was a well-practiced maneuver in such a getup.

He followed and went with her to the desk. "Howdy, Grant. Miss Marseille would like a room."

"Hello, Montana. Marseille? I believe we have a reservation under that name." Grant shuffled a couple of papers. "Here it is. We've another guest by the name of Marseille."

"That would be my brother. Is he in his room?"

"No. He's been out all day. Would you like me to let him know you're here when he comes in?"

"Oui. I mean yes. Wait. Do not tell him."

Montana's hackles raised. She better not wander off alone. She needed a man seeing to her safety.

She continued. "Reserve a table for us in your dining room. Tell him he has a supper reservation with a young lady. I want to surprise him."

Montana could live with that.

"I'll see to it the arrangements are made." Grant spun the registry to face her. "Do you have luggage?"

"I have a trunk the train depot will be sending along." She signed the book.

"Very good. I'll have it sent to your room straight away." Grant slid her key across the desk. "I've put you in the room next to your brother."

Miss Marseille retrieved her key. "Perfect." She faced Montana. "Thank you for your assistance. Until we meet again, *Deputy* Montana." She headed toward the staircase.

Would they meet again? Not likely. Merely something people said to make a good-bye not so final.

Montana turned to Grant behind the desk. "If for any reason she's not able to meet with her brother at some point today, let me know."

"I will."

Montana shifted his gaze to the stairs again.

The lovely French lady glided up as though she were an apparition. At the landing halfway, she turned and gifted him with a smile, before continuing her ascent.

Then she disappeared.

Well...that was it. The last he'd see of her. He should head back to the sheriff's office. Instead, he stood there like a dolt.

~~~

Henny rose from a chair in the White Hotel Dining room. Saul Hammond handed her modest hat to her. She pinned it atop her head. A lot of ladies left their hats on during meals eaten out, but she preferred not to. "Thank you, Saul. Luncheon was delicious. You spoil me."

He smiled. "You deserve to be spoiled. You work hard, running your boarding house."

His lingering gaze unnerved Henny. He oughtn't look at her in such a way. And she oughtn't have such flutterings in her middle in response. He was a few years older than her fifty—almost fifty-one—years, but he made her feel young again and special. Nothing could come of their friendship, not that she thought Saul would ever pursue anything more.

She pulled her shawl tight around her shoulders. "Shall we go. All that work at my boarding house won't take care of itself."

"I wish we could lollygag all day, but I too have chores at home." He poked out his elbow.

Henny took his offered arm.

In the lobby, one of the town's deputies stood, staring at the empty staircase.

"Deputy Montana?"

Seemingly startled, he turned. "Huh? Oh. Howdy, Aunt Henny. Mr. Hammond."

"Good afternoon. You seem distracted. Have you followed a miscreant into the hotel?"

"What? No. No miscreant." A flush crept up his neck.

Saul chuckled. "Let's leave the poor boy in peace." He guided Henny outside.

Once past the threshold, she caught a glimpse of a man dashing around the corner. Something familiar about the figure pricked at her. Could he be the same man she'd seen several times, watching her last fall? When he'd no longer shown up, she'd assumed him to be a figment of her imagination. If this were the same man, she had a lot of questions for him. Why had he watched her before? Was he watching her again? If so, why had he stopped several months ago?

"Henny? Have you heard a word I've said?"

She shifted her attention to Saul and pointed. "Did you see him?"

Saul glanced about. "Who?"

"A man. Remember how I kept seeing a man last fall?"

He nodded.

"I'd thought he could be watching Nicole and the boys, but they have all moved out to Shane Keegan's ranch now. Do you think that man could be trying to find them again?" She would rather the stranger was after her. Those children had experienced enough trouble in their lives. "I think I saw him, just now."

Deputy Montana exited and stopped short. "Is anything wrong?"

"Yes." She turned to him. "Remember last fall when I came into the sheriff's office and told you about a man I'd seen several times?"

He nodded.

"I think I saw him a moment ago."

The deputy surveyed the surroundings. "Where?"

"He ducked around the corner." She pointed. "But I doubt it would do any good to go after him. Whenever I tried, he disappeared as though he never existed."

"I'll take a gander anyway and let Sheriff Rix know about this."

"Thank you. I'd appreciate it."

With a nod, Deputy Montana strode off to do his duty.

Saul patted Henny's hand still clutching his arm. "My son and his deputies will get to the bottom of this. The man can't hide around corners forever."

She hadn't realized she'd had such a grip on him and loosened her hold. "I feel better knowing Edric will be apprised of this. I don't want Nicole and her cousins to have any trouble."

"And what about you, Henny? What if he was watching *you* and not them?"

"Why would a young man have any interest in an old lady like me?"

"You are *not* an old lady, and you're quite interesting. At least to me."

The fluttering inside her danced around again. She would love to relish the joy of the feeling but needed to get control of it—and quickly. A romance at this point in her life wasn't an option. She wished it were.